ALSO BY JOHN GARDNER

NOVELS
Flamingo
Golgotha
The Dancing Dodo
The Werewolf Trace
To Run a Little Faster
The Censor
Every Night's a Bullfight
A Complete State of Death
The Cornermen

THE MORIARTY JOURNALS
The Return of Moriarty
The Revenge of Moriarty

THE HERBIE KRUGER NOVELS
The Nostradamus Traitor
The Garden of Weapons
The Quiet Dogs
Maestro
Confessor

THE GENERATIONS TRILOGY
The Secret Generations
The Secret Houses
The Secret Families

JAMES BOND NOVELS
License Renewed
For Special Services
Icebreaker
Role of Honor
Nobody Lives Forever
No Deals, Mr. Bond
Scorpius
Win, Lose or Die
Brokenclaw
The Man from Barbarossa
Death Is Forever
Never Send Flowers
SeaFire
Cold
License to Kill (from the screenplay)
Goldeneye (from the screenplay)

THE BOYSIE OAKES BOOKS
The Liquidator
Understrike
Amber Nine
Madrigal
Founder Member
Traitor's Exit
Air Apparent
A Killer for a Song

AUTOBIOGRAPHY
Spin the Bottle

COLLECTIONS OF SHORT STORIES
The Assassination File
Hideaway

DAY OF ABSOLUTI✝N

A NOVEL

John Gardner

SCRIBNER

NEW YORK LONDON TORONTO SYDNEY SINGAPORE

SCRIBNER
1230 Avenue of the Americas
New York, NY 10020

SCRIBNER and design are trademarks of Macmillan Library Reference USA, Inc., used under license by Simon & Schuster, the publisher of this work.

Designed by Colin Joh
Set in Aldus

Manufactured in the United States of America

1 3 5 7 9 10 8 6 4 2

Library of Congress Cataloging-in-Publication Data
Gardner, John, 1933–
Day of absolution : a novel / John Gardner.
p. cm.
I. Title.
PS3557.A712 D39 2000
813'.54—dc21   00-032219

ISBN 0-684-82461-2

For Louisa and Annie
May they rest in peace
And may light perpetual shine upon them

AUTHOR'S NOTE

I made some notes for this book in the early seventies and eventually sold it in 1995 over a working breakfast, at The Algonquin in New York, to my editor, Susanne Kirk. I expected to deliver the typescript in the following year. Alas that did not happen because, out of the blue, I was taken seriously ill and finally had some major surgery. This was followed, with almost Job-like horror, by a family tragedy that made writing exceptionally difficult for a while.

However, finally back on course, I delivered the manuscript almost four years late. While I was writing it, the world turned and a large number of things changed. But Susanne Kirk kept the faith and waited. I thank her more than I can say for her trust and patience.

I also thank my agent, Lisa Moylett, who took me on when I was at a particularly low ebb and saw me through with constant goodwill, bolstering me up with a wonderful lack of sentiment.

John Gardner
Hampshire, UK, 2000

DAY OF
ABSOLUTION

To the wronged grant restitution,
Save us Lord from destitution,
Grant us all your absolution.
—Brother Francis of Shrivingfold (sixteenth century),
    An Alternative De Profundis

PROLOGUE

There were five scrolls with around twelve feet of papyrus to each: the sheets sometimes stitched, sometimes glued together, then rolled onto hardwood drums, with carved shafts at each end so that they looked like large bobbins. The exception was the very short one on which the covering letter had been written. We have no idea how they ended up where they did, but you can make any number of educated guesses.

Some of the names are familiar from the text of the scrolls: Centurion Titus Romillius; the girl Naomi—who dictated the diary; the dark-skinned Nubian girl Azeb; the boy called Petros, who had been brought in by Romillius, mainly to do the writing.

From the text we know that Romillius was a friend of Pontius Pilate, the procurator of Palestine, governor of Judea—the man who sentenced Jesus to death. So, Romillius was close to Pilate, and we know he was the target of an attempted coup. The murders, which were part of this conspiracy against Pilate, almost certainly took place sometime in the morning of the day on which Christians now celebrate Jesus' resurrection from the dead. The first Easter—a word borrowed from pagan times but anchored firmly to the ancient Jewish festival of Passover: that memorable occasion when the people of Israel celebrated the way in which they were released from their bondage in Egypt; a day linked so inseparably to spring sacrifice and commemoration of rebirth that it may well have been the true time of the execution of Jesus.

On the day after that momentous first day of the week, Romillius wrote the letter that appears on the shortest scroll.

How did it all come about? Who knows the truth? Pilate was the one who said, "What is truth?" But you can make healthy stabs at the truth because, for the first time, there is a detailed contemporary report.

If the murders were committed on the first Easter Day, it is likely that the prostitute Naomi disappeared directly before those brutal acts—the dreadful stabbing and slashing of the girl Azeb and the boy Petros. It is also possible to guess at what else occurred. Romillius, now a marked man, fled for his life, leaving the city of Jerusalem with the scrolls wrapped in skins, watertight and safe. It is logical to think that he took this booty to some place he had already prepared. If so, it would be nice to think that he was never able to retrieve them: that once they were hidden, circumstances prevented the Roman officer from ever going back.

Certainly the little sacred treasure trove must have lain out of sight for many centuries. From other evidence we know those same scrolls were moved by a Russian Orthodox monk called Brother Pytor—a biblical scholar, sent by the Patriarch of Moscow and All the Russias to study an archaeological dig that was taking place near Jerusalem.

We can be sure that Brother Pytor traveled back to his own country, somehow smuggling all five scrolls out of the Holy Land, just as we know they ended up in the Church of St. John the Warrior, round the corner from the Oktjabr'skaja metro station in Moscow in the spring of 1920. In the summer of the same year the scrolls were removed by the State Organs—the precursor of what later became the KGB—during the first months of Stalin's Terror: the show trials and executions from which so many were not to be seen again, including the Soviet Union's best military leaders.

It was a relatively long time before those incredibly important sheets of papyrus were to reappear. Important? Certainly, for they were finally revealed as the only contemporary account of the Crucifixion and Resurrection of Jesus: a diary of one who was there, close to the events: the first firm evidence that the whole thing really happened in the way described later in the Gospels. Or was it?

CHAPTER ONE

So it came about on a bitter and freezing Wednesday in February at the beginning of the new millennium that Charles Vincent Gauntlet married Rebecca Louise Olesker, at a civil ceremony with people pulled in off the street as witnesses. They had lived together, in Bex's flat in Dolphin Square, for some months and, in spite of the perceptible age difference, were as happy as they had any right to be, if not happier.

Bex was particularly suited, for her work was—well, let's just say that any partner had to really understand the Job. She had given up looking for a husband when she first met Gauntlet. It had always been such a letdown. Men never understood, or they wanted to know more, or they just got jealous of the Metropolitan Police Force. Being a detective chief inspector in the Met was bad enough, but to be in the Anti-Terrorist OS13 Branch was something else.

They had met at the funeral of a colleague.

"You knew old Herbie for long?" Charlie asked her. It was almost a chat-up line, and he was quite surprised when Bex said that she had done some quite wild things with Herbie. "It was sudden," she said, giving a sad little smile, her big brown eyes drooping away. "Very quick I understand." Charlie Gauntlet gave her a kind of bracing nod.

This time her eyes locked on him, lips trembling. "Happened in my sitting room." Her voice cracked. "There one minute, gone the next, silly bugger. He went from life to death in the snap of your fingers. Poor old Herb." And now she fixed him with her eyes so that he felt like an insect skewered against a mount and was totally lost to her.

"What d'you do for a living?" Bex asked him sweetly.

"Me? I'm retired. Like old Herb was, out to grass."

15

Now, if anyone asked Charles Gauntlet what he had done, he would give a wry smile and mutter that he read law at Cambridge but eventually, before he was really ready, went on to do something dodgy for the Foreign Service. Their mutual dead friend, Herbie, had worked for the same firm, only his job had been even more dodgy. "Should've died years ago, Herb," one of his other iffy colleagues had said. "Took a lot of risks when the curtain was still up."

So that was how Charlie and Bex first got together, only Charles had taken early retirement, and one of the boons he brought to the relationship—and thence to the marriage—was that he was very much an ex-government employee who knew exactly how to keep his trap shut and not ask awkward questions. He knew how to see no evil, hear no evil, speak no evil, which to Bex's mind was bloody nigh impossible.

In retrospect, the marriage was quirky because she wasn't looking for a husband. Sure, sometimes her thoughts strayed to the idea of tying the knot, then, like a sniper with a plethora of targets, she switched and considered better of it. That was until the Saturday evening when she came back to Dolphin Square and told him that, barring accidents and a change in the wind, she had five days free.

"What you want to do, then, Bex?" he growled, looking up innocent and paradoxically wise at the same time. The stare said, Okay, Bex, you want to go to the movies, or are we seeing *Les Misérables* for the thirty-sixth time and having a good cry? You want to go out and live it up—which meant have an Indian or a Chinese, or even an Italian—or you want to go to the movies? See Laurel and Hardy or Charlie Chaplin, like I first suggested?

Later she realized that Charlie, cunning bugger that he was, had led her into a trap simply by the way he looked: by his body language and the tilt of his mouth. He was suggesting that probably there was something exceptionally good to see at the movies, and after that they could have a Madras chicken with Bombay potatoes and lashings of onion pickle and it wouldn't matter.

"What d'*you* want to do, my darling? You choose for a change." She could almost taste the Madras chicken. She was a martyr to Madras chicken.

"Okay." He shifted on the settee next to her, one hand straying to her thigh, grinned, dropped his voice, almost picked it up again, and whispered, "Well, I'm getting married Wednesday if you agree."

She did a double take, then a treble. He's joking. No, he's not, the bastard. I can see it in that sly little look he's trying to pull.

Gotcha!

"Charlie?" Stern and very grown-up.

The grin widened.

"Charlie, you've set me up . . ."

"Only if you want it. Only if you want to get married, Bex. Make an honest man of me."

"You've arranged it already . . ." She remembered that he had quizzed her several weeks before: "Got to make some arrangements, Bex, for when your next leave comes up: your away days, right? Maybe we do something stupid, like take the bus out to Hampton Court. See the armor. Do something daft like get married."

She heard her own voice hurtling from a few weeks ago, "That'll be the day, Charlie. I should live so long."

He now gave her another quick grin, flashing on and off like an Aldis lamp. "So?" Eyebrows lifting, eyes dancing, winking a challenge.

She took a deep breath and committed herself.

So, the police officer and the former lawyer with special duties and dark secrets were married on that raw, cold Tuesday with a delivery-man, a lady bank clerk, a council worker, and a housewife—only you cannot marry a house so she called herself a wife—as the witnesses; and the woman registrar beamed, looking like a coiffured owl as she pronounced them man and wife.

After that, Charlie Gauntlet took Bex in his arms as though she were a fragile piece of porcelain, which she was not, and kissed her as tenderly as she would ever want to be kissed. And she wondered at the whole business: after all, we were up to our asses in platitudes about family values, on the one hand, while people had cast matrimony to the waves on the other. Nowadays people have "partners" and all that. We also have a lot of nonnuclear, single-parent happy families.

Anyway, they went out onto the ice-slick pavements and hailed a cab to take them to the little Italian place off Fleet Street, where they let the padrone into the secret and he treated them to a bottle of champagne on the house. They ate minestrone, calves liver and onions, tomatoes floating in olive oil and a dash of vinegar. The wedding cake was an apple torte off the trolley, with a fistful of cream, and they ordered brandy with the coffee.

Then they went home for the honeymoon, where Charlie announced that he had tickets for *The Flying Dutchman* that night.

"Not really the most popular choice these days, Charles," she joked.

"Who's worried by popular?"

She explained that opera was—wrongly—considered elitist by many. Particularly the current establishment, which made him glum, for he had always been politically slightly left of center. Even so, he had been a shade cutting when the prime minister and the chancellor had both chosen Madonna, Oasis, Boy Zone, and Michael Jackson on BBC Radio's *Desert Island Discs*.

"Thought they were adults," he said again now when his new wife explained the state of the musical nation to him.

"Doesn't stop me liking opera. The Spice Girls aren't obligatory, are they?"

"Let's have a little lie down first, darling." She didn't even blush, trollop that she could be when it came to country matters.

Again she was amazed at what Charlie, at slightly less than twice her age, could pull off when he tried. She had learned that if she was not greedy, and if she allowed him to pace himself, she could not want for a better, more satisfying and attentive lover.

The truth about Charlie Gauntlet was that age had not withered him. He really was the kind of guy to whom age did not matter, either to him or the people he was with. Adult women, unless they had some seriously sorry hang-up, truly did not think of him as late-middle, or even early-old, aged. Charlie was, well, simply Charlie: a man of the twentieth century who did not pin himself down, could not attach himself to a particular decade; just as, until the closing years of the century, he was never one to really ally himself to any political ideology.

His one true secret was that he was made nervous by retirement. Thought being over-the-hill was a bit unbecoming. Yet that evening Charlie had a kind of epiphany that he thought marked a watershed in his life. Going down to the cab, on Bex's orders so that she could flounce and bounce herself up a little and look nice for him, he nodded to the cabbie who muttered, "Evenin', chief," as Gauntlet slung himself into the back to get out of the cold, said his wife would be down in a minute—his wife, yes. He did not have to repeat it for the cameras: they're never ready on time, are they? Always late when you'd made reservations, had a schedule, had to get her to the church on time. Never could stick to the program, letter, second. The cabby was loquacious, and Gauntlet was in a schmoozing mood.

So, smiling stupidly, Charlie suddenly realized that he had done the trick he had been trying to accomplish since the demise of the Cold War: he had accepted it as being over. In a couple of stray seconds he had managed to embrace the truth that he had retired and need not march to the beat of the secret silent drum anymore. His smile broadened and he made a slight movement: the stirring of a cat against a leg. His eyes closed for a few seconds as he luxuriated in the knowledge that he never again had to walk the line and tread with care. It was over for him. He could pack up his troubles in his old kit bag and grin.

The only danger he had to face now was a rogue car, plane, or train, or even the attack of a mutant killer virus. No more the writing on the wall. Well, except for any ghosts that might just come a'haunting from the freezing iceberg years—and that wasn't all that likely was it?

So, Bex appeared looking wonderful and even statuesque in her big black coat with the turned-up collar that reached almost around her whole head. She pushed her shoulder next to his and moved in a snuggling motion against him as the cabbie tried to set a brisk pace under the impossible conditions of the early-evening London traffic.

Charlie closed his eyes again, sentimental old fool that he was. When he had first met Bex Olesker he had thought her short of stature, but that was only a trick of the light, for she stood around five-seven in her stocking feet, and sometimes she was clever enough to appear only five-two, while other times she was six feet tall. And then there was the hair. Always different. Sometimes long and dark, then short and honey. After that, all the shades in between. Charlie said that if she could've grown a beard, she would've done it in months that didn't have an *r* in them.

Her real color, he knew from his unique vantage point, was near black, and as Alfred Hitchcock had said to Tippi Hedren when they were making *The Birds*, "Grab at it if one flies up your skirt, 'cos a bird in the hand . . ."

In truth, Rebecca Olesker—Bex to her friends—copper of this parish, was a rangy young woman with a hint of the athlete in her long, up-to-her-armpits legs, and a definite way of moving her shoulders that would be enough to frighten off anyone planning larceny or terrorism had they seen her first.

Charlie loved the way she walked, loped really, long, soft strides that whispered if she wore a skirt. He often said to her that her thighs were like silk when they touched one another—"That's not original, Bex, but it's true."

And Bex? How did Bex view life from the sharp end of being just married? Never ever thought you'd say it, did you, Bex? Never thought you'd ever say you loved someone just like you love Charlie? Love him to pieces: love the scent of him, the maleness and the same cologne he always used, the sweet-smelling successful wonder of him. God, you can almost even smell his smile, just as the old song says, like the sun after rain. You can't put it into words. It's difficult, but you never had the talent with words. Even liked the tickle of his mustache.

Bex Olesker, wonderwoman of the Anti-Terrorist Branch, sat in the back of the taxi, lifted her head from his shoulder, peeked at him, saw the contented smile on his face, and put her head back in its nestling place, giving a sigh like a lovelorn loon, and trying to put it all into words.

"Take a card," Charlie whispered. "Any card."

When she had first met him, a hundred years ago, she had not even particularly liked him. It hit her hours later, all of a sudden, knocked her for six, with his medium height and broad shoulders: very neat the way he walked and moved. He could never be described as handsome, with his deceptively open face that had been the downfall of many an unwary man and woman in the witness box, or that safe house in which the Firm conducted close questioning—which is another word for interrogation. Once she got over that she was in love with him, she jotted down several little mental notes. Just to remember how he made her feel—like dancing down the street and throwing a bit of sunlight at her. He could come into a room and pow!—reach up, grab a handful of sunlight, and hurl it at her so that the whole room took on new dimensions. Bloody hell, Bex, is that you talking?

What would all her liberated, militant feminist friends say? More to the point, what would her mother say if she could listen in to the stream going sliding on the thin ice of her daughter's conscious waking thoughts? "Rebecca Olesker, I've never heard anything like that in all my born days," she would have said. "Becca, you're a wanton young woman."

Say it, Mum, tell me I'm a slut 'cos all I want is for this lovely, overgrown schoolboy of a man to wrap himself round me and pull me close, hold me forever. Bex was amazed to feel like this, because it really wasn't her. Nobody she worked with could possibly recognize her if they listened to this soppy cow.

So it was that they sat with shoulders touching and the ring on her left hand seeming to be out of place and very heavy as they let Wagner's opera rage and rumble over them. They saw and heard the Dutchman's ship enter Sandwike Bay with its bloodred sails and the curse that is on the captain, who must sail the oceans until the Day of Judgment unless he can find a woman who will be faithful only to him. A tall order, Bex thought, but one she could find easy enough if the man happened to be Gauntlet, who was himself thinking the same thing in reverse, but he did not let it show—at least until the interval, when he whispered, "See, you've to stay faithful to me, Bex, otherwise I turn into a lobster."

"You're a lobster already." She held on to his arm and they struggled into the bar, grabbing the drinks they had already ordered: Perrier water for her and a black coffee for her husband.

Two sips in and one comment on the tenor before Charlie heard the laugh, recognized it, and felt the short hairs rise on the back of his neck.

She saw him prick up his ears, like a meerkat. She doubted if anyone else would notice, but prided herself on her ability to spot the changes in him. Only the tiniest of movements, but to her it was a stretching of the neck, tilting of the head with the gray eyes set absolutely still.

"What's going on?" she all but whispered.

"Ghost. Tell you later." Another sip of the coffee and a turning of the head in the direction of the laugh. He was right, 120 percent, and what the hell was Kit Palfrey doing here in London of all places? They had just about run him out of this city on a rail, but that was thirty years ago. Thirty years and counting. Run him out and then suffered the embarrassment of hearing him tell the world from his new home in Moscow that he was a traitor to his country and proud of it.

Kit Palfrey, spy-about-town, more dangerous than any of them. Part of the so-called Cambridge Ring. Charlie himself had reason to remember Kit, for it was Kit who had . . . Oh, what the hell. It was over and done with now, long gone, ancient history, and he would have to dredge his mind for the details. Just a bad dream, old Kit Palfrey—and he looked pretty old now: sixty-five? Seventy? Well, he would, wouldn't he? It had happened thirty years ago. Doesn't time fly when you've been keeping secrets?

They used to say, the press used to say, and people in the Foreign Service also, that he looked like the film actor James Stewart. He certainly had that tall, thin, gangly frame, and a voice that drawled and seemed to splutter out what he wanted to say: reaching for words that were just over the skyline. But there the resemblance ended, as far as Charlie was concerned. The face was more like that of a different actor: more square, stocky, angular—Claude Rains possibly. Yes, Claude Rains's head on James Stewart's body.

Kit Palfrey was one of the group usually lumped together as the Cambridge Spies—the group that included the notorious Kim Philby—men who were recruited by the Soviets while at university, then left to make their mark in government departments. Moles, and in some cases moths, in sensitive wardrobes. When they ran to

Mother Russia, they caused a huge scandal. Well, it *was* at the time. Nowadays? Ho-hum, ancient history, and who the hell would he tell anyway? Not a soul would be interested anymore. Palfrey must've been the youngest of the lot. Well, Kit was the only one left alive, and that was certain. The others, all gone, leaving a footnote—or at best a short chapter—in the secret-history books. Especially nowadays when the television provided most people with their news: tucking away the sound bite and the two-minute story, reducing history to the level of a cartoon—except when it turned on you and slugged you in the guts.

As Charlie took another quick look, he noticed that Kit's hair was still in good condition—still long and flopping around his ears—and that he had a healthy tan on the weather-beaten face, his eyes not leaving the woman he appeared to be with, lips smiling, moving, and tipping flattery onto the reddish blond head. Oh, Kit, you were always a charmer. In the circles in which Gauntlet had once moved they rated Kit's charm at devastating plus ten. Storm warnings should be hoisted, they said, to warn virgins whenever he came into the room—not that they needed warning in the current climate.

In that split second, Charlie recalled everything. Hardly the blink of an eye, yet he plainly saw the old chief's office—ninth floor above the gasoline company in the now vacated Century House. He'd been a child then, that Monday morning in the very late sixties, a time when swinging London was just starting to wind down. London with Mary Quant, the Beatles, Campaign for Nuclear Disarmament marches, Biba, Twiggy, the Pill, and all the other icons of that turning era beginning to decelerate. Monday morning and the two anoraks from the Security Service—their sisters with whom they rarely shared anything—and the wax-skinned suit from the U.S. embassy in Grosvenor Square who had brought the news.

"Former buddy of yours as we understand it," the American drawled. "My people in D.C.'ve asked him to leave. Hope you don't mind. They'll be putting him on a flight from Dulles tonight. Here's the collateral." The hand dipped into the pigskin document folder and came up with the photographs, which were spread out on the chief's desk.

Old Kit Palfrey meeting Crakilov, Gennady, First Secretary (Military) to the Soviet embassy in Washington, D.C. The envelope slid across the table and pocketed. Caught in flagrante after all the warnings the Yanks had given them from their huge building among the lush Virginia trees at Langley, or was it McLean? There was the photograph and a few straws in the wind.

"We would suggest," the smooth suit continued, "that you give him a very hard interrogation. Sweat him, get a conf—"

The old chief's palm came down on the desk, flat and hard as his baby blue eyes. "I would be obliged if you'd refrain from trying to teach me my job," he yapped. "We've been doing this for the best part of five hundred years—since the first Elizabeth—and you're stating the obvious, and not necessarily the best way to go about matters. Kit Palfrey is a senior officer of this service, and I've yet to see hard evidence . . ."

In many ways the chief's outburst had a lot to do with the manner in which Palfrey was later to be treated. Nobody wanted to find him guilty. That was the top and bottom of it.

"The photographs—" the American began.

"—tell us nothing. How do I know they weren't cobbled together in one of your bucket shops? You've never liked him in D.C., and I'd be the first to admit that his drinking habits leave much to be desired. However, there's the possibility that Palfrey has a reasonable explanation—"

The American, who was called Ben Kemp and whose rank in the real world was colonel, let out a one-note contemptuous laugh, and one of the anoraks shook his head. "They told me you'd try to cover it up. Anything to keep it out of the papers, that's what they said at Langley."

The chief sent him packing and Charlie was dispatched to Heathrow with Gus Keene, head of interrogators. Passports at dawn and tired transatlantic commuters slewing off the early-morning arrival.

"Idiot Yanks," Kit had said when they shook hands. "Bloody fools think I'm working for the Russians."

"Are you?" Gus asked as they drove away.

"Don't be daft, Augustus. Don't be a stupid pratt."

But Gus, with Charlie in tow, put him to the question. Very hostile Gus could be when he wanted. All week they interrogated Kit with no results. Charming, relaxed Kit Palfrey laughed at them. Lunatic to even consider that he was tied up with the Reds. Bloody raving if they thought that. Barking. As for the Yanks' photograph of him with Crakilov . . . well, the envelope was simply some snaps. It was all in the log. He had been cozying up to Gennady in an attempt to turn and burn him. Could he sue the Americans for casting doubts on his loyalty?

"Christopher . . . ?"

"Kit. Nobody ever calls me Christopher. Kit, like Kit Marlowe."

He was a spy as well, Kit Marlowe. Got himself stabbed; maybe for the same business, possibly for betrayal or because of it. Or maybe that film was right and he died in a row about his bar bill. Who knew now?

Come the Friday, Gus told the boss that they would carry on with the hostile questions on Monday. Had nothing as yet. So Kit Palfrey walked away from the beautiful nineteenth-century house in Audley Street where they did that kind of thing.

Home for the weekend, according to the two Special Branch lads who had quietly followed him to the Service apartments off Marylebone High Street.

So they left him alone and there were those who seemed surprised that, come Monday morning, he had gone. The bird had flown. Gone; vamoosed; evaporated; dematerialized; done a bunk. Five weeks later Kit Palfrey resurrected himself in Moscow and immediately started to unbutton his lip about how he had worked for the Sovs since days of yore.

"I never took a penny from my masters, the Soviets. Long ago I came to the conclusion that the state of world politics demanded of me only one way, the way of Communism after the manner of the Soviet Union. I have served that ideal to the best of my ability for a long time."

At that point, Kit Palfrey entered the mythology, beginning a long and almost stately journey. Whenever they wrote books about the so-called Cambridge Spies, they included Kit and he was good value. He even wrote a kind of autobiography himself—*A World of Secrets* it was called, and a thrusting, savvy publisher actually walked from his Bloomsburg office on a Friday night, flew to Moscow, picked up the manuscript, and was back on Monday morning with a great coup.

Then the interest waned, and with the downfall of the old Evil Empire it almost completely vanished. The Cold War was won; nobody wanted to read about the secret world, treachery, or betrayal, anymore—except for somewhat boring history books. Taste shifted, the act of selling your country down the river was devalued. The world turned, the Soviet system collapsed, and the lads of the CIA, SIS, MI5, and the rest sat down and toasted each other, saying, "It's over and we won. Hooray for us!"

Yet, what would Kit Palfrey be doing in London now? Had he sneaked in? Taken the soft route via Dublin so he would not have to show his passport, or come skulking in via Paris on EuroStar? If they knew he was there, the men and women who worked in the supposedly anonymous building at Vauxhall Bridge Cross, would they care a damn? Would they shout for him to stand trial for treason, this Cold War criminal? Not Pygmalion likely.

One thing was certain—two things as it turned out—Kit Palfrey, Esq., should not have been in the United Kingdom, let alone London. The other point was that, when the evening was done and the curtain had fallen on the heroine hurling herself from the clifftops and redeeming the fabled Flying Dutchman, Charlie Gauntlet, newly married, grinning from ear to ear and looking as though he had been stunned by some cartoon frying pan, appeared to be quite unaware of Kit Palfrey's eyes on the back of his head, and oblivious to Kit Palfrey's mouth curved upward in a smile that was as sardonic as the call of a mockingbird.

One thing he did notice, but only vaguely. On the edge of his vision, Charlie was suddenly aware of another figure from his past: there and then gone, in a second, in the twinkling of an eye really. As they walked out through the foyer, jostled shoulder to shoulder with the crowd, he caught sight of a tall, slim, seedily elegant figure moving quickly against the throng.

He did not so much see Patsy Wright—once his link to those who did derring-do: the fighting hands in the more dangerous European capitals during the years when they crunched their way over the permafrost—as sense him, catch sight of his reflected silhouette against the skyline of the crowd. Charlie turned, frowning as they reached the street, his eyes searching behind him, trying to catch sight of his old comrade: there one minute and gone the next.

In the taxi, after the Dutchman's soul had found rest following true love, Bex laid her head on Charlie's shoulder again and murmured, "He wasn't looking for you, was he?"

"Who looking for who?"

"*Whom.*"

"Whom. Looking for whom?"

"Kit Palfrey, he wasn't looking for you, was he?"

"You're not old enough to know Kit Palfrey."

"Don't change the subject. I'm not old enough to remember the events, but I'm old enough to read about them. What's more, only a few years ago—a handful of years—when the Evil Empire was still evil, we had an alert out on Mr. Palfrey. Some bright spark thought he was heading up some Russians who were feeding guns to terrorists."

"So you can read. Okay."

"Charlie, he wasn't looking for you, was he?"

"Shouldn't think so. I guess he hated my guts really, though we had nobody who could break him. Not even old Gus Keene could sort him out. God knows we both tried." Pause. Count of ten. "No, I'd be very surprised if he was looking for me." Which shows you just how wrong some people can be.

Back in Dolphin Square, they did not know that their lives had been bisected by events long traveled. Each, in his and her way, was about to take up a new course, navigate to an undreamed-of bearing to plow a new furrow.

Speaking of plowing, the honeymoon continued, but was interrupted at a little after two in the morning when they were both curved like spoons lying together in velvet, just reaching out for sleep.

Bex cursed, fumbled for the telephone on its third ring, almost knocked over the glass of water, and whispered, "Olesker," into the mouthpiece.

"Sorry, ma'am," the voice at the distant end breathed. "The commander wants you in. Alchemist's active again."

She cradled the instrument, swore under her breath, then slid unwillingly from the bed's warmth, gathered up her clothes, and tip-toed to the bathroom.

Bleary, she gave herself a quick wink in the mirror and started to wash. Feeling sexy in the wee small hours. Would've given a bit of her pension to get back into bed and wake Charlie from his private dream-land.

Instead, she left a note for him—*Sorry, my love, my husband, but duty calls. Commander Bain needs me back in the salt mines. See you when I see you. Love being married to you, Bex*—and a couple of hugs and a kiss: OXO.

So, Bex Gauntlet, née Olesker, of the Anti-Terrorist Branch, headed off to work, not knowing the call of duty meant she would miss the unscheduled meeting between her husband and Kit Palfrey, but, at the moment, she had other fish to fry. Alchemist, to name but several.

CHAPTER 2

lchemist. In the early days it was a joke: a name given to the shadowy figure by the press and based on an old, and not terribly witty, comment.

"We call the man Alchemist," a detective had said at a press conference following the sudden and violent death of two Mossad agents who had been passing through London when—to use the current Americanism—they got whacked. "We call him Alchemist," the policeman continued, "because we have come to believe in his ability to turn lead, cupronickel, steel, whatever into gold. To change the base metals of bullets into gold. I suppose we could've called him Midas, but we opted for Alchemist."

By "the early days" we're talking eleven, maybe twelve, years ago. Two years went by before various law enforcement agencies linked the killings to one person, or group of people. Couldn't believe it to start with for these were all spectaculars. Shootings, but puzzling mysteries; like locked-room murders some of them, especially in the bad old days when a proliferation of splinter groups vied with one another, carrying terror into obscure places by devious means.

Eventually, from those first couple or three years they tied several deaths to one source. All were high-profile deaths: each one associated with some form of terrorism.

It was, of course, the varied nature of the targets that had everyone fooled to begin with. You don't expect enemies to get themselves killed with the same weapon and hence by the same organization.

Commander Joe Bain had been a chief super just cutting his teeth on the ways of terrorists when he put forward the theory that this was a hired gun, or guns. In London, Belfast, Dublin, Paris, Berlin,

Madrid, Jerusalem, even Tokyo, they laughed at this ridiculous theory. Indeed it was laughable because the watchword in those days was *intelligence*, but as the years passed, police forces were slow to admit this was the name of the game. Pure detection worked only in the books of Ruth Rendell, P. D. James, and the like. You collared sneak thieves, pickpockets, and drug barons—even some killers—by listening and putting people on your payroll, and if it worked for those kind of villains, it was even more true of terrorists.

Joe Bain was the man who finally proved, a decade before he called Bex back to his office on her wedding night, that the killings of an Iranian torturer, two PLO bombers, a Red Brigade informer, the armorer of an IRA splinter group, a Latin American country's chief of police with a poor record in human rights, and a senior East German IO were all inexplicably linked; like a chain.

The same weapon was used in each murder—a .38mm Smith & Wesson revolver—and the killer had left a bizarre series of clues that had, until then, been overlooked. From the bodies of each victim—one in the case of the two PLO men—they had recovered neatly typed cards each with an apt Shakespearean quotation.

In the last ten years there had been a further eight bodies laid at Alchemist's door.

The Mossad agents whose deaths had tripped the serial nature of the killings had died in a cold and calculated manner: the back of their heads blown away by the same Smith & Wesson weapon, and a card with a Shakespearean quote tucked into one of the men's breast pocket.

The police did not reveal this last piece of evidence, with its quotation, "Hath not a Jew eyes?"—a direct quote from Shylock in *The Merchant of Venice*. So the newspapers finally, in the late 1980s, dubbed him Alchemist, just as they had, in the seventies, named Illych Ramirez Sanchez, leader of the Popular Front for the Liberation of Palestine (PFLP), Carlos the Jackal (from Mr. Forsyth's book *The Day of the Jackal*). Alchemist was born of a headline, and those who used him, those who serviced him also, gave him the name, which eventually he took as his own.

This was a person—they finally had to admit—who ran death as a business, even advertised in newspapers. Genuine calls only. Any bona fide "freedom fighters" requiring the use of a trained mercenary to carry out death-squad work. Reasonable rates. Then a telephone number that, when traced, turned out to be an electronic jape leading up its own backside. But Alchemist was no joke: he was a killer without a single cause. One who, by deed, if not thought and word, allied himself to any cause for a few hours or a finger count of days.

One of the main problems was that you would not expect a terrorist group to employ someone outside their ranks, but they did. Particularly for the truly difficult targets, and nobody, on the ground or in the various centers that housed antiterrorist officers, could at first untangle the strange web.

In the beginning the wisdom said that this particular group—originally, they thought of Alchemist as a number of people: probably the Provisional Irish Republican Army (PIRA)—was filling its coffers by being killers for hire. When they traced it back, of course, this was not so. Matters became bizarre, and Alchemist appeared to be something to really fear. This was long before the cease-fires and Good Friday Agreements in Northern Ireland. The primary victims were impossible targets.

There were some twenty or thirty bodies in the last decade; but it was the first two that had thrown them off the scent for a long time.

First there was a senior officer of the Royal Ulster Constabulary (RUC)—the highly controversial paramilitary police force of Northern Ireland, now reorganized and renamed but still brimful of controversy. The RUC man had a round-the-clock bodyguard and a fleet of cars and armored vehicles at his disposal, all any man of his standing could require. Yet he died; shot dead in the bedroom of a safe house where he had planned to meet an informer in utter secrecy. Instead of an informer he met Alchemist, who not only came in through the man's window with the silenced S&W revolver, but was also close enough to lay hands on his target, leaving the typed card in a uniform pocket—"For some must watch, while some must sleep," *Hamlet*. And this in an area "owned" by the Royal Ulster Constabulary. Unheard of since the beginning of the Troubles. You did not go after an impossible victim.

Six months after the RUC officer there was the lieutenant colonel from the SAS—the Special Air Service Regiment, that most highly popular shadowy unit, which with the Airborne and the Royal Marine Commandos made up British Special Forces.

The colonel was guarded by the usual long-haired men of steel who merged into the background, and he was known to be in charge of the two-man teams that went undercover on special assignment, which in turn meant killers.

This officer, protected by killers and controlling killers, was another impossible choice. Impossible, but he made a mistake. Holed up in a cottage deep inside what was then the dangerous bandit country of Armagh, the colonel had slipped outside to meet somebody without telling his men what he was doing and why he was doing it. Unheard of and unlikely—for these men, like the Royal Marine Commandos, did not make mistakes—but it happened, and the colonel made his quietus with a silenced bullet in the back of the head, and a card tucked into his camouflage jacket: "I am fire and air," *Antony and Cleopatra.*

Even in the final days of the Troubles many found it difficult to make the real connection. Many still plumped for a team. A team of, possibly, dedicated Republicans who were shit hot at entrapment, had long memories, and could wait for the moment.

From the death of the RUC officer and the lieutenant colonel of the Special Air Service, there were many other bodies. Toward the present, another Iraqi secret policeman close to the main man; a young woman in Hamburg who had, in secret, run an aggressive fascist group and only stayed in business because she was untouchable. Then, almost a year later, two PLO men thought to have been behind the bombing of a commercial airliner. This pair met their end in Libya, where the regime sheltered them from attempts by both the United States and the United Kingdom to have them extradited. One night they did something they had never done before: went together to the house of a close friend. They arrived in the same car and died as they were getting out onto the pavement. Nobody saw it happen, nobody saw or heard the bullets, or glimpsed the figure slipping cards onto bodies.

Somewhere around the original third and fourth targets, OS13, the Anti-Terrorist Branch from New Scotland Yard, began to build the model, draw the map, plot the plan. At first they did not want to believe it because it was too bizarre. An apolitical contract killer; a man with no qualms, no ideals, and no morals willing to take huge, absurd risks and snuff unattainable victims. Having reached their conclusions, the military, Security Service, Royal Ulster Constabulary, OS13, and even the Republic of Ireland's Garda began to watch, listen, and pray.

There were people who had become involved almost by accident. Or so it seemed.

Take Theresa Murray for instance. Theresa was named for St. Theresa of Lisieux: the Little Flower of Jesus. As an infant she learned to play on this fact of life. She would go into her parents' pocket-handkerchief garden and ostentatiously smell the flowers. She would even caress them with her little hands and her mother would croon, "Oh, the joy of it. You'll be our own Little Flower, so you will."

But as Theresa—who answered only to either Tess or Tessa—grew, so she started to regard her mother and father as a pair of blinking idiots. In truth they were simple folk: he an unskilled worker at Shorts, the maker of airplanes, she a dinner lady at the local school four days a week. They lived in a part of Belfast that was almost untouched by the Troubles, for they had inherited the little house from her father's sister, the only member of this branch of the Murray family who had, until Tess, made something of her life, and that was a point as sore as a gum boil with the Murray seniors.

What concerned them was not that Geraldine had died with money and a little property, but the way in which she had come by this good fortune. Gerry had been—as Tessa's father put it—a rich man's fancy woman. True, her lover was not what could, by any stretch of the imagination, be called rich, but he had been married, so Gerry had lived with him, as they say, in sin. Oh, the shame of it.

Gerry's gentleman had owned a small bookshop just off Royal Avenue, and after he died she inherited not only the shop but also his house and a modest amount of money—a disagreeable bone of contention as far as his wife and two children were concerned. Indeed, there were many unpleasant incidents regarding the will going to probate, but to probate it went, and one action in the courts finally saw off the widow and her family.

The point was that Geraldine's gentleman friend was certainly of sound mind when he wrote in his will, "To my legal wife, Harriet, I bequeath neither jot nor tittle. The same applies to my children by Harriet. I have had to put up with Harriet's moaning, groaning, and volcanic temper for over twenty-five years, just as I have had to put up with the selfishness of my children. My wife has money of her own, and that should be enough for her and her brood."

As things turned out, Gerry Murray died, untimely, two years later. Came home after Christmas shopping one Thursday evening and dropped down dead of a brain hemorrhage: in the lavatory, of all places. Gerry never had any sense of time or place. "Died as she lived," Tess overheard her father say. "Died as she lived, with her knickers round her ankles." At the time, this had rather shocked Tessa.

But memories were strong. She still remembered the police coming to break the news of Gerry's death, and the endless rationalization of why it was not morally wrong to accept what was willed to them: the house, the money, and more money when the shop was sold. Some of the arguments voiced appeared flawed to Tessa, but voiced they were, in almost Jesuitical terms. Of course this would not be recognized by her father or mother, but even at her tender age Tess saw through the whole charade. You do at fourteen, don't you? You know the whole business of living. The facts of death come later. At fourteen you're never going to die.

By the age of eighteen, Theresa rejected just about everything held sacred by her parents, including the Roman Catholic faith. She had also got herself out of the family rut, having worked unstintingly at school to the extent that she had been able to go South, into the Free State as they called it, and win a scholarship to Trinity College, Dublin.

There she worked some more, reading law and getting herself a reasonable degree with the magic letters BA after her name. Her time at Trinity had also forged many links with people who would be useful to her later.

On the night after the newlywed Gauntlets went to see *The Flying Dutchman* and spotted Kit Palfrey into the bargain, Theresa Murray arrived in Dublin from Belfast by train. But it had taken her a staggering forty-eight hours to make the simple 150-odd-mile journey from her nice little house in the suburbs of Belfast, for she had traveled with great, almost paranoid, care and had had one terrifying scare. On arrival she took a taxi to The Gresham Hotel at the bottom of O'Connell Street, where she was treated with the usual civility accorded a regular visitor.

After calling down to room service for smoked-salmon sandwiches and a half bottle of Moët, she stripped, put on the toweling robe that came with the suite, and started to run a hot bath. She tipped well after signing the bill, then ate the sandwiches, finally taking a glass of the champagne through to the bathroom, where she took off the day's makeup and stepped into the hot water, which she had liberally sprinkled with Eau de Guerlain. Now she eased herself into the steaming bath, inching down until her whole body had acclimatized to the heat. At last she stretched out, took a sip of wine, wiggled her toes against the taps, and relaxed for the first time since she had left Belfast.

She was frightened. Had been frightened since the previous evening when things had gone very wrong. She had taken every precaution, as she always did when the Dublin lawyer signaled there was a new contract to be picked up. She checked and double-checked when she left the house. She drove carefully, using all the usual routines to make certain that nobody was following her, and only when she was absolutely certain did she drive down and cross the border into the South. Traveling back to Belfast was, at that time, not an option.

In London inside the theater the Dutchman was just falling in love with the heroine as Tess Murray turned her car into the forecourt of the Dublin Airport Hotel. Twenty minutes later she was sitting in her room thinking about going down to dinner once she had made the obligatory telephone call. She dialed the number, and when a male voice answered, she asked for Michael, knowing that it would in fact be either Sean or Fergus who was really answering. They worked in shifts manning the phone in the clearinghouse kept for Alchemist.

"Michael, it's Nuala."

It had never happened before: the pause followed by the realization that whoever was on the distant end was very drunk.

"Oh, so it's Nuala. . . . Grand. . . . That'll mean there's traffic for Alchemist." This was followed by a raucous laugh.

The fear was instant, for the clearinghouse was close to the border on the Southern side, and she knew the area was still thick with electronic scanners left by people waiting to lock onto, or already locked onto, any telephone conversation to which they took a fancy: the Brits, the Garda, the remains of the Provos, even the RUC. Whoever?

She spluttered, stalled, then shouted, "For God's sake . . . !"

"Not to worry, Nuala—and I know that's not your real name— we've been having the most wonderful piss up here. So, I'll jusht make a note that you called and—"

"Bloody fool!" she yelled before dropping the instrument back into its cradle.

What to do? What to do? This was a serious breach of security and could prove to be dangerous. In telephone conversations they never mentioned Alchemist.

In the Dublin Airport Hotel, Tess Murray had reason to be frightened.

In the final years of the century, audio, electronic, and visual surveillance techniques had become terrifyingly sophisticated. Indeed, the commander of Scotland Yard's Anti-Terrorist Branch had it on record that he felt secrets were almost phased out. People rarely even muttered confidences on insecure telephones anymore, while faxes were reduced to generalities. If you wanted to be safe, you went outside to talk, and then only as long as you were away from areas that could be overlooked or followed with a parabolic microphone.

In seconds, computer-controlled equipment monitoring several hundred telephone numbers could be alerted by a trigger word and so lock onto a conversation, filch talk, depositing it onto a microchip that stored up to a previous two minutes of the exchange, eventually delivering a recording in its entirety.

This is what had, in fact, happened during Tess Murray's dialogue with the drunken "Michael." Within seconds of her closing the line on the call, men in London and Belfast were listening to the recording, while others were reading the transcript on their VDUs. The information electronically dredged from the telephone line included the location of both parties: the Airport Hotel outside Dublin, the room number, and the supposedly safe communications house located in the town of Dundalk.

Later, when briefing Bex, Commander Joe Bain commented that coincidence had played a large part in what followed. "We can't bitch about there not being a copper about when we needed him," the super said. A Security Service officer from the embassy was at the airport, putting documents onto a London flight. His immediate boss in Dublin had him on a safe phone fast, and in less than ten minutes he was at the hotel, where he quickly identified Tess Murray and, for the next two hours, carried out a long-range surveillance that took her to the border with the North.

As soon as he was certain she was heading back to Belfast, the officer used his radio to send a coded message to the embassy. In turn, the embassy was quickly in touch with military intelligence HQ. Peace may have broken out, but some things never change.

Two other things happened during that evening. First, a two-man RUC undercover team shadowed Tess back to Belfast; while a further two-man crew moved into the Republic, setting up shop within sight of the supposedly safe communications house in Dundalk. They were there to keep the house under observation. Nothing else was going to rock the boat at this stage. The men and women at the top, with the military, the Royal Ulster Constabulary, OS13, and the Security Service (also, to some extent, the Republic's Garda and the Irish Military Intelligence), were all metaphorically holding their respective breaths.

There was another common state of mind that few would express professionally: while Alchemist was himself a kind of terrorist, few tears had been shed for the bulk of his targets. The Yard's reaction to this new turn in events was to send a new boy out—well, a new girl actually. In the small hours of the day following her wedding, Bex Olesker was briefed by her superintendent, driven to Northolt, and flown to Belfast's Aldergrove airport where, under a thick cloak of secrecy, she was moved by helicopter to Springfield Road barracks to be briefed by the ranking OS13 officer in the province.

The senior Anti-Terrorist cop on the block was also a woman: Detective Chief Superintendent Liz Liddiard, fortysomething, pug nose, full lips, untidy dishwater-blond hair, and large brown eyes ringed with dark circles suggesting that she did more at night than simply collate intelligence reports.

"You ready for this, Bex?" Liz's voice was soft and unmelodious; the voice of someone drained by the complexities of the place and the people.

"Depends. I was on my honeymoon."

"Want to go back? In my book you'd be excellent for the job, but—"

"What's the job? The commander said it could uncover Alchemist."

Count of around seven while Liddiard made up her mind. Then she gave a short nod, which dropped hair in her eyes. She sighed wearily. "Don't know, but it could well lead to something. Honeymoon?" As though this had just registered, Bex explained, adding that if it really could lead to hard copy she would like to see it through.

Liz Liddiard scratched deeply into her dishwater hair, and with probable cause, as she explained the situation in short bursts that seemed to have expunged verbs from her vocabulary—"Theresa Murray, late thirties, early forties. Nailed by acoustic telephone scanner. Possible Alchemist handler. Junior partner of the Belfast law firm Saunders, Rivers and Murray—low profile, no political affinities. Travels regularly. Might take us there; might not: Alchemist's obviously got a well-organized team. She could be high in the pecking order. As far as we're concerned—"

"And you'd want me to surveil?"

"There was an argument. Security Service wanted to bring in a team with all the bells and whistles. I said what we needed was a discreet, competent unknown face. Told them I could provide. Looks promising, but Murray's obviously heading out, so you'd have to commit."

Bex said her new husband would understand, and she would like to commit, which, under the circumstances, was pretty big of her.

Liddiard raised her eyebrows, an act that made the big brown eyes even bigger, and somehow distorted the dark rings, making her look like an opossum. "Lucky girl. Sounds like you hooked a gem."

"Price above rubies."

It was the only time Liddiard came close to cracking a smile.

They gave Bex a float and a minder and let her head into Belfast for some shopping. "Enough for three or four days," Liz told her, "but don't stint yourself. We haven't run an op in months so there's no cash shortage." Bex returned with three basic outfits including more jeans and a natty, long jacket with a flared waist and high collar: very pop-idolish. She also bought cosmetics, two pairs of shoes, and some neat underwear. They also gave her more money, a new identity—Ruth Elizabeth Nightingale—and credit cards, which they assured her would work.

She almost said, "Don't have to sing in Berkeley Square do I?" but kept her mouth shut. It was best not to add to the unoriginality when they were doing things by numbers.

Late in the day they said the target was heading back to Dublin, so they showed her some grainy photographs. Matt prints of Tess Murray with two sheets of widely spaced typing that laid out her life in the same kind of shorthand used by Detective Chief Superintendent Liddiard. The target was now coded Beecher.

"H. Beecher Stowe ho-ho-ho does it," Bex thought with a smile.

Finally it was back to Heathrow, where she boarded the late flight to Dublin, after telephoning Charlie, who said he was having an interesting time and might be going to Scotland for a few days.

It was almost eleven by the time Bex checked into The Gresham. A phone call provided her with Tess Murray's room number and the news that they had a monitoring service at work. "She's meeting a brother legal eagle at ten in the morning. Don't know where. Good if you'd tag along." Bex knew they must have some kind of secure line, for the paranoia filtered down to all levels, and the disembodied, rather sexy, deep brown voice gave her an emergency number. Unless it was guaranteed safe in a dozen languages, nobody would talk within four walls.

As she dropped quietly into sleep, Bex wondered what the hell Charles was talking about—going to Scotland.

CHAPTER 3

Coming up through layers of sleep, Charlie imagined he was nuzzling his wife's ear, into which he inserted his tongue, then, shifting his body, whispered to her, "As they'd say in South London, honey, you're the business." At this point he awoke and found himself wrapped around a pillow.

Initially he was angry to find she'd gone. Sneaked off in the middle of the party, he thought. Then, after he had read and destroyed the note, he mentally bayed to a nonexistent moon. Which all went to show that Bex had seriously misread him when she told Liz Liddiard that her new husband was of a forgiving and understanding nature.

Charles stumped around the flat for some thirty minutes muttering terrible curses. But he was nothing if not pragmatic. Slowly the fuse of his irritation began to burn less brightly, while the sting of a supposed slight became more bearable. Bex was a copper, and coppers did not work sociable hours. If anyone knew about these things, Charlie did. In truth he was nervous for his new wife, as he always was when she was off doing her antiterrorist thing. He had no doubt that her working life could be dangerous, yet he'd never hint at his concern. Charlie had become not simply husband, friend, and lover, but also, by a short head, father.

He showered and shaved, then tried to rearrange what hair was left, peering at himself in the big mirror over the handbasin: cocking his head to one side like a bird preening itself or listening for worms boring through the earth.

"And now," he murmured to himself in his earnest David Attenborough voice, "and now, the lesser-crested Gauntlet views the future with some concern."

"You're natty, that's what you are, Charlie," Bex would say to him. "From what's left of your hair to the tips of your highly polished shoes. Natty, like some ex-major of marines living the life on half pay."

He grinned at his reflection, did a little squaring of the shoulders, caught a hint of Bex's scent from the early hours, then went to find the Hoover to get on with cleaning the flat like a good hausfrau.

> LA's fine in the sunshine,
> Most of the time.

He sang along with Neil Diamond, thinking he was becoming a bit of a golden oldie. The audio was turned up so high he almost missed hearing the doorbell. But not quite.

Kit Palfrey leaned against the jamb doing his best to look elegant, and almost succeeding, his face half-lit in a hideous grin.

"What you want, Kit?" Gauntlet didn't even sound surprised to see him. They had been close, Charlie and Kit, in spite of the difference in ages. When the truth was out and Palfrey revealed as a traitor, Charlie had taken it personally. It was as though Kit Palfrey had betrayed him on a physical level: as if he'd gone around behind Charlie's back tupping every single wife and lover Gauntlet had held dear.

"A few minutes of your valuable time, Chuck."

"Don't think so, and don't call me Chuck. You come through my door, the next thing I know is I'm in the Tower for consorting with the enemy."

"Don't be bloody stupid, Charlie. I'm hardly the enemy. Or didn't anyone tell you the facts of life?"

"Give me a for instance?"

"Try Rolly Hensman for a start."

Back in the old days, Roland "Rolly" Hensman had been the office manager for all the supernumeraries—doctors, lawyers, and Indian chiefs—who worked within the intelligence community. Rolly Hensman was the man you went to if you wanted permission to fart—or so they said. In fact, Rolly Hensman really wanted to be in the thick of it. Rolly Hensman was a little jealous of Charlie's success as a holder and preserver of secrets.

Now Charlie shook his head, indicating a negative, then took a pace back and said, "Come in, but I haven't got all day."

"Very civil of you, Chuck." Palfrey walked in, dropped his body into Gauntlet's favorite chair, and rested his right ankle on his left leg, just above the knee. He wore yellow socks.

Charlie realized the damage was probably done already. That the Security Service had taken to advertising in the popular dailies did not mean that it had lost its edge. It was unlikely that Kit Palfrey had given the watchers the slip, which meant Gauntlet and his new wife would already have one black mark against them for being in the same theater as Palfrey; while this open visit to Dolphin Square merely compounded the sin.

"Don't see Rolly these days." Charlie eased himself into the chair usually favored by Bex. There was a distinct protest from the springs. "You trying to tell me something, Kit?"

"Only the obvious, Chuck. Nobody's in my wake. No one's watching in the shadows."

"'Cos we're all good friends now? Come off it, Kit."

"No. I really thought you'd have been in the charmed circle. Need-to-know and all that. But you can ring them and check up. Point is, I was never the bad boy everyone made out. When I nipped over the Curtain, I was still on the side of the angels. Always was, always have been. If you really don't know the form, give them a bell."

Gauntlet snorted, "Don't have the number anymore, Kit. I'm out. Finished. The book's closed; end titles've rolled." Three seconds silence. "But you say I shouldn't expect a visit in the night?"

"From whom? The law or our friends across the river? Nobody's going to call."

After a long silence, during which Gauntlet inspected his finger-nails, Kit Palfrey reached for the leather briefcase that he had placed beside the chair. "Like to show you something, old thing."

"Show away, but why me?"

"Why you?" Lifting the case onto his knees and fiddling with the locks. "Why not? Saw you at the *Dutchman* last night and thought,

'Old Charlie always liked a mystery, loved to join up the dots, finish the crossword.'" The catches clicked back noisily and Kit lifted the lid. "Pretty pix to start with." His hand slid into the case, fingers and thumb snapping like bulldog clips, and coming out with several matt black-and-white photographs that he waved in Gauntlet's direction.

Charlie reached over, took the pictures, his slim fingers clumsy, crawling across them, separating them sluggishly, looking down but not really seeing what had been captured by the lens.

Slowly he took in that the bulk of the images appeared to be of documents. He also quickly discerned that the written characters were mainly from the Greek alphabet.

Inevitably, in a dark corner of his mind, Charlie saw a figure crouched over a desk using a focal-length chain and a Minox to make these same photographs. "What am I looking at?" he asked, remaining dead-eyed.

"The originals." Palfrey spoke as though Gauntlet could read minds and had mastered the whole thing. Then the pause lengthened for effect, before he said, "Probably the only existing documents describing the death and resurrection of Jesus Christ written within hours of the events taking place." Slightly stunned silence stretching toward oblivion. "Possibly the greatest religious find in the history of man. Mind-bending."

Gauntlet frowned, bent his head even lower to peer at the prints, then looked into the eyes of Kit Palfrey. "You're kidding me. You mean you think these're for real? You're pulling my leg, Kit. Never."

"Absolutely. The biggest story ever to come out of the shadows."

"You believe this? You believe that these're *genuine*? Better than the Gospels?"

"You're repeating yourself. These're much better than the Gospels, Chuck. The earliest Gospel was, maybe, written a century after the death and resurrection, maybe earlier. But these were written in the weeks before, and in the days just after. They're a different kind of Gospel. More immediate. Also a touch more colorful."

The figure with the Minox was replaced by a memory. Kit Palfrey lounged in an overstuffed easy chair in front of a long window that afforded a view down Marylebone High Street. His long legs were stretched out in front of him, crossed at the ankles, displaying a pair of yellow socks, like the ones he wore now, which had jogged Charlie's memory. Yellow socks above immaculately polished oxblood shoes—talk about natty, he thought. Kit was younger and this was a remembered day, long gone, when there was laughter and happiness. In that still center of his turning world, Charlie saw Palfrey throw back his head and bray with laughter. "In the war it was a different kind of game," he said. "We should make all you deskbound wallahs do time in Moscow itself. Experience things at close quarters. In your case, Chuck, the other side of the Wall will do. Send you there for a month."

Gauntlet recognized the words for what they were: glib little stings aimed at anyone who didn't go out and earn his living dangerously. Kit Palfrey was certainly going to do time in Moscow, while Charlie stayed in London and the Home Counties advising on legal matters and occasionally cross-questioning suspects or people who had, as a famous author said, come in from the cold.

In the present, Gauntlet shifted in his chair, both physically and mentally uncomfortable, licked his lips, then asked where the documents had come from. He was slowly starting to see that if things were as Kit claimed, this could be dynamite. He brushed the thought away, not prepared to believe that it could be true. New thoughts shuffled sideways into his head. What was in it for Kit? He comes barging in with some cock-and-bull story about some contemporary descriptions of the death and resurrection of Jesus Christ. So, knowing Kit of old, he had to ask what was in it for Kit Palfrey.

Charlie gave a little puffing laugh. "Come on, Kit, where d'you find stuff like this?"

"Not to put too fine a point on it, they came out of the Lubyanka." Kit gave an on-and-off smile, locking eyes for a moment. "Well, near enough. Dzerzhinsky Square. The old KGB Religious Archives."

"Why?"

"Why? You really need to ask why?"

"I find it all a shade far-fetched, as my old grandmother would've said."

"Okay. Why? Because I had the run of the files, and I wanted to bring back a conundrum. Not good for people like us to sit around doing nothing. I knew I would be coming back so I went trawling, rooting in unlikely places. You'd be amazed at what's there. And what isn't, come to that."

Charlie nodded slowly, unconvinced. "So these pages were just filed under G for Gospels or J for Jesus?" He flicked through the prints and stopped at one that showed scrolls, with their carved handles, neatly packed in cardboard boxes: one scroll to a box. Five in all.

"They were like that." Kit Palfrey leaned across and tapped the photograph with a neatly manicured finger. "Boxed and labeled, with a sheaf of attendant notes. The documents said they were seized from the Church of St. John the Warrior, Moscow, in May 1920. According to the notes with them they had been bought in Jerusalem by a biblical scholar: a Father Pytor, who later stood trial and was banished to the Gulag, where he died."

"Victim of the Great Terror." Humor him, Charlie thought.

"Propagating the cult of an individual—one Jesus Christ. Feeding an opiate to the masses."

"So they've been lying in some damp and lonely basement, these scrolls, until you came along and liberated them? Just like that?" Charlie made a Tommy Cooper move with his hands.

"Exactly like that. I had the opportunity, the means, and the motive. My credentials were impeccable. There was even a book about me by an eminent Fellow of St. Anthony's College, Oxford; and Fellows of that spook school don't write about tat, Charles, as you well know. It says that I was probably the third most dangerous mole working within the Secret Intelligence Service for the Soviets. That's rubbish of course, but nobody's going to disillusion the general public. I don't even look like the person they associate with Kit Palfrey, Masterspy. Mole to Kim Philby's Rat—"

"Kim's *King* Rat."

"Whatever. You recognize me last night, Chuck?"

"Please, don't call me Chuck. Recognized your laugh. Bit longer over the old physog."

"There, you see. Not the same man. I've reached the stage when I look in the mirror and see my grandmother staring back at me."

"So." Charlie brought his hands together, fingers splayed slightly, the hands moving to and fro in a clapping motion, soft and not actually touching. "So, you were not the traitor we all imagined, Kit. I got that right, yes?"

"Good. Yes."

"Instead you were a double. Yes?"

"Yes."

"So when the war was over—the Cold one—and youth stone dead, you, er, you toddled safely home and brought your conundrum with you. How many boxes did you say?"

"Five. Like in that picture." Kit touched one of the prints.

"Brought 'em back to your flat in Kensington High Street. That's where you had your flat, right?"

"Chelsea actually."

"What's in a name?"

"Indeed, what?"

Charlie Gauntlet gave Kit a big smile, the kind he would use just before popping the most pertinent question to some overconfident witness. "You expect me to believe all this?"

"Told you. Give them a ring. Anyone."

Gauntlet grunted. "These scrolls, you've got 'em in Chelsea now?"

"No. *You* said that's where they were. I didn't. Actually they're on the Isle of Ringmarookey."

"Ring-mar-what?"

"'Rookey. An island. Near—but not one of—the Hebrides. Off the west coast of Scotland. The Western Isles."

"Ringmarookey. Ringmarookey. What's there, Kit, apart from sheep and randy shepherds?"

"Monks, old dear. Not Roman Catholic, but Anglican monks."

"Chanting plainsong and making CDs of themselves?"

"Very good at the plainsong, but they don't record. They follow scholastic pursuits."

"Monks?"

"Yes."

"Monks and scholars?"

"Yes. They're Hieronymean. They name their order after St.

Jerome. Geezer who first translated the Bible into Latin: a Father of the Church. They put the letters *OSJ* after their names—not to be confused with Jesuits, who use *SJ*, Society of Jesus, but I don't think there are any Anglican Jesuits—well, not officially anyway."

"And they're mainly biblical scholars, these Order of St. Jerome monks?"

"On the whole, yes. There are some scientists among them, notably Father Gregory Scott, OSJ—*Dr.* Gregory Scott as he was when he wrote his seminal work on the dating of ancient documents, *Papyrus, Parchment, and Paper: Telling the Time.* Very popular book. Best-seller. Grabbed the imagination of the public. Almost as popular as Stephen Hawking's book and much easier to read." Kit stopped, noting that Charlie Gauntlet's eyes seemed to have glazed over. "Chuck, it's fascinating stuff, papyrology."

For a brief moment a small argument went on in Charlie's head. "Where do you know that name from, Charles: Gregory Scott?" his mind asked. "Just a familiar name, that's all. Nobody in particular." Aloud he said, "Sure it's fascinating stuff, Kit. I bet Jeffrey Archer, Ken Follett, and, possibly, Steve King're soiling their underwear because Father Gregory Scott's scooped the pool. When're they doing the movie?"

"Charlie, come on. I'm serious."

"Course you are. You've taken it up, haven't you? With some people it's collecting stamps, or butterflies, with others it's learning to paint. Old Maitland-Wood—remember him, Kit? Once deputy DG of our old Firm—he's into gardening; Brian Cogger, who was once computer king, dabbles in photography; Nigsy Meadows, originally with the Far Eastern Desk, is a farmer. People who served with us, our sort of age—well, your sort of age, Kit—we all have to take up hobbies, it's compulsory. With me it's getting married. With you it's biblical studies and dating old manuscripts. Good way to spend your retirement—providing you're not spending it in jail. . . ."

"And is old Double dead?" Palfrey snapped sharply, angry. "I've told you. Ask someone. Anyone. I'm back; I'm free; I'm not Kit Palfrey, traitor."

"Sure, Kit, you're a hero. Why don't you fold up your tent and quietly steal away. I won't go searching for you; I won't even tell anyone you're in the country. I asked you before, Kit, why me?"

"Because you're here, Chuck. Because I might just have the answer to a great mystery. At the moment I'm sharing it with the good monks of Ringmarookey. Last night I saw you at the opera and I was simply filled with the desire to share this with you. Could do with an extra pair of brains, if you follow me."

"And if I don't believe you? If I really don't want to follow you ...?"

"Then you're not the man I took you to be. Remember what Winston Churchill said about the Soviet Union? He called it 'a riddle wrapped in a mystery inside an enigma.' Well, a lot of people think the same thing about Christianity, and while I was living out a lie at the end of a Moscow winter, I stumbled across what could well be the key to Christianity: the answer to the riddle; the password to the mystery; the gateway to the enigma. Further proof of Jesus Christ's life. A solid contemporary blow-by-blow report. Chuck, doesn't that make you excited?"

"Why me, Kit? And who the hell cares? Not fashionable, religion. Not cool to be a Christian anymore."

"When this gets out, it's going to be cool to be a Christian. This cracks the code. As for the other, I told you already. I saw you last night and I remembered how you were from the past. You were like a terrier when it came to problem solving. You never let go. Remembered you with affection, Chuck. Thought you'd jump at this. Dare to be a Daniel...."

"How d'you find out where I live, eh, Kit? And don't call me Chuck."

"Oh, Chuck, come on! After all these years in the trade, it's like riding a bike, old thing."

"Okay, so tell me what you've got. So far you've talked in riddles. Tell me what you have here."

Palfrey looked blank, took a deep breath, as though he were purposely being misunderstood, "Late spring '91. Moscow," he began, launching himself into a kind of debriefing mode. "To those of us in Moscow, close to power, it had become obvious that the old Soviet

Union was near collapse. The attempted coup was the beginning, and it was an engineered beginning, but that's another story. It's enough to say that the plotters tried to isolate Chairman Gorbachev in his Black Sea resort, and Yeltsin, in spite of his bronchial attacks—which require the ingestion of a lot of his favorite medicine—was on the rise. For months I'd been rooting around, trying to find something of real importance in the old archives. There was interesting stuff, but limited in its appeal. You know, big footnotes to history, stuff that would get the experts writing new books which would appeal to only a limited number of people." Kit squirmed as though the memories were uncomfortable.

"I was looking for something with wider drawing power. Don't know why I began to look through the religious archives, but I did—one Saturday evening when I was doing a spell as duty officer at the old headquarters, Dzerzhinsky Square, backing onto the Lubyanka prison. The statue of Iron Felix, the founding father of what finally became the KGB, was still in pride of place, so you can tell how early this happened, 'cos the Western press all had pictures of that statue being hauled down as a front-page eye byte: symbol of the end of an era, right?"

Charlie gave a curt nod, but Palfrey had his attention now. Gauntlet had a brief flash from the past: Kit Palfrey's famous lecture to the new intake of probationers. Old Kit really used to hold everyone in the palm of his tongue. "You want to know about spies," he always began. "You want to know about intelligence operations, and security exercises? Then I'll tell you. Think of the most immoral and scumish acts you can conceive. Think of the most underhanded, loathsome, offensive actions you can comprehend, then treble it and you'll be halfway to understanding how we operate. Forget glamour. Forget charm and luxury. Bring on the obnoxious. Exit truth. Enter lies. You are now penetrating the kingdom of the blind, the princedom of false-hoods. You have—I cannot call you ladies or gentlemen—become thieves, cheats, confidence people, perjurers, even killers. You are beneath contempt, for you have entered the secret world."

Nowadays, what with New Labor and political correctness, they couldn't have wheeled Kit out without causing offense. The world, Charlie considered, had turned into an era of uncomfortable touchiness.

In days of yore, listening to Kit, the old hands would know that this was what he really thought of the second-oldest profession, and they knew he was right, for he always drew a picture of maggot-ridden corruption that was both repugnant and, at the same time, attractive.

He was exercising that talent now, painting a picture of Moscow in the spring of '91, with the snow barely melted, and the tensions high. Without even trying, he managed to conjure up the nervous rumors, the whispers, even the cabal of plotters, drunk and inept.

Then his search: the descent into the dank storerooms below Dzerzhinsky Square where footsteps echoed and every movement was magnified in sound. It was a long, wide whitewashed cell, he said. Stone blocks, damp walls, rickety tables—the kind of thing you get from military surplus stores. Box upon box of green, moldy paper. There was the evidence of the early days of Stalin's terror. Sandwiched between the first arrests of military men and the dictator's paranoia was his personal attack on religion, the sacking of churches all done by the Cheka, which would, in the coming decades, be transmogrified into the KGB out of the OGPU, GUGB, by way of the NKVD, et cetera, et cetera.

"Mind you," Palfrey said, "there was precious little left. There were long lists—gold and silver. Chalices, patens, pyxes, monstrances, gorgeously embroidered stoles and chasubles. All detailed with the date and the name of the church from which they were plundered, and next to each item, meticulously recorded, the amount of money which the treasure had generated."

This, in itself, was informative, for it was possible to trace the countries that had been part and parcel of transactions: the United States, Great Britain, Switzerland, Italy, Spain, Portugal—interesting in that, following the richer countries, came the Roman Catholic states. The Church almost certainly buying back what had already been plundered.

Then, by the gloom of naked low-wattage lightbulbs, Kit found the scrolls. "The boxes were in surprisingly good condition, though I was concerned for the scrolls themselves. A couple of them had damp patches, others had become brittle." He recognized the ancient Greek but could not read it. He also reminded Gauntlet that he did have some experience in these matters, for Kit's father, like the traitor Philby's father, was an Arabist and an archaeologist. "Four of the scrolls were in Greek, but one—much shorter than the others—was in old Latin. The dead language that had been beaten into me at my snobby public school."

He recalled the smell: of wine cellars in rainy summer, and the prep school changing rooms of childhood, damp serge and wool, and sticky armpits. The air redolent with crotch, knee-joint, and arm-joint tang. Tincture of Sweat Glands, he called it. "Suddenly, in that freezing-cold, barren, whited sepulchre of a place, I was reading, freely trans-lating, even modernizing, the Latin. Two minutes in I prayed for it to be genuine and found that all my senses were stretched, eyes and brain lipping over the language and its meaning, my ears straining for any noise that might signal the advance of another person into the area. I swear that I could have smelled the approach of another human. I could separate one from the rats that already scuttled around and shredded precious paper. Here—!" His hand went back into the briefcase, retrieving a sheaf of typewritten notes. "This is what I read, but this is translated by Father Harry Jarvis, OSJ, and Father Hugh Pickles, OSJ: both men who could converse in Latin. Take it, Chuck. Read what stapled me to these documents."

Gauntlet put on reading glasses—"Don't really need them, but they help a little"—arranged his face into his most skeptical look, and began to read, following his guiding finger along the double-spaced lines.

My name is Titus Romillius, and I am a centurion of the Ninth Legion, moved and attached to the Roman prefect of Judea, Pontius Pilate. I am writing this explanation as I have been summoned back to Rome and know, from Pilate, that this could be a trick to replace me with another officer, for my duties have been of the most sensitive kind. Because of this, I am adding other notes to this letter. They should help anyone reading the journals.

And sure enough, there were more pages after the letter.

Already, there are those here, in Jerusalem, who would like to see me supplanted and my work destroyed.

On Pilate's instructions I have been gathering as much information as possible on the Jewish religious teacher Jesus, who was sentenced and executed only three days ago. This Jesus had a large and devoted following, and the only way I could observe the man was by putting someone close to him. Originally it was thought his followers could pose a serious threat to Roman rule. We have, over the last few years, been examining all of the terrorist groups that seem to thrive in this ripe little satrapy on the edge of civilization.

Charlie cocked an eyebrow at Palfrey. "Bit modern, Kit."

"What?"

" 'Terrorist groups.' 'Satrapy.' This fellow Romillius, the centurion, says he's been examining all the terrorist groups in Judea, which he calls a 'ripe little satrapy.' Bit modern, isn't it? 'Terrorist groups'?"

"The people doing the translation're trying to make the text easily understood. Comprehensible in the modern age. They are very expert and dedicated men. They also know their job. Father Harry wrote the software for translating old documents."

"Ah." Charlie went back to the letter.

For some time, when I first came to this place and started to study the Jewish people and their splinter organizations, their politics, and their religion, it was best for me to be removed from their leading city, Jerusalem. So I made my camp in the town of Hebron to the south of Jerusalem, and it was here that I met the prostitute Naomi.

Naomi was born into the Jewish faith, but had fallen on hard and dangerous times following the death of her husband, James. After James died, Naomi was driven from her home and lands by the treachery of her husband's family, and she was forced to leave Askelon, on the seashore, where she had spent most of her life.

So she had come to Hebron, still very young, some fifteen or sixteen years, and greatly attractive, both in face, speech, and body.

Being a prostitute, she was shunned by her own people, even though Jewish men used her in secret. However, she plied her trade mainly among foreigners—particularly Roman officers. Her price was high, so she was not available to the ordinary soldier, or the common man, and this was how I met her, in the pursuance of her trade. She was a warm, experienced, loving, and clean girl, so much so that I was in a mind to take her as my exclusive woman. She was intelligent and a good talker, though she could neither read nor write.

In the end, I decided she would be an ideal person to place close to the teacher Jesus, so I brought her to Jerusalem and instructed her in what I wished her to do. She still worked in her chosen profession, but with a limited number of clients, most of whom were known to me. I must say now that this was very difficult for me personally, as I had become most attached to the girl, who was pleasing in all possible ways. However, it was essential for me to collect information concerning Jesus, so I arranged Naomi's household accordingly.

Petros was an educated young man who worked on the fringes of the military presence in Judea, and who I knew thirsted after advancement even though he was unable to speak—struck dumb when a ship's mast fell on him during a terrible storm that overtook him as he sailed with his fisherman father, who died in the same storm. It was already well known that he ministered to those of his own sex, and I made him an attractive and generous offer. He would be brought to live with Naomi and would be available for the daily work and for the use of any clients who preferred his own, Greek, offering. Most important, Petros was to spend a minimum of one hour a day during which Naomi would recount to him all things that had happened during her past day. These things would be set down, in detail, in a journal, and Petros was charged with keeping this, and holding the results close. This is the journal to be found, written in Greek, on the four scrolls that accompany this letter.

I also provided Naomi with a girl to act both as a body servant and as a replacement in the bedchamber if a client so desired. This was a Nubian, some twelve or thirteen years of age, the daughter of the woman Abzi, who was one of the female slaves acting as servants to senior members of the legion. The girl, Azeb—or Sheba as she was sometimes known—became a great help to Naomi, even though she tended to talk out of turn and to be sullen. Naomi recounts that she was forced to punish Azeb often because of the girl's unbridled tongue.

I commend to you what Petros set down in these scrolls as it was told to him by Naomi, for she, being a woman of exceptional intelligence, has been scrupulous in recounting both her actions and feelings. In many ways, the plan I had conceived went astray, yet all was not lost by it. Naomi grew enamored of the teachings of this Jesus and became a true believer of what he communicated to all his disciples. Indeed, she came to accept him as the Messiah, as the Jewish faith had foretold. In this there is a great and deep story of both human and divine dimensions. There is much to learn and on which to ponder, just as there are many mysteries that are difficult for us to understand.

I write this in the early morning of the second day of the week. I sit on a hillside a good way from Jerusalem, and my own mind is reeling from the events that surround Jesus and what has happened in the past days—in particular the news that reached us yesterday.

At the end of last week, the man Jesus was sentenced to death by my friend Pilate. At the last minute I was put in charge of the execution detail, so we took Jesus and crucified him at the usual place just outside the city. It was a difficult, unpleasant business, and because of the Jewish religious holy festival Passover, it was necessary to make sure the condemned man was dead and buried by nightfall. I tried to be as much help as I could in the plan that had been devised and passed on to me through Naomi. This plan was to save Jesus from death by taking him down early from the cross. I do not know what finally happened, except that Naomi herself was forced to run and hide, for there were men and women who wanted to see her dead. Now Naomi is gone, her friends are dead, and Jesus is reported to have risen from the dead. How these things can be I do not know, but there is much to read in the last words of Naomi as she dictated to Petros. I must go, as I fear for my life also.

There followed a note saying that the original document had been signed by Romillius.

Charlie returned the papers to Palfrey, pushing them away as though he could not wait to get rid of them; giving the impression that a bad smell was hovering just below his upper lip. "You really think this is genuine, Kit?"

"Convinced of it."

Charlie made a shrugging gesture, big and over the top. "So, if this is for real, why hasn't the Church started to scream it from the rooftops, then? Why hasn't His Holiness the Pope had something to say—*urbi et orbi*, or whatever he does?" Come to that, why hasn't the Archbishop of Canterbury had a word to say about it? "'Cos if it's genuine, Kit, then it's proof positive that Christianity's the one true faith, and Jesus is the main man. This, I guess, would be brilliant news for the Church."

"More than brilliant, Chuck."

"Right, and don't call me Chuck, Kit." He remembered now how well Kit had known him in their past life and was aware of his own constant questioning of truth, both fact and rumor. The former head of interrogation, the leathery Gus Keene, had said of Gauntlet that he had popped out of the womb and immediately done a hostile Q&A, indicating that he didn't believe his mother was his mother, or his

father was his father. "Born with it," Gus had said. "Born with suspicion. Doesn't believe the sky's up and the earth is round unless you
can bring him proofs."

"So, why isn't the Christian Church, in its many forms, screaming
this from the rooftops, Kit?"

Palfrey sighed, after the manner of one who was unaccustomed to
dealing with people of a low IQ. "His Holiness, His Grace the Archbishop of Canterbury, and even the archimandrite of the Donskoy
Monastery, have said nothing because, as you well know, Chuck, part
of the delight of our calling is our ability to keep secrets. They haven't
said anything because they know nothing. The monks of the Order of
St. Jerome also know how to keep their lips buttoned. QED, 'quite easily done,' as my waggish old chemistry teacher used to quip."

"Okay, Kit, how long've we known one another?"

Uncharacteristically, Palfrey scratched his head. "Thirty, thirty-
three, -five years, give or take a couple. And in that time, have you
ever had cause to doubt me?"

"And have I ever had cause to doubt you? The answer to that is,
yes. With the rest of the country, yes. Whatever you say now, Kit,
you're still a proven traitor, a gold-plated liar, and a dissembler—and,
no, I'm not going to telephone anyone."

"You're saying you don't believe me?"

"Let's say you're right, I like a challenge, and this is bloody challenging. But I find it hard to believe."

Palfrey put on his face best suited to one who has been greatly
wronged. "What precisely don't you believe?"

"All of it. . . . I have to be persuaded. It's . . . well . . . what can you call
it? Glib?"

"Would the holy monks help you?"

"How the fff— hell do I know, Kit? I never knew you were religious before. I never had the slightest inkling. Never suspected that
you had a single religious bone in your brain actually, Kit."

"I didn't!"

"So?"

"So, I didn't until this. I was skeptical, until this. I couldn't conceive the mystery of Christ, until this." Palfrey was becoming more and more aggressive. Serious. Deadly serious.

"But this did the trick?"

"Yes!"

"With a little help from your friendly monks, right?"

A tiny pause. "The monks helped me understand certain things. Chuck, read it, please. Please read your way through it. It's a story that'll amaze you. I found the whole thing unsettling. Didn't know what to believe. There are things in those scrolls that are a million light-years from what we think of as Christianity. Naomi describes everything about her life, then, as she falls under the influence of Jesus' teaching, she goes through a kind of rehabilitation. I also found it too easy, Charlie. I couldn't somehow take in the history, and I realized that, for years, I'd been thinking of the Jesus story as a kind of fairy tale, and it's not! It's a true piece of history. A lot of us had some pretty half-baked teaching about Christ and the Christian Church, and I think that's why people have relegated it to a myth. It's not a myth, Chuck. It all happened and this helps prove it."

"Kit, I just find it—"

"No, Chuck, please." Palfrey's voice rose, anger flicking through his tone. "You've got married, right?"

"Yes, but—"

"Where is she?"

"Who?"

"Your wife. The woman you were with last night, the one with the great eyes and the smashing tits."

"Hey, Kit, you want a diverticulated septum, you're going the right way to get one, talking about my wife like that."

"I was paying you both a compliment. Where is she?"

"At work. She's a cop. The Yard. She's with OS13, Anti-Terrorist."

"She gets back when?"

"Maybe a couple of days. Maybe weeks. Hard to tell."

"You let her roam around out there for a couple of days?" Palfrey sounded genuinely shocked.

Charlie grinned. "Kit, things've changed over the years. Me? Me,

I'm a nineties man now. To marry her I had to give up being a male chauvinist porker, okay?"

"That means you'd be free to come up to Ringmarookey?"

"Only if I say so, Kit. With you I can still be a terrible chauvinist pain in the ass, and monks aren't my scene."

Which, in a way, was why, when Bex called him from Heathrow en route to Dublin, Charlie Gauntlet, husband elite, told her that he might be going to Scotland.

He did not tell her that, once more, he thought he had glimpsed an old comrade. Looking from his window on that London morning, he could have sworn that he saw Patsy Wright, just as he thought he had seen him on the previous evening. This time he was more distant, loitering at the edge of a far pavement. It was an eon since he had seen Patsy, and now, twice in the same number of days? It puzzled Charlie and nagged quietly in the back of his mind.

He shielded his eyes and peered toward the figure. The man standing across the street turned, and Charlie saw clearly that it was not Patsy after all. He didn't know it couldn't possibly be Patsy because Patsy was minding Bex in Dublin.

CHAPTER 4

Surprise! It was raining in Dublin the next morning—"a grand soft day."

"Soft, is it?" Bex muttered as she looked out of the window onto O'Connell Street, the gutters running with water, which was better than running with blood. "Soft? More like the fecking flood." Bex had long since become acclimatized to thinking in an exaggerated stage Irish patois when she was across the water.

It was not the prospect of getting wet that worried her, but the well-known fact that it was notoriously difficult to keep up a lone surveillance operation in teeming rain. The common wisdom was that you could not play anyone "long" in a downpour, though Bex had a sneaking suspicion that, even in monsoonlike conditions, you could probably remain well back for much longer than they taught on those thrilling and purposeful weekends run by anonymous men and women at places like Bramshill. Subjects of that kind of surveillance in this kind of weather had their own problems.

Just to be certain that today's chase-me-Charlie was still on, she dialed the emergency number. The same dark brown voice answered.

"Going to call you," he said after she had spoken. "Only thing to do is see where she goes. While she's out, we're putting some ears in her room." This, Bex reasoned, meant that they would be bugging Beecher's telephone. Bex had a feeling that this was really the work of the Security Service doing things on the sly, with her representing The Yard. No names, no pack drill. After all they still had so many "funnies" operating in both North and South that she reflected it would not come as a surprise to hear that a flock of cloned sheep had been unmasked as an antiterrorist intelligence unit.

It was raining harder than ever when she got outside, brolly extended, raincoat belted and buttoned. For a second she had a minor fantasy about the raincoat, which was really a white trench coat, and because of that quite unsuitable for the kind of job she was on now. Charlie found the coat sexy—particularly with her knee-length black boots—and had told her so on many occasions. She could have done with a warm bed now, with old Charles whispering sweet nothings in her ear and, possibly, wearing the trench coat over nothing at all and letting him unbutton it. Last summer he had dared her to go out wearing the trench coat and nothing else, apart from a tiny string of coral beads at her throat and, of course, the boots from Bally that had cost the earth.

The little fantasy and remembrance lasted less than two seconds, damped down by the infiltrating rain, which thundered like hoofbeats on the canopy of her umbrella, sweeping fine spray against her face.

Up ahead, Beecher was wearing a dun-colored Burberry and carrying a dirty-gray umbrella. Not for her any telltale hue like Bex's trench coat.

Yet Bex had her in her sights and quickly perceived that Tessa Murray knew exactly what she was doing: looking for anyone on her back. Come to that, so was Bex, just in case they had some kind of mutual admiration society on the go. She watched what Tess was up to, stopping to glance in windows examining her reflection and those of the people around and behind her; going into a couple of the shops, having a bit of a browse, buying another umbrella in one of them: a dull green to merge into the surroundings.

Bex checked her own back while she watched her quarry going through all the ancient routines of the black arts—thank you, Saint Baden-Powell, for teaching us the rudiments of the chase. Another incongruous memory faded into the back of her mind: Venice, Piazza San Marco, and in the throng of crocodile schoolkids and parties from Luton and Slough, she remembered seeing a furled umbrella, lifted high with a glove over the ferule: a tourist guide beckoning her party along, the glove almost obscene, waggling fingers in constant motion.

As far as she could see, nobody was watching her, though there might have been a car as the traffic was moving slowly, grinding along. If she was being led by the professional "watchers," it was probably an odds-on bet that someone would be watching *her* back.

She smiled at a memory of Charlie in the bath warbling "Raindrops Keep Falling on My Head" as a particularly large drip hurtled from a shop front and splattered onto her face. She muttered a silent prayer as she crossed both roads, pausing at the median looking at the ancient battleground of the GPO, still with her quarry just in view and beating the traffic by two fast seconds, getting her feet on the pavement close to Easons Bookshop and Bhs. Another smile, recalling that Charlie always referred to the shop as The British Stone Whores. It was not particularly clever or witty, but it was typical of Gauntlet, who could make her laugh with the simplest of jokes.

She glanced right again, thinking of the statuary up the street. The "Floozie in the Jacuzzi" would be wetter than ever this morning.

She just caught sight of Tessa scurrying across the bridge over the untroubled Liffey and on into Westmoreland Street, hugging the scholarly edge of Trinity with the Bank of Ireland, flush, across the way. In her head she heard Charlie singing, his cracked voice warbling his own version of "Singing in the Rain," which would make a nun blush, so it would. Dublin was having an odd effect on her, but then she had always loved the city.

She traversed busy Nassau Street and reached the foot of traffic-free Grafton Street.

And there was no immediate sign of the target.

Concerned, she slowed, eyes raking rapidly from side to side, then sliding up the street: trying not to move her head and so draw attention to her searching. The usually crowded shopping precinct was only sparsely populated on this chilly, wet morning: half a dozen scattered ahead as though God had thrown out a handful of struggling human seeds, wrapped against the rain and rolled into the street like dice, or magpies.

Out of the left corner of her eye she detected movement. She recognized the colors and was aware of Tessa Murray exiting a shop. Bex swung away, dropping her head, doing a little jig with the umbrella to bring the canopy down and block off her face, 90 percent sure that her prey would not recognize her again. To make certain, she slowed and dropped back, conscious of her pulse increasing as she felt the tension that had gone almost unnoticed until now.

She was almost level with Bewley's Oriental Café, the chip scent, parfum de bangers and mash with brown sauce full of Eastern promise.

"The rain it raineth every day," she heard, the sound of an almost forgotten, slightly harsh-voiced Feste, that sad jester, from an amateur production of *Twelfth Night*. God, she thought—"The rain it raineth every day"—she had been in love with the young man who played Feste. She had not known it at the time, but she knew it now on a damp Dublin morning heading up Grafton Street toward magnificent St. Stephen's Green. Why had that tittle of truth come back to haunt her now?

Beecher, ahead of her, turned into Stephen's Green with O'Donoghue's famous pub huddling just out of sight and The Shelbourne, grand, standing proud and expensive. Yet when Bex Gauntlet—still trying on the name for size and keeping her own for work—could see the Wolfe Tone Monument, there was no sign of Ms. Theresa Murray, only the traffic and one soiled old Rover near the curb but pulling nicely into the stream.

Love us, I've lost her, Bex thought, and in the same instant realized why she had thought of the long-lost love who had played Feste. It was not the callow boy who had played the fool that had dragged her back, but that the character Feste was sometimes in truth Charlie Gauntlet. Billy the Kid of Stratford might have written the part with one facet of Charlie in mind—that threnody of sadness that lurked behind the layers of strength and buffoonery.

"It's not sadness I feel now," Bex thought. "I'm just pissed stupid at having lost the girl. Oh, shit!"

So, eventually, after taking some precautions via The Shelbourne Hotel, she dragged her way back to the Gresham. And as she returned in the rain, down the traffic-free Grafton Street, she was oblivious to the tall, slim figure, trench coat over his blazer, collar turned up, and a soft cap rammed jauntily on his head.

He looked slightly dazed, and you would never in a million years think he was interested in Bex Gauntlet (née Olesker) as she hurried, wanting to get in out of the rain.

Patsy Wright's face was permanently bronzed, leathery, like that of a man who has spent much of his life out of doors in many different climates. As he made his way down Grafton Street, he seemed to blend into the picture so that nobody would really notice him or pick him out. He had been there, close to her a couple of nights ago, and again in Belfast. Now he was still only a few paces behind her and relieved that Charles was not around. Charlie would have spotted him by now. As Patsy would've said, "For your basic desk driver, Charlie's quite good on the street."

Patsy was exceptionally sharp himself and specialized in minding people who were being allowed to play in the deep end.

But Bex would not have picked him out anyway, for she did not know Patsy Wright. She had never seen him, never met him, but knew a little of his past alliances with her new husband. Certainly she knew that Patsy could be the best friend in the world; or, conversely, the most dangerous enemy. Charlie had left no doubt about those qualities.

"Nobody behind you? Nobody on your tail?"

"None I could see. But why would there be anyone?" She did not realize that she was pulling her mind back from the unpleasant possibility.

"You can't be too careful, so. Nowadays you can't." The car hit some standing water in Baggot Street, sending a little plume of spray arcing from the front offside wheel, and Tess felt her stomach lurch, for Jimmy Maclean had put a voice to the fear that had been within her since that stupid telephone call. Shall I tell him? she wondered. No. Why should I?

"And there was trouble, I hear. Some of the lads on the piss at the telephone." It was as though he had read her mind.

"You'd know all about that?"

"Of course. Connor Bolan gave me a bell. Honest about it. Very loyal. Took the blame for it. He was in charge and he screwed up.

Badly. I've sacked the whole team and moved the telephone out. Relocating. Changed the number, everything—and why wouldn't I know about it?"

They were heading south through Ballsbridge, past the RTE Studios, clocking up the miles toward the Wicklow Gap, which was always the favorite route for them. The rain was beginning to ease off, the sky lightening behind them.

"Is that safe, firing those boys? Won't they talk?"

"They knew nothing, except for the one lad who messed up when you called. Connor's getting new people. He'll take care of it." Jimmy paused and gave her a quick glance. "One way or another." There was no doubting his more sinister meaning.

"So." She had been up at Trinity with Jimmy Maclean, who was a famous man even then. A star now with his own legal practice. But he was more silent than the grave and knew how to organize clandestine services even back then in his student days.

It was Jimmy who always ended up with the contracts for Alchemist, though by the time the details reached him the shadowy men who wanted the service done had been filtered through a muddling maze of checks and balances.

Jimmy was always moving his base of operations, changing the unofficial telephone numbers, ducking and diving, yet you would never think it to see him in his solicitor's office—the height of respectability.

Now he was in his midforties, and Tessa had known him since the days when he was a year senior to her at Trinity. Even then there had been something about him that gave off a sense of trust and honorable credibility. He carried confidence like an aura, wonderfully turned out. Nobody ever saw him in need of a shave or haircut. In the office or in court he wore immaculately tailored suits; heavy, expensive shirts with double cuffs; quiet silk ties; and heavy cuff links that were always a talking point: ceramic copies of Victorian hot- and cold-water taps; or genuine old gold coins set in contrasting mounts; little watches that worked; or—his favorite—blue enamel circles with hands pointing *Left* and *Right*: these he invariably wore reversed.

Today, however, as on all days he met clandestinely with Tessa

Murray, Jimmy Maclean was not looking himself. He wore casual clothes, unpressed jeans and a black, scuffed, leather bomber jacket over a well-worn gray T-shirt that bore the legend *Winnie the Pooh for Taoiseach*—prime minister. He also wore aviator wraparound sunglasses. His dark hair was ruffled, his face unshaven, and he drove the battered old Rover, not his usual gleaming Beamer. For someone like Maclean, this was all that was needed by way of disguise. While people would take in the glasses and, maybe, the T-shirt, few would have given his face a second glance; fewer could have identified him as the suave lawyer who was so well known in Dublin society.

His reputation was of more than squeaky cleanliness, and few had ever penetrated the darker side of his particular moon. Tessa was one of that tiny circle and had been for many years. In her second year at Trinity, when she had suddenly found herself in need of some dodgy assistance, Jimmy Maclean had unexpectedly come out of the wood-work and to her aid.

Tess had grown up cheek by jowl with the Troubles in the North; yet she had carefully avoided publicly taking sides. As a student, she passionately believed in the Republican cause, but had the sense not to see the Provos in any romantic light. Her political faith also held to the concept of peace only through the force and violence of the Provisional IRA. To her mind, the British presence in Northern Ireland was not only unjust, but also immoral: obscene even. To some extent this was a reaction to the fence-sitting, hypocritical, wishy-washy stance of her Roman Catholic parents. However, Tessa Murray was realistic, and very down-to-earth.

When she was finished at Trinity College, Dublin, she would have to live out her professional life in the North, or possibly in the United Kingdom. From a purely financial viewpoint, London had an undeniable pull to it. So, with no illusions, she kept her head down and rarely made any committed comment allying herself with the PIRA in any of its many manifestations.

The crunch came in her second year at Trinity, in the summer when she made one of those steps along the good-intentioned path that could well lead to hell. In short, she tried to make a little bridge back to her parents. She had done it before and she would do it again, and it would always end in tears and guilt, for her ma and da really could not leave things well alone.

It was a sunny Saturday and she had vowed to stay until Monday night, but she was already revising her plans, because of a spat with her mother over some trifle that led to a melee. Tess needed to get out, so by midafternoon she was wandering along Royal Avenue, not really buying but on the brink of being reckless with money.

As she stared into the big plate-glass window of a lingerie shop at the white, black, and pink display, vaguely toying with the possibility of dropping fifteen quid on a tarty satin nightie, she sensed, more than saw, the man standing just behind her right shoulder.

Medium height, which means short of six feet, jacket and gray flannels, his shirt open at the neck, and a lock of salt-and-pepper hair falling over his right eye. He sighed and spoke. "It's a terrible problem women have in making decisions." The accent was not local but much softer, definitely from the South.

"Not necessarily," she said with a smile, and glanced back to be held for a second by his grin and the ice blue eyes. Then she turned completely and asked if she knew him. Those were the days before talks or fragile cease-fires, and though she had seen little of the violence, Tess had that caution anyone in Belfast at that time seemed to be born with; and if they were not born with it, they learned bloody fast. That is, if they had any intelligence at all.

He said, well, they knew each other now. His name was Rory Deacon and he wasn't being forward but would she come and have some tea with him because he was awful lonely and she really looked a nice, well-brought-up girl.

"You're not from here, from the North, are you?" It came out in a slightly accusatory tone, which she had not meant, and she stumbled over her tongue, wanting to justify it, then not bothering.

"No. I'm from the Free State, as folks here call the Republic. Dublin, but I have to spend the odd day up here. I travel—represent publishers: four of them, from across the water. I'm a distributor and they ask me to check on the shops here sometimes; about once a month." His eyes seemed to give a little sparkle, and the amused smile never left his lips. "I'm going back to Dublin tonight."

"I'll take you up on the tea." She tentatively pushed her hand out and told him her name. His hand was dry, with a firm grip. A man with square shoulders who looked you straight in the eye and knew what he was doing. Confident, he marched her straight into a café and ordered "tea and disgusting cakes." The waitress giggled and seemed to know him, at least by sight. "If we were in Dublin, I'd take you to Beshoff's for the fish and chips."

"I'd prefer Bewley's for some of those decadent fairy cakes." She grinned, knowing that it lit up her face.

"So what d' you do to earn an honest crust?" he asked after the tea arrived.

"I'm the female equivalent of Trophimov." It was a test question, the kind of thing that girls did to check out a man's intelligence and knowledge. Trophimov—"the eternal student"—being a character from Chekhov's *Cherry Orchard*; the remark said that she liked theater and was reasonably well read. She appreciated his daring and the audacious way he had picked her up. Yes, she was in need of male company, but she had to make sure that this was not going to be a one-way street. That he was not just a wham, bang, thank you, ma'am. She had never done it, not ever, but the last thing she needed was an all-in wrestling match here in Belfast where there was nowhere to hide.

"You're daft. Too young to be an eternal student." He passed with flying colors, but she was intent on completing the ritual and dropped another question cloaked in conversation. "Oh, then, I see Queen Mab has been with you." She opened her eyes wide and embraced him with them. Thinking back on it, she recognized her foolish immaturity and the pretentiousness of these student games.

"We're both a little old for being Romeo and Juliet, don't you think? Or are you casting *me* as Mercutio?"

"I'm up at Trinity," she said, as though that explained everything.

Passed with honors, she thought, and had a mental picture of this charmer in square and gown being handed the scroll of his degree.

"So you're reading English." He smiled at her, and she could forgive him because that is what most people would have thought.

"No. I'm reading law."

"So you like the theater?" Which was quite witty in a way, for the law has a lot to do with theater.

"Mad about it. Theater, the English language, novels. Whatever."

"Well, I can get you plenty of novels."

That was the beginning. Rory went back to Dublin that night—by train, she discovered and did not question it, because the drive was really not the safest of journeys in those days.

She changed her plans and followed him the next morning. They had a date on the Sunday night and soon settled into a pattern. She would see him on Wednesdays and most weekends, the Saturday and, sometimes, the Sunday. He had a clean little flat in Sandymount, just before you reached the railway level crossing. It was the basement floor of one of the old, larger houses and he kept it prick neat: a bedroom, bathroom, kitchen, and a long front room with a big window from which you could see the tall barber's-pole chimneys of the Poolbeg power station.

Rory Deacon took Tessa Murray's cherry in that bedroom on an agreed Saturday night a month later. She remembered lying very still afterward and wondering what all the fuss was about. Then he had her again, and this time she knew because she was more relaxed and did not have to fake a thing. In the morning they went out and walked along the strand, getting sand in their shoes, stopping to watch a lone rider galloping almost in the water, sending up spray and watching the sea come alive as the sun peeped from between the clouds, sending bright sparkles to interleave with the white froth of foam. She knew she would never forget losing her virginity and really marveled that she had kept it so long.

Rory had become someone very special to her. The horror came a month later, though she did wonder on the Tuesday morning when she broke the pattern and went to his flat and found he was not there. She had set out to surprise him and have him, but the woman who owned the house called down to her from one of the upstairs windows. "He's only here Wednesdays, and at weekends," she said with a knowing smile, so that Tessa wondered how many other girls he had brought back and deflowered in his little bedroom with the big Canaletto print on the far wall, and the little coastline crack running from the rose in the ceiling to a spot just under where she would lie and spread her legs to receive him, until she learned there were more ways than the missionary position.

"You know, in America," he told her on their second bout on the Sunday afternoon, "in some states the law says that's the only way you can do it—the auld missionary position."

"The law?"

"Look it up. Virginia for one. No oral sex and only the old one-two, man on top and girl with her legs apart. Reading law, I'd have thought you'd have known that."

"No. What's the penalty?"

"Well, they have to catch you first."

She pecked him on the nose and asked him, all innocent, what oral sex was, then rolled over, still coupled, and pulled herself on top of him. She was raw all week, but it did not stop her wanting him on the following Saturday.

When it all went wrong, they were in a pub on a Sunday night. No need to name the place, though it was right next to St. Andrew's Church and a haunt of all those international jet-setter trendies who were students.

He had to go to the North that very night and would be away until the Wednesday, so he said. They had arranged that he would leave her there, in the pub, for she could easily walk to her rooms, three minutes away, when he had gone. After all, there would be plenty of other students around. She would be safe on the streets. He was the first man who was really concerned about her protection in the city's sometimes hostile environment. She thought this was sweet, but it made more sense to her later.

Though he was due back on Wednesday she had a lot of work to do, so they would not meet again until Saturday. She felt what some would-be poet had once called "the little death each time he goes," for by then she had admitted that she was in love with him. Seriously. Not playing around or romancing a daydream. If Rory had asked her to marry him, she would have hugged him close and whispered, "Yes, please," quickly, before he changed his mind.

Later she remembered that earlier they had eaten some cold meat with a salad and some blue-cheese dressing. He had laughed when she told him that she had called it "animal cheese" when she was a little girl, because her father had said that they were wee animals, the things that made the cheese blue. It was one of the tiny handful of happy memories she had dragged along from her childhood. That, and the one holiday she remembered when her father had agreed to be an intrepid adventurer and go across the water. They had stayed for a week in Llandudno, where it had rained all the time, but the boarding-house food was great, plenty of fried stuff, and they went to the pictures a lot, and once to a concert. She was about ten, and through her adolescence Tess would conjure up that week to keep at bay the stretched nerves, the mood swings, and the terrible changes to her body that brought with them a new responsibility. It's a direful time for girls that no-man's-land of in-between. So, she remembered the animal cheese, Llandudno, and one Christmas when, suddenly, everything seemed happy and great. The mood was dashed two days into the New Year, but she clung to the Christmas memory.

Alone now, with thirty or forty other people chattering, laughing, and drinking around her, she looked into her shandy and decided she should drink up and get home. Across the room she glimpsed Jimmy Maclean in deep conversation at the bar. She had been introduced to him once, the famous man, at a party. He was impressive in that he appeared to be interested in what she said, and he remembered her name, saying good-night to her when he left an hour or so later. A great and prosperous future lay ahead of him, so they said, adding that he was incorruptible.

Tess took a long pull at her drink and thought about the hour of work she had to finish—a preliminary essay on torts. She was hardly aware of the two men who slid into the chairs on either side of her.

"We have to talk to you, Tessa." He was a broad-shouldered lad in his midtwenties with a small, elfin face that did not go with his body.

"Who are you? I don't know you." It sounded pretty lame, and she had an unpleasant roll of concern in her stomach as she leaned away from him, shrinking back.

"Ah, but we know *you*, Tess." The other man was bigger, heavier, with a blue-veined nose and the carriage of someone who has a vaguely military background: the look of a street fighter. He was older than elfin-face, though they both had unkempt hair and similar accents. Indisputably from the North, and she vaguely recalled seeing them, collecting for the Provos in some pub that had the old IRA songs going on the tape machine: "The men behind the wire" and the like.

"My name's Michael, Tess, and it's about the Brit soldier," the older one said quietly. He pronounced his name "Mee-hail" in the Irish manner.

The alarm on her face was so tangible that her right hand came up and she could almost see the look in her own eyes. "What Brit soldier?" In that moment she knew who these men were, and what they were. "Brit soldier?" she repeated, salty bile filling her mouth.

The elfin-faced one gave a cruel little smile. "The Brit soldier who calls himself Rory Deacon and says that he's a distributor for some publishing houses across the water."

She knew it was true and saw a great pit opening before her. "But . . . ?" she began, not able to look either of them in the eyes.

"Oh, there should be no buts, Tessa. No buts at all. You're not a Prod. Both Billy and I know that." It was the older Provo, Michael, talking. "What we'd like to know is what a good Catholic girl like you is doing regularly with a Brit killer soldier?" This was still in the time when the lads tried to make people believe they were fighting a holy war and it was Protestant versus Catholic.

"Are you sure?" she began again, though she could see that these men were experienced, and had no need to lie.

"His real name is Ralph Docking." Billy with the elfin face sat still as a statue, even his lips did not seem to move. "He's a captain in the Royal Marines. A commando, but on detachment to some other unit, trying to build up a little cadre of people here in the South. The kind of folk who'll give him information, spread tales, and feed stuff to the press. Illegal it is as well. Dublin hasn't authorized the gallant captain's little game, I'll be bound, and I'd be surprised if they even know he's coming over regularly. Certainly the Gardai don't know him. He's usually here of a Wednesday and again at weekends. But you know that." Billy shook his head as though it were terribly wrong for her to know. "They bring him over by helicopter. Drop him at a cottage up near Monaghan, where he keeps his car for the drive into Sandymount."

"I think we should tell you what we want doing." Once more the older fellow, Michael, sitting as still as Billy. "You drive, Tessa?"

"Yes but . . ."

"But you have no car. We know that, so you'll hire one. You'll hire one this Sunday morning and tell him that you've got a lovely surprise for him. You'll make sandwiches and stuff for a regular picnic. We'll tell you where to hire the car. Then you'll drive him to Glendalough—the glen of two lakes—because it's a magical place and a holy place. Have you been there at all, Tess?" Michael did not wait for an answer. "Magical with the remains of St. Kevin's monastery and those beautiful views. You'll give him his picnic, then you'll drive away and leave him."

"No!" Hand up to her mouth. "No! No, I won't." The tears were already scalding from her eyes. They did not have to spell it out for her to know what was planned.

"Keep your voice down, Tess! Don't be stupid now. You'll have everybody staring. Shush!"

"I won't do it. I won't." She shook her head violently and felt the silent tears down her cheeks spraying off. "For God's sake!"

"If you won't, then it's going to be a very painful life for you with no kneecaps and the broken legs. For the rest of your life you'll live in pain, Tess, and it'll all be the same. Now, you do as you're told, girl. Hire the car and do it." Michael repeated a telephone number. Twice. Just to be certain. That was where she would hire the car. "It's best you pay for it, see. We'll . . . we'll reimburse you, mind. Sunday. Right? Get there about eleven in the morning and leave before two. Oh, and Tessa, don't be foolish. Don't tell your man, now. Be your usual self, and we'll see you're looked after. Stupid things happen to stupid girls, so mind."

"I . . . I . . . I can't. It's not . . ."

Billy stuck his little elfin face with its pug nose and pointy ears into her face and hissed. "You'll do it, Tessa, or by the Lord Christ we'll know why. Got it? You'll do it."

A little spray of his spittle crossed her eyes and nose so that she lifted her hand to wipe it off, and Billy flinched as though he thought she would strike him before he turned away.

So they were gone and she knew this was the end. There was nowhere to hide from men like this, she knew it because she knew all the true stories. In the end her love for Rory would make no difference. "That's all one," they would have said in times gone by.

She was desolated, half standing, then sitting back down again, for her legs had gone to jelly and her knees were buckling and she knew she would rather be dead than do what they told her. Knew she could not do it, not in a thousand years.

She tried to stand up again in the whirling babble of conversation that went on around her, in the smoke-and-beer-breathed room. She had felt the blood drain from her face; actually felt the thick liquid blood leaving her face, knowing that her skin and flesh would look like old parchment. Tears ran down her face and nobody appeared to be in the least bit interested—except for Jimmy Maclean, who had started toward her from the bar.

He reached out for her—"It's Tess Murray, isn't it?"—and she felt his arm across her shoulder as he spun her around and propelled her toward the door. The chill evening air smashed her in the face so that she reeled back, clutching at his lapel, sobs making her shudder.

Tessa could never recall how he got her to his car, but she remembered the lights flashing by and even their arrival in Fitzwilliam Square. Later she had a picture of them pulling up in front of the great row of red-brick Georgian houses, though in memory this always seemed to have happened by day.

It was one of the great myths about Jimmy Maclean. Everybody said that he had what they called "private money." Later she learned that the only things his parents had left him when they died in the terrible air crash outside Paris was the beautiful Fitzwilliam Square house and a cottage up in west Cork, near Skibbereen. The money went to his sister, who, he told Tess subsequently, eventually loaned him a great tranche of cash to start his own practice.

On that Sunday night, Tess wept floods of tears in Maclean's kitchen while he made her sip neat brandy. She felt as though she were desperately ill; as if she should have been in hospital. All she wanted was to be nursed, looked after, cosseted.

He asked her nothing in the house. Only later did he lead her outside and over into the railed central garden, the private preserve of house owners in the square, mainly doctors these days. Oddly, her memory retained the picture of the garden correctly, by night with the high, ornate streetlamps throwing unnatural light across the trees and shrubs.

He walked her, sternly and with purpose, up and down like somebody sobering up a drunk. When he spoke and questioned her, it was in short bursts. "Now, it was the two men who came in and spoke to you wasn't it? . . . Tell me exactly what was said. . . . Now, this man—Rory Deacon—they say he's really a Brit officer? . . . Royal Marines is it?" and so on and so forth until the whole story was out, including the depth of her love for the man whose real name was Ralph Docking. The man who was to be killed. She understood that. You did not have to be a genius to know what they meant to do at Glendalough.

"I know those two, and, yes, they're serious men. They're Provos all right," he said, speaking low, almost whispering. "I have a little influence. Not much, but a little. I can try, but I can do nothing for the marine. He's as good as dead."

In the end he was not as good as dead. Tessa did not, could not, get a message to him, but she always wondered about Jimmy Maclean's part in things. He told her to be strong and brave, picking her up two days later in his car as she left a lecture.

Again they walked in the garden. This time by day, and she took note of his watchful eyes, as if looking for an assassin lurking behind the damp greenery.

"You'll hear no more from them. I persuaded them that you were innocent."

"I love him."

"Maybe, but you're innocent of knowing who he really is." Jimmy turned her around as though an invisible barrier proscribed their walking space. "You're to forget about him."

"I don't . . ."

"It'll be hard. Nothing in life is easy, you know."

A month or so later she talked with Jimmy in a pub. Thanked him and asked how she could ever repay him, thinking he would want to sleep with her: his reputation was as a ruttish fellow with the women. He wanted none of that, giving his little secret smile and telling her that he would think of something.

Years later he turned up, on a wet Friday afternoon at her office in Belfast, as though appearing like the genie of the lamp in a pantomime. Leaning against the doorjamb in her office and saying they should talk—outside and away from the building.

He drove her to the green hills south of the city and, still with a smile, told her about Alchemist and what her part would be.

She asked him how he had ever got mixed up in this and noticed that his smile did not touch his eyes as he said, "Breathe one word of this outside of me and the man himself and I'll see you dead in a ditch, Tessa."

She knew he meant it, and never a day went by without her thinking about what he might have done for her and what he might still do to her. In a way she was in love with him, though nothing ever passed between them. The details never came into the open, though she was conscious of them lurking in the shadows between them, for the Alchemist conspiracy they had entered into immersed both of their lives in the end, and this was really only the beginning of it.

If she could allow herself to see the whole business clearly, she would see the truth of it: that she had been set up from the start, chosen as a suitable case for the job. But she rarely allowed herself to think about the manner in which she was brought into Alchemist's organization. And when she did, well, all the logic went to pot. If you thought it through, the dates were all wrong: it was far too early in time for Alchemist. But how many other little conspiracies was Jimmy into, even as early as that?

It was here and now, on the day that Bex Olesker had followed Tess, undetected, in Dublin. Sitting in the old battered Rover, next to Jimmy, Tessa looked out on the raw, harsh, and brutal beauty of the Wicklow Gap and wondered at the enormity of the message Jimmy Maclean was giving her to take to the man called Alchemist.

CHAPTER 5

Kit Palfrey had sent the first few pages of the translation of Naomi's diary to Charlie Gauntlet. They arrived by courier, neatly laser-printed and in an unmarked folder, so Charlie settled down to read the pages on the plane, going from Heathrow to Glasgow. After a long and twisting conversation with Palfrey, Charlie had reluctantly agreed to visit the monks on their stateless island. Because of the beautifully printed, double-spaced manuscript, Charlie found it difficult to take it seriously. He also realized that this had been a problem with the supposed letter from Romillius that he had read when Kit first appeared, uninvited, at Dolphin Square.

Neat little Charlie Gauntlet meditated on the things he had been told, and the words he had read. If the centurion's letter was genuine, then whatever the other scrolls contained had to be more than startling. At first reading, Charlie had thought Romillius's words sounded prosaic, commonplace. But thinking about the subject matter, he realized that it was not so much the way in which the Roman soldier had written: the mundane style of the message came not only in the manner in which it had been translated by the monks, but also in the way he had read it.

The translators had put it into reasonable English, not the English of the King James Bible, which Gauntlet associated with holy writ. Reading law had brought to Charlie a love of language, and his first mentors in what had become his life's work had all been devotees of Shakespeare, so Gauntlet had come to embrace the poet's Elizabethan English. As a child, and particularly in his school days, the rise and swell of the old biblical language had become a great and seductive part of his inner life, as did the elegance of the major poets. Eventually, the books beside his bed would include the writings of Winston Churchill, which added to the luster of his interior life.

On the occasions he had been inside a church in recent years—a few weddings, funerals, and two baptisms—Gauntlet had recoiled at the flat, ordinary way in which modern English presented scenes and dialogue from the Bible when clergy had messed about with the Book of Common Prayer. He missed the immediacy of the old translation. Somehow, modern language seemed to demystify the message and made the Bible sound like a novel. It was the same with the Book of Common Prayer. The modern translations subtracted from the Bible, and the Prayer Book, rather than adding comprehension, and Charlie secretly thought the excuses—to make the great books more accessible—a load of bunkum, for the fire had gone out of both. He still got angry at idiocy, exploding with anger when some schoolmaster declaimed that Shakespeare had lost his relevance to the young people of today. "I suppose this parvenu finds it a chore to see the way the Bard put up a mirror to life in all times," Charlie fumed. "God knows . . ." He appealed to heaven.

Charlie was neither theologian nor Christian believer. He found that trying to understand that the Christ story was absolutely true was, for him, like trying to visualize infinity, eternity, space, light-years.

As he read it, he thought that, in a way, the text of Naomi's diary—as translated by the scholarly monks—came over in the same somewhat flat and impersonal style that had impregnated the letter from Romillius. Charlie had to constantly remind himself that this wasn't necessarily a fiction, but possibly a revelatory find that would explode, giving hope and certainty to all humankind. This was not easy, but seated in the comfortable club-class seat, Charlie began to read, aware that the words could well be part of a giant tapestry reaching back from the past to be active now, in the present. Naomi had dictated:

My friend, customer, and teacher, the centurion Titus Romillius, has sent Petros to me. He has explained what must be done, and young Petros seems to be the kind of man who cannot be made to blush. It is hard to tell because the boy is dumb and only communicates through signs with his hands and expressions on his face. He is lively, though, always smiling, and makes laughing noises whenever there is mention of physical gratification— by which I mean sex. Romillius was there when he arrived and Petros signaled that he thought I was pretty. This is good, for he has to work close to me, but he will only give love to the men who want a boy. Romillius has explained all this to me.

Petros was brought from an island somewhere off the coast of Greece. A brother centurion saved the boy from death and found that he is very intelligent in spite of not being able to speak. He has studied hard, and now he can understand the Roman and Greek tongues as well as my language and that of the Egyptians.

Romillius has suggested that I should first say something about myself. This is difficult for me, being a woman and therefore in subjugation to my betters. Indeed, I am a simple person who likes easy things such as watching the sun rise and set, marveling at the beauty of flowers and plants, or my husband's smile and the look in his eyes. I used to adore just sitting in the high ground above what was once my home and looking out over the city of Askelon and seeing the sea sparkle in the distance.

Tomorrow we leave Hebron and go to Jerusalem. I have never been there and am very excited as Romillius says there is already a house waiting for us and we will be safe for we shall be under his protection. Perhaps this is the true turning point in my life that has known so much sorrow in the past three years. A Nubian girl called Azeb is already at the Jerusalem house. She is young and will clean, cook, and is old enough to have men should they desire her.

Romillius says that I must tell Petros of the bad times when my husband died, so I shall do that now. My husband, James, had offended his family by marrying me, for they had wanted him to marry a girl called Sarah, the daughter of an old family friend called Isaac ben Ehud. This would have meant a great increase in sheep, goats, and land, because Sarah's father owned a larger herd than my husband, together with two fields of corn, against James's one small field.

In the end, James refused to be betrothed to Sarah, for he loved me—and I him—with a deep and strong bond. We entered into the marriage with gravity and honor.

James and his family were quite ignorant people, though James did not realize how ignorant he was. How could he be otherwise? He never spoke with learned men, so he knew no difference. Looking after herds of sheep and goats all day and night does not exercise the mind. At least my father was a scholarly man, and while he did not think women needed education, so that they might read or write, he saw that I grew up in the shadow of good talk and knowledge of the things that mattered in our faith. Even though James was an unlettered man, I loved him: he could make me laugh and give me happiness with a simple thing, like a smile. He also satisfied me in physical lovemaking. I did not need much to keep me happy, and James managed to do that most of the time, even though he was a lot older than I.

God grant us all that ability, Gauntlet thought as he turned the page.

Alas, it was to be a happy, but short-lived marriage. I did not become pregnant as we had hoped and prayed, and this was not for want of trying. I was a dutiful and loving wife to James, and we were vigorous and happy when we lay down together: something I enjoyed as much as he did.

Some of the older women I spoke with in Askelon were critical of me. They would gossip and say it was not natural for a woman to enjoy the loving as much as I—though many of the younger women agreed with my views and they looked forward to the evenings and nighttime when they could satisfy their husbands with as much ardor as I showed. Many times I heard people say that only harlots enjoy physical love. What nonsense. Now I know that the harlot seldom likes the coupling she is forced into for money—or lack of it.

One of the women, Anna, a beautiful girl, became a close friend. She was taller than I, a well-formed girl, with dark eyes and long black hair that came down below her waist. Six months or so after my marriage I spent one afternoon with her. We kissed and fondled each other on the mattress where I slept with James. Anna took the man's part first, then we changed over. It was pleasant, and neither of us felt in any way awkward. It was a nice game and there was no need to feel guilty afterward. Anna told me frankly some of the things she did with her husband, and I repeated to her all manner of acts I did with James. I think she was shocked at first when I told her what I did with my lips and mouth. I have never thought of that as sinful. Anyway, she said she would try it with her David and much fortune to her. It made James like a wild thing, though the first time I did it, he seemed angry and beat me, which was oddly pleasant as he was very masterful.

Finally I was blamed for James's death because of my enthusiasm for making love with him. I had ground corn and made bread one morning in the spring, toward the end of our first year of marriage. I let the unleavened bread cool and then took it out into the fields to James, together with a jug of wine and some chicken that I had cooked with herbs and spices. I always kept strictly to the laws of food in which my mother, who was a devout person, had long instructed me.

On this beautiful day James was with our flock of sheep and goats in the foothills outside the city; the weather was balmy with a blue sky and a light, warm breeze. I discovered James resting near an outcrop of rock, while the herd grazed nearby. He was glad to see me and we ate together, drinking in turns from the jug of wine. We were on the edge of a valley and had an unsurpassed view of Askelon and the seashore upon which the city lies.

After we finished the food, James, inflamed by the wine and the beauty of the day, and I think also by my face and body, became aroused and began to kiss and fondle me, making me want to howl with need for him. Our desire became so strong that, as we were alone in the grazing land, I took off all my clothes and gave myself to my husband, lying there on the hard earth. The warmth of the day, the fact that we lay in the open air, together with the effect of the wine upon my senses, gave me an unusual thrill, and when we reached the pinnacle of desire I cried out loudly with the joy of it. Later we talked and I considered that I was the luckiest woman in Askelon to have such a husband.

At the time we neither knew—nor would we have cared—that some of the older men from the city had hidden among the bushes to spy upon us, seeing everything we did with each other. Even when we had finished, we did not bother to dress, but lay naked on the ground, clinging to each other.

Later on the same day, after I had gone back to our small house, these same older men brought me the news that James had been bitten by a viper as he was moving the herd to higher grazing.

Some of the younger men carried him in from the herd and I tried to clean out the bite, but the poison from the snake was already so well established in his body that he died as the sun went down. The snake had been young and its poison strong and the shock so great to my poor husband's body.

We buried James the next day and I was almost mad with grief. Yet this was nothing compared with the sorrows to come. I was melancholy, downcast, lamenting and weeping as I sat with the other women mourning the death of my husband as the men took his body for burial as is the custom.

However, in the midst of all this anguish the leaders of the community came into the house, together with James's mother, and pointed at me declaring that my husband's death was my fault. One by one they accused me of being wanton, immodest, and lascivious. They spoke of seeing James and me in the open air behaving, as they said, like beasts of the field.

I had led my husband into wicked, carnal ways, they claimed, and denounced me, saying I had filled James's mind with sinful depravity so that he could not look to the safety of the flock, and indeed the safety of himself, so that the poisonous snake had caught him unawares. His mother said had he been of normal mind he would never have been bitten by the snake. I had bewitched his mind, she said, using terrible spells and incantations. It would not have surprised me if they had accused me of being some kind of devil.

This was not simply his mother's grief, trying to find someone to blame for her son's death. I was certain this was the work of the elders poisoning James's mother's mind just as the snake had poisoned my poor husband.

Later, when I was in Hebron, I met a woman I had known in Askelon, and she told me that James's young brother, scarcely twelve years old, had been betrothed to the girl Sarah and the whole of our flock given over to them. In the meantime the sheep and goats were being looked after by Sarah's father, and the corn seen to by an uncle. They had finally got what they wanted, and at the time I could do nothing but flee from the city. If I had stayed, they would certainly have sentenced me to death and I would have been dragged out to the cliff by the sea and stoned.

Charlie Gauntlet looked out of the window, down to the roiling, dark clouds spread out below at twenty thousand feet with the sun hanging bright in the canopy of sky above.

What a sad little tale, he thought. He also wondered how the monks were affected by reading of Naomi's sexual cavorting. A flight attendant, slick in her neat uniform skirt and shirt, sashayed down the aisle. As she paused to bend and speak to a passenger, the material of her skirt pulled tight across her buttocks, giving Gauntlet a pleasant little frisson of the loins. Aloud in his head he said, "No, Charles. This is politically not correct." It was all so real that he thought for a moment he had actually spoken aloud, for the young woman turned back and looked at him. He asked for a coffee, and she brought it with a foil packet of peanuts, smiling her nice, stern flight attendant's smile that made him feel slightly ashamed. In his head he had just about committed adultery with her. It made him feel guilty, as though he had been unfaithful to Bex already. He was missing her more than he ever thought possible. Charlie had been brought up in that somewhat cold, stiff-upper-lip school of the British upper-middle classes, and many of the feelings he was coming up against now were journeys into unfamiliar territory.

He sighed, then turned the page and continued to read.

After I fled from Askelon, I came to Hebron with nothing but a few coins and the clothes in which I traveled. It was here, in Hebron, that I met Romillius, who befriended me and suggested that I should sell my body and be a harlot. I had no wish to do this, but neither did I want to beg on the streets, starve, or do menial tasks, which was the only other way I could have kept my body and soul together. In the end, Romillius prevailed. I was in dreadful need of money for food and clothes, so I gave myself to the centurion, who promised to instruct me in the ways of whoredom.

He knows much about women and the many tricks they can use to please men. So I soon learned that men are possessed of incredible imaginations. You cannot put boundaries on a man's imagination, and I should think that you could not proscribe a woman's either. I learned many strange things from this soldier who had traveled all over the empire that is ruled from Rome. As a young legionnaire he had served in Gaul and lived in Britannia.

Romillius told me about his travels, of how wild and brutal some lands could be, and how hostile. Even so, he had experienced much at the hands of women. There were stories about some of the women warriors who became willing partners to soldiers in places like the north of Gaul. It had taken many years for the women to be trusted, for in the early days they would feign friendship, hiding a knife or similar cutting instrument near the bed. Then, later, when they had a soldier in thrall with the wiles of their body, they would unsex him with the knife and run away, hiding in the woods where they had to be hunted down like animals.

Romillius taught me that both men and women will be excited by many odd and different things. There is no sense to this. Some even enjoy pain, humiliation, and religious-like rituals in which they are bound with cords and ropes. I remembered something of this when James had beaten me after I had kissed and sucked at him. He had pretended to be stern, but at the same time he became very aroused. I recalled that I did also.

It is strange the imaginings of men and women, and the way in which these thoughts will set fire to desire.

The centurion, who is a senior officer, told me of many things that I could hardly believe, but later I found them to be true. He taught me the ways in which I could stimulate men, using my fingers and palms, also my tongue and mouth. Lying with him, I soon learned that men could be excited by touch, and he showed me the various places on the male body that are sensitive to stroking and pressure with the fingertips.

I had long known that men could be stimulated by what a woman wore, or how she smelled. Romillius, whom I now loved with a depth I had never thought to feel again, instructed me with regard to unguents and scents, bathing oils, and even clothes.

He gave me items of clothing made of soft material, even silks, which made me feel like a woman of great riches. He explained to me that some men enjoyed undressing a woman—sometimes they would get more pleasure from this than the complete act of loving. These things were all new to me. Things I neither knew nor could even guess at.

Yet Romillius is a keeper of secrets.

Gauntlet sat up and began to take notice, wondering if this was the start of a revelation that had been hinted at by Kit Palfrey. Later on the day he had visited Dolphin Square, Palfrey had admitted there was another reason why he had chosen Charlie to confide in.

"So, you saw me at the opera and thought you'd like to talk to me for old times' sake, huh?"

"Something like that." Palfrey gave Charlie a quick, lopsided, quirky smile, then repeated in cockney, "Sunink like that."

"Ho? Yes, sure, Kit. I wouldn't believe you if you swore it on a stack of Bibles."

Palfrey went silent and became very still. Gauntlet remembered moments from the past, clearly recalling Kit Palfrey going still and silent just as he had now. Whenever Kit went like this, it was always the precursor to a revelation, so Charlie jumped in with both feet, and total recall into the bargain.

"I can't believe you, Kit. Couldn't believe you if you paid me a million dollars. It's what deceit does in the end."

"Believe what you like, Charles." There was anger in the way Kit spoke. "Get out the thumbscrews, polish up the rack, oil the iron maiden, or break out Skeffington's daughter."

"In your eyes, Kit. That's where it shows. You've got these baby scorpions, scuttle behind your eyeballs when you're trying to hide something. I've seen it before, and it's there again, now."

Palfrey grinned again. "I gone deaf, George."

"You what? What are you talking about? George?"

The stillness had returned to Kit. This time it was more marked, stretching between them like a garden path loaded with traps and water jokes to snare the quiet and unwary. The silence stretched, became taut, then Palfrey turned away, unable to look Gauntlet in the eye. Charlie began to speak again, but Palfrey made a kind of quick hissing sound.

"Wait!" Kit's voice struck out, almost a shout, and he raised his hand, flat, palm outward, pushing at the air. Dramatic and overstated. "For heaven's sake, wait. Yes, I chose you, Charles. You were not that random. I picked you for your brains. No, that's not true, you were elected because of the way you think."

Kit paused, as though he needed to catch his breath. "Okay. So you'll know soon enough. When you start reading, you'll know. Charlie, you're like a bloody woman, won't leave things alone. You're like a woman nagging on to find what you've bought her for Christmas."

"This is a Christmas present?"

"Don't be feeble. No, Charles. Listen to me. Your mind works in a special kind of way. You nag at problems; you have a knack of seeing what's behind the things people say and do. You're expert at reading the runes, Charles. What psychics call cold reading."

Kit went silent again for a moment, then took a deep breath. "There's an old story about a former archbishop of Canterbury who remonstrated with a cabbie for swearing. He said, 'You should rid yourself of that dirty habit!' And the cabbie said, 'Habit, guv? Swearing's not a habit, it's a bloody art.' Charlie, you've developed a bloody art of questioning everything. You won't let go. You dig and delve. Worry at things until you find an answer."

Charlie raised his eyebrows.

"When you were cross-examining me, before I took the dive—did a runner to Moscow—I pleaded with my Soviet control to get me out. I told him, and it was the truth, that I could only hold out against you for a few more hours. I warned my control in the Firm as well. That I was a double was a deep secret, but you can be so bloody persuasive."

"I can?" In his mind, Charlie thought, He has almost charmed me from my profession, by persuading me to it. Then he couldn't recall where the quote came from. *Timon of Athens,* he thought later.

"You know you never give up. I've watched you with others. You get straight to the heart of things. You suss out secret agendas quicker than a mine detector. It's as though you've got your own personal radar."

"And I need that personal radar now?"

"You'll see when you start to read the thing, 'cos the centurion had a secret agenda."

"Ah."

And was this what Romillius was coming to now in the written-down spoken words of a prostitute in Hebron, around two thousand years ago? Give or take the odd hundred. Were they finally getting down to cases? Charlie wondered. If these scrolls were real. If Naomi actually lived in the Palestine of Jesus of Nazareth, if that was a fact. Well, he swigged the last of the coffee and read on.

Yet Romillius is a keeper of secrets. He has told me what he does, and almost how he does it. Indeed, he was moved from the Ninth Legion to do a special service for the emperor. His work is to discover dangers in our land. He listens, he seeks out men and women who will give him good information. I can speak of it here because it will go no further, Petros being dumb. It will be written down by Petros, who is smiling at me even now while I am speaking. I can reveal Romillius's work because, in the end, it will be Romillius who will read this, and I know that I am already helping him do his work.

The people of Israel are beset by dangers because we are who we are. I know this for I have heard my own learned father talking of it. Our chief priests and the Sanhedrin*—our religious council—disagree about so many things; our teachers, those who interpret the Holy Book—the Scriptures—all disagree because there is so much we *can* disagree about.

Within our faith, customs, and rituals we have divisions. Because we are the Chosen People of Jehovah, we are not loved by many from other races and beliefs. There are also threats from others. The forces of Rome occupy our lands. This, in itself, I am told, is dangerous. People who are not from among the Children of Israel—foreign to our ways and our faith—are not content to live under the yoke of Rome. They rise up against both the Roman garrison and the civil governors set over us by the emperor.

There is discontent. Soldiers and officers of the emperor are attacked, even killed. Because of this, we are in danger. Fear is engendered by the Zealots and others called after Sicarius, which in the Roman language means "assassin." The Sicarii carry hidden knives and kill as lightly as they would swallow wine.

Also, because of this, Romillius, and his helpers, must be

*Sanhedrin—the Greek term for "sitting together": a council formed on the orders of the Roman executive for the administration and judicial running of Palestine.

watchful. My duty will be to get close to one man who has set himself up as a teacher, possibly a prophet. His name is Jesus and he comes from the village of Nazareth. Some even say that he is the Messiah, the God made man whom Jehovah has promised will come to Israel and lead us into a new time of understanding.

This Jesus already has many men and women who listen to all he teaches. They also say that he can perform miracles. So, I must gain his trust and bring my report back to Senior Centurion Romillius. I am to be his spy and I shall work hard, for I think I would follow my centurion to the grave. I only give myself to other men because he demands it. Soon I shall meet with this man Jesus and do what my Roman love desires.

Charlie Gauntlet almost shivered, the aircraft lurched, and he saw that they had begun their descent into Glasgow. They would soon be coming in low over the rough, undulating ground, which always produced a bumpy approach. He wondered if all he had read was indeed the truth. If it was, then Kit Palfrey had stumbled over a historical and religious bombshell. In simple language, if it was true, then Naomi had been recruited by Roman intelligence to infiltrate the most sacred inner sanctum. She was the mole in Christ's citadel.

There was a number for Charlie to ring once they landed. This would put him in touch with a private pilot who would fly him to Ringmarookey miles off the coast, and way to the north of Ireland. Charlie would rather be flown out there than do the trip by boat. He hated boats and lived in terror of the humiliation of seasickness.

Funny, he thought, the last time he had worked with Patsy Wright they had done a trip by boat. That had been quite an adventure, but old Patsy had been one for adventures. Why was Charlie thinking of him now when he didn't even know if Patsy was gainfully employed by the government anymore?

In the old days, in the wonderland they inhabited where the currency was secrets and the trading was in treachery, Patsy Wright, ex-officer, slightly down-at-heel, slim, blazered, old regimental tie knotted at his throat, walked the stealthy streets and smoothed a safe pathway for people like Charlie Gauntlet. Patsy had been a fixer, a watcher, a man who arranged matters, saw to it that everything was in place, or cleaned up after someone had made a mess. Nobody better than Patsy Wright. Even back then Charlie had sometimes wondered exactly how far Patsy was told to go. Funny, he thought. Funny, I miss old Patsy.

CHAPTER 6

When she was with Jimmy Maclean, Tessa would often experience a flash of suspicion—sometimes only for a second or so but deeply skeptical nevertheless. That she recognized this as paranoia did nothing to alleviate the concern and well-entrenched anxiety; and here it was again, as he pulled the dirty old Rover off to the side of the road, surrounded by the brutal beauty of the Wicklow Gap. She would never even admit to the thing that disturbed her: the old idea that perhaps Maclean had been responsible for the trauma and agitation in her past. Yet she never allowed the thing to formulate in her mind. She snuffed it out before it had a moment to get into sharp focus.

It is a valley, the Wicklow Gap, that snakes through the mountains that form the backdrop almost wherever you are in County Wicklow. The road on which you navigate through the valley even takes you to Glendalough, of dreaded memory for Tessa, and the sprinkle of houses that is Rathdrum. The mountains dominate, and the crags and bluffs remain beautifully forbidding no matter what the weather.

They always came this way because it was truly safe to talk in the Gap. The peaks and rock faces made it secure. Jimmy maintained that if you were out in the open in the middle of the valley, it was impossible to be overheard: even sensitive directional mikes were difficult to use in this terrain.

Now, out of the blue, the name came into her head: Rory Deacon—whose real name, according to a couple of Provos all those years ago, was Ralph Docking. She hadn't thought of him in a decade, so why now? Mentally she shook her head, as though physically throwing off the thought. Rory Deacon: he had disappeared as though he never existed. Vanished. Gone.

In the present, rain clinging to a strong breath of wind was blown up the valley like gunsmoke. Jimmy stirred in the driving seat. Stirred, coughed, then spoke.

"This time it's madness. Impossible."

"Oh?"

"Oh, indeed. My worry is that he'll go for it; and at the same time I hope he will. It's a paradox. These are new clients and they have some very serious provisos."

"Well, show me."

He nodded, as one hand went to unlock the glove compartment. "Can you believe this?" Sliding the photograph out and turning it over.

Tess flinched as though she were the target and bullets had just ripped through the windscreen. "Jesus!" she said, her voice almost lost so that she repeated it. "Jesus God!" One gloved hand to her cheek.

Rarely was anything written. Little was actually spoken. Anything that was scribbled down was always destroyed. Faxes were never sent. Here, at the beginning of a new century, privacy was a thing of the past and they went to enormous lengths to protect themselves.

"You see what I mean?"

"But who would . . . ?" She looked hard at the picture. The president of the Federation of Russian Republics stared back at her, the ghost of a smile around his lips, but the eyes dead, like glass eyes in a dummy. At the president's shoulder, his scandalously young new wife seemed to be elbowing her husband out of the way.

President Oleg Bortunin—who had been elected in that extraordinary time of changing presidents following Yeltsin and Putin—had been a hard-drinking, mercurial, slickly tough politician until his dour, stolid wife had suddenly died. Oleg, everyone knew, had a tipsy, roving eye, but this did not prepare anyone for what was to follow. Three months, almost to the day, after the demise of his wife, the president announced his remarriage.

At the time people quoted *Hamlet:* "Thrift, thrift, Horatio! The funeral baked meats did coldly furnish forth the marriage tables."

The new Madame Bortunin was half the president's age, a product of the worst girl-power excesses of the West, and caused a violent storm of reaction on her first appearance with her new husband. Dressed in the briefest of skirts, giving the cameras not only a view of exceptionally lovely thighs, but also a flash of crimson pants, she seemed to tower over Oleg. This was mainly due to the heavy platform boots and the hair: blond, piled high in a swinging, top-knotted tassel. The photographers went wild, and the tabloids shrieked headlines such as "Bortuzza Marries Spicekova Girl" and, from *The Sun*, "Oleg and Anastasia," for the bride's given name was indeed Anastasia. Every newspaper in the Western world, from the *New York Times* to the recently revived *London Daily Sketch,* which had nothing to do with news as we know it, displayed this bizarre marriage as something beneath contempt.

Wrongly.

Within a week it was revealed that Madame Bortunin was not the mindless bimbakova that she appeared. Anastasia was, in fact, the product of New College, Oxford, where she had not only won herself a first-class honors degree in political science, but also a considerable Ph.D. in psychology. Yes, she was a brazen sex cat, but she had claws and a steel trap for a brain.

The president was swiftly admitted to a private hospital in Switzerland, from which he eventually emerged looking incredibly fit, tanned, almost young, and bouncingly happy. From there, the president and his lady instituted a new and vital program of changes, setting the ailing Federation on a new tough course, which, if the Bortunins did not swerve, could well be Russia's final salvation in this third millennium. Nobody doubted that the silk-and-lace-covered iron fist of Madame Bortunin was working Oleg. He had become the most expensive vent doll in the business.

"Her as well?" Tessa asked.

"Of course. You can't have one without the other." Maclean nodded crisply, then opened the door and eased himself out into the drizzle, turning up the collar of his bomber jacket. Tessa joined him, shrugging her shoulders as she tugged at her collar, turning her back to the windblown rain. Carefully Jimmy tore the photograph into confetti and let it dribble away from his fingers. Together they stood watching the mist obliterate the tops of the mountains.

"Who?" She asked quietly, meaning, Who had contracted the killing? Just as they never spoke the name of the target, they had a rule about contracts. The man they called Alchemist had a series of edicts that were nonnegotiable. For instance, they always had to know who was putting out the contract, making the running. Part of Jimmy's brief was that he had to meet representatives from the organization who wanted Alchemist's services. The meeting had to be very much one-on-one, and on their part the contractors had to establish bona fides long before that meeting took place. It was essential, for if a terrorist organization could discover the way to Alchemist, then law enforcement or security forces could also sniff out the path and home in on the star of the show.

It was relatively simple to make the initial contact, but very difficult to follow through, establish the facts, and make the face-to-face meeting. It took time and patience from both parties, and Jimmy had never gone into the precise details with Tessa.

What she knew was that the early stages were negotiated by using the small-ads services in daily newspapers. Oddly, while they were careful to the point of obsession about speech and written messages, the opening moves were always played out in plain sight. A kind of code was quickly established, and noncommittal letters would go to and fro between nameless associates and faceless agents.

The next stage was always the testing time. Tessa did not know it, but Jimmy Maclean used many men and women who had been exposed to military or police experience and training. These were people who were familiar with the meticulous routines of covert trade and fieldcraft in a way that was intuitive.

Maclean thought of these people as his personal "watchers," to use the old Security Service slang. These "watchers" were usually not intercognizant; neither did they know the true nature of their work. Many of the people doing this job imagined they were part of a private detective force used by several firms of solicitors.

Once Maclean had fingered the contact man, or woman, several surveillance teams would be put into play. For weeks at a time they would keep the subject under constant observation, drifting around the fringes of this person's world, like pilot fish around a whale, not only keeping an eye open but also an ear. It was essential for the agents to be listeners as well, and their priority was to establish that the contracting organization was the genuine article. Early in Alchemist's career it became a golden rule not to accept any approach as genuine until it was proved to be 110 percent unquestionable.

Only after this had been done did Jimmy Maclean order his people to go to the next stage, and this also took time, for they rarely followed the same procedure twice. However, the one action that remained constant was that the team, working like stalking-horses, would cut the target away from his, or her, associates and minders; making sure the contact became vulnerable, even if it was only for a minute.

Often the mark would not even know what was going on, and the experienced watchers were able to do it again, then again, so that they could make use of the moves either to lift the target off the street or give him instructions.

So far, these methods had been stunningly effective, with Maclean's people running rings around both police and security forces. At this time, with the year 2002 almost within spitting distance, the rise in crime across Europe and the demands of taxpayers for government accountability had reduced the number of police and military personnel who could be fielded by law and security agencies.

There was also the added problem of financial limitations. Now that the old Soviet Union had completely disappeared, there was less to spend on large-scale policing or intelligence-gathering operations. An idiocy gripped many countries, and few would forget that within days of the fall of the Soviet regime, there had been serious calls from within the establishment of the United States to close down the CIA.

In other countries, members of governments began to reduce the once wide powers of their security forces, and those law enforcement agencies that had run such things as surveillance and listening services. This had started as far back as the early nineties with the role of the British Metropolitan Police's Special Branch, once the mailed fist of the Security Service, changed almost out of recognition.

Jimmy Maclean, though, was not tied by restrictions of manpower. If a situation demanded twenty men and women on foot, he would put twice that number into the field. Neither was money a problem for the Alchemist organization. Difficult targets could only be removed for a great deal of money. The murders of the senior RUC officer and the SAS half colonel had cost many millions, most of which was profit, and all of which had been raised via criminal practices on the fringes of the Provisional Irish Republican Army, while the more recent killings of the Mossad agents had been funded personally by a Middle Eastern head of state.

Taking Tessa by the elbow, Maclean turned her away from the wind and began to stride slowly over the uneven ground.

"Why is obvious. But who?" she asked, raising her voice. He shook his head as though trying to rid it of some memory. "Who?" she asked again.

"A group calling themselves the Sons and Daughters of October." He repeated it in Russian. "I met with their man in London. He's actually a Chechen, but the organization's basically Georgian, the womb of Russia's organized crime." In his mind a series of pictures telescoped and overlapped. The man they had singled out had been stocky, barrel-chested, and with skin pitted like the surface of a planet. His name was Chermyet, Illych Antonovich, and they knew he had been active on behalf of the Communists. Openly he was one of the many who said that it would be better to have Stalin in power again than the slipping, sliding, and mushy chaos of the new and recent regimes. Yet they also knew that Chermyet was on good terms with the constantly expanding Russian Mafia. He had even traveled to the United States and stayed with a Mafia boss's father-in-law, in Brighton Beach.

When they did cut Chermyet out from his bodyguards and had a fifty-second whispered conversation—"Be ready, outside your room, two oh two, at the Cumberland Hotel, at one in the morning, tomorrow"—he had briskly nodded. He was in London talking to some highly suspect Ukrainians with links to drugs and prostitution. These people were the newly crowned princes of crime and were now undoubtedly beginning to square off with what was left of London's East End gangs and those north of the Thames.

Nowadays, the criminal gangs of Europe had made use of both the Economic Community and the slick advances in technology. In the main they were computer and Internet literate, while the gun had long given way to the cell phone. In the current climate, millions were stolen on telephone links every week, and further millions made through the old staples of loan-sharking, prostitution, drugs, and crooked gambling.

Chermyet and his colleagues wanted the favor of a high-profile murder, and they were willing to pay over 3 million, in sterling, for the job. At one in the morning he had slipped out of room 202 in the Cumberland, hard by Marble Arch, and was taken to a safe house near Paddington Station. Many of the old houses around that area had been diced and sliced into small apartments rented monthly by whores who advertised in telephone boxes and men's public lavatories as far away as Cambridge Circus. Jimmy owned a couple of these houses off Praed Street, once the casbah for the porn-book trade. He never tired of telling associates of the man who had turned up at one of the places claiming to be responding to "your advertisement in the Oxford Street underground gentlemen's convenience."

Now, Jimmy described the contact, so that, in turn, Tessa could describe him to Alchemist, for their principal was a stickler for detail. It was part of both his dogma and liturgy, and there was good reason for it. A minute part of Alchemist was infected with paranoia that held that, somewhere along the line, a face from his past would close in, looking for unspecified revenge. A description of any contact was an automatic necessity, and to her credit, Tess always took this part of her duties seriously.

"He's a short, muscular man, broad shoulders, very big in the deltoids, and his thighs look thick and springy with power. Square-faced, skin like a relief map of the moon, thick neck, light-haired, cropped to the scalp. He also has very distinctive clear blue eyes. Walks like a boxer, stands like a boxer come to that: one foot in front of the other. Graceful on his feet. Walks as though he's about to attack. You know, a tough kind of swagger, moving at the shoulders. He fancies himself as well, very taken with his animal magnetism, as they used to say. Not likable. Wouldn't care to meet him alone and on the wrong side, because I suspect he's fast, cocky, and can probably handle himself very decently." Maclean closed his mouth tightly, as though he could smell the Russian close to him. "If the boss knows him, I guess that description'll open the doors. If not, we've got pictures. To be honest, Tess, we didn't like dealing with him, though he's obviously the bollix, as they say. If we still had the Provos coming to us for help, I'd have turned him down. But as things are . . . Well, the Good Friday Agreement hasn't done us any favors."

Chermyet had answered all the questions openly. It had been chilling to hear him talk of murder, maiming, blinding, or castrating with as much emotion as a cabbage. Jimmy had a permanent picture of him with his beer-swelled gut and hairy hands spread on thighs as he sat in the whore's small parlor and talked.

"You ask why we will not do this thing ourselves? You *have* to ask that? Then you are fools if you cannot tell why we will not do it. It is much too dangerous for us. Also it must be done outside Mother Russia herself. We cannot afford any trace back to us. This is essential."

The room smelled of an expensive deodorant, and not until later did Maclean realize the scent came from Chermyet himself. When the deal was done, the man removed his shirt to reveal a million in high-denomination sterling, hidden in pockets sewn into the shirt. The deal was for a further million to be delivered within twenty-four hours, and the remainder on completion. "Though if they don't pay up, I don't see that there's much we can do about it," Maclean said, laughing. Tessa felt uncomfortable at times when frivolity ran hand in hand with the serious, terrible business of murder.

They offered Chermyet a whore and secretly videotaped him humping her with a laboriously grim determination. None of Jimmy Maclean's people would ever have done this.

Now, in the present, as they walked in the blowing fine drizzle in the Wicklow Gap, Jimmy told Tessa that the Russian had claimed the president had been the real power behind the attempted coup in 1991.

"Why did you think there were a few suicides and the rest were never prosecuted?" Chermyet had said with an unpleasant laugh. "These idiots were manipulated, and I don't think many people even guessed what had happened. This was the overthrow of the lawful government. To kill the president, and his young, lecherous wife, is very dangerous, but if your man can do it, and get away, it is worth our entire future. There will be more contracts for you afterwards, and many other things we can plan together."

Maclean spelled it out for Tessa in case she still did not understand. "This fellow's a died-in-the-wool, true dark red, trad Communist, who wants the old order back at any cost. I suspect it's because he likes being part of the ruling classes; likes the kind of order it brings. Doesn't care for all these jumped-up men and women making their fortunes. And he's clever enough to use the Mafia and their money. In the end it'll be them going to the wall, but he doesn't care how or whom he uses. The man's as criminal as the Mafia bosses, and more ruthless."

As he talked, Jimmy had a clear picture of the interpreter he had used with Chermyet, a small academic whose terror showed in his eyes and hands. Jimmy again smelled the scent and saw the room crowded with the four of them: Chermyet, the interpreter, Jimmy Maclean, and his minder who had helped pull the Chechen from the hotel and whisk him down the Edgeware Road for the meeting. The room was gloomy, decorated in purple with clashing cheap pictures on the walls and a crucifix out of place above the headboard. In his ears Jimmy could hear the rhythmic thud of the bed while the man who was paying to have his president assassinated boffed the whore for the unseen cameras. "We took movies for the insurance," Jimmy told Tessa. "It's a shame, but we need people like this now." He gave a single bark of a laugh. "The one person Chermyet seems to fear is his wife and her friends. He cheats on her with almost excessive old middle-class care."

"What about these provisos? You said there were some serious provisos."

"There are. They have to be killed with a gun—the prez and his Spicey Girl. I don't suppose that'll be a problem. Preferably a bullet to the back of the head: 'execution style.' But the main thing is that they want it done when they're in London, for the talks with the Americans and the Brits. That's in ten days."

A summit, hosted by the British PM with the American president and senior advisers had been scheduled two months before. "Lucky we pushed when we did. There's obviously a time limit on this;

though I suppose it'll make things easier if it's on home ground. They obviously want it to send a message to everyone."

"And Alchemist gets most-favored-assassin status if he pulls it off." She walked two paces, her strides matching those of Maclean. "But why do it at all, Jimmy? It can't turn back the clocks."

"Ah, well, they think it can. They're convinced that Lenin'll come waltzing out of the mausoleum, that Stalin'll thrust aside the stone in the wall where they've got him tucked away. He used the word *restoration* several times. You'd think they had a direct line to Uncle Joe, not to mention Beria and the other hard-liners. This fella's harder than steel."

"Jesus!"

"They think *He's* on their side as well. He actually spoke of Christianity as being the first true Communism."

"I always thought it was the opiate of the masses."

"That's football now. This is New Communism with a vengeance. Could be that we're in for the civil war everyone said would come after glasnost. Pity nobody spotted Chermyet and his chums pulling the strings."

"I'd better get myself off to see the man then." She automatically glanced at her wristwatch.

"On your way tonight? The usual flight to Bern?"

She did not confirm it, but Tessa already had her ticket. She did the trip regularly: seeing Alchemist at his lakeside retreat.

As they walked back to the car, heads down into the wind, a motorcyclist—a robot figure, black leather and helmet—came slowly along the road stopping and calling out to them as though asking directions.

Jimmy hurried over to the idling bike. "And?"

"There *was* someone. A woman. We thought she was maybe interested, but she was going to The Shelbourne. A date. This fella came in and they wrapped themselves around each other. It's some affair and she just happened to come out of The Gresham after the lady. Taking the same route."

"We know who she is?"

"A nobody from across the water: Coventry. A Mrs. Ruth Nightingale. They knew her at The Gresham because she's over every month. Has something to do with a bank, they say."

So, Jimmy Maclean and Tessa Murray went away happy and with few worries, but they always traveled carefully and with constant glances over their shoulders. They really should have been more concerned; in the midst of the complex lengths to which they went to protect themselves, they had hit one small, unseen bump. Maclean felt satisfied that his team, who were good people—four of them former Garda detectives—would not put a foot wrong. He had been concerned about this particular job from the moment he'd watched his boys and girls part Chermyet from his minders and slip the word into his ear. He took it for granted that his folk in Dublin had checked and double-checked, that the ex-Garda boys had used their contacts in London to tag down this Mrs. Ruth Nightingale and pin her to the board like a butterfly.

But they had not. Luck had latched onto Bex Olesker. Her name was indeed down as Mrs. Ruth Nightingale, and she had given an address in Coventry. This identity had hurriedly been stuck on her in Belfast before she flew out from Aldergrove back to Heathrow. The ladies and gentlemen of OS13 were painstaking and, on this occasion, just that tiny bit more careful than Maclean's people.

A Mrs. R. Nightingale indeed existed. She also stayed in Dublin, at The Gresham, about once a month, and she was connected with banking. OS13 had made sure that Mrs. Nightingale of Coventry was not in Dublin. So, when the former detective identified himself—illegally—as a Garda officer and asked the duty manager if he could see the registration cards of people who had booked into The Gresham in the past twenty-four hours, he had discovered Tessa Murray and Ruth Nightingale were the only ones. The duty manager, when asked, said yes, of course she knew Mrs. Nightingale: she was a regular. This was also true. Alas, the manager had not been on duty during the previous evening, so she had not set eyes on Mrs. Nightingale. If she had, she would have given a little squeak and said, "Oh, no, that lady's not the Mrs. Nightingale I know."

*   *   *

When Bex walked out from Grafton Street into Stephen's Green and found that her bird had flown, she did not even pause. Bex was 99.9 percent sure that Tessa Murray was in the old Rover pulling away into the stream of traffic. Bex was also 99.8 percent certain that she had someone on her tail. She had seen nobody, identified nobody, but she was, like so many women, blessed with an intuition passed to her through her father's X chromosome, and finely honed in the service of her country. If she were a betting woman, she would have put money on there being someone following her, and she simply prayed that her other sense was accurate: that this was a little Security Service operation.

As things were, she did not falter, but kept walking steadily toward The Shelbourne Hotel, and once there she marched in, sat herself down, ordered coffee, and gave a good imitation of a young woman whose date had not turned up. She tapped her foot, drummed her fingers, and took constant glances at her watch. At last she was rewarded. A familiar face appeared: a member of the Security Service named Dicky Winters, who was dressed as a man-about-Dublin, wearing a British Warm over a checked suit, a lime green shirt with a yellow silk tie, both from Charles Tyrwhitt, and a smile that said I-am-a-lecherous-and-roving-dog.

That he was well-known to Bex was not an accident. That she greeted him as the man of her dreams was, again, her intuition, but it did the trick, and everyone went home satisfied.

Back at The Gresham, Bex took a call just after 3 P.M. "She's booked out on a flight to Bern tonight. Bern via Brussels," the dark brown voice told her.

"Wonder where she's really off to?"

"We think you should find out so we've whistled up a seat on the same plane. I'll be over with the tickets. I'll call you when I get there."

"Will I have company?"

"Someone'll be loitering along with intent."

"Oh, good." She grinned at the telephone as she replaced the receiver and then tried to call her brand-new husband. Charlie was not at home, so she rightly figured that he was on his way to Scotland. Of course, she would've still liked to know why.

CHAPTER 7

Kit Palfrey had given Gauntlet a number to telephone after landing in Glasgow. This put him in touch with a pilot who flew regularly to deliver food, wine, and people to the monks in their monastery on the island of Ringmarookey. The pilot was not authorized to fly mail, so that went by sea, much to the disgust of the holy fathers.

The pilot sounded a very English Englishman on the telephone. Charlie knew the type. "Upper-class twit," he told himself, and was then surprised when *he* turned out to be a woman. The name, he already knew, was vaguely androgynous—Hilary. He had assumed this was a male pilot, as you always presupposed firefighters, policemen, and accountants were men, unless otherwise specified—particularly if you still thought like a male chauvinist porker, which Charlie did for much of the time. But in these days of political correctness one had to be careful. Never assume, was what they had taught in the firm he had previously worked for. It was a lesson never learned: a road not traveled.

"Hilary Cooke—with an *e,*" the young woman told him: all five foot two of her. Five foot two, green eyes, russet hair, snub nose, Carly Simon mouth, and coconut breasts. Charlie mentally christened her the piña colada babe. He had absolutely no doubt that she was a babe, for the eyes were as big as saucers and she moved in a provocative way, even when she was flying an airplane. They shook hands and he said, "Of course. Cooke with an *e,*" as though this were a grammatical rule.

Lovely bum, he thought, like two brass rubbings.

"You come here often?" They were taxiing out in the minuscule Cessna, and he had really meant to ask if she flew the route regularly.

"Oh, yaah. Had to take the f-in'—pardon my Ethiopian—instrument-rating exams four times before I passed though. Damn antifeminist instructors. I was only lost for half an hour. Had an hour's fuel left so I didn't see the problem." Then, quickly to ground control: "Oscar Mike, say again, Control."

Charlie noted that she pronounced *hour* "are." All in all our Hilary failed to inspire confidence. On takeoff the Cessna lurched alarmingly and dropped a wing just after becoming airborne. Gauntlet glanced at his pilot and saw her mouth shape a silent expletive while deep scowl marks appeared on her forehead and between her well-plucked eyebrows.

When they reached the cruising altitude of five thousand feet, well below the dome of thick cloud, Hilary Cooke began to talk again as though takeoff had been merely an interruption in an ongoing conversation. "Yaah, those damned instructors, all they wanted to do was screw me."

"How terrible!" Charlie was not used to such candor from women he had just met, particularly babes. "What you do about it? Report them to the pilots union or whatever you call it?"

"No. Some were quite nice. I slept with two of them, but it made no difference. They still wouldn't pass me until they were good and ready."

Or until you were good and ready, Gauntlet thought. He found it oddly disturbing to have a woman he hardly knew describing her sexual attitudes without hesitation. With the subtlety of a climbing boot he tried to change the conversation. "You know the monks well?"

"There're only two of us in the air-freight and taxi business out of Glasgow who get into Ringmarookey." She took her eyes off the instruments and gave him what might have been meant as a soulful look. Really it was the one she usually reserved for the monks. "Actually that's not altogether true. There are only two of us with small enough aircraft to get in. Not much room on Ringmarookey."

"Thought it was more than sixty square miles."

She explained that she was talking about the landing and takeoff space. "I should call it the runway, but it's not dignified enough to be called a runway." The good fathers, it appeared, had hacked gorse, heather, scrub, and brush out of a flat area close to the monastery walls. She assured him that on a calm day there was plenty of room to take off and land. "Hour and a half we'll be there." She spoke loudly above the engine's roar as the plane jigged along. "You goin' to join up?"

"You what?"

"You goin' to be a monk?"

"In your dreams."

"Sorry. Just bein' polite."

Ringmarookey lies to the west of Scotland, some twenty-five miles out past the Outer Hebrides. Sir Francis Drake made one reference to the island, calling it "a pebble thrown into the wild ocean," and, indeed, it could be a turbulent place, for there is nothing to prevent Atlantic storms from sweeping across its mostly flat, "ungovernable terrain," as Abraham Ortelius, the sixteenth-century Flemish mapmaker, described it. "No man," he wrote, "would willingly wish to live on this knob of scrubby stone and rock. I would fain live in a coracle, at the mercy of the deep, than on this brutal raft."

Seeing Ringmarookey for the first time from the air, Gauntlet agreed, wondering why anybody could banish themselves to this remote place. Then, as the Cessna tipped and banked over the southern end of the island, the sun slid momentarily from the clouds, bringing the island to life so that it became a rock-encrusted green, red, and gray jewel surrounded by the foam and waves of an inhospitable sea: the angry stone outline like a drying scab at the edge of a wound set in a blue-gray body.

A great scar, a crescent about a mile and a half long and almost a mile wide, was visible at the southern end of the island, as though a mechanical digger had gouged a chunk from the earth. This was, in fact, the remains of the quarry from which the stone had been cut for Ringmarookey's one structure: the Monastery of St. Jerome.

From the quarry to the monastery walls the monks had neatly tilled and planted the earth. Half of it had been seeded with grass over a long period, and now sheep and cattle grazed happily. The remainder was quilted out in plots that were obviously handed over to individual monks responsible for growing vegetables for the refectory table.

As they lost height, heading north up the western coast, Charlie had his first clear view of the monastery itself, a brown and gray Gothic complex that reminded him of his Cambridge college—St. John's.

A chapel, topped by a chunky Norman tower, was at the heart of the building. In turn the chapel lay within two cloistered courts, the inner backed onto turreted buildings that, Gauntlet was later to discover, housed the monastic quarters, loggias, and grass studded by occasional park benches and a pair of formal rose gardens.

All this, Charlie took in as Hilary Cooke prepared for the landing, dipping the Cessna into a sharp ninety-degree turn to the right, bringing them to the west of the northern tip of the island. They were coming in low over the sea and Gauntlet felt his stomach lurch. His hands were wrapped tightly in white-knuckled fists, and he was conscious of swallowing hard as he clearly saw the small oblong of green that marked the boundaries of the makeshift runway. From where he sat he had severe doubts about the length of the chopped-out flat area.

The Cessna crossed the boiling surf and the cliffs, with Charles still biting back the fear in his throat, as Hilary the daredevil aviatrix shouted something about being too high. The aircraft's nose yawed to the right as the left wing dipped in a sideslip. She throttled back and quickly lost height. Just in time, it seemed, the Cessna leveled off, and with a reassuring bump the gear thumped onto the resisting ground. "Jolly good, eh?" Hilary drawled as she pumped the brakes, slowing the aircraft.

"Fantastic." He was simply happy to be alive.

Glancing to the right, he saw the monastery rising like another cliff face. From the air there was only the impression of size. Suddenly, on landing, there was a mammoth building. Charlie thought briefly that he should not have been surprised to find the monastery so massive, for the huge quarry to the south reflected the amount of stone that had gone into the building. The Cessna taxied back to park some fifty feet from the gatehouse, where he now saw Kit Palfrey standing with a tall, thin, black-cloaked figure, both of them clinging conspiratorially to the wall, almost merging with the stone.

The little aircraft was dwarfed, like a toy, next to the outer cloister with the height of the chapel tower looming up against the lowering sky.

"I have a few things for the father superior," Hilary said as she switched off the engine. "I won't be goin' back for an hour or so. If you want to cadge a lift."

"Unhappily I fear that I'll be staying; and it's not really my scene." He did not even smile to lighten the load but spoke as he felt. It was many years since he had come into contact with organized religion, and his view of the monastic life was colored mainly by such movies as *The Nun's Story, Shoes of the Fisherman,* and, dare he think it, from back in the dark days, *Brother Orchid,* with Edgar G. Robinson, in black and white. Charlie felt that if he knew more about religious orders he would probably disapprove of them. He gave Hilary the intrepid birdwoman a lopsided smile, thought briefly on how much he missed Bex, then walked slowly toward Kit Palfrey. In his head he heard Mick Jagger singing "Sympathy for the Devil."

"Allow me to introduce Brother Simon." Palfrey was hunched into a very 1930s dark coat with a little velvet collar. He appeared to be suffering from the cold, which blew in from the east on a wind as serious as it gets outside of a force ten.

Charlie took his right hand from the pocket of his leather bomber jacket, wished he had not, then extended it to clasp Brother Simon's bony paw. Charlie's other hand was gloved and clutching the Adidas sports bag in which he carried his overnight things: his change of raiment as he thought of it now. In this place everything was rapidly becoming biblical.

"He's in charge of the gate," said Palfrey.

"I also do the phones and mail." Brother Simon all but grinned. This showed a smidgen of pride that caused Charlie to give the monk one of his penetrating looks, as if he were trying to gaze into the man's soul. Later, Brother Simon said to the assistant porter, Brother Crispin, that he felt "the little neat one would make a good novice master. He's got a look that put the fear of God into me." It was something that Charlie sometimes did to people. A much younger girl had once told him, "It's your immaculate turnout, Charles. Your size. And if you don't smile . . . well, you can be dead sinister if you don't smile."

Brother Simon was a beanpole of a man with a beaked nose and wild, dark, Italianate hair. In the world he had been a toper, addicted to strong drink with the kind of dedication usually reserved for love and marriage. To be fair, though, he had found God, who must have delivered the spiritual equivalent of a short, sharp shock. Quite suddenly Simon had eschewed the hooch and entered the Order of St. Jerome. Now he was all efficiency and business. "It's good to meet you, Brother Gauntlet." Members of the order always prefixed names with brother, sister, or father.

"Oh, please. Don't stand on ceremony. Please, Brother Charlie."

"No, Brother Charles, I think," Palfrey muttered without enthusiasm.

"Sure, Kit." Gauntlet's face lit up with a grin, and he quickly gave Palfrey a broad wink.

"Come, Brother Charles, Brother Kit." Pause. "Let's go in out of the cold." Brother Simon pushed against the heavy oak and iron-banded door and led them into the gatehouse, a wide, stone-slabbed entrance hall with a high, ornate ceiling and heavy Victorian furniture. In the middle of this huge hallway stood a big oak table scattered with copies of *The Church Times*, *The Tablet*, and incongruously, *Homes and Gardens*.

"The father superior insists on *The Tablet* for the book reviews, and—unhappily—*The Church Times* for the recipes."

"And *Homes and Gardens*?" queried Palfrey.

"Don't even ask, Brother." Simon's right eyebrow lifted, with a mind of its own. He took two steps toward a closed door to his right, then changed his mind, swinging around, slipping the lions' head clasp on his cloak, then doing an ungainly pirouette and sailing the cloak around him so that it billowed and lifted: a theatrical gesture revealing the gray habit he wore as a lay brother. The cassock was cinched around his waist with a black leather belt from which hung a six-inch, plain wooden cross. Later Charlie learned that lay brothers were distinguished from priests by both the color of the habit and the black and silver crucifix worn on the belt by priests. Postulants and novices were identified by three-inch, plain white crosses.

Simon gathered up his cloak, oblivious to the somewhat camp gesture he had just performed.

"Should've been a dancer," observed Palfrey.

"Ah, a good job Father Benedict wasn't around. Father Benedict is the novice master, and he's quite capable of letting anyone know when they've committed an act of unacceptable behavior. Behind his back the novices call him the Beast Master. Mortal sin, I should imagine. He hasn't been with us long, but I believe he was born fully formed, in his habit and everything."

Charlie looked at the painfully small radiator and thought, Cold as a witch's . . . No . . . charity. . . . Cold as charity. Aloud, he asked if it was as cold as this everywhere, or did they make a special effort to welcome visitors with an arctic blast?

"Well, Brother Charles, now that you mention it, the chapel and refectory are pretty chill, and you'll get 'fair shramed,' as old Father Whitehead would say—a Somerset man—if you walk around the cloisters at this time of the year, but the cells are kept a little above freezing, and the guest lodgings are positively luxurious at a steady fifty degrees Fahrenheit. We stick to the old currency here—Fahrenheit, miles, inches, feet . . ."

"Rod, pole, or perch?" Charlie smiled.

"Precisely. And the King James Bible." Brother Simon gave a short, sharp nod of agreement. "Well, I'd best let the father superior know you're here. He'll want to meet you, I'm sure—just up his street, the scholarship you've set him. You've put the cat among the pigeons here, I can tell you. The diaries have set the novices in a fine old stew. Did you know the first five years are the worst when it comes to the temptations of the flesh?"

"Never had the problem myself," Gauntlet lied. "But I can see it could lead to difficulties in an enclosed society like this."

"Verily, verily, Brother." The tall monk returned to the door on the right of the entrance and, after an indecisive pause, opened it.

Before the door was firmly closed again, Gauntlet briefly glimpsed a roaring fire, a comfortable armchair, and a table piled with papers surrounding two telephones: one red, the other black. "Nice little caboose," he muttered.

Palfrey grinned and nodded. "The temptations of the flesh obviously come in several different sizes. Some like it hot."

"And who can blame them? Talking of which, what am I hearing behind Brother Simon's words?"

"Don't know what you mean." Palfrey, deadpan, marble arch.

"I'm sure you don't. But what, Kit, do I represent? Yon Simon implied that *I* had put the cat among the pigeons. What am I, Kit? Am I not retired? Have I come down as a representative of the Office? Because, if I have, we could be in trouble. The Office doesn't take kindly to people posing as card-carrying members when they're not."

Palfrey looked away, then glanced pointedly at his watch. "I must make haste. I have an appointment with our translators, Father Harry and Father Hugh."

"Before you go . . ." Charlie laid a hand on Kit's arm, the muscled fingers making Kit wince.

"Okay. Right, Charles. Right. Yes, you *are* here to give everything the imprimatur, so to speak. Add a bit of weight. I must fly. Catch up with me after you've seen the beak."

"'The beak,'" Gauntlet repeated without feeling as he watched Palfrey whisk his way through a door to the rear. Suddenly Charlie felt cold again and it had little to do with the temperature of the gatehouse. This was the chill felt when you are suddenly alone in a hostile environment, and the monastery gathered around itself a feeling of intense alienation and loneliness.

Then the gatekeeper's door opened and Brother Simon returned, his lips locked in a mirthless smile. "The father superior is ready to see you now, Brother Charlie."

"Oh, good." He wanted to quote from *Hamlet*, "For this relief much thanks; 'tis bitter cold, and I am sick at heart." He was not a complete fool, though, so he kept quiet and allowed the beanstick Simon to shepherd him out into the first cloister, then on through passages and doors until they stood at the father superior's threshold. Charlie felt as though the monk had put him under some kind of arrest. Was it the porter's attitude? His manner? The way he moved and spoke: a tugboat to Gauntlet's liner?

"Brother Gauntlet, Father Superior," Simon intoned, ushering Charlie into the bleak, book-lined room.

"Ah. Good. Sit ye down, sit ye down." The figure that untangled itself from the captain's chair behind a military desk with green and gold skivers was as tall as the porter: a gaunt, severe-looking academic with long, slim fingers, a smooth, bald pate, dark satanic eyes behind strong lenses, and a straight, patrician nose that would not have looked out of place on Romillius.

Behind Charlie's back the door closed with a whispered, "I'll await you, Brother."

"So. Charles Vincent Gauntlet. It's been a long time."

Gauntlet peered at the face that beamed down on him as a lost man will study terrain; searching for some tiny detail that will tell him exactly where he is.

Father Gregory Scott's voice was almost harsh. "You don't remember Scott of the DP camps, Second Lieutenant Gauntlet?"

The "DP camps" did it. The displaced persons camps that had sprung up across Europe in the wake of the Nazi turmoil. Some of them still existed in the early fifties. Charles Vincent Gauntlet, ridiculously young and just starting to shave bum fluff from his chin, had been posted to Germany as security officer at a DP camp close to Frankfurt.

"That's why I knew the name, Gregory Scott," Charlie muttered. "Of course." He was vaguely aware of the voice, but would never have recognized the man. The voice would have caused some disquiet in him, trying to place it, for the kind of work he had pursued for most of his life relied a good deal on memory.

"I was older than you even then—still am, by a good few summers." The father superior chuckled. "But I remembered you straight away, Charlie. I knew you as soon as Kit mentioned your name, and it didn't surprise me to hear what you had become. You had a very tidy mind, Charles. You liked things to be in their proper places." Scott chuckled again, a hand slicing up to run across his sleek, bald head. "That was another life. Long before I was drawn to this, and long before I was called to the religious life. You don't recognize me, though. And you could never know what a profound effect you had on *me*. Sometimes I think I would never have studied documents, their ages and their owners, if it had not been for you."

"Why so?"

"Because, even as a young man, you were able to read people like books. I watched you; the way you cocked your head to one side as you listened. And your intensity. You had, even then, the great ability to concentrate on the person you were with. You used to say, 'I don't listen to the words. I listen to the music.'"

"That wasn't original."

"No? I'm really quite surprised you didn't recognize me."

Gauntlet gave a long sigh. "No, but I knew the voice, Greg—Father Gregory." The voice was a distant memory for sure, but now even stronger recollections returned. The damp, clinging rain and the dreariness of the place where Major Gregory Scott had been his CO. The wire; the ramshackle wooden buildings; the hospital beds; the squaddies with closed faces; the British doctors and nurses; the officers, such as Gregory Scott, constantly questioning the men and the women who tried to hang on to the shreds of dignity, or, conversely, the fiction of their lives, in that terrible place. Yet most of them had seen more dreadful places than a DP camp.

Gauntlet also knew that, all those years ago, Major Gregory Scott had taken his time before he had any trust in the adolescent officer who was Charlie Gauntlet: a different young man in a different world.

"I . . . I remember your sergeant—in charge of the other ranks. A color sergeant, yes? Color Sergeant Hammer." Silly, the name stuck in his throat because he was talking to an elderly monk who looked away and did not meet his eyes. They both had sins, he thought. Both retained the trace of old sins: sins neither would like to see dragged out again for public scrutiny. Together, and in words not spoken aloud, they formed their own collusion about Color Sergeant Hammer. "Hammer of the North, you called him."

"Yes. So I did."

Gauntlet saw Scott as he had been, young and tagged by the war's horror, a swagger in his step and vanity in the way he wore his uniform, the angle at which he cocked his cap over one eye. For a second, Gauntlet saw the young major with a jet-haired woman and knew what they did together in the CO's quarters of the DP camp, which he had been able to smell for the rest of his life. And now, the young officer who had taken the woman to his bed was the old monastic priest who sat behind the desk, his eyes sad and reflective.

There were other things Charlie remembered—serious, important things; things he would have loved to talk about now, but instinctively held back; waited for the moment, holding on to some tiny vital facts in case he needed leverage. In particular he thought of the two military police corporals who had been an integral part of life in that camp. He remembered them as big men, almost giants. Which of course they were to someone of Charlie's stature.

"I was able to confess and receive absolution once I became a Christian," the priest murmured as though he had second sight and could read what Charlie saw with the eye of his recall.

"Lucky for you." Charlie spoke quietly. His own sins of the time bore in on him, clear photographs tattooed to his memory. He wondered if it was true that they were stamped into his soul. "I cannot find forgiveness so easily," he said in the here and now.

"You think it's easy for anybody?" Scott looked Charlie in the eyes, smoothing his bald head with his right hand yet again. "There is more than just a recitation of some magic words, by a witch-doctor priest. That's a problem with Rome you know. They don't mean it, but they give the impression that it's all easy. The doctrine and the ritual make it appear to be simple. It isn't of course. It isn't for Roman Catholics any more than it is for Anglicans. There is a little word called *contrition*. You really have to be disgusted with your own sins before you can hope for absolution, and there's nothing easy about that. There has to be contrition and penance. Absolution comes in the middle, but I believe it can take years. Then, time will cease. Time as we know it will end."

Gauntlet nodded. "And who will know what dreams we'll dream. It was a dreadful time."

"The time won't let you off the hook."

Charlie saw Sergeant Hammer lying dead as Scott stood impassive at the man's feet. Again he quoted Shakespeare: "The times are out of joint."

"Always. God won't forgive you because of the history of your days." Father Gregory sighed heavily. "Yes, we've both changed, but it's good to see you, and to see you at a time when we're looking at something very positive about the Christian faith."

But Gauntlet allowed the chance to slip by. He was still mired in the past: in the camp near Frankfurt. "Hammer," he said again. "Color Sergeant Hammer." Repeating it. "We both have cause to remember him."

"And Corporal Day. Shortest Day, the lads used to call him."

Gauntlet looked up with a broad smile, as though the priestly monk had granted him some great favor. "Shortest Day. They called him Christmas Day as well." Charlie recalled that the nickname Shortest or Shorty was a joke in itself, for Corporal Day was a man built on a massive scale—something akin to the Colossus at Rhodes, he thought: around six foot three with huge shoulders, great arms with hands like hams, and a nose from which an original bald eagle's beak could have been designed. "Used to harass the men. I would laugh." The man's forehead was wrinkled by a zigzag scar.

"He's visited me here, Corporal Day." Almost an aside. Then, Scott raised his voice: "Grip your rifle, lad. Grip it like you'd grip your mother-in-law's throat, lad." It was an odd, uncanny imitation of a man glimpsed for a short time only in the adolescence of Gauntlet's life.

Charlie nodded, then looked up and saw the priest was staring at him, his eyes gleaming, watering, and his mouth opening to say something. Gauntlet watched him change his mind, alter the words that had been ready in his brain. Instead, the priest said, "It's good, and strange, to meet you again, Charles Vincent Gauntlet. You've come to put the stamp of authenticity on this incredible diary." It was almost a question. Not quite. A millimeter off. "You probably know, there was a time when I was able to help him—Kit Palfrey, I mean . . . but that's all gone now, hasn't it?"

113

Really? Charlie thought. This is news to me, and at the same moment he realized that Gregory Scott had deliberately eased him down the path toward "Shortest" Day to take him away from Color Sergeant Hammer. Again he saw the body with the look of surprise frozen on Hammer's face.

Charlie bumbled with his hands, wrapping them around each other, interleaving his fingers. Helped Kit did you? he thought. Aloud he asked, "You believe it, then? You believe this dictated diary? It's real?"

Gregory Scott inspected his fingernails, then opened a drawer in his desk, bringing out a round glass dish piled high with Jelly Babies. "Have one." He gestured toward Charlie.

"You own them?"

Gregory lifted his eyebrows. "Technically, yes."

"But a monk isn't allowed to own anything, Father Superior. Isn't that right?"

The smile played around the old man's mouth as he inclined his head. "Technically, yes," he repeated with a laugh. "You were always shrewd. Now you've blossomed into what our Father McKay—who is a Scot—would call 'a very canny man.'"

Gauntlet moved in the chair, making himself more comfortable, settling himself in the room, glancing around, taking in the books and the large, heavy crucifix that hung above the father superior's chair. "You believe it, then? This Naomi's diary? It adds up?"

"Yes. Yes, if you'll officially vouch for Mr. Palfrey, I'll profess the writings're authentic."

Officially vouch for Kit? What the . . . ? Aloud he said, "You can be sure?"

"No, of course I can't be sure. There are inconsistencies; I don't understand why the thing's been preserved in the form of scrolls, but, yes. Yes, I'm as certain as any trained man can be. I'd attest to them being written during the early part of the first century. How were you always certain that people were lying to you while others told the truth? Kit Palfrey tells me you were very good indeed at putting people to the question."

"That's different. They were there. The events were close. I could smell them. There was . . . intuition."

"Which is blind faith. My take on them—as young people would say nowadays—my take on the scrolls is fifty percent intuition, and fifty percent forensic. The papyrus, the way it was made; the ink; and most of all, the way the young mute scribe, Naomi's amanuensis, wrote his Greek letters. He was very professional."

"Amanuensis?"

"Well, that's the correct term for the lad Petros, isn't it? An amanuensis is one who assists, takes dictation, helps prepare a text. From the Latin *a manu*, one that is at hand."

"I suppose so. Convenient, a mute secretary, isn't it?"

"As convenient as a dumbwaiter." Scott laughed, and out of his past, Charlie remembered that the man's laughs were infectious.

"For Christians this would be a huge proof?"

"Oh, just another couple of bricks. We have the proofs we need." Scott made a swatting movement with his right hand. "People are revising dates all the time. Let me tell you something. At Magdalen College, Oxford, there're three small pieces of St. Matthew's Gospel. Experts used to date them from the second century. Now it's suggested, and many scholars believe, they're really from early first century—the same as this manuscript. If that's true, then whoever wrote St. Matthew's Gospel was probably around when some of the reported things happened."

"The same with this?"

"Yes, but are they telling the truth? That'll be the next question. We can never satisfy everyone."

"So, if you were a betting man . . . ?"

"Which I'm not and never have been."

"You'd put your money on Naomi the prostitute, with her Roman officer who worked for—no, who was—the intelligence service."

"Yes, and young Petros the dumb scribe, and Azeb, the Nubian girl. It's far more believable than the idiotic book that says that the Bible contains coded messages: prophecy about the Cold War, the Berlin Wall, and the Kennedy assassinations. People bought the thing by the boatload. I suppose they wanted to believe a fiction posing as fact. Personally I found it rather obscene, in the true meaning of the word. It reduced the Holy Book and put it on a par with the quatrains of Nostradamus."

Gauntlet gave a noncommittal grunt.

"Yes." Gregory Scott fixed him with his eyes. Charlie turned back at him, recalling that the man's eyes could make you uncomfortable. "Yes, well, you should also know everything this text is beginning to reveal. Let me tell you about Petros and his style." Gregory went on to describe the characteristic *Häkchenstil*, the "hooked style" because of the hooks—the *Häkchen*—that characterize the way in which the Greek letters are written. The "hooks" are usually an indicator of an early period when dating papyri. He also explained that it had been necessary for the two scholarly translators to decipher occasional lapses into tachygraphy by Petros. The young man had obviously been well trained, for tachygraphy is the name given to several different types of shorthand in use across the Roman Empire in its ancient days.

"Charlie, how much of Naomi's diary have you read?" Gregory Scott finally asked.

"Only the first couple of pages. The girl's description of how she came to be on the game . . . Oh, I'm sorry, Father."

"Don't be. 'On the game' is perfectly acceptable. Why shouldn't it be?"

"You're a priest . . ."

"So?"

"So . . . well . . . I was going to ask the people who're doing the translation . . . is it Father Harry and Father Hugh?"

"Yes."

"They are monks, yes: they've taken vows—poverty, chastity, and obedience, yes?"

"Of course."

"Holy men?"

"What do you mean by *holy*, Charlie?"

"Men set apart. Dedicated to God."

"What's the problem?"

116

"They're translating these texts. By a prostitute. This Naomi, she talks much about sex, this woman: she's mad about sex."

"That's natural, it's her job."

"But . . ." Charlie squirmed. "These two men, the monks, priests . . ." It crossed his mind that, possibly, he was being very naive.

"They are also two of the world's best scholars when it comes to biblical Greek and Latin."

"Yes, but what the woman is describing. You call that—how do you say it?—you call this *mortal sin*, yes? I worry that . . ."

The father superior smiled. "My dear Brother Charlie. I think I see what you're getting at, and may I say that I am touched by your sense of—how can I say it?—awe?" Gregory leaned across the desk, put out an arm, and touched Gauntlet's right shoulder. "You are being very protective, concerned that in reading the woman's innermost thoughts she might corrupt my brothers in Christ."

"I suppose that's what I'm getting at, yes."

"The sins of the flesh, Charlie. They are not the worst sins. Sometimes I think that people imagine fornication and adultery to be the most besetting of all sins. They are serious, but there are worse things. Oh, and I am certain that they pose difficulties to Fathers Hugh and Harry. They cause me problems, at the age of seventy-five, for in the sere and yellow part of my life, the autumnal years, I still experience difficulties. The imagination can be a wild and furious thing."

Charlie bumbled again, searching for the right words. "There is a great altercation in my mind when it comes to the Bible and, well . . . sexual explicitness."

"You ever wonder how all these folk begat other folk? The Bible's full of sexual innuendo. It contains more lust, murder, rape, and desire than most modern blockbusters."

"Not where Jesus is concerned."

"You think Jesus, as a man, was a prude?"

"How can I tell? I don't know, but it makes me—what's the right word?—uncomfortable?"

"Uncomfortable and somewhat caring. Monks know the score, I promise you."

"Yes, but I wouldn't like to think that we were leading them into mortal sin."

"Let the scholars look after their own souls. It's between them and God. I have a much greater concern."

"Yes?"

"Indeed, yes. Let us grant that this document is genuine. That it is written by a woman called Naomi who was a whore employed by the officer Romillius, head of a Roman intelligence-gathering unit. I have read more of these diaries than you have. I am much more concerned about this Naomi's IQ; her intellectual capacity; her acumen and her motives. You see, the very fact that she reduces so many of her thoughts into purely sexual imagery is, in a way, suspect. I feel that she has very limited intelligence, so possibly has less insight. She may not realize the full extent to which she is being used."

"You mean we should be wary of what she says?"

"Very. But I only speak with a little more knowledge than yourself. We should read more." Scott rose from behind the desk, striding toward the door, with his habit flapping around his ankles, making a rippling noise. "Shall we go and see how the translators progress? Let you read more? There are some shocks and surprises in store, I can tell you that already, and Naomi allows herself to be dominated by the Roman officer, doesn't she?" Scott tugged at the door, surprising the porter, Brother Simon, who had been standing a little close, even with his ear pressed against it, for he leaped back, his face confirming his guilt.

"Ah, Brother Simon, you have heard enough? I have spoken to you about this before!" The harsh edge of the priest's voice stung like a slap, and Charlie saw him for a moment as he had been back in the early fifties in the DP camp. Gregory Scott's voice cracked again, biting the air. "Come, lead the way to the study room being used by Fathers Hugh and Harry."

The three of them marched, in brisk pace, through passages and cloisters until they reached a light, airy room near the large library: white walls and no decorations except for a five-foot crucifix high on the far wall.

Two of the walls were taken up with big computer screens, printers, scanners, and other hardware. Light flooded down from large overhead gantries, and Charlie must have looked surprised for a tall, florid-faced, muscular monk strode over and put out a hand. "You must be Charlie Gauntlet." His voice sounded perpetually amused. "And, yes, we've been dragged kicking and screaming into the twenty-first century. I'm Father Hugh. This is Father Harry." The other monk was equally tall with the face of a man who was once good-looking but had been devoured by the world. Father Hugh's eyes were those of a man rapidly growing tired after years of poring over books and documents. They sat, with Kit Palfrey, at a plain oak table, and it was Palfrey who looked up from loose pages of the translation and whispered in some reverence, "Charles, this is incredible. Right from the heart. We're reading the thoughts of one who touched Jesus. Read. Please read."

Kit passed a handful of pages toward Gauntlet, who took them, sank into a chair, and began to read.

CHAPTER 8

Last night, when we stopped to rest on the last part of our journey from Hebron to Jerusalem, my soldier, Romillius, took me, outside his tent, under the stars. He is fierce, brave, bold, and fills me full of divine fire. For him I would willingly give my soul: even today when I can feel the pain and the bruising on my rump where he plowed me against the hard earth and stones. I wish he would claim me only for himself. I will try to lead him, but in the meantime I shall do his bidding.

Once again, Charlie found himself slightly shocked that a woman, a couple of thousand years ago, could have expressed joy and pleasure in sex. He realized that he was giving himself a wry, silent smile in his mind, hearing Father Gregory's voice saying, "Yes, Charlie, for you sex was invented in the 1960s, wasn't it? Before then nobody really enjoyed it, you guilt-ridden old devil you. Like the poet said, it was invented just before the Beatles' first LP."

After the loving he talked to me for many hours, telling me what extra services he wishes me to perform once we get to Jerusalem. I now know it has to do with the man Jesus, who is from Nazareth and who is certainly a prophet and holy person. Already many are saying that he is also a worker of miracles.

A man called John caused much stir in his day by cleansing people, baptizing them, giving them a ritual washing, in the river. This John hailed Jesus as the Messiah—the one who our prophets say will come to free us from the shackles of the Roman invaders; and the one who will lead our people into peace and everlasting life. I cannot know of all these things for I am a woman without learning and the other skills given only to the rich and powerful. Yet I am gaining knowledge from Romillius.

He has told me of the fears that beset the emperor and his military leaders in Rome. In many parts of the Empire there are uprisings or plots against the Romans. It is important for the leaders, the officers and members of the governor's household, to be aware of what goes on. Now I am given a place of great trust, for Romillius is charging me to bring him whatever I can discover from both Jesus and those who follow him. He explained to me that they must all be forewarned of any plans to either hinder or harm the Roman presence here. More, I am to be given gold and silver to do this, and I shall try to be worthy of the trust that is placed in me.

We came into Jerusalem this afternoon, and Romillius told me that today was the day the Romans do honor to their goddess Venus. Tonight for us it is Sabbath, and I am doing all I can to keep to the law, though this is not easy for me.

To be in this city is wonderful and I cannot wait to go out into the streets after Sabbath is over. The house is much larger that I expected, very clean, and in a narrow street near the Temple, which I have yet to see properly. There are rooms for all three of us, another at the back for preparing food, and a large space above, enough to accommodate many people. This entrance hall is decorated in a lavish manner, and after the Roman custom. Romillius explained that he might have to use this house as a safe place to keep people in danger, or those whose faces he wishes to hide from the public. After all, it is paid for out of military funds.

As we came into the city, we saw some great and lovely villas with gardens full of color, beautiful trees and pools of water, around which we could see men and women in the gardens being given food and drink by servants. I would think myself lucky to be just a servant in a house like that.

Azeb appears to be a nice, quiet girl; short, but with a fine body. Though it is possible that she has a willful side to her, for she showed some anger on being sent by me to buy food. She made it plain that she did not wish to go. I dared not go myself, as it was almost Sabbath. I know what my fellow men and women can be like when it comes to whores like me. I sometimes think that people in my profession frighten my fellow Jews.

When Azeb returned, I found her surly and it was necessary for me to show her that I am the mistress here. I slapped and beat her hard with the palm of my hand, and she did not try to resist when she perceived that I was much stronger than she was. She cried out in pain and shouted for me to stop, but I knew I should not show mercy. She wept pitifully, but I threw her onto her bed where I commanded her to stay. She turned onto her face and sobbed when I left. My hand really stung from the beating I gave her, so I tremble to think what her rump is like. Bruised I should think. She will soon learn. I shall ask Romillius to get me a thin rod so that my hand will not be hurt next time. Oh, how she howled! I hope she learns her lesson soon, for I dislike having to punish her, but you should not show mercy to these kind of people.

Romillius returned shortly before the start of Sabbath, and he tells me that nobody will come here tonight, but he is sending a man to me after Sabbath is over, tomorrow at dusk. This man is an officer of the Sanhedrin, the Jewish council set up at the command of the Romans; he is also a steward to Caiaphas the High Priest. My lord told me that it will be an honor for me to serve him. I replied that I have all the honor I require by serving my lord, and I thought he would strike me in anger. He bade me watch my tongue. Then he told me that I should be ready to leave Jerusalem in two days' time. Word has reached him that the man Jesus is to be at a wedding in Caana near the Sea of Galilee. Romillius says that this would be the best time for me to draw close to the Nazarene.

Last night after I had gone to my bed, the girl Azeb came to me and lay down beside me. She showed that she was ashamed at the way she had behaved and she came to me in the only manner she knew. For her young age she is very experienced and has been taught well. Strange, but I find being with a woman is sometimes more pleasant than being with a man.

We awoke this morning entwined one with another. Her kisses were delightful on my mouth and wherever else she gave them, using her tongue to great purpose. Oh, she *has* been well taught. To my lord, who will read this, I say that you should not be angry with me, but if you are, then that will be punishment enough.

The high priest's officer, Thomas, came to me after Sabbath ended. He is a scrawny, unpleasant man who tells me that his wife refuses to take him to her bed for he has impregnated her no less than six times. Of the children, only three have survived. He has evil-smelling breath and his hands never stop moving. He became aroused quickly and seemed very proud of himself, spending as much time fondling himself as he did me. He took me twice in a short time, but I was able to think of other things while he brought himself off. There is no thought, in these men, of giving me gratification, though it is different with Romillius.

I am excited by the thought of what I must do for the Roman Empire. If I do well, I shall ask Romillius if I can become a Roman citizen. Perhaps he will even take me to Rome when he goes back.

Last night, Azeb came to my bed once more and we kissed and held each other. I thought much on Romillius and my plans for the future. Late in the night, Azeb sang to me. She told me it was a song her people used to soothe babies into sleep. She has a pleasing voice, though I cannot understand the words in her tongue. We are trying to make up signs with our hands and arms so that we can understand one another more easily. I did not sleep soundly as I am excited about what will happen in Caana.

My lord Romillius came early to the house and spent time with me telling me what I must do. There has been much commotion for men known to the Romans as the Sicarii tried to kill the governor, Pontius Pilate, only the plot was discovered before they could carry out the plan. Everyone lives in fear of these men who kill using daggers. They cause terror among people living in towns and cities. It appears it was Romillius who received the news of the plot and went with soldiers to the house where these criminals were gathered together with a woman. There was a fight and one of Romillius's soldiers was wounded, while one of these lawbreakers died.

This woman had a supply of oils and unguents to make her skin smooth and sweet-smelling. So Romillius brought to me a sealed alabaster jar of thick oil perfumed with the root of spikenard that is expensive, but he took it from the house where they had found these villains. Now he has thought of a clever scheme for me to use the oil when I see the man Jesus. I leave for Caana in one hour with two men who are to escort me. They are soldiers who are under Romillius's command and who do not wear a uniform, but present themselves as ordinary citizens.

Charlie came to the end of the page and glanced up to see Father Gregory almost snapping his fingers to take the page from him.

Father Harry reached over to give more pages to Charlie, who looked squarely at the father superior. "I thought you'd read all this." His tone was accusatory.

"We've done more work on it," Father Harry said. "There were passages in this that were slightly ambiguous and we've tidied it up." The monk leaned back in his chair pinching the bridge of his nose between the thumb and forefinger of his right hand. "I don't know how conversant you are with the Gospels, but if this was written at the same time as the events took place, there is a serious anomaly."

"Anomaly?" Gauntlet repeated as though he did not know what the word meant.

"Yes. Anomaly. A divergence."

"I know what it means." Charlie spoke quietly but with a hint of humor, as if wagging his finger at the monk.

"It's different. Different to the Gospels."

"Doesn't conform to the Gospel narratives as we know them." This from Father Hugh, whose voice had a dry, dusty quality. "In St. Matthew's Gospel some of the things described here take place at the house of Simon the Leper in Bethany. Here everything happens at the wedding in Caana of Galilee: the miracle of the water and wine, the anointing with the perfumed oil, and the washing of Jesus' feet. In the Gospels they're recounted as separate incidents. There is an attempt to set matters right, but it's a departure. New."

Gauntlet nodded, took the next sheaf of papers from Father Harry, and continued to read.

Romillius has explained important matters to me. Jesus has told his closest disciples that he will be put to death and buried, but after two days, and on the third day, he will rise from the dead and come among them.

This is strange and frightens me. I am to use the oil that Romillius took from the woman who was arrested to anoint this man as if for burial. My lord says that will be the best way of getting close to the prophet, for there are very few women who mix freely with the prophet's disciples. I am told that his mother, called Mary, is often with him, also a girl from Magdala and some serving women. Yet Romillius tells me I shall have no difficulty in getting close to the man. I must make myself ready.

I have seen him; touched him; spoken with him, this man Jesus who comes from Nazareth. Now I have talked for a long time with Romillius, who tells me that I should include the answers to his many questions when telling all this to Petros.

The journey to Caana was arduous, but I rode behind the man called Aurus, clinging to him. In the night we camped outside Caana and I slept a little. In the morning they gave me bread and a cup of wine to drink. I was able to wash in a stream and change into my white robe, the one Romillius gave to me in Hebron, the one with the blue thread stitching on the hem and sleeves. Having taken a comb to my hair and washed my feet before putting on my one pair of good sandals, I presented myself to the two men, who said that I looked clean and modest. Felix did not meet my eye when he said he thought the centurion was a lucky man, while Aurus muttered something about the officer being stupid not to claim me as his one true woman. I did not say that there are only three women of Israel who have ever become free and married to members of the Roman army. That is what Romillius tells me anyway, and I think it is true. It holds out little hope for Romillius taking me with him to Rome, but I shall still find a way to ask him. Indeed, I have discovered such a way, haven't I?

Charlie smiled to himself as he read. If the translations were accurate, then Naomi was being cheeky and dictating to her advantage. Nothing changed did it? Some years ago he had dealt with a prostitute the Firm was using to turn and burn a suspected agent—the Cold War was still going strong when this happened. The girl was just as cheeky, always going for the main chance to ingratiate herself with the powers that be.

I walked into Caana and quickly found the house where the wedding was to be held. It had a garden with many flowers and trees, while, inside, the rooms appeared to be large and clean. I talked with the women who prepared the food and were ready to serve the wedding party. Only one woman seemed suspicious of me, asking what I was doing there and where I had come from. My answers seemed to satisfy her, so I busied myself in helping the others, who seemed pleased at my assistance.

Soon I had learned a lot from the conversation. The house belongs to a man known as Simon the Leper, who is rich and also has houses in Jerusalem and Bethany. I was told that Simon had invited Jesus and his closest pupils to the wedding of his daughter for two reasons. Not only had Simon been cured of leprosy by Jesus—a great miracle—but also the bridegroom's family comes from Nazareth and are well acquainted with Jesus' mother, Mary, and his father, Joseph.

The girl who told me this—and others agreed—said there were many puzzling stories about this prophet and teacher.

There were tales about when he was born, a number of strange events: a bright star in the eastern sky that appeared over the place where Mary gave birth, and the appearance of heavenly beings to shepherds near the town of Bethlehem.

It is also said that he was born in Bethlehem because Mary and Joseph were in that place for a census taken more than thirty years ago. There were no rooms or lodgings to be had, so Mary, Jesus' mother, had the child in a stable behind the Bethlehem inn. Others maintain that there was no census at that time: that this was simply a convenient story invented to conform to the scriptures. Older folk say that strange things *did* happen, though there was no census, and few can recall any bright star shining over Bethlehem. However, there are men who remember the child being born and clearly recall talking to those who claimed to have seen visions.

I have been told by others that Joseph is really not Jesus' father, and that Mary was made pregnant by a priest called Zacharias, who is the father of John the Baptizer. Of course I cannot tell if there is truth in this, or if it is just foolish talk. However, an older woman tells me that Jesus *was* born in Bethlehem because that is where Mary and Joseph lived. The house was crowded with visitors so Mary went to a nearby cave, where animals sheltered, and gave birth there. Later, the whole family moved to Nazareth.

Another odd circumstance is that three sages, princes, came and presented the baby with gifts of gold, incense, and myrrh. These things, they tell me, are all signs from the prophets of old and bear out what has been said concerning the coming of the Messiah, as written in our most holy book.

Another of the women spoke of an even greater mystery. She has heard a story from many people concerning the circumstances of Jesus' birth. Some say that Mary was not made pregnant by Joseph, that she was still a virgin at the time of conception and that an angel appeared in a vision telling her that she would conceive by the Holy Spirit and remain untouched by any man. This is not only strange but miraculous if true. If it is not true, it would mean something else entirely, and Jesus could be what they call a false prophet.

The wedding was late in beginning because Simon told everyone they must wait until the Nazarene arrived before things could begin. Certainly before the couple made their oaths to one another, and before they were blessed. So we waited, and there was much talk of Jesus, and excitement at his coming.

Jesus finally arrived with five or six of his closest disciples, who walked near to him and with one in front and one lingering behind. They move like soldiers guarding a great dignitary and their eyes are watchful, as though they fear for their teacher's life.

As for my first thoughts when I saw the man Jesus, I had imagined him to be either a tall man with a striking appearance or a man like the old prophets, wild of hair and beard and eyes. He fitted neither of these descriptions.

Not tall nor short, this Jesus carries himself in a quiet manner that is at odds with the way his disciples behave around him. His hair is dark and cropped close, while his beard is neat. Like his hair, the man's eyes are also dark, almost black, and when he speaks it is in a commanding tone. He does not judge and is not harsh, as one imagines the old prophets, but there is a sense of power and authority in what he says and does, and I would not like to be at odds with him as he gives the impression of having control over himself and others. This is the inner dominance that he wears like a cloak.

Jesus did not strut or push himself forward, yet everyone at the wedding, from the bride and groom to the governor of the feast, Simon himself, or even the lowest serving girl, showed him great respect. In speech Jesus keeps his voice low, so there are times when a listener has to strain to hear. This is not so when he is speaking to a crowd. On these occasions, they say, he turns himself into a good, clear, and forceful speaker: not one who shouts at the people or gestures with his arms and hands, but one who shows dignity and believes and knows of what he speaks.

Jesus' mother was with him and a younger woman also called Mary, but these two kept apart from the men, though at one time I did hear Jesus speak a little sharply to his mother.

Before I was able to make my approach to him, there was another strange event. While I was helping the other women in preparing the wedding feast, there was an accident to some of the big wine jars. These were balanced on pieces of wood stretched between square-sided stones, and in the crowding two of the jars became dislodged, fell, and were shattered with the wine pouring out over the courtyard at the back of the house where food was cooked. Toward the end of the feast, as I was getting ready to do as Romillius had instructed, someone sitting near to Jesus said loudly that they were running out of wine. Jesus heard this and sharply told the serving women to fill up the jars by the door with water. These jars are those used for the ritual washing before taking food.

They filled the jars with fresh water, brought from the well at the back of the house, in the courtyard where the wine jars had been broken. When the jars were filled, Jesus told them to draw out water and give it to the guests. People made much of this, saying what good wine it was, but I think it was just water and nothing else. One of the women said she thought Jesus was having a joke with Simon. Even so, I became most concerned that he would be angry when I approached him, but I did it.

I went across to him quickly, almost running. As I went, so I broke the seal on the alabaster box. "My lord," I said, and he gave me such a look that I was moved to tears. I ran some of the oil into my hands and rubbed it into his hair and onto his forehead. The scent of it was strong and filled my head, making me dizzy.

He looked at me again, drew in a long breath through his nose, then nodded and smiled—the first time I had seen him smile, and all this made me start to weep with joy. I knelt before him, bowing down so that my tears fell onto his feet—he had kicked off his sandals—so I grasped around for the hem of my dress, to wipe the tears from his feet, but as I did so, my hair came untied from the comb and fell down over my face so that I simply dried my tears with my hair.

One of his disciples, who had been watching me, keeping a close eye on what was happening, came quickly and put his hand on my shoulder as though to pull me away, but Jesus stopped him. "No," he said quietly. "Leave her alone."

Simon the Leper came over from his place and asked what was wrong. When he smelled the spikenard root and saw the alabaster box, he spoke sharply and said that I was foolish, that I had wasted good oil. "That could have been sold. We could have given the money to the poor!" he shouted, but Jesus glared at him and, speaking roughly, told him that what I had done was a symbol. The words, as I remember them, were, "Simon, the poor you'll always have, but I won't always be here. This girl has anointed me as if for my burial. When you speak of the good news of the kingdom of God, you should tell what this girl has done. See to it."

Simon the Leper asked him to stop me weeping and get me up from the ground. Jesus spoke again a little angrily. "No!" he said firmly. "You didn't greet me with a kiss, but this girl has kissed my feet many times. You didn't wash my feet, but she has washed them with her tears. Don't criticize her."

This time he did not smile when he looked at me, grasping me by the shoulders and saying, "Go, daughter. Go and don't sin again."

My body shook, and I shed more tears. This is a man of great influence. I trembled for it was like looking into the eye of God himself and I do not know what to do anymore, for my daily bread is sin. Also, I fear for Jesus' safety. He appeared to be quite serious when he spoke of his death and my anointing his body for burial.

As I walked from Simon's house, back toward the place where I had arranged to meet Aurus and Felix, one of Jesus' disciples, a young man called James, ran after me and asked my name. I told him that it was Naomi, and he smiled and nodded.

"My lord is anxious that you hear him teach," James said. "He says there is only one sure way to the kingdom of God, and that is through believing in Jesus. In two days' time he will be in the place where he was born, Bethlehem. He will teach there and pray. It would be good if you could be there."

I told him I would be there, for not only did I know Romillius would want me to go, but also I felt deep down inside myself that I wanted to hear Jesus teach.

Charlie was no theologian; come to that, he was not sure if he could claim to be a Christian, and his churchgoing was erratic to say the least. Yet now, sitting in this cold room within the monastery, he recognized that what he had read could well be a handshake across the centuries. He thought also that the Jesus described here was not the gentle Jesus, meek and mild, beloved of Sunday-school teachers.

In the back of his head, tucked away in a far corner of his mind, he heard a flourish of strings: a great fanfare of violins, violas, cellos, and basses, a Wagnerian opening that almost touched his spine with a charge.

If this is true, he thought, if it is really honest, then I can put my hand out and almost touch this wanton, naive, simple woman and, in turn, touch Jesus Christ.

He looked up, locking eyes with Father Gregory. "Is there more?"

"Oh, yes. There's much, much more. This is only a beginning." The father superior took in a breath and opened his mouth to say something else, but before he could speak, the ground under their feet quivered, and the walls shook, as though a small bomb had landed nearby.

Displaying remarkable agility for his years, the father superior lunged for the door, and as he pulled it open, they all heard shouts coming from the far side of the wall.

CHAPTER NINE

The man they called Alchemist was a former captain in the Special Air Service who had thought to better himself by transferring to the Royal Marines. He had served and fought in many parts of the globe, a brave and skillful soldier trained to within an inch of his life. However, less than a year after completing his service, and coming up against the civilian experience, he developed a chip on his shoulder that threatened to become a deformity. True, he had tried to sign on for a further five years, but this had been denied him.

In reality, the events of the last decade of the century opened several dangerous mantraps for anyone like Alchemist. The fall of the Soviet empire and its aftermath had caused this man's early retirement during the downsizing of NATO forces. A grave miscalculation had been made, and that, combined with individual concerns for the future, led many men and women to leave the armed services of their own accord. This, in turn, caused a knock-on effect. Manpower in all forces dropped to a dangerous level. So, less than a year after Alchemist left the Royal Marines, there were moves to bring back recently retired personnel so that the Royal Corps could be restored to full strength. Alchemist was not even offered a chance to return, and this certainly angered Richardson—for that was his name—pushing him almost to the edge of obsession.

If Tessa Murray had known the full story of Ronald Brinsley Richardson, she would certainly have asked him about her former lover—her first true lover—the man whose real name, she had been told, was Ralph Docking. She also knew that Docking was a marine, and had she asked Ronnie Richardson, he would have told her everything about Captain Docking, RM. But she did not know Ronnie (Door-Die-Ron as he was sometimes known to officers and other ranks with whom he had served) was a former Royal Marine, so she did not ask him. Tess Murray assumed he was SAS, and he admitted to it, so that was all one, as Shakespeare would have said.

Richardson had first conceived the idea of "assassin for hire" long before he completed his service with the Royal Marines. The idea first came as a glimmer in his mind when he served on detachment to "The Group," as 14 Intel was known: that most covert of military intelligence-gathering units operating just under the surface in the North of Ireland, even during the long and complicated series of truces toward the end of the millennium. At first sight it seemed to him a possibly astute career move, particularly in the light of his self-knowledge. Killing had never worried Richardson, while his advanced standard of covert fieldcraft and the use of small arms gave him every possible requirement for the job.

Also, he was blessed, or cursed, with an uncanny talent for making himself visible or invisible at will. To those who eventually hunted him across Europe and the Middle East, Richardson seemed to have the expertise of a medieval magician, for he appeared to possess the ability to pass through locked doors and solid walls. He was also a master of that dubious Special Forces art, silent killing, which, combined with the other skills, made him a formidable enemy.

In many ways, Alchemist was a man born out of his time. If he had reached maturity in the earlier half of the previous century, there would have been plenty of opportunities to indulge his lethal talents. Major wars are the workplaces of men and women with an aptitude toward murder.

When Richardson first toyed with the idea of committing himself to the life of a serial assassin, it was simply a mental exercise: academic, a series of brain-cudgeling mind twisters, dealing with abstracts that could never become realities because there was no possibility of ever moving into the realms of fact.

Until he actually did it.

After that happened, it soon became clear that he truly liked the planning, the careful working out of the logistics and a design of battle, particularly when the kill was to be in Europe.

As an adolescent he had grown up in rural Berkshire, in a tiny village, a Roman Catholic enclave, the people of which seemed to be frozen in time with their faith. So his favorite memories were of the rolling downs, the endless cornfields, woods and copses of his youth. His pleasures were simple: watching badgers, otters, foxes, and other wildlife. Smelling grass after rain; trees and wildflowers at dusk on a hot summer's day; biting into a stripped corn husk; or seeing the sharp gray-and-white picture of a bitter winter evening, with smoke rising straight up from cottage chimneys.

Even his first recollections of sex were locked into fields, woodlands, or hedgerows. His contemporaries all carried out their initial navigation around lithe, warm teenage bodies in the open. Not for them the backseat of a car, or the parents' front room. Like his friends, Richardson explored the mounds and curves, the paradoxically firm and yielding flesh, under blue, Sunday-afternoon spring and summer skies, or hard by an early-evening hedgerow.

His first woman was had on springy turf deep within a wood, close to a rushing stream. When the girl cried out as he entered her, and again on reaching her first climax, he heard also the wind soughing in the trees and the trickling bubble of water over rocks. For Richardson, the Alchemist, a walk in the fields could bring him face-to-face with sexual thoughts: trees and running water would arouse him as easily as a glimpse of thigh, or the imagined fantasy of flesh moving under thin clothing.

Like so many daydreams, the plans for a kill remained, for years, only in the mind. That was until Richardson met Maclean; accidentally—or so it seemed—in the Savoy's American Bar.

They were both in London, staying at the same hotel. Jim Maclean wanted some cigarettes; Ron Richardson was waiting for a girl. The pair of them were there together in the bar just after it opened, one of those rare coincidences where truth is stranger than fiction.

Richardson quickly discovered that Maclean was a successful lawyer, specializing in British tax law; and Richardson presented himself as a creator of adventure stories, historical empire-soldiery yarns, and similar writing-by-numbers pastimes.

Maclean knew intuitively that this was a front. Sixth sense was, possibly, the most important piece of glue that finally bonded the pair. He let Richardson run on for several minutes. Then:

"You haven't actually had a book published, have you?" Speaking in almost a whisper, looking slant-eyed at Richardson, who sipped his drink and did not return Maclean's questioning glance.

"Well . . . possibly not . . . but I'm working on it. I do have this great idea." Richardson shifted in his chair, elegant in an Armani suit showing almost an inch of cream cuff and links made from a pair of antique gold coins. There was never anything cheap about Ronnie Richardson. The smile was devastating as he went on to describe the premise of his "book": a man not averse to killing, with experience in special forces, hires himself out to ideological terrorist organizations. "He would take the heat," he explained, lighting a cigarette and ordering another round of drinks using only body language. "He'd slot only the truly difficult ones." For *slot* read "kill": SAS-speak.

"You really think they'd pay him to do that?"

"If they have access to money, yes. You've got to remember that terrorists are your basic amateurs. There are targets they don't even attempt because they appear impossible—targets they'd love to take out. Look at the times they've cocked-up real spectaculars."

"I don't call Pan Am 103, or Oklahoma, amateur cock-ups."

"I do. Neither was surgical. There's nothing professional about big-bomb jobs; nothing sophisticated about them. They're catchall operations that don't require real skill."

"And *your* assassin'd be a professional?"

"Of course. The highly trained professional soldier can do the impossible—and get away with it."

Jimmy Maclean appeared to think for a long time before he replied, "Only if he's exceptional and has the right intelligence."

"Goes without saying," Richardson volleyed back. "You can't do anything like this without detailed intelligence. Watchers up close. On the ground. Listeners. Recorders. Photographers. Mapmakers even."

"But you'd have to test it against real life. No good writing a thick-eared novel unless it bears some examination when set next to truth.

Unless it's based on reality. Could it happen, d'you think?" Maclean sounded truly convinced, which was a plus.

"I intend to find out. I propose to write the book. Live it maybe." This last was the true giveaway, and Maclean did not miss it, for he was an intensely shrewd man who, even in his early twenties, had stored up allies. Many people owed him favors, even their lives.

So, at that moment, Maclean decided to put veracity to the test. Not that he was prepared to start asking the imponderable questions just yet. Richardson, on the other hand, did not shirk from probing. "You could possibly help." He looked up with bright, intelligent eyes that Jim was later to think of as "Ratty's eyes from *The Wind in the Willows*." "Perhaps, as a solicitor, you could work out some foolproof way such a man could get paid. That'd be the real trick: how to commission him and pay him without beating a path to his door."

"Ah! Yes! Mmmmm!" Already electric patterns were activating Jimmy Maclean's brain.

Eventually he said, "It has to be part of the illusion of life. To do what you propose, one would have to construct two visible worlds, like a set of Chinese boxes, or a mirror cabinet which looks empty but is really secretly full of all kinds of stuff." From there the solicitor outlined the bare bones of a plan that was the first step toward the structure they later manipulated with such success: the brilliant scheme that allowed complete control over anyone who approached the system used by Alchemist's support organization.

It was almost eighteen months before the two men—the killer soldier and the lawyer—came together again. By that time Maclean had devised the unbeatable system and already knew where to put the necessary surveillance hardware and software: the radios, scanners, cell phones, scramblers, voice-distorting mikes, automatic telephone exchanges, recorders, night-vision glasses, infrared- and thermal-imaging gizmos, and the rest of the ultra-gee-whiz gear so necessary for Alchemist's success.

Maclean's initial investment was in time, and a relatively small amount of money. During that first conversation, as he listened to Richardson explain the plot of his "book," Maclean felt the hair rise on the nape of his neck. At that point, he made certain that the man he had met by chance knew how to get in touch with him again. He was 99 percent certain that his own life probably depended on doing business with this tough, coiled spring of a man. Once this professional killing machine was set in motion, Maclean reasoned, all traces of preparation, such as the Savoy conversation, would be wiped from the slate by gun, knife, poison, or bludgeon unless both parties were engaged in work for the future, becoming mutually dependent.

During that first casual meeting, Richardson baited the trap, then reappeared one July evening in Dublin, with a telephone call and a "You won't remember me" line of chat that sent Maclean off twitchy to dinner in the wilds of County Wicklow. There, over gazpacho, grilled sole, and summer pudding, the assassin-elect came clean and the solicitor told him he had known all the time.

So it began, and almost by design Alchemist's first clients were one of the wealthier offshoots of the Provisional Irish Republican Army. These paying customers asked for the deaths of a senior Royal Ulster Constabulary officer and an SAS lieutenant colonel. These men had been under a death sentence for months, yet had eluded several assassination attempts. Experts had tried to bomb and shoot them, yet, perpetually ringed with steel, they had seemed to live charmed lives. Both killings had to be unattributable to the principals, and by this time Richardson had made up his mind how he was going to signal his own presence: by the coup de grâce shot to the back of the head, and the Shakespearean quotation on the body. Originally he had planned for this item to be in the victim's pocket, but haste in the first killing had determined a tiny deviation.

Oddly, the first murders had similar aspects during the opening phases. Early in his planning Richardson had found foolproof ways to crack into the supposed secure telephone system of both the RUC and the British army. So certain of their own safe communications were those two organizations that they had long ceased to take simple precautions when using the "screened phones." Both the RUC superintendent and the SAS lieutenant colonel had a similar Achilles' heel. Women. Or at least one woman each.

Both men were married, and their dangerous liaisons were carried out by using police and military safe houses; claiming that the women were informers. So it was relatively easy for Richardson to listen to the secret, and somewhat licentious telephone conversations between the men and their lovers, eventually turning plans to his own advantage.

In essence he used identical modus operandi in both cases. He hid within the agreed meeting places hours in advance of the times the lovers had arranged to meet, then telephoned the woman, almost at the last minute, using a code word to call off the assignation.

In both cases the men had walked straight into the entrapment ("Almost with their cocks in their hands," as Richardson later told Tess, who in a bizarre way had become fascinated by the mechanics of murder) and had been dispatched by bullets fired from the silenced Smith & Wesson revolver. "Nowadays there's so much publicity for H & Ks, nine-millimeter and even twelve-millimeter automatics, that the ancient, good revolver seems outdated," Richardson said.

Alchemist's escape had been made good by some clever misdirection: a small explosion in the case of the superintendent, and shots from a well-contrived booby trap operated by remote control: the trigger on an elderly Stirling submachine gun, activated by the kind of device used to fly model airplanes. In the ensuing commotion, Richardson had got away, while in the aftermath the full truth was never revealed by those close to each of the two men. Both had exceptionally loyal cohorts, and that did not hurt Alchemist's reputation. Hence the word of mouth that allowed him to walk through walls.

As for the relationship between Richardson and Maclean, during and following the first two killings it had been all downhill and a matter of trust. Now, several years later, they corresponded only through Tessa Murray, who carried detailed letters in her head from Dublin or London to Switzerland.

Ronald Brinsley Richardson now lived in simple luxury in a pink villa hard by the water's edge, with its own little boathouse and a garden sloping down to a small private beach in the town of Brissago just on the Swiss side of Lake Maggiore.

After her meeting with Jimmy Maclean, and their conversation in the Wicklow Gap, Tessa Murray headed for Switzerland followed by Bex Olesker and another friendly watcher, plus an unseen wraith of a person whom neither of them knew was also there until almost too late.

CHAPTER 10

Rebecca Olesker, having lost her quarry on that damp Dublin morning, returned to The Gresham Hotel and the man with the dark brown voice, who was now there in person: tall, muscular, and handsome as his speech—though he did not speak this time. Instead, he stood next to her in the elevator and produced a small leather notepad with the paper clipped neatly into brass-edged slots. On the top sheet he had written:

> Please accompany me into the street. This is an official instruction from Detective Superintendent Elizabeth Liddiard.

Bex gave him a cheeky smile, pressed the button for the ground floor, and nodded cheerfully.

Out on the pavement, in the wet again, he extended a large black umbrella and bent his body at the waist while sheltering her from the rain. "A turn around the block, I think." The voice matched: deep colonial brown and lovely, with the resonance of an echo chamber.

"What's going on?" Bex asked, concentrating on trying to remain relatively dry.

"Apart from you losing sight of Beecher?" His eyebrows lifted in a classic I'm-one-helluva-wag look.

"If you know that, then you probably know where she's gone, which makes me redundant."

"Far from it."

They reached the corner and he put out one hand, touching her arm to signify that they should turn right. "It'd be best just to give you the message as it was passed on to me. Ms. Liddiard says would

you please not lose her this time—Beecher that is. If you do, she'll
request your transfer to directing traffic." He switched his nice smile
on and off. "Not quite in those words though."

"I can imagine."

"Good. We more or less know her direction—up to a point anyway.
How's your German and Italian?"

"Nicht Hinauslehnen! Pericoloso di morte!"

"Brilliant. I've got tickets for you. You'll be on the same flight as
the lady. Leaving from Dublin this afternoon, going to Bern, changing
at Brussels."

"Where the sprouts come from."

"Oh, indeed, yes. The tricky bit'll be Bern. That's the part we don't
know about. She's got an open ticket that'll take her on from Bern.
That's it, we don't know any more."

"Broken our crystal ball, have we?"

"No crystal balls, no Ouija boards, not even a pack of Tarots. Just
the passkey and enough mechanics to do a swift search while we put
ears on the telephone. She had the tickets hiding in plain sight. Obviously kept an appointment this morning and expects to move on to
Bern this afternoon. I imagine she plans an overnight there and on to
wherever in the morning. I think it's probably quite important for
you to be on her back all the way. I'd make that a fairly high priority
if you don't like the thought of waving at cars and buses."

"What if the tickets are a plant? What if they're to throw watchers
off the scent?"

"They're not. While you were busy losing her, London ran a check
on airline computers, and she's done the trip before. Regularly. Each
time within a month of some spectacular."

"You're saying that from here she goes on to meet Alchemist?"

"Quite possibly. That's what the glamour boys think; and if they're
right, he lives somewhere south of Bern."

"No educated guess?"

"Could be anywhere. Ms. Liddiard thinks you should let usual surveillance go hang. Just be someone traveling in the same direction.
Don't try to hide. Just be there."

"She'd know of course. And we all thought the old tradecraft and stuff was a thing of the past."

"Nothing's ever wasted."

"What if I do turn up someone else?"

"You give us a shout. Well, not me, but London."

She looked at him as the rain trickled down the ribs of his saturated umbrella. "Who're you working for?"

"Commander Bain as far as you're concerned."

"Funny. Never met you before if you're OS13."

"Oh, come on, Rebecca. This is illegal as hell. Nobody's counting and Joe Bain'll get the collar if you run Alchemist to earth."

"What kind of backup do I have?"

"You're deniable, but we've got guardian angels out in the field. If it gets hairy, someone'll rope you in. They've been close all day, but I doubt if even you could spot them. We're not going to let you come to any harm."

"Promise?" She opened her eyes wide in what Charlie called her "doelike bimbo mode."

"Absolutely." He flashed his teeth in a Colgate grin. Insincere as a tart's declaration of love. White against his coffee-colored skin.

They were back in O'Connell Street before he handed her the AmEx wallet containing her airline and Swiss-rail tickets. Outside The Gresham he touched her shoulder lightly and wished her luck. So she took a cab up to Grafton Street and went straight to the now amalgamated Brown, Thomas & Switzers, the old, established Dublin department stores, and equipped herself with the accessories of disguise: a reversible raincoat, two soft, crushable hats, three scarves—including one expensive Hermès—and a pair of heavy-framed, clear spectacles that she lifted from a display stand, fully cognizant that she was breaking all rules of tradecraft. On her way out she bought a slightly larger garment bag with a waterproof, zippered compartment that would take the new reversible raincoat and other items as well as war paint, and the bits and pieces necessary to sustain life for a modern executive woman. Most of the things she bought were for emergency use only: if she needed to use the simplest of disguises.

She did not look twice at the tall, slim man wearing a trench coat and a cloth cap set at a jaunty angle. He saw her, though. Saw her and was latched onto her the whole time. God was in her heaven and Bex had a guardian angel.

Back at the hotel she rang the contact number of the OS13 office at the Yard and was told that, yes, Joe Bain had okayed the operation, though not in so many words. What was actually said was that her car repairs should be completed by the end of next week. All very Le Carré really. The girl fielding calls for Bain told her they had been on to the factory and the part they required was on its way. "There's no need to worry, Mrs. Nightingale. Your insurance is going to cover everything."

Well, that was nice, she thought. Very secure that made you feel. It took her only ten minutes to pack the garment bag and explain to reception that she had to check out unexpectedly and to ask them to keep her overnight case. She paid the bill, then took a taxi, which dropped her off at Dublin International a good two hours before the flight was due to leave for Brussels.

A helpful check-in girl told her she could get away with taking the garment bag onto the aircraft as hand baggage; the flight wasn't full, and, yes, they would be on time. Bex went through to the restaurant on the groundside and treated herself to a wholly inappropriate meal of sausages and fries with bread and butter and a cup of strong tea. Twice. To blazes with the cholesterol and calories.

As she ate, Bex suddenly realized that she missed her new husband very much. She wanted to call him but could not because heaven knew who was watching. Nowadays they did not even have to see you dialing a number to get it. A brand-new little electronic gizmo could pick up the number from a hundred meters away. She'd had it demoed at a recent high-tech weekend. "The old spy cult has a great deal to answer for," she said to the techie, who muttered something about fact being stranger than friction. "You mean fiction." He gave her a supercilious little smirk.

"I know what I mean," she said, and the techie gave her a sour look.

Replete, she headed through to the airside, showing her Nightingale passport. At the gate she found a seat giving her an uninterrupted view and began to watch for the arrival of Tessa Murray.

There was one Garda Special Branch man, looking every inch a cop, sprawled in a seat nearby, sticking out like the proverbial spare what-sit at the nuptials. Later an entire team turned up—two men and a woman, young, playful, and actionmanish—though Bex could not have said for sure whose side they were on. They could easily have been Security Service on an away day, or equally Tessa's own people keeping an eye on their asset.

Again she wondered what the hell Charlie was up to in Scotland. If that was indeed where he was. Couldn't be much of a sweat: after all, he was retired. When they called the flight, bang on time, Tessa had not even shown. In fact, Bex was ready to off-load herself when Murray turned up, almost the last to board. What was the old TV ad? "Murray mints, Murray mints, too good to hurry mints."

As it was, Bex had to look twice. The woman she had followed that morning looked early middle-aged, slightly dowdy, and would not have turned many heads. The Tessa who now arrived looked sleek and svelte, trim in a claret pantsuit with denim-blue accessories. That would've looked really nice in the eighties, Bex thought. Tessa's long black hair trailed onto one shoulder, giving her a hint of the gypsy, complemented by the large dark eyes and heavily beringed fingers. Somehow the look did not go with the briefcase and overnight bag, which could easily have been by Gucci. For the first time Bex was able to study Tessa with a pinch of envy. In another time they could have been friends. Certainly, Tessa seemed to have the élan and poise that made the new Mrs. Gauntlet feel the prick of covetousness. Certainly, as Tessa took a seat in business class, she looked very much at home. Even the flight attendants fussed around her. Sod her, Bex thought. This morning she was all wily and streetwise, while this afternoon she's got that most elusive quality, old style. Makes you sick.

It was already getting dark by the time they reached Brussels; and black night with a hint of rain when they landed at Bern—home of Einstein, Klee, the bears, and that bloody clock tower, Bex thought as she moved quickly, leaving the aircraft well before Tess. She lingered on the Jetway, bending over to examine a nonexistent problem with her right shoe until Tessa Murray passed by, not even slowing as she headed along the corridor: good strides and the confidence of a much younger woman.

Tessa traveled light, as she always did when visiting Ronnie. The overnight bag only held essentials, for she had a full wardrobe at the Villa Myrte, which had long been a second home on the lakefront. From Brissago's ferry dock you walked in the direction of Italy, up the main road for almost a kilometer. The villa was on the left with its red-tiled roof and the balustraded balcony that ran the length of the ground floor looking out across Lake Maggiore at the curve of the mountains on the far side.

Next to Richardson's Paris apartment, the villa on Maggiore was Tessa's favorite place in the world, and she would have liked to be able to get on to Locarno, and thence Brissago, that night. But it was late when they got to Bern, and she knew from experience that it was always better to break the journey. "I'd rather have you here refreshed and a day late than have you jumpy and tired after the long haul from the Bern bears," Ronnie once told her during the first months when she was establishing a pattern of visiting her "brother."

She went through passport control, smiling at the dour officer who did his little conjurer's move, flipping the document open, glancing up for the reality check with the photograph.

As she walked across the concourse and out into the damp night, Tessa recognized several people who had been on the flight from Dublin and Brussels. A pair of businessmen, a middle-aged couple who could have been illicit lovers—if there were such things these days—and the thirty-something woman in sensible shoes, well-cut raincoat, and a Hermès scarf tied loosely at her throat. There was also a tall, slim, once attractive man—airline pilot, captain—his raincoat slung open around his shoulders, navy blue uniform crumpled, cap at a studied angle, and a well-worn and scuffed black leather overnight case bulging in his hand.

In recent years, Richardson had taught Tessa Murray how to sort professional hunters from the innocents so she could alert herself to possible danger at least 80 percent of the time. In Dublin, as she arrived late for the flight, she had spotted the surveillance team and a lone Garda plainclothes cop. Now, as more people came out of the arrivals and baggage halls, she extended her mental antennae and, with studied care, made a visual sweep of her immediate surroundings.

Two uniformed policemen sporting automatic weapons were just inside the terminal. Outside, a lone, officious-looking cop kept the peace with an evil eye and strong body language.

The businessmen were away quickly by cab; the middle-aged lovers—the man looked jumpy, she thought—hesitated, as though they were not sure if they could afford the luxury of a taxi. The woman in a raincoat was definitely ambivalent, unable to make a decision, going to a taxi and speaking with the driver. Tessa looked up toward the airport bus stop where a young couple and three more solitaries, two men and a woman, had joined the waiting line. She didn't even notice where the tall one wearing the cloth cap had gone, but he had disappeared, and this last fact left-footed Tess, who liked to keep tabs on everyone traveling around her.

She stood back just as another clot of passengers came out onto the pavement: three couples, one of them with children—the woman carrying a baby ("Make certain it really is a live child," Ronnie usually counseled. "It's good technique to be carrying a child")—two more women, and a young man dressed formally in a suit with a tailored topcoat trimmed with a small brown velvet collar. His shoes shone like mirrors, and he looked out of place, like someone inappropriately dressed at a party, but he did not trigger any of Tessa's alarms. For some reason, though, she had become jumpy after realizing that slim, flat cap had vanished. Maybe? she queried.

She hesitated, then strolled over to join the growing queue for the airport bus. If she became alarmed, she could always change her mind and take a cab at the last minute.

By the time the bus arrived, she had recognized a handful of her fellow passengers from the flight from Brussels, including the woman in the raincoat. Nothing suspicious, except for the missing cloth cap and blazered man with the lived-in face. The driver had now arrived, as humorless as the passport control officer. She paid her fare and took a seat toward the back of the bus.

There was a small problem with the raincoat-and-Hermès girl, who seemed to be having language difficulties. "He wants to know if you have other luggage," she called out. The driver was being unusually obstinate for a Swiss. More often than not they liked to speak their fluent, faultless English, but not this one, who addressed everyone in thick, singsong *Schweizerdeutsch*, asking about luggage as they proffered their fare.

When they were all on board, the driver climbed out and loaded the baggage into the compartment behind the rear seats, making a song and dance of it. The rain became heavy as they set off, and a lot of early-evening traffic was on the roads. Through the wet-dotted windows the lights became starbursts, and the driver handled the vehicle with exaggerated care. Tess thought he was a real pain: an attention-seeker determined to make heavy weather of everything: you could almost hear him sighing in unison with the windshield wipers, and somehow, this seemed to make the short journey more arduous.

Half an hour later they reached the Bahnhofplatz, coming to a halt outside the information office that was firmly shut against the night. The couple with children alighted and were greeted noisily by relatives, a man and a woman who looked like models for Tweedledum and Tweedledee—short, fat, with red, aggressive faces.

Tessa hefted her overnight case, climbed out, and quickly sought the comparative shelter of the arcade of shops and offices, crossing the road on the corner of Spitalgasse, opposite the somewhat straitlaced and forbidding Church of the Holy Trinity. She was vaguely aware of other people behind her as she went through the doors of the little guesthouse she always used when passing through Bern. Early in their relationship, Ronnie advised her to use small, unobtrusive hotels and guesthouses. "Stay away from luxury in continental Europe," he'd said. "It's very difficult to get lost in a six-star hotel. In America it's easy—and in England also. Unless you're very well known to the executive management, they don't even recognize you. But on the Continent it's different. They've more of a history of secret policemen. In most countries they still check and look at the guest lists of big hotels—so much for the E.U. In Switzerland, always stay down; never go the luxe route."

She smiled at the girl behind the cubbyhole of the reception desk who knew her, but could never remember her name.

The girl smiled back and said, "Ahh, Frau . . . ?" Pass friend, she thought as she gave her name. "Nicholas," she told the girl, taking the little registration slip and writing *Thomasina Nicholas. Passport Number* . . . Between leaving the aircraft and walking into the hotel, Tessa had done a quick change. All her documents now showed her as T. Nicholas. Even her luggage tags were changed, quickly slipped off and on during the walk from the baggage hall to the bus.

"I can still get dinner?"

"Yes. Yes, of course. We don't start serving for fifteen minutes."

Someone came in behind her, but she did not even turn and look.

"In the morning, a call at seven please. I must leave at eight-thirty for the train."

"As always, Frau Nicholas." Sliding a key across the little counter. "Enjoy your stay with us. Room twenty-one."

As Tessa turned toward the little lift, she saw that it was the rain-coat-and-Hermès girl who was behind her. She smiled and tucked the thought away in her suspicious mind.

As for Bex, she asked if they had any rooms for the night. They had, and a few minutes later she was in one: small, comfortable, and clean with outrageously heavy furniture and windows overlooking the street. Outside, the rain was starting to ease off and the road below shone from fractured little bombshell reflections exploding from the black surface. At a distance, about a mile or so away, the sweep of car headlights around some bend dazzled on and off like a flare, while necklaces of lamps swung in the wind and looked like tracers. Far away, a red warning blinked on and off from a high building. There was a sense of World War I déjà vu in what she saw.

She looked out on this scene of trench warfare by night and suddenly her husband, Charlie, leaped into her mind: a huge wide-screen version in glorious Technicolor, with a score by Bruckner and Charlie's voice caressing her thighs. She realized that his voice could do that—caress her thighs. It was a Gauntlet trick and she had not realized it until now.

Bex, in this moment of revelation, knew also that this was not good; this was dangerous given what she was doing; foolhardy, because thinking about Charlie could distract her from the one thing that really mattered—tracking down Tess Murray and using her as radar to light up Alchemist.

So she pushed Charles from her mind, then wondered at her ability; marveled at the ease with which she could banish her beloved so completely from her consciousness. She shrugged, grinned at her streaked reflection in the window, then went to wash and change before going down to dinner.

However intelligent, we all live relatively blinkered lives: restricted by our bodies and experience that cannot be shared, for which of us fully shares that inner life with another person? Psychiatrists may probe, but as Bex's husband once remarked, "Why spend money on psychiatrists when you can listen to the Mahler Second?" It was something he'd had in common with their mutual friend who had died and so led them to each other at his funeral.

As she turned from the little washbasin in the tiny bathroom and walked back into the bedroom, Bex suddenly experienced one of those incomprehensible out-of-body, out-of-life experiences. Feeling naked and vulnerable, she seemed to have suddenly leaped into someone else's body, as though she did not recognize her own familiar limbs. All of a moment she seemed to have become a terrified soldier in Flanders, 1916 or 1917. Night black and sticky as tar. Out in no-man's-land, out near the wire, and unexpectedly a flare went up and she/he/she stood stone still as the light curved against the black velvet, painting a new swaying clarity over the winter mud and the terrible barbed, curling strands. She was utterly lost, with her breast bare to the vicious machine guns until she shook herself clear of it and came back into the hotel room and the present.

Over the next few frightening days she would recall this weird time warp, as though something from her distant past had come accidentally skittering through an invisible wall and a parallel world into her present, leaving her shaking and shocked with fear.

Rebecca carried no weapons except an old wooden matchbox, which a hard, nut-brown little man who had pioneered silent maiming across the free world had taught her to use with devastating cunning. In her handbag she also had a six-inch nail file—she could not do the sums to put that in what she called the new money of centimeters. She kept the nail file in a protective pouch as it had been ground into a razor-sharp stiletto.

Bex had seen horror caused by gun, knife, and bludgeon. She wanted never to carry anything lethal, at least never until now when she would have given a lot to feel protected. It would be a while before she felt safe again.

In a room almost directly below the one occupied by Bex Olesker, Tessa Murray wiped cold cream off her cheeks as she prepared to put on a new face, as her mother would have said. As she drew the cotton-wool ball across her jaw, exposing clean skin, so she thought of death. Thinking of death took her along another road, the one that led to Ronnie Richardson, her lover.

Out of nowhere she wondered, what if she had been wrong! What if she *was* wrong? What if she was upside-down inaccurate about God? If that was so, then the dead might indeed rise up to be judged and enter into life everlasting. If that was so, then she had made a catastrophic miscalculation.

If she was inaccurate, not only would she be in mortal sin, but her lover, her dear Ronnie, would be out of reach, for he would surely be deep in mortal sin. She had long ago understood the unhealthy and frightening aspect of their love; she adored a man who was calculating and quite ruthless; a man who snuffed out lives without a second thought. Indeed, he had pride in his work.

Once, a year or so ago, she had asked why they could not just come out and settle down, buy a house in some favorite part of the world and spend the days together, indulging themselves, living it up, making whoopee. He had said that is what they *would* indeed do when the time was ripe. She had pushed a little stronger and he had become angry, putting on that frighteningly cold attitude and lowering his voice to arctic proportions.

Theresa Murray's problem was that at times she had a conscience, and she was aware that this could bring about a terrible end. She loved

Richardson with a passion as strong as a thick metal hawser designed to take huge weights. She loved him with a desire that knew no bounds, and a depth way below the seven-mile limit.

Taking all this into consideration, she paused sometimes to reflect on the possibility of his having an immortal soul and, if so, just what the outcome might be. At the moment of death could he—and by extension she was asking about herself as well—be absolved in that twinkling of an eye?

As she applied blusher, she knew that she missed him most dreadfully when she was away from him; and she looked forward to their reunion as a small child anticipates Christmas. She longed for him now, in the guesthouse in Bern. She could have wept for him, she became wet for him, and her stomach turned over. This was not at all good for Tess Murray. It almost warped her judgment. But not quite.

When she went down to dinner she saw the girl who had been on her flight—the one who had worn the raincoat and the Hermès scarf. Tess smiled at her, and the girl smiled back, inclining her head, acknowledging her.

She saw her the next day, also, when the train took her on its winding route—through Thun and Brienz, then up through the snows to the St. Gotthard; down to Bellinzona and a hint of warmth to come with the palm fronds on the platforms, and so on to Locarno, almost to Italy. On that train Tess should have thought twice.

Between Thun—with its Frankensteinish *Rathaus* snuggled below the sinister castle—and Brienz she stood in the corridor and again saw the Hermès girl, who squeezed by, smiled, and quipped, "We must stop meeting like this."

Tessa thought, I wonder . . . ? And by the time the train pulled into the Locarno station she *had* thought twice about the young woman.

Once they had arrived in Locarno, Bex remained only a few paces behind Tessa when she boarded the ferry. So, here they all were in the Canton of Ticino, the Italian side of Switzerland: that part of the country where the ferries ran year-round on the lakes because of the hairpin, snakebend roads that became slow and crowded in both winter and summer. Bex felt a small pang of not altogether pleasant nostalgia as they plowed across the smooth lake, for the last time she had been on Lake Maggiore was when she was only fifteen years old.

Nor were they alone, Bex and Tessa. An unseen third person had looked and listened, made telephone calls, and like a psychic entertainer reading the minds of his audience, traveled to Brissago by a slightly earlier ferry and so arrived before the other two, ready to crash into their lives. But that was almost part of a different story.

In turn, yet a fourth man, with no connection to any of these people but a long and close connection to Alchemist, had sought Ronnie Richardson down the years of the last decade and across the continent. He knew where Richardson was and planned to confront him face-to-face to put an end to an old, festering wound. At that moment, as the ferry nosed down toward the lakeside town of Brissago, this fourth protagonist, whose name was Leonard Saxby, did not spot or suspect Tessa Murray, Bex Olesker, nor the near invisible watcher who waited onshore.

Saxby was deeply focused on his target. It would have been better for him had he used his eyes, ears, and the sixth sense that works as a human radar. For he was far too close to events over which he had no control and had not even the tiniest inkling that he was headed toward a devastating crash site.

Over the mountains, lakes, and seas, back on the island of Ringmarookey, Charlie ran with monks toward a different kind of wreckage.

CHAPTER 11

In spite of his age, the father superior reached the door before Gauntlet, Palfrey, or the other two monks. It crossed Charlie's mind that Gregory Scott had thrived on the monastic life. Though he looked a bony wreck of a man, his reactions were the quickest of any of them.

"A bomb!" Palfrey muttered as if to himself as they reached the door and crowded into the cloisters, bunched dangerously together. "It's a bomb!" Almost under his breath as they surged forward.

In a sort of Greek chorus Fathers Harry and Hugh began chanting, "Who'd want to bomb us? Who'd bomb us here?" As though someone might well want to detonate explosives near them at some other location.

The words were repeated and overlapped and combined with the click-clack of heavy monastic boots on the cloister flagstones. Gauntlet thought he could have set the piece to music—"Who'd want to bomb us; bomb us here; who'd want to bomb us, bomb us?" Ad nauseam, like a tediously written church anthem.

They reached the gatehouse to find the great oak doors open, swinging in the bitter wind that battered against them, squealing on their iron hinges like trapped animals. Outside, there was smoke and wreckage, against which the dark monastic figures were silhouetted like a seventeenth-century painting of a military skirmish.

Hilary Cooke's little Cessna had come to a spectacular end. Deep gouges in the earth marked where the aircraft had slewed off the runway leaving the cropped scrub at an angle of ninety degrees. The tailplane had been torn away and now leaned, moving in the wind close to the runway. Some fifty yards farther on the wings and center of the fuselage were concertinaed into a tangle of metal and fabric, while the nose and the engine had careered on to smash into the monastery wall, the propeller blades bent and shattered, having chipped out slices of stone, the whole gushing flame and thick smoke.

Roughly halfway between the wings and nose, a pitiful little mound of wreckage marked where part of the cockpit had come to rest, and Charlie saw several of the monks, some with the skirts of their habits pulled up to their waists, running toward this debris. Taking a deep breath, Gauntlet pounded across the turf toward what had once been the cockpit.

Closer to the wall, he could see why they had felt the ground move and shake. Where the aircraft had hit the wall, burying its nose into the thick stone, shredding its prop and exploding, could just as easily have been the concussion point of a shell from a siege gun. The huge blocks of stone had been shattered, cracked, and blasted through as though by a powerful charge.

Charlie's nose wrinkled involuntarily, as if he could detect the sweet roast-pork smell of burning human flesh that was the reek of an illusion. In that instant he heard deep from his mind a snatch from what he thought was a Bruckner symphony—though he could not be certain—and saw the sudden flash of a large wooden inn sign lurching on its hinges with a V-shape cut deeply into one corner. Much later, he recalled this odd image had come from childhood. The inn sign was from Robert Louis Stevenson's *Treasure Island*: a vivid picture conjured up by that most graphic teller of ripping yarns and brought into the present by the battle scent of smoke and the squeaking of the heavy monastery door.

No wonder they had imagined it was a bomb, he thought, realizing that other scenes and scents from his early adolescence were crowding into his brain: memories of the first time he had visited Berlin in the late forties, when you could still smell death thick in the air mingled with the singed redolence of wood and paint.

No hard and fast rules govern aircraft crashes and explosions. The literature bristles with million-to-one shots: a man walking from the epicenter of a massive detonation, while everyone else was incinerated; the lone woman staggering naked from the factory where two hundred of her fellow workers perished when a spark ignited tons of explosives; the child torn from its mother's arms, the lone survivor, as an aircraft blew itself to pieces in a cornfield.

So it had been with the Cessna, and somehow, either by design or freak, Hilary Cooke had survived, huddled now in a gray ball lying in a small indentation between the wreckage and the wall.

The gawky Brother Simon stood over the prone form, his face a stricken mask, while he flapped his arms up and down like an animated scarecrow. "She was taking off!" His voice pitched high as Gauntlet and the father superior reached him. "She opened up the engine and was almost airborne, then there was this bang and the plane swerved and came apart. It was horrible." Simon's eyes glistened with shock and he flapped his arms again as though trying to get himself airborne.

"Useless," the father superior puffed, dropping to his knees by the still body of Hilary Cooke, who lay facedown on the rocky ground. "The lad's absolutely useless in a crisis."

Gauntlet moved in on the other side of the girl, and gently they turned her onto her back.

She groaned and Charlie leaned forward, taking his handkerchief out trying to clean up her face, streaked with oil and smoke. He stopped, wondering at his need to attempt to make the girl more presentable, realizing that he had few medical skills that could really help her now.

Her skin was like thin-stretched parchment: gray, almost opaque. He had seen dead people with more life in their skin tone.

"Make yourself useful, Brother Simon," Father Gregory growled. "Get in touch with the mainland. They'll have to send a rescue helicopter with a doctor."

"Yes, Father. Immediately, Father." Simon sounded like someone out of Chekhov. "Is she . . . ?"

"I've absolutely no idea, young Simon. Just do it." Father Gregory laid his hand across the girl's bruised forehead and murmured a prayer, looked hard at Charlie, who was still trying to clean up the girl's face, and said quietly, "That's not fashionable, you know."

"What?"

"Handkerchief. People use tissues nowadays. They don't carry handkerchiefs around anymore, people don't."

Charlie grunted. "That's just the kind of information I can't do without."

"What d'ye think?"

"Don't know how I've lasted without knowing about handkerchiefs."

"I mean, what d'ye think of the girl? Hilary?"

"I'm not expert in these things. Don't think we should've turned her over. Don't think that was a good move. You were giving her the last rites, weren't you?"

Gregory nodded, muttered one more prayer, and made the sign of the cross. "Reflex action. A priest sees someone badly injured and he goes into the prayers as though a doctor's whacked him on the knee."

Hilary lay curled and limp as though she had made an impression into the earth, which was impossible, for most of it was solid rock. There was little substance about her body. Her head lolled and her limbs seemed almost detached. There was no sign of blood, however, and her breathing seemed deep and natural. Charlie tentatively felt her arms and legs for broken bones. He found himself being unreasonably concerned about her and supposed there was something he very much liked in her. He had found her quaint—that was the best word for it. Quaint and offbeat. Things that he admired in people because they were characteristics that he shared ("You're neat, Charlie. Neat and a shade weird," Bex had once said of him). Now he was worried that Hilary might have some terrible internal injury and was about to die on the cold, rock-hard ground. Jesus, he said to himself; then realized that it was a prayer, not an oath.

Young girls, he thought. I hate it when young girls get killed. For a moment he felt quite frantic, then he was aware that the father superior had motioned most of the monks away, though little groups of them still worked on the bits of wreckage.

The smoke stung at Gauntlet's eyes, and when he screwed them up, the monks in sight changed shape, became mobile Giacometti sculptures, skeletal, thin, and emaciated. They appeared to move jerkily, like marionettes. A few weeks before, Charlie had watched a pop group on television, fascinated by the oddity of the hip-hop, near spastic movements as they danced. The fans crowded around the group, seemingly in ecstasy at the strange jerking way these young people danced with exaggerated movements, taking huge steps as though they were negotiating a series of small fences on the apron-sized dance floor. Now, through his blurred vision, the skeletal monks looked as though they were doing the same odd steps.

"They're getting a helicopter up quick as a flash." Brother Simon was back, still flapping, breathless.

"You have no medical personnel?" Charlie asked of Father Gregory.

"Wouldn't you know it?" The grizzled old priest made a face that, for a moment, turned him into a gargoyle. "Father Martin's our doctor. Took sick last week. We had to send him to the mainland. He's pretty poorly." Shaking his head. "We desperately need new blood."

"What's wrong with your Father Martin?"

Gregory wrinkled up his face. "Old age. He'll be ninety-four at Easter."

For a second or two, Charlie reflected on the wisdom of a community of aging men living on an inaccessible island. He presumed that the younger brothers did most of the heavy work. "What you need," he began, "is a district nurse." Then, catching the stern look in the father superior's eye, he turned to Simon. "What did you actually see?"

In little staccato sentences, the beanpole young man told how Hilary had said she would be getting back to the mainland—"She used to jest with me a little." Charles thought Simon's use of the word *jest* was somewhat contrived. "She did today. Said there was room if I wanted to come back to Glasgow with her. She said there was room in her plane and in her bed."

"Simon! Ye'll stop that coarse talk!" Father Gregory sounded like a loud illegal firework. "Ye'll stop it at once."

Brother Simon looked as though he wanted the ground to swallow him up.

"Get on with your story." Quietly, from Kit Palfrey, who had come up softly behind Father Gregory.

"I like watching Hilary landing and taking off." Brother Simon sounded almost halfheartedly defensive. You like watching Hilary, period, Charlie thought. Hils with the little turned-up nose and the freckles, and the neat jelly-mold breasts. Yeah, get in there, Brother Simon. Brother Simon, sensual keeper of the gate.

Pause. Deep breath. "She's got guts, that girl," Simon said. "Spunk! But something went wrong today. She was fine, then about halfway there was a bang."

"From where?" Palfrey was suspicious. Gregory reached over, distracting Simon, motioning the younger man to take off his cloak to cover Hilary. "Shouldn't have moved her," Gregory muttered as though he had just come to this conclusion.

"Get on with it! The bang. From where?" Palfrey again. Charlie detected a hint of urgency.

"I don't know, but that's when the smoke started."

"From the engine?"

"Maybe. It all happened very quickly. Oh, Lord, it was terrible." Simon still sounded and looked as if in shock. White-faced. Trembling. Tears filling his eyes. "It was some kind of explosion. A fire I think. The plane just sort of . . . disintegrated. Oh, poor Hilary. Will she be all right?"

"Pray for her, Brother Simon." Gregory's head was down against the wind that streamed in from the sea, bleak and brutal. "Go on with you. Round up others. Go to the chapel and pray for her instead of standing around cluttering up the landscape."

The father superior sounded like one of those muscular rugger-playing Christians, more biblical fundamentalist than sung mass. "Go on with you." His voice rose like a sergeant major drilling on a parade ground.

"Yes, Father." Simon shrugged, then started to slink away.

Father Gregory looked up and caught Charlie's eyes, saw there some incredulity, and said sharply, "Charles Gauntlet, what're you looking like that for? Prayer's the one thing we people in the religious life do well! It's the one thing we really know: praising Almighty God and interceding on behalf of humans who are too busy or just can't be bothered. That's what people don't understand." Gregory paused, looking about him, then, taking a deep breath, plunged on. "A few years ago I saw a television program with some young, smart-alecky girls saying that nuns and monks were people who could not cope in the real world. Bah, have you ever heard anything more stupid? They have no idea, people today, of what a calling is. We're God's shock troops, His commandos."

Gauntlet again started to say something, but the father superior had not done. "You modern people. You don't believe in prayer any longer. Well, I'll tell you—both of you—that, while God's not dead and He still listens, there're not enough people getting on their knees and talking to Him. God's will is always done, but there's immeasurable good done by intercession."

Charlie looked away, and his eyes followed Simon, who plodded back toward the gatehouse as another monk, tall and almost as thin as the gatekeeper, started to talk to him. The monk was wagging his finger at the younger man as though it were an exercise for his muscles.

"There's one of your monks giving young Brother Simon what you might call a wigging." Charlie lifted his head with his chin tilted.

"Tall man, could double for Death if you put a scythe in his hands?" Gregory did not take his eyes off the girl's face.

"Sure. Could also play Yorick at a pinch."

"Father Benedict, our novice master. A holy terror. He's a Christian version of Attila the Hun, or maybe the reincarnation of Torquemada. Secretly I think he leads an organization dedicated to bringing back the knout."

"Yes." Charlie nodded. "Brother Simon has spoken to me of this man."

"Well, perhaps he'll get the real work done: the prayers said. Price above rubies, a good novice master—and they're not any good unless they're feared by novices and monks alike." There was now conviction in his voice that caused Charlie to glance quickly at Gregory's face: set and unsmiling.

Gauntlet's eyes still watered from the smoke. He passed a hand over them, wiping away tears with a knuckle as he looked back at Brother Simon being harangued by Father Benedict. As Gauntlet did so, the view appeared to change for a moment and he saw clearly who the novice master could have been. It was like drawing a curtain back to reveal his past, and he could also see himself as he had been all those years ago.

"I know Father Benedict, don't I?" Gauntlet looked up at the father superior.

"Maybe. How would I know? Another country." The old man would not hold Charlie's gaze.

"But I am right, yes?" In his head Gauntlet thought of the corporal at the DP camp. Corporal Knight: the control freak, the one who had worked close to the dead Color Sergeant Hammer. "Corporal Knight. MP, friend of old 'Christmas' Day; 'Shortest' Day; Corporal Day. Knight and Day incorporated, we used to say. Knight was there when Color Sergeant Hammer died, remember? Remember? It's Colin Knight, isn't it? Laurel to Day's Hardy. We always said they were like chalk and cheese." Knight had been thin and dark, Charlie saw him clearly, superimposed on the form of Father Benedict. "Day was the one with the accent, built like a brick shithouse, jagged scar across his forehead."

"No need to be crude, Charles." Gregory's slap-on-the-wrist voice.

As he spoke, Hilary Cooke appeared to stir. A long sigh, followed by a groan that would not have disgraced the Disneyland spook house; then a series of little snorts combined with shaking the head to and fro.

Charlie leaned forward again, touching her face and examining nose and ears for any traces of blood.

"Wharrappened?" Her eyes opened, then closed. "Blurriell!"

"Gently, Hilary. You're going to be okay." She had hazel green eyes with gold flecks. Pretty eyes, Gauntlet thought. Pretty girl. For no particular reason, he suddenly imagined Hilary in lacy green underwear. Dirty old devil, he considered correctly. Careful, Charles. Keep on thinking like that, you'll get a stiffie and Bex isn't here to take care of it, so hard cheese.

"Doctor's coming. Be here soon, then they'll take you back to Glasgow in a helicopter," the Father Superior soothed. "Can you hear me, Hils?"

"Atelicopters." Her head lolled again and she went off on another short course in death. Then the breathing became regular and stable, and as Charlie glanced up, he caught Kit Palfrey's eye.

Palfrey winked and gestured, moving his head, motioning Gauntlet to join him away from the monks tending the injured pilot.

"I want you to go with her." Almost in a whisper. They were several feet from the group: Father Gregory with Fathers Harry and Hugh kneeling around the girl, whose jeans—Gauntlet noticed for the first time—were torn down one leg, and whose fur-lined leather jacket had a rip in the shoulder.

"Go with her where?" Charlie frowned.

"Back to Glasgow. I need someone with her."

"Why?"

Palfrey lowered his voice until it was almost inaudible. "She's been working for me. Keeping an eye on the holy boys."

"Keeping an . . . ?" As Gauntlet said it, he caught Kit's warning in his face and eye, saw that the grayness was a reflection of the North Sea in midwinter; saw it was deeper than the sea; felt the stab of coldness that told him that Kit Palfrey was not to be trifled with: that this was not a game but something far more serious.

"I've got two of them. Hilary and a bloke called Rockwell—'Romeo' Rockwell they call him. Also flies a Cessna out of Glasgow."

"Romeo Rockwell? Why Romeo?"

"You guess, Charles. The guy's dark and swarthy. Thinks he's quite a lover . . ."

"But there's not much there," Gauntlet completed.

"I'll give you his number. He'll bring you back here as soon as you know she's out of danger, or . . ." Kit left the worst possible situation unsaid.

Charlie's ears hurt badly in the cold, making him screw his face up. "Why?" he asked again, like a two-year-old child. "Why are you doing this, Kit?"

"I just need someone around to make sure the girl's okay."

"There're things called telephones, and radios." Gauntlet did not relish the thought of a helicopter ride back to Scotland, then the palaver of bumming another plane ride out to the island.

"There are reasons . . ."

"Come on, Kit, what's going on?"

"Not yet."

"Tell me or I'll walk out on this now. I'll go to Glasgow with Hilary and never return. I'm only in this for the fun of it. Don't need you to do the prima donna bit." A pause as Gauntlet sucked in air. "I was with Scott just after the war. He's got other little helpers. There's a corporal was in the same mob and he's here. Novice master. It's like bloody old home week, Kit."

Palfrey hunched his shoulders against the cold and gave Charlie a fast sideways look. "Something's wrong," Kit muttered. "Can't put my finger on it, but maybe I shouldn't have brought the scrolls to this place. It seemed best, though, with Gregory here and all."

"The girl? Hilary? She's working for you?"

"I told you."

"I check that with her?"

"Of course. Tell her you remember Chris the Lizzie pilot."

"Chris the Lizzie pilot?"

"Should do the trick, yes."

Gauntlet turned to his right and caught sight of Father Gregory Scott, head half-bowed, face set and impossible to read as his novice master, Father Benedict—grim-visaged death on wheels—talked at him, nineteen to the dozen, his mouth moving as though he had to enunciate with exceptional care, like talking to someone who had to lip-read: face within inches of Gregory's. As before, Gauntlet realized this was not a new scene, but something he had already experienced in the distant past. Something in the past mattered to someone: Gregory Scott for one, and the former corporal—Knight, Colin Knight.

As Charlie took in the tableau, so the years again rolled back and he recalled an autumn afternoon out in the camp for displaced persons near Frankfurt. Time was peeled back from Gregory Scott's face, and Charlie saw him as he had been in the early 1950s. With the memory, other facts crowded in. He had not thought of those days for many years; now he remembered details long forgotten: several things swam back into his mind with such sharpness that Charlie was even ready to question the facts. Were these real? he asked himself. Are the memories accurate? Did these things really happen as I recall them now? Was Gregory Scott truly as I recollect, or is this simply a muddle of facts inaccurately dragged back from wherever they have been lying dormant?

"I'll go to Glasgow. See she's okay." Gauntlet looked into Kit Palfrey's eyes, saw that little worm of treason move, then vanish. "I'll make a couple of phone calls while I'm there." Pause. A slow count to six. "Kit, has this got to do with the efficacy of Father Gregory's religious beliefs?"

"Maybe."

"Give me the Romeo feller's number. I'll be back as soon as possible."

Palfrey rapped out a number and Gauntlet fed it into that area of his mind equipped with a mnemonic he used to remember numbers.

"Get me some more pages," Charlie snapped back. "I'll have time on my hands. Time to read. Pass them on."

Palfrey gave a little, almost insubstantial, nod.

When Gauntlet returned to the injured Hilary, he found that she had recovered consciousness enough to talk a little. She could not use one leg; the left arm and shoulder gave much pain; her chest hurt, she said, and her head was still fuzzy. She sounded weak and miserable. Not together. Frightened.

The father superior said he would be happier if they could get the girl inside, out of the biting wind. To that end he was already organizing some of the younger monks, under Father Benedict, who seemed wary of Gauntlet. Wary, shifty, sharp, and unforgiving. Charles did not take to the novice master, and the feeling was obviously mutual. He wondered if the man recognized him from the past. There were so many pictures of that time crowded into his head: Major Gregory Scott; the sinister Corporal Knight; the dead Color Sergeant Hammer; and the massive, brick washhouse that was Corporal Day and was probably someone completely different now.

Brother Simon arrived with four other young, capable, and muscular novices carrying a canvas stretcher; Father Benedict took charge, instructing them on the art of lifting an injured person. Charlie reflected on the novice master's abrasive personality, magnified by a disagreeably harsh, nasal voice, which had that astringent quality specifically designed to grate and rattle the nerves.

Charlie also noticed that two of the younger monks wore a single stud in the left ear. A small cross hung from the studs. Surprised, he saw that Brother Simon was wearing a keeper in a recently pierced earlobe.

In spite of all this, the younger monks were remarkably gentle and efficient. Hilary was obviously in great pain, yet they managed to make her comfortable on the stretcher and carried her into the warmer gatehouse. Charlie's overnight bag was still there, and he made a weak joke about not yet having checked into his cell. The whole time, he was very conscious of Father Benedict's eyes on him, drilling into the back of his skull. If looks could cripple, he would be on crutches for the rest of his life.

Turning suddenly, he saw Benedict move quickly from beside Hilary, where, a second before, he had been trying to reach under her body. For the first time, Charlie noticed that she was lying on a large shoulder bag, the strap of which was slung around her neck.

Just over an hour later, as Gauntlet continued to question his memory of times long past, the helicopter arrived. Kit Palfrey sidled up, handing a file folder to Charlie, slipping it to him in an almost covert manner.

So, they chopped up into the scudding clouds, bouncing around like a fairground ride, finally making Glasgow in the late, dark afternoon after a bumpy, noisy, and ragged kind of journey.

It was drizzling—a fine, almost cloudy mist soaking everything, and Charlie rode in the back of the ambulance with Hilary. He had some vague idea about asking her what she really did for Palfrey as well as fly, but she had been in agony on the flight and they had given her a strong painkilling injection that moved her a long way from consciousness.

In the hospital, he waited for over an hour in a crowded casualty department where young doctors and students battled anxiously against a tide of injured drunks, idiot driving accidents, bits of domestic abuse, assorted wounds, and sudden illnesses. The young housemen and casualty staff, though dedicated, had the look of shell-shocked officers. Gauntlet had seen those faces years before in the streets of Berlin and in that DP camp near Frankfurt.

Eventually a doctor sought him out: a harassed girl who looked about fifteen years old and wore a badge that said she was Dr. P. Pippet. Her bruised eyes indicated that she had been working for too long without a break.

"Mr. Gauntlet, you came in with Ms. Cooke. The airplane accident."

"Sure." Good way to describe Hilary, he considered: Hilary the airplane accident.

"She's going to be okay." The doctor flicked a strand of rogue hair out of her eyes. "There's a compound fracture to a leg. Broken arm. Dislocated shoulder—we've put that right. Four ribs and concussion. We'll have to keep her in for a few days. Should be longer, but we can't spare the beds. We run out so quickly these days. Beds, I mean. I presume you can look after her when she comes out?"

"I'm not even a close friend, Doc. Just happened to be around when the accident . . ."

"Oh!" For a moment the child doctor was nonplussed, but she recovered quickly. "Oh, well, don't worry, we'll talk to her. Fix something." She gave him a little twinkle with her eyes and the corners of her mouth, then turned and hurried away: a medical fireman trying to extinguish a four-engine blaze with a glass of water. To himself Charles thought, Thanks a bunch, Pippa Pippet.

He checked on visiting hours—was told anytime—and the ward to which Hilary had been admitted—C7—then went outside to use his mobile to book himself a room at The Central, before taking a cab off to The Ubiquitous Chip, one of his favorite Glasgow haunts, for an early dinner.

The serving staff were all young and helpful, as were most of the diners. He found it refreshing, particularly after Ringmarookey and the monastery. He recalled someone once telling him that monks were often like manure because they did most good when they were spread over a wide area, and smelled when lumped in one place. He did not suppose the members of the Order of St. Jerome would see it like that. He grimaced, realizing glumly that he would be stuck in Glasgow for at least twenty-four hours. He had begun to regret this involvement. After all, there was little in it for him.

Charlie Gauntlet made a point of keeping clear of people whom he had known during his long, and for the most part bizarre, time with what was generally known in government circles as the Office or the Firm. Now, in the privacy of his hotel room as he nursed a glass of passable zinfandel, he dialed the number of an old acquaintance with whom he had spent many secret years.

"It's Charles," he announced when his friend picked up.

"What's goin' on, old Charles? Long time no see or hear."

"You know me. Like the four wise monkeys."

"Four?" Arthur, the friend, should have known better.

"Sure. See nothing; speak nothing; hear nothing; and fart nothing."

"Oh, yes." At least Arthur did not dignify the crudity with a snigger. "To what do I owe this pleasure?"

"Wondered if you still have your old contacts."

"Some." Not being pinned down.

"Remember a few years ago, mate? Remember, I walked you across some old photographs? Tour of the displaced persons camps, circa 1949–53?"

"Yes. As I recall, you were looking for snaps of yourself with wicked Nazis you finally interrogated."

"*Snaps!*" Charlie smiled. "Was the word I wanted. Snaps, yes. Still put your hands on them, old horse?"

"Easy as pie, Charles. How many you want?"

"Selection taken at the one near Frankfurt. The one where I was stationed, remember?"

"Not really, but it'll be marked up."

"Someone took quite a lot of candid camera shots there. Got everybody to watch the birdie. There are even some of your old mate Herbie Kruger."

"He died."

"I know. I picked up the girlfriend. You'll do the pictures?"

"Good as done, old thing. You collect 'em or shall I send them?"

"Great if you could courier them to me. I'll pay, of course."

"Courier all the way to Scotland?"

"No." Charlie rattled off the Dolphin Square address, then grinned.

"You got one of those cute bits of electronics plugged into your phone, haven't you?"

"Turns me into a mind reader, Charles."

"Easy as falling off a log, yes."

"Easier. This official, old thing?"

"Perish the thought . . ."

"You're not doing anything naughty are you, Charles?"

"Don't be stupid. I'm out of it. No, I just saw someone I thought I recognized. Difficult to be sure, so much whatsit under the bridge."

"And water as well, yes. How's Bex?"

"Mrs. Gauntlet to you."

"I'd heard. Surprised." Charlie had been once bitten in a marriage that proved loveless. It was said that he would never tie the knot again.

"Had to make a respectable woman out of her."

"You old dog. How's she enjoying married life? Hey, you up in Scotland on your honeymoon?"

"Whoever went to Glasgow on their honeymoon? No, she got called back to work. You know how sentimental the Met can be?"

"So you're minding someone else's business until she gets back, eh?"

"Something like that."

"As long as you're not crossing up the Office."

"No way. Listen, these're from your private collection, right?" Arthur had a legendary collection of photographs, which, over the years, his family had built into an impressive list. During World War II, for instance, relatives had taken cameras out into the field and provided the nucleus of a unique database of images. Like Gauntlet, Arthur had returned to private life after years in government service, but he now ran a thriving business providing unpublished pictures to authors, magazines, newspapers, publishing houses, film and TV companies, plus security and intelligence services when they asked nicely.

"Pix and Mix. I'll get them to you as quick as I can. You staying at that place under your own name?"

"Haven't got another now I'm a civilian. Be in touch, chum." Charlie did not want any rambling schmooze on the telephone. Rambling schmooze was careless talk, and that cost lives.

He took a cab back to the hospital, and when he checked in at the nurses' station at C7, a trim-waisted sister was looking through Hilary's notes and said, "She'll be okay." The sister had short ash-blond hair set in a deep, smooth wave with a mannish parting. Charlie reckoned her hair would never be out of place, and in spite of a no-nonsense manner she looked as though she had at one time been seriously beautiful. "Your Hilary'll be in for two or three days."

"Not *my* Hilary, Doctor." Where hospitals were concerned, Gauntlet made it a habit to promote people. He always addressed sisters as doctors, nurses as sisters, and ward maids as nurses. A kind of creative upgrading.

"You're not a relative?" She raised one eyebrow, which made her look very come-hitherish to Charlie.

"Just passing through. I came back with her from Ringmarookey."

"You were with the monks?" The tone was actively suspicious.

"Again, just visiting. I've got to go back there tomorrow. Back to the monks."

"It's no a natural life, monks."

"Wouldn't do for me, but they seem to thrive on it. They also say it is a most natural life, so what do we know?"

"Yes, well. It's a pity you'll no be in Glasgow for a wee while. Your Hilary needs visitors. She's a bit low. Probably shock."

Everything about the sister was trim: the crisp navy blue uniform, the shoes and dark stockings. Even the laminated badge with her photograph and name: *Sister Louise Marks*.

Sister Marks was the kind of woman who would linger for years on the border between youth and middle age, working hard on the figure and getting the respect she demanded with the glint in her clear hazel eyes. She'd be as neat out of the uniform as she was in it, Charlie thought as he went through to the ward and found Hilary Cooke's bed.

She was not the happiest of campers, Hilary Cooke.

"I brought fruit and chocs. Thought you were probably a fruit-and-choc kind of girl."

"Fruit and nut more like." She gave him a weak smile, looking deathly pale and obviously very uncomfortable encased in two cumbersome plaster casts: one from her left upper arm right up to the damaged shoulder. Her right leg was not only in a plaster but also suspended at a nasty angle.

"In movies that's the way they always have the leg." Charlie grinned. "Also someone usually lets it fall with a crash!"

She nodded, not amused, and he pulled up a chair, sitting down, touching his fingertips together in little exaggerated movements, not unlike the "genteel" mannerisms of Oliver Hardy. "I'm flying back to Ringmarookey tomorrow," he began. "Wanted to make sure you were okay."

"I'm alive, but not very happy." She looked as though she needed a few months of R&R, with a lot of TLC thrown in for good measure.

"I think they're going to let you out in a couple of days."

"A couple of weeks, actually. That's why I'm not very happy."

"Never say die." Gauntlet was really not terribly good at sick visiting. "Sorry," he said, trying to put matters right, and they both ended up laughing. "See, I had to come in. Sort of ask you some questions." Another nervous laugh, then an attempt at quirky humor. "Kind of interrogate you. Bring out the screw thumbs."

"Thumbscrews?"

"Yeah, like I said. Thumbscrews and the iron maiden."

"Hardly me." She gave a rueful little smile, and Charlie saw that she was really quite attractive in a Doris Day, hearty-tomboy, and freckles kind of way.

"What happened?"

She closed her eyes, sighed, then said that she had been given no warning of the crash. "I think it was a small explosion in the engine. I was just about to rotate and get the old crate into the air when all hell broke loose."

Old crate, Charles thought. World War II slang. "Can you sort it out?"

"The folks from Farnborough'll be asking that." She tried to shift on the bed, tried to make herself more comfortable, but it did not work. "And I reckon I want to know as well. Very unpleasant. Never been in a real prang before."

There it was again: ghosts of the RAF and World War II. Prang.

"Could it have been done accidentally on purpose?"

"I . . . I . . ." She wrinkled her nose and scowled as though this thought had not come to her before. "I reckon it could've been. It felt like some kind of explosion. But who the . . . ?"

"You tell *me*, Hils." As he said it, Charlie recalled the scene of the crash: Father Gregory looking grave and worried. "Can you hear me, Hils?" he had asked the semiconscious girl. Did this mean he was on close terms with the young pilot? Charlie thought it was about time to come clean.

"Hilary, I'm working with Mr. Palfrey. He said you were doing some jobs for him as well. True or false?"

"Who wants to know, Mr. Gauntlet?"

"Call me Charlie, Hils. I also remember Chris the Lizzie pilot."

"You knew my pa? Hey, that's . . ."

"That's what Kit Palfrey told me to use. To give you my bona fides."

"Oh. Oh, yes. Mr. Palfrey knew my pa. He was in the RAF at the end of the war. Flew Lizzies for Mr. Palfrey's crowd."

The penny dropped. "Ah. Lizzies, sure. Got it." A Lizzie was a Westland Lysander aircraft: big radial engine, high, odd wing above a greenhouselike canopy, fixed undercarriage with little spats. During the months and years before the D-day landings to free Europe from the Nazi occupation, Allied agents had been flown into occupied Europe in Lysanders. They had an alarmingly short takeoff and landing capability, and the pilots who flew them from the so-called Moon Squadrons relied on faultless navigational skills and an ability to land in, and take off from, French fields by insubstantial moonlight.

Lawks, he thought, what did people know about that time nowadays? They got on Le Shuttle or rode a ferry into France and roamed at will. They probably couldn't imagine those old days when to be on the continent of Europe was to be among enemies. Unthinkable now. Outdated and unthinkable.

"You're pretty young to have a World War II pilot as a father." They said of Charlie Gauntlet that he was the kind of man who would always query your birth date if he didn't think the numbers added up.

"I was an afterthought." She gave him her best wide-eyed grin. "Pa didn't meet Ma until the fifties. They had my brothers bang-bang-bang, then a dry spell. I didn't arrive until well into the swinging sixties. Must have been all those Beatles songs and the rising hemlines."

"One of the Cookes with an *e.*" Gauntlet gave her a sly smile. "Always the worst kind, with an *e.* Known for it. So what you doing for old Kit Palfrey?"

"Watching people?"

"Who?"

"The father superior and the demon novice master, Father Benedict."

"And what did you find out, Hilary Cooke with an *e*?"

"That the pair of them go back a long way. Maybe even to the war. Benedict's relatively new here. Came less than a year ago and took over as novice master when Father Ambrose died. And he speaks incredibly good English for a foreigner. You'd never know unless someone pointed it out."

"Who pointed it out, Hils?" That was odd; as far as he could recall, Corporal Knight was British, though he could be wrong. It was Day who had been undeniably foreign.

"Mr. Palfrey. Well, he said it could be that he was from Abroad." She said it as though Abroad was the name of a foreign country.

"Okay, anything else?"

"They didn't trust me. Gregory accused me of tampering with his mail."

"And were you?"

"Of course. That was part of the deal. Peep in the mail. Did a rather botched job on one envelope, which led to the old superior Superior getting on my case."

"Learn anything?"

"Palfrey knows. Yes, Gregory has a very handsome fortune tucked away in an offshore bank."

"What d'you call a fortune, Hils?"

"Around three million sterling."

"That's a fortune."

"And Benedict's got land and money. Conventional. Locked away in a Swiss bank."

"Doesn't mean a thing anymore."

"Doesn't stop them informing him that a monthly payment hasn't arrived two months running."

"And where's *that* from?"

"Grozny, Chechnya; or Tiflis—Republic of Georgia."

Gauntlet heard a lot of bells and whistles going off in the back of his head. "And he doesn't trust you either?"

"Wouldn't like to be left alone with him on a dark night. Wouldn't turn my back on him."

"Maybe you already have, Hils."

"Oh, shit," she said calmly, as though it were an aside like "It looks like rain."

"You want to talk some more? You look all in."

"When're you going back?"

"To the holy fathers? Sometime tomorrow."

"Romeo taking you?"

"I suppose. Haven't arranged it yet."

"I should. Romeo tends to get booked up." She gave him a wan little smile. "Can you come in again?"

"Sure. Rest now, eh?"

Back in his room at The Central, he tried telephoning the Dolphin Square number, but all he got was the tape, so he tried the advanced feature, dialing the number and then bleeping in the code. There were six messages. Three from one of Bex's friends—"Bex, where *are* you? I'm only in town for three days." Tough, Charlie thought. There were two for him. Waterstones had now received the book he had ordered. Only he had not ordered any book.

"Curious," he muttered, then dialed the number Kit Palfrey had given him for the pilot, "Romeo" Rockwell. A disembodied female voice told him he had reached Rockwell Aviation and he should speak

after the beep. He put on his telephone voice and left an uncomplicated message giving the hotel and room number. He also said he
needed a flight to Ringmarookey on the following day. Afternoon
preferred.

He replaced the receiver and prepared for bed.

Then he opened the file with the latest pages of Naomi's journal.

CHAPTER 12

The bells kept her awake. If you had lived there for some time, maybe all your life, you would get acclimatized. But not if you had arrived in the late afternoon of a winter's day after a long rail journey followed by a bit of uncomfortable tailing.

The lakeside town of Brissago has one hotel, standing almost on the lake, with the church set just above it, giving guests an unenviable proximity to the bells that toll each half hour. In bed, Bex became convinced that the bells were tolling just for her. This was the main reason for her nocturnal telephone search.

She had already called London with a quick situation report: four lines of text that could be fed into the magic machines to give her exact location and an outline of the facts as she saw them. She expected a reply within hours. In fact, it was pretty well essential that they got back to her soon. She did not fancy operating in either Switzerland or Italy without some kind of sanction—particularly from the Swiss, who were known to be a shade touchy when it came to another country's law enforcement agencies taking liberties in their backyard. This status would only be further compounded by the presence of someone from Belfast in the frame, for Tessa Murray's name would now be posted on many search lists. Even in these times when a permanent cease-fire had been achieved, the Irish were more than a mite touchy over security. And who can blame them?

London now knew that Bex had not only Tessa in her sights, but also someone, presumed to be Alchemist, within touching distance. So Rebecca Louise Olesker—or Gauntlet, depending on where you stood—had every reason to expect reinforcements, an arrangement with the Swiss Security Service, and most probable of all, instructions to back off in favor of some kind of specialist team. Maybe she would have to go via Belfast so that grimy Liz Liddiard could do a short debrief.

Whatever, it was reasonable to assume that she would be ordered back. PDQ before she got trashed. She was not naive enough to imagine that she had arrived in the town without being detected by Alchemist. They had in fact locked eyes. Also, she figured—rightly as it turned out—that London would take immediate steps. What she neglected to see was the time lag before the senior officers of OS13 would snap into action.

So, in the dark, slow waiting time of night, Bex kept the demons at bay by allowing herself to be filled with curiosity about her husband and his reasons for being in Scotland. In many ways it was the thought of her imminent return that prompted this nudge in Charlie's direction. In short, she really wanted him there, in Dolphin Square, when she got back, not swanning around, roamin' in the gloamin', or knee deep in heather and haggis.

Yet when she did track him down, with the help of a trusty diary that contained several flimsy pages of hotel numbers, she found he was out. At this time of night? she queried. Beware the green-eyed monster, Bex.

Outside, in front of the hotel, with the church looming above it, there is a short paved area leading down to the water. So close is it that on a clear, calm day the church is reflected in the lake, and the ferry stage is a gray finger of planked wood cutting into the green-glass water. When the steamer is in, you embark and disembark by passing under a metal arch proclaiming the town's name, and you walk over the creaking wood almost straight into the hotel.

In summer you sit outside, eat, drink, and watch the ferryboats as they chug crisscrossing the lake to Italy and back. If you do that, there are other delights, for across the lake the huge breast of mountain rises, green and cow-dotted in summer; white, running down to green in winter; and as the year progresses, it provides a constant light show on its meadows and rocks as the sun shifts from dawn through its phases until the shadows chill the day and the view at dusk is an altered state.

Here, though, when winter has yet to sniff the first hint of spring, there is a bleakness, for the place is not whole out of summer.

So it was, around four that afternoon, that Bex had boarded the ferry in Locarno, and as soon as the ship slipped her moorings and began to make way briskly out onto the lake, Bex hefted her garment bag and made for the nearest washroom. She emerged as they were turning toward Ascona, the new raincoat reversed and belted over her thicker jeans and the waisted, slightly flared, black jacket she had bought in Belfast. Since leaving Ireland she had worn soft, low-heeled shoes for comfort; now, wanting to gain a little height, she changed into sleek blue pumps with taller heels. She had bought those in Belfast also, on her little shopping spree, and she knew Charlie was going to label them her fuck-me shoes. She smiled to herself as she crammed down the darker of the two felt hats and, with the heavy horn-rimmed spectacles on her nose, returned to her spot forward, looking like a very different girl to the one who had come up the gangway in Locarno.

Glancing into the forward saloon, she had a clear view of Tessa seated near the big sliding doors; saw how she sat and remembered it: how the woman seemed to put all her weight onto her left buttock; back straight but her chin tilted arrogantly.

They stopped at Ascona: two people off, three on. Then the steamer began its shore-hugging approach to Brissago, and she saw the Murray girl stand up, wrap her heavy coat around her, and make her way over the gently rocking deck to the starboard side, where she joined a knot of passengers by the rail, close to where the gangway would be slid out. The engines died to idle and they moved softly up to the landing stage, bumping the heavy buffer tires lashed to the woodwork.

Bex sidled aft, moving along the windows of the lounge, and cutting across to the starboard side just as the first passengers began to make their way down the little ridged gangplank. She hung back at the tail end of the dozen or so people in front of her and made heavy weather out of carrying the bag.

Tessa was well ahead of her, a hand brushing hair from her face, and her steps high and sexy, her legs taking wide paces as she strode off to the left of the hotel, toward the main road. Bex caught sight of her turning—again to the left—as Tessa reached the top of the slight incline up onto the road. She was heading toward Italy.

Bex dared not risk leaving her garment bag at the hotel, for she would need it if Tessa led her over the frontier. How the hell did you follow someone along a main highway carrying a case? She slid the strap over her shoulder, shrugged, and stepped onto the gangway: the last passenger to leave the steamer, shoulders squared and her own prancing walk—her seven-league-boots stride as she called it—trying to shorten the space between her and the target. The blue shoes did not help.

Only one main road travels through the town of Brissago, and Tessa Murray was still visible, moving fast as though she had no cares in the world. The road hugs the sweep of the shoreline, passing a scatter of villas as it goes on above the lido, then past the tobacco factory on the right before it crosses the small border post into Italy.

She walks like a bloody giraffe, Bex thought. Those long, high paces, almost kicking from the knee. Certainly she was off in a world of her own, not even a glance backward as she seemed to quicken the walk, as if she were late for an appointment. She gestured, looking at her left wrist, and Bex wondered if she actually was late for a meeting.

Then Tess slowed as she approached the villa on the left: more cypress trees, terra-cotta roof tiles, a low wall, and a wrought-iron gate. Bex, almost twenty yards behind her, could see the front door, heard it as it scraped open. Bex stopped, bent and pretended she had a problem with her shoe, squinting up as the man came out of the front door into the dusk, reaching out as Tess closed the gate and dropped her bag as he appeared, wrapping his arms around her: pulling her to him, one arm sliding around her waist in an acquisitive movement that left nothing to the imagination. You saw it and knew, immediately, how these two people would be spending their evening. He kissed her, hugged her close, but his head came round over her shoulder, eyes raking the road as a Fiat bustled along noisily from the direction of Italy followed by a little truck with three workmen, chilly in the back, catcalling and whistling: laddism on wheels.

Bex sensed the man's eyes on her, trying to gauge the threat. Then she saw him turn away, an arm flung around Tessa's shoulders, his other hand going for her case and ushering her through the front door. Bex straightened up and started to walk on, telling herself to look purposeful: five yards now from the low wall and metal fence, the boundary marker enclosing the property. Bex glanced toward him and knew, somewhere in the back of her consciousness, that something was wrong. She saw the man turn again at the door, looking straight at her before he closed it. No sign of Tess Murray, who had disappeared into the darkness of the hall.

She realized that her body was tense, heart racing, expecting him to react, leap toward her or hurl a bullet from the doorway. But she had passed the farther edge of the wall and fence, catching sight of the little ceramic nameplate—*Villa Myrte.* Clear and away? she wondered, feeling the tension building in her head and aware of her muscles stretched, tendons like bungee cords straining.

Almost unconsciously, Bex quickened her pace, alert in case he had returned to follow her, but there was no sound, no hint that he was even watching her with suspicion.

She walked on, spotting a little café some thirty or forty yards from the villa, across the road. *Café National* it proclaimed in crimson lettering above the door. In summer there would bougainvillea up the trelliswork and a lattice awning over space for some sixteen or seventeen tables, deserted now, abutting the main building, lit behind a large, steamy window and from which some unconvincing pop group played and sang in an Italian attempt to ape an American band.

She waited for three cars to sweep past in the direction of Italy, glimpsing the driver of the first one, hands tight on the steering wheel, face anxious and hair awry, talking to himself.

She crossed the road as she came abreast of the villa, glancing toward it, seeing an archway to the left of the house and thinking to herself there would be steps beyond, down to a boathouse and the lake. In her head she even imagined that she could hear a boat bumping against its mooring. She had heard the door closing, or thought she had. Certainly nobody appeared to move inside, though she thought she could sense the man's eyes on her again.

Since passing the villa, she had repeated her description of him in

177

her mind, burning it in like doing mathematical tables in a school-room; locking it into her memory. Conning it by rote: a mantra. Late forties; five foot seven, maybe eight; broad shoulders; military car-riage, very conscious of squaring the shoulders; and moving with hands balled into fists, thumbs down. Face, slightly Germanic, good bones, straight nose, wide mouth, light eyes, probably blue, couldn't see; lines below the eyes giving a slightly tired look. Complexion, well tanned. Light hair, well groomed, short and styled. She would make a drawing when/if she got back to the hotel. She could reproduce him on an E-fit, complete with dark blazer and khaki slacks.

Her hands were cold. She realized this as she opened the café door and heard a little jingling sound. A tinny, bell-like electronic alert, presumably for the girl in the black dress and ludicrous little white apron who studied something—probably a women's magazine—from behind a little counter. Her uniform was like something a whore would wear to entice clients, turn them on to get it off.

She looked up, unsmiling, and greeted Bex with a bored "'Serra" and a questioning look, as though she wanted to get a flying start on the order. It was a glance with the head cocked to one side and eye-brows raised.

Bex smiled and used halting Italian to order a coffee. The girl nod-ded, batted her eyelids, and went through a beaded curtain with all the animation of someone who was performing forced labor and really wanted to be somewhere else—maybe in a different season and on a different planet. Bex's mother had been fond of a phrase describing that particular walk—"Moving around like dead lice're dropping off her."

Bex chose a table against the wall, felt the stifling heat from the lit-tle tiled stove in one corner. The young woman who had gone in search of coffee was dark, swarthy even: late teens, early twenties; thick, heavy hair inclined toward greasiness. Very Mediterranean, yet the Café National seemed to be hankering after the lakeshores of Geneva or Zurich, or even the pastures of the Bernese Oberland. Large old cowbells were arranged along the main wall, after the man-ner of flying ducks, while a couple of Swiss Railways posters showed tourists on a mountain road meeting a woman in national costume, and a couple dining by moonlight looking out on a lake encompassed by mountains.

The waitress returned with remarkably good coffee, which she served, then retreated to her magazine, occasionally looking at her watch and glancing toward her customer as though she suspected she would abscond without paying the bill. She smiled only once, when Bex paid and left an overgenerous tip, feeling that she had been blackmailed and could have suffered physical harm had she left less.

"Allora," Bex began her staggering Italian again. Brazenly asking about the villa across the road, the Villa Myrte? No, it wasn't for rent, no. An English owned it. A man who wrote. A scribbler. Yes, a Signor Hungerford—the girl pronounced it 'Ungerford, with an accent on the *Ung*. Antonio. Tony 'Ungerford.

Ah, well. Bex did a sad little shrug as she reached the door. The lights from two cars, moving slowly from the direction of Italy, swept across the front of the café. For a few seconds they illuminated a figure walking toward Brissago on the other side of the road: a tall, slim man, a light trench coat wrapped around him and belted tightly; a dark, soft cap on his head. He moved almost like a dancer, and Bex thought there was something familiar about him. Yet he seemed to have disappeared when she crossed the road, swallowed up in the night.

Though fearful of the return past the villa, she saw nothing to suggest it was chancy to pass by. There were signs of life, a glow from the rear of the house that filtered through doors and arches, and a faint suffusion of light—a candle possibly?—somewhere upstairs. She met no other people on the road, but was passed by several cars and one large long-haul lorry, before she reached the hotel where they greeted her as though turning up unannounced at five-thirty in the afternoon of a February day was absolutely normal. Yes, they had rooms—she wondered what she would have done if they had been closed. Certainly she questioned what she was doing there at all, for how do you keep watch on a lakeside villa a quarter of a kilometer along a lone road?

She tried to sound casual; said she had been here once before, long ago as a child. There was a house toward Italy. A Villa Myrte? Oh, yes, of course, the English colonel. It was sad, he had died suddenly two years—no, three years—ago. Mrs. Harrison had gone away. Yes, they thought she had gone to live with her unmarried daughter in Trieste. The Villa Myrte? But certainly, another Englishman lived there now. An Englishman who wrote crime books: how you say? Thrillers? Yes, the manager laughed and called him *Piccolo Scroccato*, literally, the "little scratcher." Though there was nothing *piccolo* about this *scroccato*. No, they did not see much of him. Only sometimes when he went to Locarno on the ferry. Occasionally he took a glass while he waited in the summer.

And Bex knew she was not off the hook yet. The English scribbler was a professional. You didn't have to pass exams at Police College to know that.

She bathed in wonderfully hot water, sluicing the grime and ache of the day from her skin, and downstairs, in the large dining room, ate raclette, succulent lamb chops, with rösti and green beans, a salad with a dressing that cleaned the palate, leaving it fizzing; followed by a peach flan with thick cream for those who just did not care about cholesterol.

Only when she got to bed did the bells begin to disturb her. First the bells, then anxiety regarding Tessa and the man who called himself Hungerford.

She must have managed about an hour's sleep, then the bells woke her. After that she dozed and then woke completely around midnight. As she came awake, she had one clear thought in focus. The man she had glimpsed on the road. The slim man in the raincoat, wearing a flat cap at a jaunty angle, was somehow familiar. She had a feeling that she had seen him earlier. Dublin? No, earlier than that, she thought. At the opera? Strange, because she also remembered Charlie suddenly turning his head as they left the theater. She had followed his gaze and caught a flash of the same figure on the edge of the crowd.

Her mind turned in random circles, following a haphazard stream of consciousness. She thought of years ago and the sound of school bells. When she was very young, she had attended a village school where they had retained the old Church of England school building with its formal playground, and a little exposed bell incorporated into the churchy design. They had still used it. She saw herself, hair flying and kneesocks falling, as she rushed along the pavement to avoid the stigma of being late.

That led to her early religious beliefs, those strange, half-formed ideas of God and the chocolate-box Jesus so many children come to believe in through Sunday school and Bible stories not rooted in any sense of time or place.

The Jesus she had learned about in her early teens was basically a white, middle-class, English Jesus. A Jesus whom you thought of as preaching at the parish church on a Sunday morning and returning with the vicar to eat a roast-beef-and-Yorkshire-pudding Sunday lunch. A "Lord put beneath thy special care, one eighty-nine Cadogan Square" kind of Christian. That was what her whole family had been then.

She dialed Charles again. He was still not in his room. "That his wife again?" the hotel operator asked. Then, "The night porter says he's gone up the infirmary."

So now she worried. Could he be ill?

An hour later, Charlie was still not in his Scottish room, so she was there, within a stone's throw of Italy, sleepless, with nobody to talk to, not even on the telephone.

Finally, Charlie picked up at just after three o'clock and they had hardly exchanged a couple of sentences before Bex's hotel room door suddenly opened and her worst nightmare descended.

CHAPTER 13

Charlie read, lying on his bed at The Central Hotel, Glasgow:

I have just heard from Romillius that the man Jesus is said to have performed another miracle. I could be wrong about the thing that happened at the wedding. Now everybody tells the story of how Jesus turned the water into wine. Even Romillius has heard of it. He came to see me tonight and asked if I really thought this was true magic. I told him I was not sure and that, at the time, I thought it was a joke. Now there is a story that Jesus has cured a blind man, and also that he has raised a man called Lazarus from the dead.

That was as far as Charlie got before his eyes drooped and he slid into a deep sleep. The events of the day had taken their toll, and he did not wake until the phone rang just before midnight.

"Mr. Gauntlet?" A woman.

"Who wants him?"

"This is Sister Marks, Mr. Gauntlet. We met when you came in to see Hilary Cooke this evening. She told us where you're staying. I'm sorry about this, Mr. Gauntlet, but she's asking for you."

He sat bolt upright. "What's really wrong? What's happened to her?"

"Nothing. She's fine, but she says she needs to talk to you. She hasn'ee really been herself since the other fellow came to see her."

"What other fellow?"

"The monk. The Ringmarookey monk. Yon Father Martin."

Father Martin! He'll be ninety-four at Easter, the father superior had said. "The old monk? The doctor? The one who's ill?"

"Must be a different Father Martin. This fellow's no what you'd call real old. He's a bit of a muscle man. A man mountain really. A huge fellow."

Charlie was dressed and halfway downstairs to the summoned cab when his telephone began ringing again. After having tried large hotels in Aberdeen and Edinburgh, Bex had struck lucky in Glasgow. Now the hotel operator told her that her party was not in his room. The operator made this sound very suspect, and Bex, speaking from the hotel in Switzerland close to the lakeshore, asked if she could leave a message. She was simple and to the point: "Would you tell him his bride rang." Then, in answer to the operator's questioning tone, she added, "No. No, I can't leave a number."

Within minutes of his arrival back at the hospital, that morning in Glasgow, Charlie was wearing his interrogator's hat.

"I'm sorry to get you out in the middle of the night, Mr. Gauntlet. I wouldn't normally do this kind of thing, but I was really rather alarmed." Thus Sister Marks, who looked as shipshape at two in the morning as she had when she first came on duty. "I've put her into a side ward, on her own. She really hasn'ee been herself since the monk talked with her."

Sister Marks shepherded Gauntlet along the corridor and into a clean little room done out in institutional green. Hilary Cooke lay propped up on pillows, nursing a box of tissues. She looked, Charlie reflected, more like a young, frightened rabbit than an intrepid bird-woman. Her eyes were traced with red while her nose ran damply. The flybabe that was Hilary Cooke seemed to be regressing toward neuroticbabe.

"How now, Hilary Cooke with an *e*, what's the matter?" He perched himself on the edge of the bed, which sagged slightly under his weight.

"Your Mr. Gauntlet's come to see you." Sister Marks stated the obvious, patted Hilary's hand, and left, all in a series of fluid, economical motions.

"So what's going on?" he asked, a question that seemed to release a fresh wellspring of tears. "Look, I'm not so good at this comforting business."

"Then why've you come?" she wailed. "It's late. And you don't really know me."

"No, it's early in the morning. It's not late. It's early, and I do know you because, whatever the problem, I've been there. I promise you. Cubs' Guide's honor. Whatever."

"I think I'm underinsured."

"You ain't going to get your plane back, then. And that's not the whole story, is it? In fact, I doubt if it's a valid reason at all." He took a deep breath and noted that she would not look him in the eyes. He thought of a line from a half-remembered poem, "the voice of your eyes is deeper than all roses." "Listen, Hilary. You've been working for my friend Mr. Palfrey; you had a bad accident—in shock I would think, still—and you had another visitor after I left earlier. Who was he? And what's really going on? Tell me and I might be able to help. Don't tell me and I definitely can't."

She wiped her eyes with a couple of balled-up tissues that she began shredding between her hands. She sniffed again, looked down, then up. This time she did look at him and he could see the fear, and he wondered why Sister Marks had bothered him. This was a straightforward case of shock.

As he stared at her, he found it difficult to think of Hilary as the girl who had piloted him out to Ringmarookey. She did not look capable of operating a child's scooter let alone an aircraft.

She sniffed again, looked away, then back. "I don't think you're going to like it." Her hands were tense, almost white-knuckled.

"Just tell me."

"I've been . . . well, very stupid . . . I think . . . I've been reporting to Mr. Palfrey, but I've left bits out."

"You been selective with the truth, Hils."

"Yes, and I haven't told him what might be the most important thing."

"Which is?"

"Well, it's two things really. First, I've been reporting stuff back to the father superior as well. I also run private errands for him and I think that's maybe disadvantaged me."

"You've been playing both sides of the street: that's the technical term for it, Hils. That's always dangerous whatever line of business you're in. What kind of errands you do for Gregory?" Gauntlet's face had gone blank, devoid of any expression. It was a trick he had learned many years before. "Never give 'em a hint," a cunning old barrister had told him. "Listen to whatever's behind the words they speak. Read the body language." They said of this lawyer that he could find, to quote William of Stratford, "tongues in trees, books in the running brooks, sermons in stones."

In plain talk, he could read people, get under their skin, divine the way their waters ran, and pull their deepest fears from a pause. Charlie Gauntlet had learned some of the tricks from him, and he was the man who wrote the book.

"What kind of errands, Hils?" Charlie asked a second time, recalling that Father Gregory had called her "Hils" as she lay injured in front of the massive monastery. Charlie had noted it in the invisible notebook of his mind. "Hils, what kind of errands?"

"I took messages. Carried letters. Picked up things from a bank."

"Bank in Glasgow?"

"No. South. On the border."

"Concerning someone's account? His account? Father Gregory's account?"

"Yes. Gregory Scott's account. Accounts really." She gave the address of the branch of a bank in the border town of Melrose, some forty miles south of Edinburgh. Unaccountably the words of an Elton John song passed soundlessly through Charlie's mind.

"More than one? More than one account?"

"Yes, I noted three. There were three different accounts I serviced." She looked up at him and he saw that she was angry with herself. "I wouldn't be telling you this if I didn't think it had put me in danger."

"Yes, you said he had money. So, you serviced three bank accounts?"

"Yes."

"Doing what?"

"Taking letters to the bank. Putting money in. Drawing money out—or at least I took it to be money. He implied it was money. I also left things to be picked up."

"What kind of things?"

"Letters. Documents. I saw a pile of letters once. In his office on Ringmarookey: in the monastery. He said they would be dealt with by the bank. Picked up."

"You took money from him? From Gregory Scott, the father superior? You took money from Ringmarookey?" His expression shifted slightly. For a second he was aware of a puzzled look crossing his face, quick as a neon blink.

"Yes. Several times."

So, Charles wondered, where did that money come from? There was no open trade on Ringmarookey. "Checks, I suppose. That's what you mean by *money*?"

"No. No, there were sealed Jiffy bags. Mailers stuffed full of cash. You could feel it. I'm talking megapounds. This wasn't the Sunday collection for matins, right?"

"And you took money to him as well?"

"No. I took letters, some in envelopes sealed with wax. My guess was that he had mail sent to the bank. I thought the bank sealed it in these big white envelopes."

Charlie grunted. "Anything else?"

"I posted letters for him."

"Ever look at them?"

"I looked at the addressee sometimes."

"Well, I wasn't asking if you steamed them open!"

She seemed to think this was funny, smiling for the first time.

"You remember any of the addresses?"

"They were mostly for abroad. Difficult abroad names. Russia, I think, some of them."

"Any have names like eye tests?"

"Yes. Yes, how did you guess?"

"I know a little bit more about Gregory Scott than you do. Or, I suspect I know more." He sucked his teeth audibly. It was an irritating habit, he thought, then grinned to himself. Those monks've got some irritating habits, he thought. "Hils, how long has this been going on? The banks and letters and stuff. The money?"

"Ages. Ever since I started to do the Ringmarookey run. Well, once I got to know the father superior. Three . . . four years."

"Mmmmm. And you've never hinted at this to my friend Kit Palfrey?"

"No, and I should've."

"Why should you? What's suddenly so different?"

Her lip trembled again. "I'm frightened, Mr. Gauntlet. That's why I got the sister to phone my mum and dad. They must be away somewhere. She can't get hold of them, and I'm dead scared. I . . ."

"All right, you're scared. Of what, or of whom?"

"The monk who came to see me after you left."

"And who was he?" The reality of the situation was that Charlie himself was getting a mite twitchy for her. His long memory had already turned up ghosts from the past, and he did not like what he was hearing now.

"I've seen him on Ringmarookey, but never spoken to him. He's kind of weird. Tonight he said he was Father Martin, and he wore the OSJ habit." She dropped her head back against the pillow as though she was dead beat. "I mean, yes, he must have had connections to Father Gregory. He did have connections 'coz he knew I'd been ferrying the money. But . . ."

"He threatened you?"

"Well, I was worried after the crash. I mean, if I think back, that was no ordinary accident. I think someone had been messing about. . . . That I was meant to crash. Then this big bloke—"

"Father Martin?"

"Well, I don't know. That's what he called himself."

"He threatened?"

"Kind of . . . sort of threatened. Father Gregory used to tell me all the stuff I did for him was absolutely confidential. That I mustn't talk to anyone about it. But this fellow . . . Well, he was pretty up-front about it. Really frightened me, and I got to thinking, I don't really know whose side he's on. Don't really know if there are sides at all."

"But he threatened you?"

"He wanted the letters."

"What letters?"

"He wanted the ones I was bringing in from Father Gregory."

"Didn't know about this. Not a mind reader, Hils."

"No. Sorry. Gregory gave me a pretty thick sealed manila packet. I was to leave it at the bank."

"And where is it now?"

"I've got it here, under my pillow."

Charlie saw the leather bag and remembered her lying on it, the strap round her neck, and how he had caught Benedict trying to reach for it.

"I told him it got burned up in the crash. He asked if I'd told anyone about what I did for Gregory. I said no, of course not. He did say he was a friend of Gregory's. That's what he called him—Gregoriev. Said if I breathed a word of the confidential business I did for Gregoriev, I'd wish I'd never been born."

Charlie nodded her along.

"He said I'd wish I'd been killed in the aircraft. Then he asked about the crash itself. Did I think it was sabotage?"

"And did you?"

"Only after he left. I thought back about it. Realized it wasn't quite straightforward. But I was worried by then, because he started to get very heavy. Unpleasant actually. Very unpleasant. You don't expect that from a priest—from a monk. Said he wanted the documents, the letters. Said he had to make sure they were safe. That's when I got a bit bolshy—"

"Whoa, Hils. This monk, what sort of age was he?"

"That's difficult. I mean . . . ?"

"Yeah, I know. They all look the same. Like penguins. What size this guy come in, Hils? Big?"

"Exceedingly. I mean he's *really* huge. Massive."

"Age?"

"Difficult. Don't know. Like you, he's one of these people you can't tell his age. Could be fifty, or . . ."

"A hundred 'n' fifty?"

"Yes, but realistically I think he's a well-preserved sixty-some-thing."

"Ah, very old, then. Ancient?"

"Not these days. I'm not as stupid as I look."

Charlie turned this over in his mind. Looked at it and thought the age could be about right. "So an extremely large monk priest. Has hair, yes? What, black with a lot of gray?"

"That's about the size of it. And he has a big hooked nose. Large. Beaky."

"Aquiline?"

"Like a bird."

"That's aquiline, Hils. Bird beak, like an eagle, right?"

"Right."

Go for broke, Charlie thought. It was a coincidence of course, and who knew what changes had taken place in over thirty years. "He have a scar, this monk?"

"You know him?"

"Tell me about the scar, Hils."

"On his forehead. A kind of zigzag."

"More like the letter *M*."

"That's the one."

So, Gregory Scott was surrounded by the bullyboys of old.

Charlie rocked to and fro, as though he were about to start keening. "Hils, this business about the package of letters." In his head he drew a picture of the big monk, huge with his grizzled beard and hands like hams. "Hils, didn't Gregory ask you if they were okay? When he was with you after the crash?" It seemed to make sense that Gregory would ask about the letters.

"He may have done. I was pretty well out of it. You know that yourself, Mr. Gauntlet."

"Charlie."

"Charlie. You were with me in the chopper, weren't you?"

"Yes, you were out of it." She had dipped in and out of conscious-ness in the helicopter. He saw her in his mind: eyes opening and clos-ing; the chill of the rescue chopper; the noise; the smell of antiseptic and aircraft interior. Military aircraft have a special smell to them: part fuel, part the dope they use to paint the planes; metal. There was also the smell of oil: oil for weapons, he thought. Even the medical equipment did not completely blot out the military scents. "So, he really frightened you, this guy? This monk? More frightening than Father Benedict? Now, he's really scary."

She nodded, as though worn-out. Then her eyes brimmed again. "I think someone tried to kill me—the aircraft. I think maybe they'll try again. Mr. Gauntlet, you are official, aren't you? I mean, well, Mr. Palfrey was telling me the truth, wasn't he?"

"Sure. Course it's official," he lied, surprised as ever at his ability to use such an authoritative tone. But, then, most of his working life had been one of lies and double-dealing. That's what he did best. "I think I'd better take a look at this packet of papers, Hils, don't you?"

She looked uncertain, frightened again. "You're sure it's . . . ?"

"Kosher? Absolutely. Two hundred percent, Hils." Flat, as though he were trying not to look as he lied.

She reached into the bag and pulled a package from it. A thick, good-quality manila envelope, bulging and firmly stuck down. A name was on the front—*Arthur Howells, Esq., Manager*, it said. Manager of the bank's branch in Melrose. In his head, he heard Elton John again. Recognized the song, "Border Song." Gave a little grin, then stuck his right forefinger under the flap and ripped the envelope open.

The first thing he realized was that money had begun to spill out onto the bed. Large-denomination notes: pounds, dollar bills, hundred-dollar bills. Quite a lot of cash. There was also a second thick, sealed envelope. A deposit slip and a folded letter on good heavy rag paper. He sorted through the cash, then looked at the deposit slip. It showed seven thousand pounds and four thousand dollars. Not huge, but enough. "How often you do this, Hils?"

"Once a week. Oh, money?"

"No, teddy bears, Hils! What you think I mean? Of course, money."

"I suppose every other week. Sometimes there's nothing for a whole month, then every week or two. In winter it's often patchy."

"Patchy, yeah, sure. I think someone's doing some clever account-ing somewhere. Dead creative!"

The carefully typed letter to the bank manager read:

Dear Arthur,

Hope all goes well. Enclosed for account 892451. Also the let-ters for forwarding. Beridi will pick up the usual. Hope to see you sometime in the spring.

Sincerely,

It was signed *Gregory*. A flowing, rather fussy and flowery hand.

"So, is this Beridi the priest?" The name was oddly familiar.

She frowned. "What Beridi?"

A noise caused them both to look up, startled. Sister Marks put her head around the door, asking if either of them wanted a cup of tea.

"Ask her," Hilary muttered.

Gauntlet held up a hand. "Sister, I've got a question." Then, turning back to the patient: "So, ask her what?"

"About the priest. The monk. Father Martin."

"Ah! I see. Sister, the big fellow who came to see Ms. Cooke after I left . . . ?" Charlie gave her his standard grin, the one that said, I'm a bit of an oaf but be nice to me and I won't be any trouble.

"What about him?"

"You know who he was? Regular or what?"

"Never seen him before. Name of Father Martin. Asked for Ms. Cooke by name. It was very late. We don't have specific visiting hours anymore, but I don't think I'd have let him on the ward if he hadn't been a priest. Did I do wrong, dear?" The last directed at Hilary, who bit her lip and gave a little shake of the head. Almost to herself she said, "Very big he was. Exceptionally big, that monk."

Charlie's face was turned away from Hilary so she could not see the way he turned down the corners of his mouth and raised a quizzi-cal eyebrow at the nursing sister. "Tea'd be great." He grinned. "Only a tiny drop of milk for me. Lots of sugar though. Very unhealthy." Good, Charlie. Grin for the cameras. Twinkle.

Hilary wanted her tea weak—always a bad sign in Charles's book. For Charlie, tea was almost as important as the Japanese ritual. One of Charlie's bright sayings among his old colleagues had been "Tea is the ninth sacrament of the Church of England. Either the ninth sacrament or the eighth deadly sin. One or the other."

Hilary also asked for something for her head. "Splitting," she said, putting hand to forehead. "Like someone's cleaved it with an ax."

"Cleaved it?" Sister Marks gave a little moue. "Must be bad. I'll get you something."

Charlie continued to go through the packet, putting the money back in the envelope together with the letter to the bank manager and then starting to examine the second envelope. On the front, in the father superior's writing, was the one word: *Beridi*.

He glanced up as a tired-looking student nurse came into the private room carrying a small tray with two mugs brimming with tea. The young nurse looked about ten, Charlie thought as he gave her a welcoming smile. "Long night, uh?"

She gave him a smile as weak as Hilary's tea, nodded, brushed a strand of dark hair from her eyes, and said in a surprisingly grown-up, rather throaty voice, "I'd rather be on nights than days."

There was no further explanation, and Charlie waited for her to elaborate as she gave him another exhausted smile and headed for the door. "Drink your tea and shut up," he said, looking at Hilary.

"I didn't say anything."

"Then let this be a warning to you."

She slurped tea, pulled a face, and suggested that it might be dishwater.

A moment later the nurse was back bearing pills for Hilary's headache, waiting until she saw the patient swallow them with another mouthful of the disgusting tea.

As soon as she left, Charlie ripped open the other envelope. It contained several sealed envelopes of a similar quality to the paper that the father superior had used for the bank manager. None of them were addressed, though each had one name neatly written in the top right-hand corner where it could finally be obscured by a stamp.

He flicked through the envelopes, asking Hilary as he went.

"Know an Alex, Hils?"

"I remember a letter to an Alex. About a month ago. I posted it for him—for Gregory."

"Remember the address?"

"Somewhere in London, I think."

"That really narrows it down. How about Petor: P-e-t-o-r?"

"Plenty of Peters, no Pet-ors, though."

"An Igor?"

"They've got an Igor up the monastery."

"I don't think it would be this one. Not the same Igor." Then he thought of Mel Brooks and muttered, "Eye-gor." Hilary gave a snort, which obviously caused her some pain.

"How about Kenni—with an *i*?"

"Never."

"Would you believe Rudolph?"

"No. No, I wouldn't believe it. Nobody gets called Rudolph."

"I don't think these are real people. They're what we call in the trade pseudonyms, that's what these are. This geezer Beridi has to know who these people are. How about this one?"

"What trade?" For a moment she appeared to be bright and alert. Then her eyes drooped again. "What trade, Mr. Gauntlet?"

"Wine and cheese, Hils. Wine, cheese, cartography, baked beans, for buying and selling. All kinds of stuff. International imports and exports, know what I mean?"

"No."

"Okay." He looked down at the papers again. "Anton?"

"Knew an Anton once, years ago. Never did me any good."

"Valery?" He spelled it.

"Knew a Valerie."

"No, this is a guy. I'll have to read these. Peep and pry." He slit open a remaining fat envelope and withdrew four sheets of A4 paper. They were four typescript pages, undoubtedly an extract from the scrolls of the woman Naomi, with a memo pinned to them. "This is the latest take," it read, "first draft only." The writing was definitely in Father Gregory's hand. Charlie intended only to glance at the typescript, but the first words caught him.

Romillius, whom I love above all men, I am speaking these words to you, and Petros has assured me that he is writing only what I tell him.

I have now spent the past three days with the man called Jesus, and I have heard what he teaches. I implore you, Romillius, listen to me. This man means no harm to Rome. Now listen to me, for I believe that Jesus of Nazareth is either the one true messenger from God, or he is a fraud, a liar, or a madman. There can be nothing in between, and—like all his disciples—I believe him to be the Chosen One; the one of whom our prophets have long spoken: the one who is called the Messiah; the Christ; the Anointed One, who will be our salvation. He promises that all who believe in his teaching, and who come to him, will also in the last be spared and will be granted eternal life in the light of God.

I know I am an ignorant woman. Few know it better than I. I acknowledge that I am a sinner: for I do not know how I shall come to salvation through God our Father, for I cannot give wholly of myself.

When this Jesus teaches, there is nothing unusual about him. I have seen others who shout and saw the air with their hands and arms, who are full of great gestures and make their voices swoop up and down like birds, or make their hands into fists and beat a table, or the ground. He speaks, for the most part, quietly, but he speaks with a command I have never experienced before. It is as if he knows God face-to-face. God, he tells us, loves all creatures, but He loves mankind (humankind) above all others. Also, He chose the people of Israel to be the ones through whom He should make Himself known to the whole world: to everyone.

All He asks of us is that we should keep His commandments, and love Him. In return He offers the sure hope of salvation, life instead of death, peace and eternal happiness.

This Jehovah—which is the name we, the people of Israel, call our God—wishes everyone to live in love, peace, and harmony with one another, and he, Jesus, the Son of God, offers us the way to God, through His teaching: His Word.

Romillius, my beloved, I do not know what to do. If Jesus is truly God the Son, as I believe, then I am doomed. He bids us keep to the commandments, yet I cannot. I am a fornicator and adulterer, and this is the only manner in which I can make my way forward in the world. I have no skills and no learning. My husband has been taken from me, and I do not know what to do.

Jesus says that I must be sorry for my past sins; then to go and not sin again. It is not enough simply to keep to the rituals and forms of our religion, he tells us, but we must truly seek forgiveness and put our sins behind us. If I am to do this, I cannot see how I am going to exist.

Romillius, you have already told me of the way in which our high priests, and members of the religious court and council, have pressed your friend the governor, Pontius Pilate, to move against Jesus and his followers. I speak here of the Sanhedrin, which you—our lords and masters from Rome—have set up as an authority. If they have their way, it will be the Roman military who will proceed against Jesus, and this will be unfair. The chief priests, the elders, and those appointed to the council called the Sanhedrin fear Jesus because he preaches against the way in which they teach and carry out the faith of our fathers and forefathers.

Please, I implore you, warn Pilate before it is too late. It would be unjust to Jesus if your people move against him, take him, or punish him, for he is no threat to Rome. Jesus is a force only for good. The other day you said that Rome was curiously concerned because they feared Jesus could raise an army to overthrow Rome's military here in Judea. Romillius, my love, if Jesus formed an army, it would be an army of peace. Beloved, hear me, please. I weep as I speak this to the boy as I am so bowed down with the idea that I shall not find light and peace through Jesus, the Lord: our Way to God.

Charlie glanced up and saw that Hilary had slipped off to sleep at last. He looked down at the typescript again and thought to himself that if there was an ounce of truth in this manuscript, then the woman Naomi was crying out from the heart.

He found himself trying to visualize her, alive and speaking animatedly to the lad Petros, and for a brief moment his imagination drew the picture for him. This was eerie, for his inspiration gave him a clear vision, for a few seconds only, of a tall woman with striking features and long, dark, glossy hair. Her lips were almost unnaturally red, and her large black eyes opened wide as though she could see Gauntlet, suddenly and in her own time some two thousand years before. Then the illusion in his head faded, though he still seemed to be able to catch a lingering scent—spices, the afterglow of spikenard that he had once been given to sniff some years ago in Jerusalem.

This blinked revelation from the past quite unnerved him. The woman in his head had been so convincing, it was as though she had occupied space near to where he stood. There was even a trace of smell, a change in temperature, so graphic that he had to shake his head to clear the picture. Madness, he thought. Charles, your imagination'll be the death of you, his voice said silently in his head.

He gathered together the papers, smiled at the sleeping Hilary, and went quietly out into the corridor. Sister Marks was at the little nurses' station at the end of the passage. She still did not seem to have a hair out of place, though incipient lines under her eyes had started to signal fatigue.

"She's gone to sleep, at last. I must've had a boring effect."

"Oh, good, Mr. Gauntlet. I'll look in on her presently. Sorry to have got you out, but—"

"No, don't be sorry." He held up a hand as though trying to stop traffic. "I'm worried. The bloke, the priest who came to see her, knows things he shouldn't. He was a bit unpleasant. I think we should try to keep a watch on her. Will the hospital security . . . ?"

"I'll try them, but I have my doubts. They're not exactly flush with people on the ground. They also have to spend a lot of time in casualty. It can get dangerous down there at night."

"Please try them, Sister, and I'll report it to the proper . . ." He was going to say *authorities*, but that sounded contrived, pretentious. "The proper people."

She thanked him again and he told her he would be leaving Glasgow in a matter of hours. Privately he thought it might well mean he would have to change his plans and hang around for a while. The events of the night had made him unusually jumpy and edgy. Was this, he wondered, an overreaction? The crashed Cessna was serious, yes; but some pushy, big monk coming in and making unspecified threats . . . Well? Then he thought about the whole business of Father Gregory Scott and the bank accounts. He knew things that he reckoned others did not know about the father superior of the Order of St. Jerome. People change over the years, but Father Benedict was still around, Corporal Knight as he'd been in an earlier incarnation. And Charlie was pretty sure that the big fellow was Knight's sidekick, Bertie Day. Talk about old home week.

A couple of cabs were loitering out front with the ambulances. One was waiting for a doctor; the driver of the other said he was free, so Charlie took the cab back to The Central Hotel and to hell with the expense.

Nobody seemed to be around in reception. He loitered for half a minute, then went straight up to his room, dumped the manuscript, letters, and money on the bed and dialed the OS13 number at Scotland Yard.

Being the antiterrorist branch, OS13 had a round-the-clock operator, and when this officer picked up, Charlie asked if by any chance the commander was in. He was, but did he have anything that warranted waking Commander Joe Bain at this time in the morning? Charlie reflected that he could probably leave it to the duty officer, who happened to be a sergeant.

Without alerting too many people, Charles wanted to get some kind of protection for Hilary, and he was quite willing to jeopardize Kit Palfrey, with whom he was still supping with a long spoon. He first told the sergeant that he was Bex Olesker's husband.

"Heard you'd married her. Congratulations. How can I help?" Which was a promising start. So Charlie went further, spinning a tale that dodged in and out of truth and, in the end, did not compromise either Kit Palfrey or the monks of Ringmarookey. He reported the facts concerning the crashed aircraft, to which he added a cock-and-bull tale about some terrorist activity that was almost certainly a hangover from Northern Ireland. There were just enough facts for the sergeant to agree to the patient having some form of protection. In the end it would be up to the local police, but Charlie felt much happier by the end of the conversation.

Still sitting on the bed, he began to go through the letters, intent on opening them, if necessary, and certainly leaning on Gregory Scott if the situation so demanded.

He was holding one envelope, as though weighing it in his upturned hand, when the telephone rang.

He picked up. "Gauntlet."

Silence. Nothing from the other end but the noise of an open line. Then he clearly heard the distant receiver being replaced. He jiggled the telephone cradle, and when the operator came on, he asked if she had put a call through to him. She had. He asked more. It was a man. A local call, she thought. Local call, foreign voice.

"Really thick accent. Oh, Mr. Gauntlet?"

"What kind of accent?"

"Oh, what they call Middle European. Also . . ."

"Yes?"

"Your wife . . ."

"What about my wife?"

"Well, she said she was your bride actually."

"She would do. We're on our honeymoon."

"Oh?" The operator found this a shade difficult. "I thought you were on your own, sir."

"Sure I'm on my own."

"But your honeymoon . . . I . . . But . . ."

"Sure, it's the latest thing, didn't you know? She stays in one place, I stay in another. One day maybe we'll get to meet. She leave a number for me?"

"No, sir. In fact she specifically said she couldn't leave a number."

"Okay. Put me through to reception, will you. I have to check out."

Of one thing he was certain. When somebody calls you in a hotel and puts the telephone down, there is only one reason: the caller wants to know if you are at home so that he can come round and duff you up: fill you in.

This wasn't coincidence anymore. Corporal Bertie Day, as he was all those years ago, didn't hide anything. Bertie's real name was Dayosolavek, of course; it was Beridi Dayosolavek, and he had a Mittel European accent as thick as pigswill.

Glasgow's Central Hotel backs onto the railway station, so having paid his bill, Gauntlet left by the exit leading onto the main concourse. From there he walked to the taxi rank. Glasgow, like all large cities, does not sleep. In the small hours the pulse slows, but you can still get around. Two black cabs were on the rank, and he took the first one out to the airport, which was almost deserted, yet provided twenty-four-hour facilities for bathing and generally cleaning yourself up. So, at three o'clock in the morning, Charlie Gauntlet treated himself to a warm bath, for he had always found it a pleasure to lie in hot water and allow his mind to skate freely over his problems.

At this moment Charlie could not make up his mind. He need not be involved in this—whatever this was. He muttered to himself, flicking at the hot tap with the sole of his foot, "My trouble is trunky. I'm a nosy beggar. Trunky trouble. I just have to know what's going on."

A large portion of his common sense told him to give up and go back to London. Just wait there for Bex to reappear. That was really the most reasonable thing to do, but then . . .

But then . . .

He closed his eyes and gave up the battle, letting his thoughts drift.

London would be best. Funny, the girls in London were the most striking he could remember since the sixties when the capital swung. Now, the young and lovely women seemed to stride confidently through the streets as though they owned the planet, which, in a way, he supposed they did. He was incredibly lucky, he acknowledged, to have ended the century with a woman like Bex. Yes, he should go back to London so that he would be there for her when she got back from whatever she was up to.

On the other hand, there was a great desire for him to be in at the kill. Kit Palfrey, onetime traitor-of-the-month, a dodgy character to say the least, had dragged him into a series of mysteries. Charles accepted, scooping up some water and allowing it to trickle down the graying hairs of his chest, that he wanted to know how the story turned out. What happened to the woman who called herself Naomi and lived at the time when Jesus of Nazareth walked the highways and byways of Judea? If the writings were real, it might shed light on the greatest mystery facing humankind. If it was not real, if it was a fraud . . . well, why would Kit Palfrey even be bothering with it? Bringing those fraying bits of paper back from Moscow would do nothing for Palfrey. Even if they were to be hailed as a breakthrough find, unlocking doors to secrets, old Kit Palfrey wouldn't benefit. They wouldn't declare Palfrey for pope or heap the world's riches upon him; and, be fair, Kit had always appeared to act to the tune of his conscience. There was nothing in it for him, and it was a damned good story.

In the end he decided to let fate make the final call, lying in the bath until after five in the morning before getting out, drying himself, shaving, and dressing. That done, Charlie went off and found coffee. A couple of hours later he used his BT phone card and dialed the number for Rockwell Aviation here at Glasgow Airport. If someone answered, he would take it from there. Otherwise he would get himself onto the first flight to London and let the monks stew, together with Kit Palfrey and Hilary Cooke with an *e*.

Ralph "Romeo" Rockwell was at his desk, having just flown back into Glasgow from a taxi run to Heathrow. Yes, he could take Mr. Gauntlet to Ringmarookey. Give him an hour to juice up, file a flight plan, and all that. As it happened, weather and local traffic delayed them for several hours, during which Charlie experienced great discomfort, sensing eyes on his back and possibly feet ready to trip him up as he loitered away the time. One thing he did was buy a stout envelope and, in one of the lavatory stalls, seal up the money, letters, and stuff he had from Hilary; address it to himself; guess the weight, buy stamps, and stick on too many; and pop it in a pillar box. He was not going back to the island with any evidence on him.

What with one thing and another, not until a little before one on a gray, chill afternoon with a hint of snow in the air were they airborne, heading back to the monastery. Taciturn, he thought, easing himself into the cramped cockpit of the Piper Archer. *Taciturn* was the word to describe Romeo Rockwell, a short, stocky young man whose dark, somewhat tangled thatch of hair hung low over his brows, making him tilt his chin a shade as though he strained to see the way ahead. He had the sulky good looks of a pop idol, and about the same percentage of know-it-all-done-it-all arrogance, which did not endear him to Gauntlet.

If Rockwell was a man of few words, he gave much confidence as a pilot. His hands and feet had a steady sureness over the controls, while his eyes moved constantly. He would nod when it saved him speaking, yet his speech over the radio to the controllers was clipped and clear.

Charlie considered that Mr. Rockwell revealed little of the Lothario that Kit Palfrey had made him out to be, and much more the professional, safe, confident pilot that he truly was.

When they had first met in the flesh, Rockwell swiveled his eyes without moving his head and asked if they were expecting Charlie.

"I've only just come back, and, yes, they're expecting me."

"Oh, yes? I always have to ask because they're not partial to unexpected guests. Don't like people dropping in on them. If you were just there, how did you get back?" His accent was not Scottish, more Geordie crossed with Surbiton.

Charlie told him, and Rockwell smirked. "Poor old Hilary. Bit of a Pilot Officer Prunella, Hils."

Gauntlet made the connection. The old Second World War RAF term for an inexperienced or dim pilot was Pilot Officer Prune, depicted in cartoons as an upper-class twit. "Not her fault." He found himself defending Hilary Cooke.

"Never is." This time Rockwell did not even raise his eyes. "Hilary is the kind of pilot who attracts incidents. Got lost on her first solo. Just a circuit, but she managed to lose herself."

"Seemed to be doing all right by the monks."

"Sure." Rockwell obviously had little time for Hilary Cooke. His tone was dismissive, and Charlie got the impression that the man was not really at ease with the monks. He wondered if Hilary had been stealing the bread from Rockwell's bowl by being in well with the Order of St. Jerome.

Before leaving, Charles had left a message on the Dolphin Square answering machine telling Bex exactly where he was heading. He also told her about the photographs that should be arriving—"Whiz them on up to me, sweetheart"—though he had a distinct uneasiness about her. He had felt this restless concern since daybreak. "Beware big monks," he added to the message, not really knowing why he should leave a warning. The enormous monk was here and now in Glasgow.

Indeed, the man who called himself Father Martin was aware that Charlie Gauntlet was already on his way back to the monks of the Order of St. Jerome in Ringmarookey. Eyes had followed neat little Charlie across the railway station and out to the airport. Eyes were on him now as he sat in the Piper Archer heading over the sea, and eyes would be waiting for him on his arrival at the Monastery of St. Jerome on the windswept rocks.

CHAPTER 14

It was a bad dream, of course, a dream so vivid that Bex almost felt the pain and smelled the sweat on the bodies. Considering her fatigue in the early hours, it was strange that she had eventually fallen into such a deep sleep. There was no warning. After tossing and turning for what seemed like hours, she suddenly slid into oblivion. As she slept, she dreamed this nightmare that seemed all too real.

First she dialed the hotel in Glasgow and this time Charlie picked up. He even seemed pleased to hear her voice.

"Been worried about you, sweetheart," he said. And that was as far as it went before she thought she was going to die.

The door to her room opened, and she did not even have time to cry out before they came fast, noiselessly, into her room. Like robots they were on her, immobilizing her before she could fight back. So her instinct told her she was about to die. In that time she also realized the attack was from Tessa Murray and the man from the Villa Myrte. The man was probably Alchemist, she thought, and if it was indeed him, then she would surely die.

In the vivid dream, at one moment she was quietly talking to Charles on the telephone, then the two shadows were there. Not a sound. They appeared to glide over the parquet floor. Unstoppable. Terrifying.

His forearms held her down: one tight over her throat, the other low, hard across her thighs just above the knees. He was a powerful man, and all her strength was sapped in a matter of seconds.

A smaller, softer hand went to her face, rolling out thick duct tape, pressed and stuck hard and gummy over her mouth; then another length was peeled down over her eyes. She grunted and tried to move her facial muscles, but even this taxed her strength and spirit. Her mouth and eyes stung as though nettles had been flicked into her face.

Then came the sharp prick of a needle in her forearm followed by thick darkness. Of course, it being a nightmare, she came round and knew exactly where she was—in the Villa Myrte. She could not have explained how she knew this, but she thought it might have had something to do with the smell: pleasant, a tincture of June roses overlaid with lavender. The room was somehow familiar: a plain stripped-pine table stood under the window, and the room obviously caught the sun all through the morning. Two pictures were on the wall: one was a reproduction Turner, the other a good try at Constable. She even wondered if Alchemist needed to be reminded of the beauties of his motherland.

So, Bex sniffed the scent and felt the sun through the window. And she heard voices and knew that they were seeping in under the French doors that led from the living room at the roadside of the villa.

Her first thought was "Well . . . good . . . I shall have time to compose myself." She knew there was no chance of living. Rarely had she been frightened of death, for it was a fact of life. She simply thought, "Bugger it, I fancied living with old Charles for a bit longer. Fancied seeing him through; looking after him; having years of companionship."

Her mouth was dry as a desert road; her head pounded; eyes smarted under the tape while her lips felt cracked and sore, twisted by the pressure. They had secured her hands, and when she tried to move, she felt metal biting at her wrists. Shackles of some kind. Handcuffs maybe. Bex still thought she was going to die. Heard the click of a coffee cup on a saucer and longed for something to drink; almost smelled the toast, her hearing so acute now that she clearly detected the sound of teeth taking a bite. So her own mouth mirrored the intake of breath to catch the crumbs flaking from the bite and savored orange marmalade, and the charcoal taste of bread almost burned, because that was how she liked it: well done.

The pain in her muscles was intense. She knew cramps would finally overcome her calves and bring horrifying hurt to her body. She concentrated, through the soup of agony, the fog of thumping head, and the drifting clouds of distress, centering her mind toward the voices in the next room.

As she had resigned herself to inevitable death, the voices surprised her and eventually gave her a way out of the horror.

"Ah," said Tessa Murray through the doors. "Ah, there's the bell. I wonder who this can be?"

And the bell was huge, its tone lasting, filling her head and coming through the walls and window from Brissago's church.

Bex woke in a lather of sweat, surprised that she was in bed at the hotel. Outside, the sky was that shade of blue that spoke not of warmth but of the illusion of warmth that comes on a cloudless day in winter: a morning edged with frost, and the smoke from chimneys rising straight. Her watch said that it was a quarter to nine.

Her hands flew to her face and she was relieved to find herself without restraint and with no tape on her lips and eyes. The dream had been so strong that she thought she could feel the trace of the tape gum burning her tongue and its stickiness on her skin.

She remembered telephoning Scotland, and she quickly sought out the notepad on the night table. Deciphering her scrawl, she dialed with the international code, and from Glasgow's Central Hotel she learned "Mr. Gauntlet left this morning, madam. Gone off to the Isle of Ringmarookey where the monks live in that monastery of theirs, by the way."

"Ringmarookey!" she said softly, aloud, thinking it all sounded romantic. "Ringmarookey," again, as though tasting it, wanting so much to be there with Charles. Yearning for him. Didn't know what the word *yearning* meant until now. If London said she could leave today, then she might head up to Scotland. They might even get to complete their honeymoon north of the border. She felt the unmistakable palpitation low down at the crux of her thighs in anticipation. Then she felt a twinge of guilt. At her age she shouldn't feel like this. It was the way her generation had been brought up to think.

She showered, soaping her body, lingering over it and wishing Charlie were there to wash her back. The nightmare remained with her, a strong memory, leaving an unpleasant depression in its wake. For a moment she wondered if her dream was something psychic: a portent of things to come. This she dismissed almost in the same moment as she considered it. Bex was a thoroughly practical lady and did not really hold with matters psychic.

Yet the scent of doom remained. She seemed to be shrouded in unease, a most terrible sense of dread enveloping her, as though an evil poison flowed and mixed with her blood.

She dressed in jeans, a thick silk shirt in pearl gray, and her now favorite, Belfast-bought, waisted dark jacket. With her face on, Bex was finally ready to go down to breakfast. Yet even that was an effort.

She missed Charles fearfully; wondered when she would hear from London, thought about her new husband on this unknown Scottish island once more, and again wished she were there. Never in her life had she missed somebody else so dreadfully, not even when she'd first gone off to boarding school at the age of ten.

The dining-room double doors were of wood and glass, ornate and fussy. Inside, it was warm, heated with reckless disregard for the ecology by a large wood-burning pot-bellied stove. The padrone, whom she had seen in this same room over dinner last night, came toward her, greeted her in English, lead her to a table halfway down the room, asked how she felt, if she had slept well, and told her that it was dry but cold outside—as if she hadn't already worked that out for herself.

A scattering of guests were planted around the big, polished room. A silent couple in their late forties faced each other without speaking. The third year of marriage is usually the breaking point, not the seventh, but this couple looked as though they were on lap twenty-one and their faces told a sad story, as old as time and cold as freezing fog.

Three men, identifiable the world over as commercial gents, nursed sick headaches from last night's booze, terrified of what the day might not bring.

One lady sat apart, lonely: schoolmarmish, angular, heavy-breasted with restless, empty eyes. Another woman, younger, fair, plump, and forty, with a cheery smile for everyone, almost a come-hither twinkle, was also alone at the far side of the room, munching away on fresh rolls, spread thick with butter and preserves. Her body language said she would not be alone for long, or she would die in the attempt.

A family, noisy at a window table, looked like something from a French comedy movie: father, seedy; mother, dowdy; children arguing, strident; and funny uncle, a droll with constantly shrugging shoulders.

Into this walked Bex, poised, elegant, and trying hard not to be noticed, knowing suddenly that for some unaccountable reason she had become more visible in this small, pleasant hotel dining room. It was as though the fact of her recent marriage had been leaked to every person in the room, and each one was smiling, eyeing her with lascivious intent, telling her they had watched as she popped into the laced filigree of her bra and drew on the silk, soft white, tight little pants after her shower. Or, possibly, it was just Bex, unprepared for many pairs of eyes wheeling on her, a stranger, in that morning dining room.

Again she felt the chill of doubt and the horror of despair. For no reason at all she recalled breakfasting in a hotel in Cambridge with Charlie, who had taken her there for a weekend of long walks and strolls around the colleges. They had bought some old prints, and she now wondered what had become of them. That had been a year ago, and she was conscious of her bewilderment at thinking of the incident now.

The others glanced toward her, then away, hanging for a split second in silence, then the room relaxed again and the chatter was resumed.

A dark, tousle-haired waiter, all hands and teeth and a little woman's waist, descended on her like a shark, deftly picking up the words *rolls, coffee, preserves,* and swinging away with a series of gestures, waiter's semaphore, to one of the juniors, instructing coffee to be brought as he dropped a basket of rolls and croissants lightly onto the table. Bex cracked a roll, smelled the soft yeast wonder of the bread, thought to hell with weight and poured the strawberry jam thick on the butter, bowed her head in gluttony, and savored the sinful delights.

The coffee came, and she—to use her own thoughts—"hoovered it up." Then, raising her head and reaching for a second roll, she saw the schoolmarmish woman rise from her table and plod toward the doors. She had that outflung bust and bottom that makes a female look completely off-balance, somehow freakish: an S-shape with legs.

Bex glanced away as the woman reached the double doors, then back again. She had disappeared, but the doors swung open again to reveal Tessa Murray, in black leggings and a navy blue, thigh-length jacket, all hanging strings, toggles, and such over a white, stylish cambric shirt, like a tabard. Bex first thought that Tessa looked medieval, with one hand stuffed into the big black leather bag swinging from her shoulder. Then she saw Tessa's eyes lock with her own, froze as she saw the lips move, head turning a fraction as the padrone asked if he could help; saw him nod, smile, gesture, and watched with a momentary sensation of hopelessness. Tessa Murray was heading for her, straight as a cruise missile and, she thought, just about as dangerous. Bex pulled herself out of the few seconds of fear, mentally shook herself like a shaggy, old dog heavy with rain and mud. She half rose . . .

"Sit down." Tessa flapped a hand in front of her. "You either know who I am or you don't! That doesn't matter. Shake hands! I'm talking to you. Think of the fuss you'll cause if you don't act naturally."

Bex felt the girl's hand very strong in hers and sensed that she was being physically assaulted. Pain slid angrily through her fingers, almost cracking, as the other woman gripped Bex's hand as though in a vise.

"Just listen to me," Tessa hissed. Her voice was not overpleasant. Bex registered that she had the marked accent of Northern Ireland: "Jest yew listen ta mey." A female version of Ian Paisley on an irritating day.

"I have a pistol in the bag. My hand's on it and I have a finger wrapped around the trigger. I'll not hesitate. I'll use it."

"What the . . . ?" Bex began, sounding, even to herself, like someone wrongly identified.

"Don't know who you are!" Tessa continued, unrelenting, sharp. "Don't much care. But you were on the plane coming into Bern; you stayed at the same hotel as I did; then you were on the train to

Locarno with me; and you turned up here last night; followed me to the villa where I'm staying. Could be a coincidence; don't know, but we have to talk with you. Right?" Tessa was smiling as though Bex were an old friend.

Bex smiled back. "Get the fuck out." In the back of her mind she sought out the answer to how she could and should react. If I weren't a copper, she pondered, how would I behave? If I were totally innocent what would I do?

Tess smiled back charmingly. "I really mean it." Teeth gritted in a ventriloquist's grimace. "If you don't stand up and come with me, I'll just gun you down. My brother's waiting at the villa. Now, are you ready?"

"I want to swallow the rest of my coffee." Pick up the cup and get her full in the face with scalding Colombian brew, she decided, before the reality took over and her old instructor whispered in her ear, "Never put innocent people at risk. If there's any chance of chummy pulling a trigger, make sure there are no members of Joe public about. Worst PR job in the world, some suit or anorak taking a risk that puts Joe up as a target."

"Touch your cup and half of your stomach goes. Just stand up quietly, nod in a friendly way, and walk toward the door. Okay?"

Slowly Bex stood up, pushing her chair back and putting a little distance between her and the edge of the table. She nodded, a curt bob of the head, and again the old instructor, the little nut-brown man, told her, "They usually make a fatal mistake with handguns. Sometimes they move in too close. Never try it if they're two paces or more away. Disarming a jumpy idiot with a gun's only feasible when they're up close."

"Turn around and start walking." Tessa smiled and nodded. There was no option. "And please, don't even think about heroics. I really would prefer to settle this quietly."

Bex nodded again, smiled at the padrone, and hesitated just long enough to rule out any move at the doors. In the bare, functional hotel foyer she turned toward the main exit and so passed out onto the lakefront. The fresh morning sat up and slapped her in the face.

People waited for the ferry: a group of some ten or eleven folk, two of the girls in national costume; a nun who looked incredibly happy; and a priest, hobbled with age and gleaming with holiness. In Switzerland it is always busy on Sundays.

Bex felt the chill passing through her clothes and wondered if she could get lost in a crowd between here and the villa. No way, she decided. She felt two large drops of sweat detach themselves from her armpit and splatter against her rib cage. Fear scuttled through her stomach and inched its way up her neck, into her hair. Creeping. Dangerous. Her hand moved to her head, scratching, back muscles moving, squirming.

Immediately, she increased speed in the hope that Tess would try to catch up and so give her the advantage. She glanced over her right shoulder and saw the girl remained a good five or six paces behind.

"Where d'you want me to go? I don't understand . . . ?"

"Just go the way you went when we got off the ferry last night. Up the slope to the road, and then turn left."

People were out and about but not in large numbers. For the most part they wore Sunday clothes because in this part of the world they still did that. Catholic countries seemed to remain constant while the Protestant lands appeared to have dissolved into myth, legend, disbelief, and the more outrageous demands made by specialist shops dealing in fairies, stones, sacred groves, sentimental Victorian angels, and the whole hodgepodge of New Age quasi-religious mumbo jumbo.

Tessa stayed a careful five paces behind Bex, who felt it was no accident that Tessa had come for her at this hour in the morning. A couple of times Bex thought about making a run for it, crossing the road between cars just slowing as they came into Brissago from the direction of Italy. It was never safe, though, and she again tried the dodge of speeding up. Tessa Murray stayed on station, and Bex thought that in the end it would be best to bluff it out. She had nothing on her that would lead them back to the police, she was sure of that, so she slowed her walk, glancing behind her. "Where exactly do you want me to go?"

"Just keep walking. I told you, my brother's waiting for us at the villa."

Brother? Bex thought, then aloud asked, "Which villa?"

"The one you walked past last night."

"I walked up here to a café. I had coffee there. Up here on the right, across the road."

Tess came closer, but not nearly close enough. "Keep going," she urged quietly, and Bex remembered Tessa's high-stepping giraffe walk of the previous evening.

The terra-cotta rooftop of the villa was just visible behind a stand of cypresses. In the distance a promontory of land fingered into the lake. Far ahead, about a kilometer down the road, lay the tobacco factory and the frontier post. On the far side of the road cars had pulled off, and children ran around the trees or stood, staring into the cold blue sky. Bex remembered a moment in the movie of the musical *Oliver!* where young Oliver Twist sings a song from a window about a beautiful morning, the camera walking London streets under just such a sky.

There were soldiers at the crossing. Bex thought about it, then dismissed the idea. Just go along with Tess. They can prove nothing. Let's just see how it develops. This way at least she might learn something. The pavement ahead was empty, but traffic had become almost nose to tail in the direction of Brissago.

Far away the sound of the steamer's horn blared twice across the water as it put in to Ascona.

"The villa here, on the left." Tessa was hard behind her now, yet not quite close enough for Bex to do anything. The traffic unclogged itself and the road cleared. They moved out of sight of the people across the road.

"Where your brother's waiting?"

"Yes, but you know him now, don't you?"

Alchemist, yes, Bex wanted to say. "Don't know him from Adam. Nor you. What did you say your name was?"

"I didn't. Just keep walking."

Her dream came back and Bex felt the tape over her mouth, her eyebrows sticky from where her eyes had been covered. The dream had been incredibly tactile and the memories were strong in her senses. The fear moved again.

About fifty yards, in old money, from the Villa Myrte now. "Look,"

Bex said, softening her voice, "isn't this a bit melodramatic? I really don't know why you've picked on me, I—"

"You don't? You *really* don't know what this is about?"

Oh, sweet Jerusalem, her dream was going to come true. She was going to die in that lovely villa by the quiet lakeside. Well, if that was the case, she really should go down fighting. But Bex had almost reached the low gateway, and she saw the front door of the villa was slightly ajar.

"Keep going!" Tessa, closer than ever.

Bex wheeled around ready to fight if she had to.

Tessa Murray stood, legs apart with the automatic pistol, visible for the first time, held at arm's length, her hands steady, with her cold dark eyes wide open and looking unblinking across the sights. Nobody was on the pavement behind her. As a car came into view, she lowered her arms, keeping the pistol close to her body, near her waist, turning a little to shield the weapon from eyes in the car.

"Come on, move yourself. We want to hear what you know and how you know it. We might even let you off with a slap on the wrist if you cooperate."

The urge to live, the possibility that she would not be killed, grabbed at Bex, though she knew there was no real alternative. Tessa moved closer, jabbing at her with the muzzle of the little gun. "Get in, will you! Move!"

So, Rebecca Louise Olesker crossed the threshold of the little house she'd entered in her dream. This time it already smelled of death.

Tess Murray pushed her hard against the wall of the neat little hallway. Bex took in the layout—the big mirror in an old gilt frame, and a low table with a telephone, to her left, then the archway leading deeper into the house.

Tessa thumped Bex on the shoulder, pushed her face into the wall, harshly whispering, "Spread your legs! Hands flat on the wall now! Get yer fecking feet back!" She had Bex well off-balance very quickly, hands against the hard wall and taking all her weight with arms extended. She kicked out viciously at Bex's ankles, spreading her legs wider. Then she shouted, with an abrasive laugh, "I'm home, honey. Home is the hunter, home from the hill!"

Calling to her "brother," Bex thought.

And Tess moved to the left of Rebecca and kicked a door open. Instinctively Bex knew the door led to the room at the front of the villa. She heard Tess involuntarily sniff the air and caught the whiff of blood and excreta that comes with sudden, violent death. Then Bex heard the screaming from Tessa, followed by the moaning: "Oh, no! Ooooh nooooooo!" Keening; rocking. "Sweet mother of Jesus, nooooooo!"

Bex flexed her arms, did a push-up against the wall, pushed herself off, and caught Tessa unaware, blindsiding her, a cupped right hand going hard for the left side of the girl's head, smashing into the ear with some force, the cupped hand sending a nasty, painful shock wave calculated to damage the eardrum.

Tess yelped, fell to one side, tried to recover, dropped the pistol, and smashed her shoulder against the doorjamb. She was still wailing, "Dear God, who would do this? Oh, no! My God! Noooo!"

It came out a long "Nuuuu!" And Bex swooped down, lifted the pistol from the carpet, and paused for a split second as she saw the man whom she thought had been Alchemist on his back, sprawled, unnatural, like an effigy to be burned on a Guy Fawkes's night bonfire. He still wore the dark blazer, its front soaked in gore; the head lolled back, the face a mush of blood where bullets had torn the features away; more blood spreading over the floor. She remembered some Shakespearean quote about not realizing someone had so much blood in him, not using it aloud as she recalled it came from *Macbeth* and it was bad news to quote from the "Scottish play."

She swiveled, turning and bringing the little pistol to bear on Tessa, and saw that the woman was half against the wall, drooping and bent, limp with shock, her face parched white, lips trembling, arms hanging down.

"Up," said Bex, low and very cool. Then the front door batted open and the slim, tall figure leaped into the entrance hall, his navy blazer undone, trench coat flapping around his legs, iron gray hair falling over his brown, leathery face in open concentration. She could not have explained how she knew that this was the man who had disappeared in front of her last night, but she knew.

Bex turned, brought the pistol up, but the man simply slapped the weapon to the ground in an almost lazy movement, but with incredible strength behind it. Taking two long paces forward, he brought back his right hand, chopping down firmly on Tess Murray's neck. The Irish girl had no idea what happened: she simply slumped forward with a little moan.

"Name's Wright, DCI Olesker, *Patsy* Wright. Come to get you out. Think we should really make a mad dash for the border." He glanced into the little sitting room and saw the body. "Oh, yuck. This is very nasty, ma'am. Please, I think I'd better give you a lift."

"How do I know . . . ?"

"You don't, but neither of us has the brief to be here. I thought I was simply lifting you out of a dangerous situation; now someone's got himself separated from life. This could be . . ." For a second he seemed lost for words. "Could be . . . well . . . unpleasant."

But Bex looked unconvinced. "Sorry, but I really have to stick around. I—"

"Please don't make me get violent again. London told me you'd married old Charlie Gauntlet. True?"

"How do I know that you didn't nip in here and shoot the life out of the fellow before I arrived with little Miss PMS?"

"Because I rarely shoot people. Come on, let's move. Charles would want it, you'll see." He had her by the wrist, pulling her through the door, and she suddenly became aware of what he had said on his arrival. "*Patsy* Wright?" she asked. Her lovely Charles had talked of Patsy Wright: a legend he was. "A man you don't want to be without in a ticklish situation, eh?" Charlie had often told her. "Saved my life a couple of times, Patsy. Hot as mustard and twice as accurate." Whatever that meant.

"Take my word for it. Patsy Wright in the flesh. Come on, and I hope you've got your passport."

"Yes, I . . ."

"Then come on!" He yanked her out to the gate, then across the road to a little scarlet and silver Terrano II that was parked neatly, pointing toward Italy.

Ten minutes later, they crossed the frontier and the long, lithe

214

Patsy Wright grinned at her. "How d'you like joyriding in a fast Nipponese car, with a young fellow-me-lad like me, eh, sport? Make old Charles jealous, what?"

For the first time in days, Bex laughed. Though, on looking down, she saw that her hands were still shaking. "Isn't the Murray girl in danger?" Her voice was small and she felt her stomach turn over.

"Well, by the look of things, someone didn't like her boyfriend, that's for sure. You didn't pick up anyone else on your tail?"

She told him she had seen nobody and again realized as she said it that she *had* in fact seen Patsy himself a couple of times. "You were watching me in Dublin, weren't you?"

"Guilty. I was with you at the opera as well."

"You were at the *Dutchman*? I wondered."

"Yep. They told me to move in closer that night."

"You saw Kit Palfrey then?"

"Oh, indeed. There are those in London who are very interested in Mr. Palfrey."

"Even though the old Evil Empire is dismantled?"

"Especially now that the Evil Empire is dismantled." Patsy gave her what her mother would have called an "old-fashioned look." "Very short of cash, Kit Palfrey. In need of a loot injection."

Another half hour and they were at the western end of the lake, in Stresa, which, Patsy said, reminded him of a huge British tearoom, quickly adding that this was not original. "Read it somewhere in a guidebook and thought it was apt, the Brit tearoom line, I mean." He said Stresa was a great stopping-off place for package tours visiting Lake Maggiore, cheaper than the Swiss end, and a good center for day trips. He was relaxed and chatty as though lifting lady coppers from danger and looking at the recently dead was nothing out of the ordinary. "There's a blandness about the place that reminds me of old, established British southern-seaside towns," Wright drawled, and the comparison made Bex smile, but did not quell the butterflies in her stomach, nor the afterburn of that morning's frightening experience.

She dragged the conversation back to the matter in hand. "I meant, was it wise to leave Tess Murray on her own?"

"I don't suppose she is. You were on her back, and my brief was to watch you. But I don't for a moment think we were on our own out there. Thought I caught a flash of Mickey Herring and Fatty Brimstone along the way, in Dublin."

"Mad" Mickey Herring and "Fatty" Brimstone were a pair of hard men known to the Anti-Terrorist Branch as having tenuous links with intelligence in many of its forms: mercenaries of the secret world.

Patsy drove down toward the lake and parked the car on the via Duchessa di Genova, close to the small hotel in which he had booked a room on the previous evening.

Squinting at the girl, he saw a still lingering suspicion in her eye. "I really am here on duty. I've been following you around for days. You're like a bloody yo-yo, DCI Olesker."

"Talking of yo-yos, you wouldn't happen to know where my dear husband is now?"

"With a mess of Anglican monks on a godforsaken little gobbet of rock off the west of Scotland, and I get the impression that he shouldn't be there. He's no longer under any discipline, and all kinds of odd things are going on."

"Ah! If you're talking about a place called Ringmarookey, he wasn't there last night. He was in Glasgow. At the Central Hotel. But he left sometime this morning." She went on to tell him of her abortive telephone calls during the night.

Patsy shook his head as though this information was a great wonderment, but made no comment, except to tell her not to touch anything, as he would have told a small child, before he disappeared into the nearby small hotel.

He was back again, clutching a small overnight airline bag, and moving at a swift trot. "Your husband's on the move again, and your presence is requested back in London. That's where we're heading." He started the car and handed her a piece of fax paper.

To: TP Cowley, it said. "Cowley?" she asked.

"Flag of convenience. Might as well call me Chicken Madras." He started the car and sought out the best way to get to Milan as Bex read:

To: TP Cowley

From: Managing Director

 Your friend's husband has been wandering around but is now headed back to the Holy Island. This is a little too close to people who are of interest. We suggest that his wife should follow and you should accompany her. Call me soonest on arrival London. Your friend should talk to her MD.

It was signed with the initials *MJB.*

"I take it they're looking out for the Murray woman, and they're talking about us going to Scotland."

"Well, it's not the three little pigs, darling. Yes, you'll have a great time with the monks I've no doubt. As for Theresa Murray, I think she may be quite important, so I guess someone'll be sniffing around after her."

Neither of them would have believed the truth at this point: that the man they called Alchemist lived and was, like them, on his way to Milan, having plowed across the lake in his sleek little motorboat with Tessa sitting, glum, beside him.

Patsy showed no great haste in driving the A8 autostrada to Milan, and from there to the Malpesa airport.

Seats were available on a late-afternoon BA flight into Heathrow. So, in the early evening, Bex, accompanied by Patsy Wright, arrived back in London and headed straight for Scotland Yard. By the time Bex got in to see Commander Joe Bain at OS13, he knew that Alchemist still lived, moved, and was about his business.

CHAPTER 15

So how could devious Ronnie Richardson, with trim Tessa Murray by his side, be zipping across Lago Maggiore in his raffish little motorboat? Bex had seen him lying dead in his own blood only an hour or so before, so how did he manage this resurrection? Indeed, Ronnie's life was unraveling, though far from over. To understand all the twists, turns, and coincidences, we must move down two snakes, as Charlie might have said: meaning go back a couple of days.

We are at the guesthouse in Bern on that inclement evening when Tessa Murray arrived from Dublin with Bex on her tail. Tessa has had dinner and returned to her room.

Soaking in her bath, with warm water lapping at her nipples, and a glass of Moët & Chandon at her lips, she thinks of the young woman she had more than noticed on the flight from Dublin: the one in the stylish belted raincoat, with an Hermès scarf pixie-hooded around her head. Tessa had seen her before all right. Clocked her, as the argot had it, in drenching rain that morning up Grafton Street. Marked her and noted her, now knowing that she was not there by chance; knowing also that she was the enemy. In the years that had followed her recruitment by Jimmy Maclean, Tessa had become what she liked to call "one of the sharpest knives on the street"—pause for four beats before she always added—"next to our Man of course."

She had learned nearly all she knew from "our Man," from Alchemist, who virtually took over her life from their first meeting, which was in Venice of all places.

Early on, Maclean had told her their principal needed to see her, probably meet her as well. He told her where she was to go, ordered her not to deviate from the instructions he gave her. Should he wish to talk with her, Alchemist would make himself known. Of course, at that time they didn't call him Alchemist. If anyone is interested, they referred to him as Greaper—as in Grim Reaper.

Tessa was to arrive in Venice on a Monday, and a room would be reserved for her at Ca' Fórscari in the tiny Calledella Frescada.

"You've been to Venice?" Jim asked.

"Never."

"Oh, how I envy you: the first time with all that light."

It was a week after Easter, in a mild spring, when the city was just starting to fill up, though not yet unbearably. On the Tuesday morning she was ordered to go to a tiny café almost opposite the Stock Exchange carrying a copy of *Un Ospite di Venezia*. She had to arrive at exactly twenty past midday and wait until a table for two became available. She would order coffee, then wait for exactly half an hour. If nobody made contact, she had to leave but go through the same procedure over three consecutive days. If by then nobody had approached her, Tessa was to return to Ireland.

Maclean also gave her an empty matchbook from the Cippriani, torn irregularly in half. Her contact would offer the matching half as his bona fides. It wasn't exactly James Bond stuff, but what is in real life?

Later, Tessa would admit to having been dazzled by the time and place. The scent of Venice had not yet reached the ripeness of summer, but the tourists were already out in force, and the young men from the Stock Exchange, shirtsleeved and Gucci-shoed, leaned against the wall across from the café and stripped passing women with their eyes.

On that first day Alchemist arrived just as Tess was preparing to leave. Afterward she realized that she had seen him walk past some ten minutes earlier looking steadily at her: tall, fit, slim, languid in jeans and a denim jacket over a chambray shirt, his face tanned in a way that made her think not of beaches but of ski slopes. An understated toughness about him immediately made you feel safe. This, of course, was one of his biggest assets, and one he worked at and embellished.

"You're just going?" he asked, leaning forward to air-kiss her on both cheeks as though they were old friends. Tess caught a whiff of expensive cologne and thought of a night years before when she had allowed a wealthy young client to take her in a Dublin hotel. She remembered putting a hand behind his ear and being put off by the roughness of his skin, which seemed to contrast violently with the scent of the cologne.

"Stay while I have coffee." Richardson smiled and wrapped her up with his eyes. It was more of an instruction than a query, and as he spoke, he slid the other half of the matchbook toward her across the table. It was as though a charge of electricity passed between them. When she thought about it, this was not completely accurate: too much of a clichéd thought. What traveled from one to the other was not so much static as an almost tactile sense of power. She found it both stimulating and almost physically overwhelming, as though her body had been taken over by some delicious nerve gas: a benign poison that removed free will. She would come to think of it as enthralling her, shackling her to Richardson.

She would tell nobody, not even Maclean, how she felt, nor what had happened. In a way she hardly even admitted it to herself in the beginning, for she felt guilty and a little ashamed. The truth remained. Ron Richardson had an immediate effect on her. When she thought about it years later, she realized that it was similar to the way she had reacted to the young Docking, but there was no testing period, no fencing with words to discover this man. He was immediately revealed to her as a person with great power, and he knew by instinct that she had almost instantly been aroused. Before the day was out he was making love to her with a vigor she had experienced only once previously. It was like a drug, and it held her captive across all her years.

At that first meeting he casually handed her an airline ticket and told her the flight left at four that afternoon. He would meet her on the plane and they would travel together. She agreed instantly, without even looking at the destination on the ticket. Only after she had checked out of the hotel and was in the water taxi bouncing across the lagoon toward Marco Polo Airport did she drag the ticket out and see that she was heading for Geneva.

That night, in the suffocating heaviness of a Swiss five-star hotel, they forged the link that was to bind them together for the rest of their lives.

"Calvin has a lot to answer for," she told Richardson after the first bout of lovemaking, and then he revealed a terrible gap in his knowledge by missing the point by several hundred years, thinking she was talking about a strip-cartoon character—Calvin, a small boy with his stuffed tiger called Hobbes—instead of Geneva's great religious leader, John Calvin.

She never referred to it again, her unnumbered senses signaling his lack of humor when it came to the gaping holes in his education. Achilles had his heel and Ronnie had his patchy knowledge. In the end, Tessa's intuition led Ronnie Richardson to accept her as his main link to the real world.

In the early days, Jim Maclean had spelled out the danger, carefully revealing the risks and the morality of working for a professional murderer. Never once did Maclean try to dissemble by cloaking the reality with political language. For instance, he never referred to Richardson as an assassin. "He's a man who's not bothered by the ethics of life and death," Maclean told her when first explaining the concept of what Richardson viewed as his career. "Some might imagine him to be a monster, but he's certainly not that. I don't think he takes any pleasure or delight in killing, he's simply not as other men. To him there *is* no moral issue. He views it merely as his job."

"He must be able to differentiate between right and wrong."

"Probably, but not necessarily," Maclean told her. "Somehow he seems to avoid the moral issues entirely."

And that was how it was: an acceptance of him for what he was, and the deep animal need that passed between them like a stab of lightning. Tessa Murray and Ronnie Richardson, she thought, now and forever, like the ads for a long-running musical. With the thought came an unbidden picture of some unspecified retirement cottage: chocolate-box art with roses round the door, everything she did not want.

As she lay in her bath in the Bern hotel on that night when she arrived with Bex riding in her slipstream, Tessa relived what had followed her first meeting with Alchemist: how he had patiently taught her what he called the fieldcraft of death.

Over three weeks, they had moved from Geneva back to Venice, then to Paris and London, eventually ending up in his secret villa, at that time on the shores of Lake Lucerne. Two years later, following a concern that the Lucerne place had been compromised, he bought another house—the Villa Myrte, close to Brissago, on Lake Maggiore. The evergreen myrtle grows in abundance along the shores of Lake Maggiore.

During their initial time together he taught her the way to move unseen—first through cities, then entire countries; how to train her senses, developing that second sight that now worked like a radar screen in her mind. They played the serious kind of tag in the streets of Paris, where he had contacts in a private detective agency whose employees acted as shadows for him, thinking that they were helping to train tyro surveillance officers.

He also made it fun, and she would remember the lessons vividly: foot-padding in the Bois de Boulogne, hide-and-seek in the Louvre, then out into the Tuileries Gardens; passing the parcel in the Musée de l'Armée in the Invalides; and cowboys and Indians along the cloistered arches of the rue de Rivoli.

In London he taught her other skills: the cunning of the sneak thief, the expertise of a forger on the fly, the deftness of a pickpocket, and—above all else—the proficiency of one with eyes everywhere. During this schooling, she first set aside any guilt that remained. If called upon, she admitted that she might, herself, be able to kill without a backward glance, though she knew she would have trouble with the accountability.

This original training had pecked at her antennae in rain-slashed Bern, so that she picked up not only the scent of Rebecca following her in plain sight, but also other shadows that clung to Tessa, unseen, but on the periphery of her consciousness. Tessa was totally aware.

With Bex following her from Dublin, Tessa was quite clear about what was going on. Lying in her bath, she thought maybe this was the final result of the idiots who had broken security on the telephone when she was at Dublin Airport.

So now she wondered if it was worthwhile trying to rid herself of the girl straight away. Leave in a few minutes, get a cab to whistle her down the wind, hop to the next point, and rest there. No, this girl was trained—possibly police, she correctly reasoned (though she could not have told you why or how she thought it)—so they might as well travel cheek by jowl. Once there, in Brissago, she could see what Ronnie had to say about it. She rarely called him Ron, a diminutive he disliked almost as much as Ronald. Tessa was ultracorrect in calling and thinking of him as Ronnie all the time.

After she'd dried off in her en suite bathroom in the Bern hotel, Tessa had gone over to the window and looked out on the wet, depressing night and seen along the slick streets traces of being followed: she counted the same car slowly passing five times through the Bahnhofplatz: a little, dirty-gray VW with extra wing mirrors and a long whip aerial, the license plate partially obscured by mud but just enough there to note that it was local. How official is this? she asked herself, trying to remember where the nearest consulate had a residence. She heard Ronnie's voice in her ear: "In Switzerland it doesn't matter. They can get people in day or night, easy as pie." And she knew it was true because all security services did it: crossed borders, hired cars, kept safe houses. Had not Ronnie shown her exactly how it was done?

So the next day when Tessa saw the girl on the train, she was in no way startled. She would have been more concerned had she found herself alone on the journey. The only thing that gave her pause was the presence of other distorted shadows, not seen clearly. Until too late of course.

"Who's that on your tail?" Richardson muttered when he came out and embraced her, lips close to her ear as they rocked together in front of the villa.

"Been with me since Dublin. I think there're others as well. But the girl's been there all the way. There's a lot of movement around, darling. A carload in Bern last night. None of it feels right."

She felt his facial muscles move against her cheek. "Fun and games're off then."

"Only after dark, surely?" With a wicked little chuckle she snaked her arms tightly around his neck, pushing her pelvis hard against him. She worked her tongue into his mouth, licking behind his gums, pushing hard, hoping he would force her indoors and take her before any further dangers revealed themselves. But after one kiss he gently released himself. "This is how I've survived," he whispered. "Taking immense care. You know how it's done, Tess, so let's do it properly."

They stood together, far back from the window in an upstairs room, watching as Bex went up the road and crossed over to the café. Then he led Tessa into the garden on the far side of the villa, and as the daylight bled away, she told him about London, the targets, the time limit, and the weapon.

"President and Madame Bortunin," she said, and he growled a one-note, deep grunting laugh.

"By firearm. In London during the ten-day visit. The state visit with the Yanks in town as well. That's next week."

"Damn! Double damn!" Ronnie scowled, his face becoming almost a caricature of itself. Anger flared in his eyes, and his mouth was askew.

"Shots to the head preferred."

He laughed the grunting laugh again. "Old faithful hard-liners?"

"Ukrainians. Call themselves Sons and Daughters of October . . ."

He lifted a hand and she stopped muttering.

"I know who they are. Well-funded prima donnas." He shrugged. "If they want to build some message into it, why don't they take the risk and do it themselves? Crazy."

"You're not going to do it?" Her voice had an undertow of relief.

"Of course I'm going to do it. It's a job." He paused as though reconsidering. "Tell you what. I'll do it if we're able to get out without being seen by whoever this woman is, and whoever's sticking to her back. Smells professional. I don't think it's a cowboy outfit." He inclined his head in the direction of the road. "You may have to come with me. . . . God, I wish you'd been more careful." Looking at her sideways, not moving his head. "Damn," he cursed again quietly, acknowledging the implications of being tracked down to this hiding place, which he had loved for so long. Sometimes he wondered if he could have real emotional love for another person, only for places to which he could never return.

She put a hand on his arm, trying to draw him closer, but it was like pulling at a standing stone. "Ronnie"—urgent now—"can't we call it a day? Can't we just up and go? Leave? Begin life somewhere else?"

For a second she thought he would capitulate. Then: "No." A shake of the head. "Not yet. Not quite yet."

The girl, he confirmed to her, was police-trained. He knew it by the way she moved when she came out of the café; by the restless, searching eyes and her loping stride. "Where there's one, there'll be others. But there's something else." His intuition had flicked, like the needles on a piece of electronic equipment. There was danger out there; he had spotted an insubstantial shadow ahead of the girl, moving with a military jaunt.

They would not be able to rest tonight, he said. It wasn't just the cop. "You felt it yourself, Tess." He said he could sense it everywhere; in his bones and his brain. And she was jumpy. "It's not just the journey," she said. "Not simply the girl and too much coffee."

This went deeper. Something else, she said, and he nodded, thinking of the other shadow. If there're two of them, they'll have some backup nearby, he told himself. Aloud he muttered something about being alert.

Ronnie created a hide for himself in the big bedroom looking out over the lake, while Tessa watched the front of the villa. Before they began the watch, he called the hotel down by the landing stage. He was looking for an old friend, an English girl, he told them. Thought he had glimpsed her on the boat—the ferry from Locarno. Yes, there was one English lady, they said. The name? Certainly, they had the name. A Ms. Nightingale. Did he wish to be put through? No, that wasn't the name. He must have made a mistake.

Tessa prepared flasks of coffee and sandwiches. There was bread, butter, Sandwich Spread, some ham, cheese, and a couple tomatoes in the fridge as well as the makings of a Bolognese sauce Ronnie had planned for dinner. Incongruously, she made neat little triangles, cutting off the crusts, laughing at herself for doing such a thing, keeping the triangles for herself and cutting doorsteps for Ronnie.

So they settled down for the long night watch. She sat away from the window in one of the upstairs rooms, looking onto the road, the small two-way radio in her lap, maintaining contact every half hour or so.

Between the cars slashing the darkness she thought of a Rembrandt painting, dramatic lighting, the colors sharp, as though she were looking at it through the window. Then, for no apparent reason, she recalled an incident from years ago, heard the words—"Oh, no. No, it's much worse than that"—tried to place them, then remembered. She must have been about fifteen because she knew what was what, but still went to church with her parents. There had been a scandal: something to do with a priest having fathered a child. She heard it being discussed in low, urgent tones. As they came out from mass, the woman in front of her leaned forward and said to the priest standing by the door, "Oh, Father, isn't it terrible about Father Xavier? It would have been better if he had died." The priest, still wearing the vestments—a gold-trimmed, green chasuble over the alb—raised his hands in horror. "Oh, no. No, it's much worse than that."

She had wanted to laugh and had to hurry away lest the priest see her smirk. She tried to make sense of his logic and failed; remembered looking at the vestments, seeing the maniple dangling from above his left wrist, admiring the beautiful needlework.

There had been an inevitable row with her mother and father. Later, through a closed door, she heard her mother tut-tutting, "Silly girl, if only she'd kept quiet, father would've been spared this fuss. Now she's humiliated him and maybe he'll be unfrocked." It had taken Tess a moment to understand her mother spoke of the girl whom the priest had made pregnant. It was an unwritten law at that time that you never accused a priest of such a thing—a habit that had taken long to die.

From somewhere else in the silt of her memory she dredged up the fact that the priest concerned had not been cast into outer darkness, just moved away to another parish, sent to the South. She had seen him one afternoon, years later in Dublin, a weasel of a man with the shifty eyes of a pickpocket, though he was into picking at things more valuable than those carried in your pocket.

In the streetlights on the far side of the road she saw two women walking quickly as though they feared the shadows, and she realized that she was carrying a terror deep inside her: a fear of what this night could bring; how it might affect the future. More cars went past, gathering speed, and she looked at her watch, tilting her wrist toward the light filtering through the window. Two minutes to midnight.

In the rear bedroom, overlooking the terrace and the grass sweeping down to the lake, Ronnie Richardson waited.

At four o'clock in the morning, Lenny Saxby—the unexpected player—rose from the water and splashed ashore bent on vengeance. He wore a wet suit and face mask. In his right hand he carried a waterproof bag that contained a Glock nine-millimeter automatic pistol. In his head he carried a grudge almost fifteen years old.

CHAPTER 16

Lenny Saxby was a trained soldier, a former member of the Special Air Service. It had been his whole life, and Ron Richardson had taken that life from him. That was how Saxby reasoned. He had been a boy entrant, straight from school, learning a trade—armorer. Later he served with the Green Howards, rising through the ranks and eventually transferring to SAS. Lenny had been a sergeant major and Ronnie Richardson was his troop commander all those years ago. There had been a stupid death: one of those useless, silly, unnecessary deaths. The man's name was Edwards and his fatality so public that, out of the Service, in the real world, there would have been no doubt that it was manslaughter. This death was almost a cliché, for Edwards was shot dead by his sergeant major. An accident . . . but . . .

There had been four of them together out on a field firing range, in Wales, not far from Brecon Beacons. The whole troop had been on an escape-and-evasion exercise, and Richardson, the troop commander, Sergeant Major Saxby, and Troopers Edwards and MacRoberts had come together at dawn, their first meeting since the exercise had started.

Their rendezvous came after six long, strenuous days and nights in the field under deadly serious conditions, including the use of live ammunition. The rest of the troop were spread out over some fifty square kilometers, making their way in pairs to the RV. Edwards and MacRoberts were the first to clock into the small copse close to the road down which they expected transport to arrive. Everything they had done over the past week had been under strict rules of engagement, laid down by vigilant umpires, and everything they had done carried more than a hint of danger. On these kind of exercises people took the gloves off. You could get destructively mashed up if you got caught or if it came to close fighting. Now, for the first time that week, they could relax. Though they didn't.

Richardson and Saxby had been waiting in the wood for six hours in a soaking, cold drizzle that had undoubtedly slowed their reactions: blunted their edges. They were both tired.

Edwards and MacRoberts had operated together throughout most of their time with the regiment, and neither Richardson nor Saxby had reason to believe they were anything else but close and mutually reliant, trusting soldiers. But today, exhausted and edgy, they were bickering when they arrived, and things quickly got worse.

To start with, Richardson took little notice, though he became aware that the squabble was bitter almost from the first exchange. There was none of the good-natured needling you'd expect from a couple of hardened professional soldiers.

"You bastard. You've been bloody seeing her, en't you? Eh? Eh, MacRoberts, you slimy bastard? It's true, en' it? Fuckin' true."

"So what if it is?"

They were both truculent, cocky, and quickly the dispute went from shouted insults to blows, with both Richardson and Saxby in no doubt that the men were in that most serious of conflicts—a quarrel over a woman. The details really do not matter now, but she was a local girl called Lucy. She had been going out with Edwards, but it now appeared that she had been cheating with MacRoberts.

As the only officer present, Richardson should have stepped in as soon as he realized this was a potentially dangerous business. Later, at the court of inquiry, he admitted that the matter got out of hand with the ferocity of a bushfire. The two men came to blows alarmingly quickly, exploding in merciless brutality: flailing fists and weapons, grunts, kicks, stifled cries, and thuds as they rolled on the ground locked together, both using their considerable skills of combat, out of control now and swamped by fury.

When the first blows came, Saxby shouted orders at the two troopers, commanding them to stop, his voice audible over some distance.

But Edwards and MacRoberts had lost all sense of discipline, and MacRoberts looked as though he would kill Trooper Edwards, who was already bleeding badly from a cut above his right eye. Now Saxby, aware that things had got out of control, took an understandable, if foolish, action. He drew his nine-millimeter H&K automatic pistol with the intention of firing a warning shot to shock the men out of their reciprocal fury.

Afterward, Saxby could not explain why his weapon discharged prematurely. He had known it was loaded and cocked, he said, but his thumb was feeling for the safety catch as the barrel cleared his holster. "My forefinger must have tightened on the trigger, and by some oversight the *safety* must've already been off," he admitted at the court of inquiry, the words coming out in a formal, cold, matter-of-fact manner that raised the eyebrows of at least two senior officers. What was not in dispute was that the automatic had fired and the bullet had hit Edwards in the right ear, killing him instantly.

"Jesus!" Saxby croaked standing over the body. "Jesus, I knew that bloody woman'd be the death of one of them. I knew it."

And this was the unfortunate crux of the matter: Saxby's previous knowledge of the state of things between Edwards and MacRoberts concerning Lucy Smith. As a senior warrant officer Lenny Saxby should have reported exactly what he knew to his troop commander. Any friction, serious or imagined, between men working closely together in the field could put everyone at risk. Sergeant Major Saxby should have known better; should never have hesitated or even got himself into this position. Saxby, however, had a besetting sin, a chink in his armor, which was his vanity. For all his undoubted military skills, Lenny imagined that, as far as women were concerned, he was a true Jack the Lad. Tall, well-built, with looks that were described as ruggedly attractive, and thick blond hair that he wore a shade too long, giving him the appearance of a rakish pirate. Unhappily, Lenny Saxby was also an additional side to the already unequally loaded triangle of Edwards, MacRoberts, and the fickle Lucy. The girl had been making out not only with the two troopers, but also with their sergeant major, whose second marriage had broken down less than a year before.

As he prepared for the court of inquiry, Saxby went to Richardson, pleading with him not to answer any leading questions concerning Saxby's involvement with the girl.

"You know it was an accident, boss. That's what's really at the bottom of this. If they get wind I was involved with the little scrubber, it'll turn things into a circus and they'll throw me to the lions."

"Len, how can I hold out? MacRoberts heard what you said, and the girl's been blabbing her mouth off all over the place. Let's see how the whole thing goes down."

But Ronnie Richardson was more concerned with saving his own skin. As the only officer present, it could easily have been argued that the responsibility for the death was his. But he made certain that nobody even suggested this by the way he phrased his written report. Saxby, he hinted, had infringed "good order and military discipline" by not disclosing everything concerning Edwards and MacRoberts's serious disagreement over the girl.

"If I had been in full possession of the facts regarding the girl, my senior NCO, and the two other ranks, I would probably have had one, or all three, of them transferred to another troop," Richardson wrote before really sticking the knife in. "In fact, as far as Sergeant Major Saxby is concerned, I would seriously have considered a disciplinary board to judge his fitness to remain in the regiment."

The court left no doubt concerning apportionment of blame for this accidental death. Within a week of the findings being published it was suggested that Saxby should take early retirement on half pay.

So he left the regiment and the army, which had been father, mother, wife, and mistress to him. He left as an embittered man whose only reason for living now was revenge, though he did not become wholly aware of it for a while.

Richardson had no illusions about his own situation. Indeed, there was a large question mark concerning Captain Richardson's motives for an application to transfer to the "Bootnecks." People indulged in loose talk, but two things are certain: first, throughout his life Richardson rarely looked back, and the accidental death of Trooper Edwards hardly ruffled his conscience; second, it was the exact opposite for Leonard Saxby. The memory of Richardson's evidence and its outcome preyed constantly on his mind.

In civilian life Saxby drifted, quickly becoming unsettled and rarely holding down a job for any length of time. He was envious by nature and within a few years abandoned any responsibility for his actions. He saw Richardson as the complete and sole cause of his downfall, therefore the reason for his current circumstances. This one conclusion overran his mind, sending him into a life of obsession revolving around one aim: revenge.

By this time, Richardson had dropped out of sight and into his well-padded life as an assassin for hire. So, when Saxby came looking for him to exact revenge, he could not be found—which caused the obsession to spiral, eventually becoming manic, then profoundly psychotic.

Now, Lenny Saxby had a daughter by his first marriage, and the daughter, Tracy, was blessed with both intelligence and ambition. This landed her a serious job with the international conglomerate Siemens.

Based mainly just outside Newcastle-on-Tyne, young Tracy, at age twenty-two, became a rising star who seemed set fair until the company had to close down its big British-based operation and she found herself suddenly deprived of both job and future.

Unlike her father, Tracy Saxby clung to her ambition. With Siemens, she had traveled through most of Europe, in particular France, Germany, and Switzerland, making many contacts in the world of business, particularly in the buzzing area of international finance. One of these contacts was with the bank Credit Suisse, which eventually offered her a job as assistant manager (investments) in their London office. This she accepted and was told the appointment would start with a nine-month course in their Zurich office. On arrival among the legendary gnomes, she discovered the bank had rented a pleasant little villa for her on the lakeside, big enough for three or four people.

After a few weeks, Tracy began to get a conscience about her father, whom she hadn't seen or called as often as she should. These qualms were the direct result of a long, rambling letter Lenny had written to congratulate her on the new job.

This led to her telephoning and inviting him to come over and stay for a week or so. "I mean, we could go out to dinner in the evenings, spend Sundays together. It would be nice."

"You really want me to come?" He knew that he had been less than a good father and felt, not truly guilty, but certainly a sense of shame: a job not completed.

"Of course, Dad. Please." Tracy sounded quite genuine, as though she was trying to forge a new bond with him.

Perhaps a break would do him good, he thought: recharge his batteries, renew his vigor in the search for his nemesis, Ronnie Richardson.

He found Zurich oppressive with its temples to the Swiss franc and the somewhat dour men and women who seemed to go about their work with a resigned and serious air. But he liked Tracy's villa and trips out on the lake during the day. He also enjoyed the restaurants, talking with his daughter in the evenings, sometimes late into the night. The trip started to take his mind off the enormous bleakness that had pervaded his life.

After a week or so, Tracy suggested that he should come to the bank and take her out to lunch because she had a particularly long lunch hour that day. He arrived a little before noon and sat alone, being eyed suspiciously by cashiers and the one security man.

Then, just as he was becoming uncomfortable and thinking he should have waited outside, he heard someone speak in English.

"Ah, Mr. Hungerford, how nice to see you. You've come to see Herr Schenk?"

"Yes, he's expecting me I think."

Saxby knew the voice. Would have known it anywhere. He glanced up and to his right. Ronnie Richardson was being shown into an office, welcomed by a tall, grave-looking suit who was nearly smiling a welcome.

Len Saxby's brain seemed to drain; his vision clouded with blood, then blacked out. Slowly his sight returned. He stood up, felt his legs shaky under him; his sense of balance deserted him so that he clutched at the nearby wall. He must have looked terrible because the security man came over and spoke to him in his singsong *Hochdeutsch*, but Saxby waved him away and blundered into the street.

(How Ronnie, who had this almost wizardly facility for spotting danger a mile away, was not aware of Saxby's presence is difficult to explain. He did not know until much later how Saxby had picked him up, and even when faced with facts, he refused to believe them: as you will surely see. One can only put it down to a sudden lapse of concentration as his mind shifted onto the question of finance on entering the bank.)

Tracy came down the bank's steps, followed outside by the security man in his crisp and correct blue uniform. "You okay, Dad? You ill or something?"

The security man spoke to her, his head bent near her ear and his lips moving urgently.

"Deiter says you look ill. What is it?"

"Nothing. Bit faint. I've come over faint. Be all right in a minute. Haven't had anything but coffee this morning."

"Dad, you're not looking after yourself. Come on, let's get some food into you."

She steered him toward a restaurant frequented by bank staff and ordered his favorite pork chops on a bed of pasta. Lenny Saxby had to concentrate hard to hold down his need to ask questions about the man who called himself Hungerford. He was conscious of the twitch in his mind being transferred to his cheek and left eye. He was short of breath and had to force himself to make small talk.

"Your mum would've liked it here, Trace."

"You ever hear from her?" She knew that normally her mother was a taboo subject.

"No, and I don't want to hear her news, Tracy. Please, just let it lie."

The conversation stuttered, hesitated, then dried up.

When the coffee was served, he casually said he'd seen an Englishman being welcomed into the bank. "Hungerford, I think they called him."

"Oh, yes, he's a writer. Well looked after by the bank. Rather a prize I think. Lives somewhere on Lake Maggiore and comes up to see the great Herr Schenk every couple of months or so."

"Who's Herr Schenk?"

Herr Schenk was the top account manager, who dealt only with the seriously wealthy.

Later she asked him how he planned to spend his afternoon.

"What . . . ? Oh, maybe I'll go out on the lake."

She sighed, concerned, for her father seemed distant. Somehow his body was there with her, but his mind had moved away, concentration gone. Yet that evening he seemed completely changed. "It's as though he's suddenly got a new lease on life," she told the dark, hunky cashier who was trying to get into her pants. At the time she thought that maybe his luck was starting to change. And her father's luck as well.

So it began. Now he'd found Richardson, there was a new and furtive purpose to life. Once he had traced his quarry to the pink and white villa teetering above the lake, Saxby's whole being altered, his mind consumed with the mechanics required to eliminate the perceived designer of his downfall. His target, he decided, would have to die in the most efficient manner of his devising. He owed it to his military training.

He first spotted Richardson in Zurich during the early summer of the year previous to the discontented winter when the newlywed Bex Gauntlet tracked Tess Murray from Dublin to Bern and onward. So Saxby's plan had several months to mature. The stalking of Ronnie Richardson was followed closely by the setting up of what Saxby, deep in his secret self, thought of as death by stealth.

Those months were spent arranging the hardware and carrying it to the final destination. He had been lucky not to be detected immediately, and by the time he finally traced Richardson to the lakeside retreat outside Brissago, Saxby knew that his onetime comrade was quietly displaying every facet of a man carefully watching his back; a man great with caution; suffused in cunning; fomented in fear.

Lenny had no idea of the enormity of Ronnie Richardson's secret, but he knew it existed, just as he was certain the man would rightly die for the sorrow he had heaped upon the head of his judge, jury, and executioner.

Over the next few months Lenny Saxby made a number of visits to Switzerland, always giving himself a reason to be there. First it was to see his daughter while she was still in Zurich, then, devious journeys to the canton of Ticino, taking pains to vary the route, mostly by train, for that was the cheapest way, staying in different places and keeping himself distant from his target.

Later he told Tracy that he was taking a look at Switzerland while he had the chance and the excuse.

"Sort of fallen in love with it, Trace. Such a different country. So many things going on. Not like old England." He even managed to rent a couple of rooms in Ascona to which address he mailed pieces of his stripped-down Glock (which is conveniently made of a durable plastic) and so avoided the dangerous business of bringing the weapon through a Swiss customs point where the uniformed men were unsmiling, taking themselves seriously.

In Ascona, where they were used to artists, he became an artistic photographer, hiring a small fishing boat fitted with an outboard motor. He would sail out and take photographs of the lakeside with an expensive camera. Many of those photographs were of the Villa Myrte from the lake.

He also made a number of covert reconnaissance sorties, swimming into Richardson's boathouse, then tracing the pathway up to the rear door of the villa.

Here he encountered indications that the owner was intent on maintaining privacy. Invisible eyes ran a three-tier barrier, safer than razor wire, around the outer perimeter of the villa's grounds, and Lenny used his considerable expertise, learned and sharpened back in the SAS, to deactivate the sensitive mechanisms. Then, over three nights, he examined the sophisticated electronic alarms on the doors and windows.

It did not take him long to discover that these electronic guards on the main house were beyond his skills. Indeed, they would have defeated most burglars or criminals, for Ronnie Richardson had not relied solely on alarms and triggers available on the commercial market. With ingenuity he had adapted many standard systems so that they were booby-trapped. Anyone tampering with the doors or windows would most likely trigger a secondary or, in some cases, a tertiary device. The alarms were sensitive as nervous black mambas and twice as deadly.

Common sense and the tracing of extra wires told Saxby that everything was linked to some central control and, certainly, through telephone lines to some monitoring center, for the outgoing lines were linked to the main alarm.

Having been able to interrupt the unblinking electronic eyes in the garden, he could at least get to the rear door of the property without alerting anyone. From the hours of watching and taking pictures from the boat, he knew for certain that his target lived alone and slept in the large rear bedroom, overlooking the lawn that ran down to the lake.

He reasoned that should he activate the alarm by smashing in the back door, Richardson would not wait timidly for the police to arrive, but would head down the stairs to tackle an intruder head-on. In those circumstances, Lenny decided, an armed interloper would have the edge. He would shoot and kill his nemesis as soon as he appeared.

So he watched his own back, knowing he had prepared himself as well as possible: never getting too close, setting everything up so that he would make his move on an unlikely night in the cruelest winter month of February.

To put things into perspective, though, Lenny was not to know what else was going on. He spent a weekend in Ascona in the days directly before Tess, followed by Bex, made the journey to Brissago.

On the night that Tessa rested up in Bern, Saxby was in London to meet a man he knew only as Donnaugh and collect items from him in a pub on the corner of Broadwick Street where it turns sharply into Lexington Street. On that night he paid a quick two hundred pounds for one small stick of *plastique* explosive and a twenty-second fuse, the fuse pushed tightly into a slim, crimped metal detonator that would provide the initial force to touch off the eruption of the *plastique* and blow the deadbolt on the back door.

There was a touch of irony here, for the pub was called the John Snow after the great nineteenth-century Dr. Snow, who identified cholera as being spread through the contamination of water—in particular the water from a public tap near where the pub stands today.

When Saxby flew out the next morning—while Tessa and Bex were traveling by train from Bern to Locarno—the fuse and detonator were snug in an umbrella handle, while the *plastique* was molded into the interiors of a thick, flashy metal pen-and-pencil set that he handed over for examination with change and other metal items before going through the Friskem scanners at Heathrow.

Lenny arrived in Ascona a couple of hours before Tessa left Locarno, and he immediately started to prepare for the end game. He had no thoughts of what would happen after it had taken place. The only picture in his mind was of Ronnie Richardson dead, with a couple of nine-millimeter bullets in him.

It is quite possible that, under normal circumstances, he would have got away with it: exacting revenge by taking the life of the man he held responsible for his own disillusioned, sorry state of mind. Yet through an unhappy quirk he chose the worst night of the year to carry vengeance to its final conclusion. Richardson was alerted, not to Saxby, but to a possible threat posed by security and law enforcement agencies operating without the knowledge of the Swiss authorities.

From the rear bedroom windows, Ronnie watched the dark shape pause for a good ten minutes as he disconnected the electronic beams down by the boathouse.

"He's heading up the path. I'm going down to deal with him," Tessa heard her lover's voice low in the earplug of the tiny two-way radio.

She acknowledged the message, and Richardson slowly pushed himself back from the window and glided from the room. On the landing he cocked the Browning pistol and gave an extra twist to ensure the noise-reduction unit was fully screwed home.

On the ground floor he punched in the deactivating alarm-code number on the keypad that was fitted inside a small cupboard between the stairs and the front door. He then moved silently to stand at the most convenient point in the passage to the rear door. The blackest, darkest place lay at the top of two steps directly below the turning of the main staircase. From there he had a clear view down the wide passage that ran the breadth of the villa. Between him and the back door were two archways to left and right, and a pine table on which stood a big china vase that had been turned into a lamp. The pink wash of the walls was gray in the darkness, and Ronnie could smell his own sweat.

Outside, Lenny Saxby put down the big cocked Glock, held the tiny flashlight in his teeth, and extracted the *plastique*, which he rolled in his fingers, making it into an irregular ball that he pressed over the keyhole, pushing so that some of the explosive forced its way in. (Just as they taught you up in Hereford when you first did the course, Len.) From his belt he took the fuse and detonator, checking to make sure the fuse went tightly home and that the bias-cut end was clear. Carefully, he inserted the primer into the center of the *plastique* and reached for the Bic lighter he had bought in London yesterday for this very purpose.

In the darkness, Ronnie again made certain the safety was off on the Browning, slid his forefinger onto the trigger, and placed his right wrist over the left, bringing both hands up and aligned with the door some five to six paces away.

Len lit the fuse and in one movement scooped up the Glock and flattened himself against the wall.

In the hallway Ronnie did not expect to fire the Browning. He really did not foresee the events that were now seconds away.

The *plastique* exploded with a flare of fire and a dull, jarring *whumph*: low on the register, shaking the walls.

Ronnie turned his head away and then back as he realized the door was open, flicked outward like a piece of cardboard. He saw the movement of smoke being cleared out of the way by a body quickly passing into it.

Lenny stepped through the door sideways, just as you were taught, offering the smallest possible target.

"Stop! Stand still or I'll shoot!" Ronnie said firmly, repeating it fast in Italian.

"Jesus!" Lenny breathed, bringing the big Glock up and toward the direction of the voice.

"Christ!" came the response as Ronnie saw the movement, spotted the weapon through the darkness, smelled the explosive smell, and fired two shots in quick succession—the standard double-tap kill. They sounded like a couple of *phutt-phu* noises, like someone expelling air through lips from puffed-out cheeks.

Above, in the front bedroom, Tessa did not even hear the shots, only the stumbling crash as Lenny was hurled backward into that stream of darkness from which nobody has returned, the Glock arcing through the air to hit and crack the big china-vase lamp on the pine tabletop, sending it crunching against the wall.

What seemed like a deafening silence followed in the wake of the little explosion, the two shots, and the clatter of Saxby's death. Then

Ronnie moved, compact steps, not wasting time, knowing exactly where to go and what to do. Both hands still up on the pistol, elbows tucked in; he went to the main switches in the hall, illuminating the passage: liquid light poured onto the pink walls, and at the end the shattered door and the obscenity.

Nine steps to the back door and the body, kicking the Glock up the passage out of the way, the Browning still moving in the direction of the useless heap straddling the doorway. He heeled at the body, hard, then lugged it over with his foot, arm still extended and fear swamping his nervous system.

"Shit!" he gasped. "Lenny Saxby! What the hell . . . ?" and his mind went into an overdrive of questions. After the past, how could Lenny be working for the security service or the police? What the hell was going on? Did the local cops know about this? What kind of backup was out there in the darkness or on the lake?

The telephone began to ring and he slipped back through the passage to the hall.

"Pronto?" he breathed.

At the distant end, the telephonist at the alarm-monitoring service asked what the code was, and it took Ronnie a couple of seconds before he realized that blowing the door must have triggered the silent alarm down the phone line.

He parroted back the number, adding that there had been a stupid prank. The operator was not amused and still asked, automatically, like a robot, if Signor Hungerford wanted the police to come out.

Tess came down the stairs as he replaced the receiver. "We're going to have to get out of here." As he said it, he thought of how he might use the body to get out clean: dressing it in his clothes, then blowing the face off with a soft-nosed bullet. At least it would give them a few hours' start—if their nerves held, and if nobody else turned up. Jesus, he thought, it must've been Saxby out there last night keeping close to the girl. Then, with a lurch in his stomach, he saw why Saxby might be working for them. They knew who he was. Somehow they had cracked it and knew that Alchemist equaled Ronnie Richardson—onetime SAS, sometime Royal Marine—and that it takes one to know one. That had to be the reason for Saxby's presence here: the only explanation.

He told Tessa to stay there in the hall and went down to the back door again, bent over Saxby's body, then reached down and pulled him inside. His bullets had caught the man in the right side, both within a few centimeters of each other. Ronnie thought they must have passed straight through the rib cage and possibly into the heart. Had to be something like that as Saxby seemed to have died instantly. The eyes were open, glazed, and had no hint of fear in them. He literally couldn't have known what hit him.

By now a plan was almost fully formed in Ronnie's mind, usable only if no backup appeared or the local law didn't show. If they had tracked him, knew who he was, Ronnie wouldn't be a fool; wouldn't try to shoot it out with them. What could he expect? Maybe ten years? Fifteen? Or would they try to take him out? Make it look like a battle to the death? Well, at least it would be quick. Ronnie was not afraid of dying. As with anybody, there were occasional moments of fragmentary fear, but death was some kind of new beginning, he thought. "The last enemy," he said aloud.

Tess called to him from the stairs, asking what he had said— "Couldn't hear you, love."

"I may be blown," he said, going back into the hall, looking up and giving her what passed for a sheepish grin. Then he told her of his fears; about Saxby; then the various options as he saw them. He went through the possibilities to test the water: using the body; bringing the girl up from the hotel; making their escape. As he spoke, he knew that his mind was in confusion.

"You're absolutely certain the girl's a cop?" Tess asked.

"I don't know. I'd swear she moved like a cop, they all have that way of walking: sort of flat-footed. I'd have put money on it." As they talked, he moved from room to room, watching both back and front. Expecting a motor launch to come roaring across the lake, floodlights shattering the darkness, or a fleet of police cars screaming up from the direction of the town. He wondered if any of the neighbors had heard the small explosion. Doubted it, the nearest was too far away.

"And you're certain about this fella, what'dya call him?"

"Saxby."

"Saxby."

"Lenny Saxby? What about him?"

"You're certain he's working for MI5 or whatever they're calling it these days?"

For the first time, Ronnie seriously started to question it.

"No old scores to settle?" Tessa had come up close to him. For a second he thought of that Shakespeare play, the one about the Scottish king. He had seen a production in modern dress, and Macbeth and his lady had moved around just as Tessa and he were doing now.

"With me? Lenny and me? Old scores?"

"No, Lenny and the pope. What d'you think, Ron?"

He thought about Edwards's death on that cold, damp morning; Saxby standing over him with the pistol. Richardson's refusal to tone down the evidence. Saxby's face as they left the inquiry. Stone-faced. The face of a man who could kill. No, Ronnie rejected it, then brought it into the open. "He might harbor the odd grudge."

"Enough to want you in a grave?"

He thought about it again. "Maybe. I don't know." If you wanted to be optimistic about the situation, it was a great theory. "Not Lenny, no. I mean, he did a stupid thing, but . . ."

After a while:

"So you want me to go down and bring the girl back here?" Tess sounded cool and in control.

"If you think you can act as though it's me lying here with my face blown off. If you've enough bottle to force the bitch back here."

"I'll frighten the bejasus out of her." Tess sounded hard, psyched up. I've taught her well, he thought. Aloud he said there was nobody out there. Nobody on the lake and only normal traffic moving along the road to Italy. Could Saxby have . . . ?

"You won't do anything to his face until I've gone down to the hotel. I'll try and get her in her room."

"No." Ronnie was adamant. "No. Meet her in public. Best not to face her until there are people around. Reason with her. Frighten her to death."

"Give me a gun, Ron." Tess grinned, anticipating the danger and the buzz it would bring.

He looked startled, for she seldom called him Ron.

"If it's dodgy, I'll finish her off here. Put her lights out and then we'll go and see to the Bortunins in London. Make some money, eh? For the pension fund, what?"

Tess gave him a tiny shake of the head, as though she knew it was no good trying to argue. She made coffee, and he brought her an automatic pistol. "Cattle prodder for that cow," he said, laughing. They drank the coffee and waited, then at last she left and he got to work getting an old blazer onto the body, wrestling with the stiffening muscles. Then dragging it into the room at the front of the house and firing two silent shots at close range straight into the side of the face.

He thought of other men he had seen dead and others he imagined. His head buzzed with the symbols of death.

As things turned out, Tessa put on a convincing act, but they were both shaken by the sudden arrival of the backup. Ronnie was upstairs cheering Tessa on when the little car screamed to a stop across the street and Patsy's gangly figure came through the open door. It had surprised Ronnie because he was still thinking of Lenny as the shadow.

The whole thing left them jumpy, twitchy, so that they hardly spoke to one another during the ride up the lake in the motor launch. Tessa had a stinking headache, and her left ear was numb and deafened from the cupped-handed blow from Bex. Ronnie brooded, remaining silent until they were in a hired car tooting toward Malpesa, the nearest of Milan's two airports. "You were bloody good," he told Tess. "You've got more bottle than a liquor store."

"I've been well trained, so." That girl who had been terrified of the two IRA hoods in Dublin seemed to have come from a different planet in another time.

In Paris that night—entering with new, untraceable passports—they searched the news Web pages and surfed the TV channels without seeing anything that could be linked with a death by shooting on Lake Maggiore.

"We might've muddied the waters for just long enough." Richardson looked tired. "I really should've killed that girl when we had her."

Tess inwardly shuddered. He sounded as cold-blooded as an alligator. "I thought you were being a bit too clever for your own good," she said, not expecting a response.

Ronnie was not used to criticism from Tessa. Bloody political correctness and the empowerment of women, he thought, dismissing it as it crossed his mind. Don't get yourself out-of-date, Ronnie, he told himself. Maybe it was really time to stop, for he hadn't seen the cavalry coming in its little scarlet and silver Terrano II. Hadn't spotted its existence. Hadn't detected Lenny Saxby either, come to that. Couldn't really put it all together yet. Found it difficult to believe Saxby had the balls to try to take him out. Mistook Saxby for some secret heavy. God, the guy must've been on the property more than once and he didn't even know. Hadn't detected him. Ronnie had meant to install CCTV at the back, but never got around to it. Bad. Very bad. Over the hill? he wondered.

On the *Sky News* from London they were talking about the forthcoming visit of President and Madame Bortunin. Already some of the Yank contingent had arrived. Smooth suits alighted from black Rovers in front of Downing Street, and the PM came down to greet the newly appointed U.S. secretary of state with a kiss. She was fair, glowing with health and good grooming, slender and winsome, the new secretary, which made a change. "Best figure ever to come out of Washington," said one of the presenters, and his female colleague gave him a filthy look on camera.

"Have you *got* to do this one?" Tessa asked yet again, her voice scratchy with concern.

"We've taken the money."

"You can give it back Ronnie, please."

"No, it's what I do well." A grin, looking away, for he really wondered if he did do it well anymore. He supposed that, for him, this was the ultimate test.

"Make it the last one then."

"Probably, yes. Possibly."

Maybe she was right. It wasn't the money. Ronnie Richardson had lately—within the last few hours—become conscious of age. Time's wingèd chariot. He tried the schoolboy grin again knowing it wasn't boyish anymore.

He called a police contact in Geneva who knew him only as the man who paid him a large sum of money, in cash, each month using the name Paramour. The contact said he'd check it out. "The Locarno area?" he queried.

"Maggiore. No, make it all of Ticino."

"I'll call you back." Which he did an hour later. "Only odd thing, there is a reported sighting of a known British security hack crossing the border at Brissago. Last night. Back again this morning and out with an unidentified British female."

"Known? How known?"

"He's not exactly welcome in Switzerland. Got caught with his hand in an illegal wiretap in '89. We don't stop him, but it's always noted."

"Where was the wiretap?"

"Old history. Basel. Don't know if he still works for the Brits."

"Description?"

The police contact rattled off an immediately recognizable description. "Patrick Wright. Known generally as Patsy."

"Don't know the bugger. Can you get me an update on him? I'll call you tomorrow." Ronnie scowled again as he put down the telephone. "We'll take a look-see in London. See how it lies. See what's going on. Who's watching what, hearing what, and all that."

So, that's how things stood. Ronnie and Tessa heading quietly into London with the killing of President and Madame Bortunin much on their minds; Bex Olesker and Patsy Wright coming in from Switzerland, via Italy—Milan—picking up instructions to go pull Charlie Gauntlet out from among the monks. ("These monks kosher, sir?" Bex asked Commander Joe Bain. "Kosher as spoiled gefilte fish," Bain said with an odd look. But what did he know? He had just spoken at length to his opposite number in Zurich, alerting him to a body in Brissago. That had been more than a shade embarrassing.) Now he carefully briefed Bex and a couple of hours later summed up, "I'm sure it's a coincidence, Charlie being there with the dread Kit-Kat, but you can see it poses a problem to our security brethren."

"And some." Bex nodded.

"We thought it best for you to go up and pull him out personally. I mean, it's as good an excuse as any: gives you the right kind of cover. There's some confusion."

"As well there might be."

"Indeed, what with all that money coming and going. Maybe the Revenue should have a team there."

"You really just want me to lift Charlie out? Really, that's all?"

"Well, no. I want you to hang on in London for a day or two. You see, Bex, our friends made the man who picked up the Murray woman when you lost her in Dublin. They know who he is and they want to pump him dry." That posed a problem, Joe said. The "friends" needed to give him a heavy interrogation, flush him out, drain him, and that would mean sidestepping the law slightly. "Just hang about, would you."

"Yes, sir. Okay." As Bex understood it, "funnies" were going to lift the man who had driven the battered Rover in Dublin. Lift him, she thought, then give him a drug-assisted interrogation. In the early years of the twenty-first century the techniques of chemically assisted interrogation had advanced incredibly. In the bad old days of the Cold War, people spoke loosely of sodium pentothol as the "truth drug," giving the impression that all you had to do was shove a hypo in the subject's arm and ask the questions. It was more involved than that, and a good deal more hit-and-miss. But nowadays, like every-thing else, new drugs were on the market and even newer sophisti-cated techniques. You could not expect anyone to stand up to interrogations nowadays; there were many ways of prizing the truth from people without resorting to violence. With the new methods had come a backlash. Political correctness had reached an idiotic high, and human rights activists caused endless problems to law enforcement agencies.

"You'll have that fellow Wright with you," Joe Bain told her. "He's a handy man to have around. A very present help in trouble, they say."

"I'll bear that in mind, sir." And she did.

And Charlie? Charlie sat quietly under the huge, vaulted roof of Ringmarookey's monastery chapel, his mind whirling with possibili-ties and wedges of worry. But mainly Charlie was angry.

In truth, Charlie was furious because the monks had kept him locked up for over twenty-four hours.

CHAPTER 17

The fathers and brothers of the Order of St. Jerome sang in swelling and dipping Gregorian plainchant:

Before the ending of the day,
Creator of the world we pray.
That Thou with wonted love wouldst keep
Thy watch around us while we sleep.

It was just after midnight and intensely cold in the chapel so their breath clouded with every line, making it seem as though the monks were smoking heavily during their devotions. Nobody slept, apart from a couple of elderly monks, unmoved by prayer, dozing in their stalls; and Charlie Gauntlet was in no way soothed by the music nor the sentiments expressed by the collective monastic brotherhood. This was the first time he had seen the entire order gathered together in one place, and a right motley crew they looked, he thought. The older men mainly had those crumpled, alligator-lined faces, lived-in with a hint of sanctity. Once you breached seventy-five, even the most villainous of men could pass for a saint.

In the suffused, dim light of the chapel, the middle-aged and younger monks mostly seemed to have either wild or haunted looks deep within their faces. Only a few of them projected any sense of peace, and some had a hardness about them that Charlie instantly recognized. It was a look he had seen on faces in the arcane professions—security and intelligence people—the world over. He thought he could see it in Brother Simon, whom he had ceased to trust.

Toward the back of the ranked stalls he spotted Fathers Hugh and Harry, who appeared to be completely focused on prayer. As though they had somehow become divorced from the congregation, they knelt, eyes closed, transported and totally tuned in to some distant signal upon which they placed their full trust. Charlie reflected that this must be an incredibly happy state to live in: complete faith, unreserved engrossment. He envied them.

> O let no evil dreams be near,
> Nor phantoms of the night appear,
> Our ghostly enemy restrain,
> Lest ought of sin our bodies stain.

What sin? Charlie asked himself. Deep, dark, and unwholesome sin, he thought, but maybe that was uncharitable. He wondered if there were in fact phantoms of the night or any ghostly enemies lurking about, skulking out of the moonlight. Charlie was not just annoyed, he was downright angry, and in this furious state a whole sheaf of images gamboled through his mind, casting gargoyle glances, thumbing long noses and stretching their mouths out of shape with inserted thumbs.

He had arrived late on Friday afternoon, and it was now the very early morning of Sunday. For a little over twenty-four hours Charlie had been kept incommunicado. He had every right to be angry, but he was equally disturbed, not only at his incarceration, but also by the motor yacht.

As Romeo Rockwell had brought the Piper Archer into Ringmarookey, Charlie had spotted the harbor, which had gone unnoticed on that earlier, more unsettling landing with Hilary Cooke at the controls.

A breakwater and a quay slid beneath their left wing in an elongated L spearing from the jagged western rocks. They passed over it at around two hundred feet, and Charlie glimpsed a sleek oceangoing motor yacht tied up, lashed fast to bollards set into the stone quayside. He could clearly see several men and women busy, swarming over the deck and the quay: working, loading, and unloading.

Another ship was also on its way in, small, wooden, and bobbing on the swell as it came past the breakwater.

A line of poetry came into his head, dredged from faraway schooldays—"Quinquireme of Nineveh from distant Ophir." Masefield, he thought. "Cargoes." He hadn't thought of that poem for years. Back in his teenage time it was a favorite, that and "Do you remember an inn, Miranda?" Who wrote that? He could recall neither its title nor the poet, yet he knew it because when he was in the sixth form—so long ago now—he had been in love with a girl called Miranda. She was at nearby St. Helen's, a lovely, leggy, games-playing, Betjeman kind of girl with muscular legs and clear eyes.

They bumped softly onto the scrubby grass, yet his mind stayed with the ships.

Charlie did not know why the yacht and little harbor struck him as suspicious, but they did, even though he was aware that boats regularly plied between the coast and the island. There was a mail boat, for instance, nothing odd about that. He gave a mental shrug and allowed his thoughts to return to the irritation he felt at his treatment on returning to Ringmarookey.

Once on the ground, scarcely out of the aircraft, Charlie requested an early and urgent meeting with the father superior. Brother Simon, in his capacity as porter, said he would inform Father Gregory immediately. Then he had taken Charlie to his room, which was neither welcoming nor convivial: bare, functional with an iron bedstead, and a corner with washing facilities. All very basic and unprepossessing. Looking back on his arrival, Charlie realized that he had been hustled along, as though Simon could not wait to get him to the cell.

He unpacked a few necessary things, putting the red folder containing the small sheaf of transcript pages onto the bed. Then he went over to the metal door with its Judas squint and an elongated cat flap at the foot. He would, he thought, take a walk along the cloisters and visit Gregory Scott in his office, beard him in his den. But the door was locked, firm and unmoving. Go to jail, he thought, go directly to jail; do not pass Go; collect sod all.

He tried shouting, but nobody came near. Then, after an hour or so, a tray was pushed through the flap at the bottom of the door. A flask of coffee and some warm, buttered toast were on the tray, together with a note typed on thick, heavy paper.

"Dear Brother," he read:

I am the novice master, responsible for the internal discipline of our order. You will be sleeping in one of the cells we maintain specially for temporary visitors. If you are not comfortable, please tell someone, who will see that your concerns are passed to me.

You will find that at certain times of day, and throughout the night, the door to your cell will be closed and locked. This is because we like to keep you apart from those who are permanently here on Ringmarookey. You must understand that, being from the world, you are likely to, unwittingly, carry unwanted conceptions and ideas with you. These ways of the world, natural to you, are not natural to our brethren trying to put the world behind them. Please understand that it is important for us to segregate you for the sake of men at the hardest stage in their conversion to our order.

One of the younger brothers will see that you are escorted to the chapel for the Divine Office.

God bless you.

The note was signed *Father Benedict, OSJ,* and it made Charlie even angrier. The argument was spurious, particularly when you considered the work of such people as the father superior and Fathers Harry and Hugh. Bullshit, he thought. Evil, rancid, stinking bullshit complete with a split infinitive. Scholastic monks had to live in both worlds. This was not what they called an enclosed order. He knew about these things, Charlie Gauntlet.

Now he was left with nothing to do but eat the toast, drink the coffee, and go through the latest extract from Naomi's diary. The toast was burned and had gone leathery, while the coffee had the consistency of thin dishwater. Charlie sighed, prayed that his young wife was safe from the prowling hosts of Midian, stretched himself on the bed, took up the folder, and started to read.

Romillius, whom I love above all men, I am speaking these words to you, and Petros has assured me that he is writing only what I tell him.

He had previously read this passage—Naomi's plea to Romillius, advising him to do everything in his power not to bring Jesus and his followers into a head-on clash with the authorities. He had read it in the hospital sitting with Hilary. He nodded and fast-forwarded himself.

Naomi had been away from Jerusalem to hear Jesus teach, and she went through many of the words familiar to anyone brought up within listening distance of the Christian faith, particularly anyone who had lived close to the Church of England. How quickly we forget, he thought.

Jesus also made us laugh. He says that people will easily condemn others without even noticing their own sins. "Often," he told us, "you will draw attention to someone who has a speck of dust in his eye, while you are walking around with a huge wooden beam sticking from your own eye." This we found very funny, but of course it is true. He also speaks of the difficulty the soul must have trying to make its journey to the kingdom of heaven. He told us we must not think that, just because we are descendants of the Israelites who came out of Egypt and are the Chosen Ones, it will be easy to walk straight into the kingdom of God. Some, he says, think of paradise as their right and due. "I tell you," he warns, "in many cases it'll be easier for a full-grown camel to pass through the eye of a needle than it'll be for you to enter God's heavenly kingdom." While this was funny, making us laugh again, it is very serious. Many of our teachers become immersed in the law and the right and good ways in which we should live our lives. They also imagine by doing things properly, keeping to the laws of food and the rituals of the Temple, we will automatically be with the Lord God, our eternal Father. Jesus teaches that this is not necessarily so. These are thoughts that make me reflect on my own life, my own shortcomings, and particularly, my own sins.

Romillius, it seems that it could be very wrong for me to love you as much as I do if I cannot love the Lord our God with equally great passion and fervor. This, if I understand Jesus, is what he asks of us. No, he does not ask it, he demands it. The love we must have for God, without whom we are nothing, has to be total and consuming. This is the heart of what Jesus teaches: we must believe in him, for only through him can we find salvation and the kingdom of God. I implore you, Romillius my beloved, please come and hear Jesus, at least listen to what he says. I truly believe that he is revealing things to us that give us the opportunity to redeem ourselves: a way to be absolved of our sins.

Naomi continued, repeating familiar parables—those picturesque and simple stories used to demonstrate deeper truths. The Prodigal Son, the Good Samaritan, the Talents, the Lost Sheep, the Wise and Foolish Virgins, came tumbling out taking Charlie's mind back to the time when he was first faced with the eternal philosophical questions: those of belief and unbelief. He had never taken the final leap embracing either a religious ethic or a firm sense of atheism or agnosticism. Somehow the situation for him had never been either a simple or clear-cut choice. As with so many other options, Charlie remained sitting on the philosophical fence. Now, reading the old parables freshly dressed by Naomi's words seemed to make them more immediate. As with so much of this strange document, Charlie appeared to be faced with a choice between accepting a fairy tale or literal truth.

Naomi also quoted several things Charlie could not recall from his scant biblical knowledge. "Today, Jesus taught us that reaching God's kingdom is in the natural order of things. Just as flowers and the fruit of trees die in the winter, so we die; and as the same flowers and fruit are reborn in the spring and summer, so shall we be born again into the holy kingdom."

Time ticked slowly past. Still nobody came to get him for either the Divine Office or to see the father superior. Every three hours, the fathers and brothers left work, relaxation, even sleep, to join together to sing matins, lauds, terce, sext, none, vespers, and compline as well as the daily celebration of the mass. In the dedicated religious life, this is usually a given, whether the monks—and nuns come to that—are of the Roman Catholic, Orthodox, or Anglican persuasion. Each of these short acts of worship follows a pattern, so that as a whole they make up an endless wheel of prayer and praise.

Some religious orders have slight deviations. The Sisterhood of the Poor Claires, for instance, dance some of their worship; London's Tyburn Nuns play football and snooker; while the Order of St. Jerome included special readings, during meals, from the letters of Father William McConochie, who founded the Anglican Order in 1887 on the island of Ringmarookey.

What matters to those who set their lives apart is the tradition of worship and praise. But this did not help Charlie, who, around eight in the evening, had another tray pushed under the door. He was awake and shouted for assistance, saw the Judas squint open, then close again.

On the tray were a bowl of vegetable soup and a stale-looking piece of bread, together with a clear plastic flask of water, which Charlie thought might well damage his health. It was a cloudy white color, which finally settled into a thick sediment at the bottom of the flask. The soup was bland, unseasoned, and had the paradoxical effect of leaving him feeling more hungry than he had before drinking it.

At a little after ten o'clock the one overhead lightbulb went out. Charlie's mind went back to his mum and the time when he was very small. For a second he wondered if this was some kind of defense mechanism: a conscious retreat to the safety of childhood. He reckoned that his mum had introduced him to jokes—"Where was Moses when the light went out? In the dark." Ha-ha.

Uncomfortable and cold, Charlie tussled with sleep and finally won, descending into a land of strange, troubled dreams where everything was insubstantial. The landscape, he quickly recognized, was straight out of a computer game called Lode Runner II. You operated a tiny man, collecting gold pieces on great, complex, and beautiful islands that floated in space and were inhabited by killer monks who, if they caught you, would cut you in two with a karate chop. Strange plants and shrubbery snaked around ornate and weird buildings, while water leaped into the air from elaborate fountains, and fire danced behind grilles.

He woke with the dreams intact, still present in his mind and body just as breakfast arrived under the door. A bowl of cereal, two slices of leathery toast, one cold and congealing rasher of bacon, and a cup of lukewarm coffee, black with what appeared to be a large part of the *Exxon Valdez*'s oil slick on its surface.

Charlie stamped around the cell, realizing that some light exercise was called for to keep the cold from his body. Eventually lunch arrived (a slice of gray meat and what looked like a genetically engineered pear). The hours dragged slowly round to the familiar leathery toast and tea, followed some three hours later by soup and stale bread, identical to that which he had been given on the previous night.

As each dose (Charlie's thought) of food arrived, he would set up a clamor, shouting and banging at the door. Again the lights went out at around ten. Charlie lay on his back, once more wrapped in the blanket. He had, since childhood, understood that easily losing your temper was a negative act. People with short fuses end up more stressed and physically harmed than those who remain calm in even the most frustrating circumstances.

So he stretched out on his back and did the thinking man's version of counting sheep: trying to recall whole passages of poems or books. He began with simple poems, then graduated to Shakespeare. At Cambridge he had been a member of the Marlowe Society, playing Polonius in *Hamlet,* ending up memorizing the whole play. In his head in the darkness now he met Hamlet's father's ghost on the battlements of Elsinore and followed, line by line, the great poetic tale of indecision. He was in the graveyard, finding the jester Yorick's skull and quipping with the gravedigger, when a key turned hurriedly in the lock and the door clanged open.

It was Brother Simon—he of the gangly, beanpole body—flustered, gesturing haphazardly, arms windmilling, face red, voice burbling, "Brother Charlie, I'm so sorry. You've been left here for a day—"

"A little more." He did not feel very brotherly toward Simon. Instead he felt unusually hostile: not himself at all.

"My deputy, Brother Crispin, was supposed to see to you." Simon claimed that he had been on a twenty-four-hour retreat, compulsory once a month: a long period of silence and contemplation in the chapel of The Holy Name, just outside the monastery walls, up in the southeast corner. "I've just come back and found Crispin isn't well, been in the infirmary since late yesterday. I'm so sorry. . . . I couldn't wait to get you in here, and then I left without . . ."

Charlie did not really believe Brother Simon but was not going to say so just yet.

"What about my request to see the father superior?"

"I told him. Last thing I did."

"And I'm still waiting around in limbo."

"Charlie, what can I say? Will you come to compline?"

"What happens if I say no?"

"I can't make you come. Don't even know if you're a believer."

"What if I do come, but don't want to return to this cell after chapel?"

"Up to you, Brother. All I can tell you is it's more comfortable in the cell, and a shade warmer than the chapel. There's nowhere else you'll get a bed for the night. I'm terribly sorry about what's happened."

"I've been fed regularly, how did they . . . ?"

"You'd be on the list."

"It wasn't very good."

"We're hardly five-star, Brother."

"Hardly two-star."

"You coming to chapel?"

Charlie felt quite dizzy. Bog-eyed, bleary, and unsteady, he was led through the cloisters and into the chapel for compline.

"That meeting with the father superior," he grunted as they neared the chapel doors. "It's important. I really need to talk with him."

"I can't do anything about that now, Brother Charles." Brother Simon sounded truculent, as if apologizing had freed him of any further responsibility.

"Look." Charlie thought of himself as being blocked from the real world. "Tell me, Simon, is the father superior going to see me or not?"

"I'm sorry, Charlie, I just don't know. The father superior doesn't take me into his confidence, Brother." Simon gave him an enigmatic shrug, followed by an exaggerated gesture meant to show him the way through the chapel doors. Simon looked more like an actor playing Walter Raleigh telling the first Queen Elizabeth to use his cloak to keep her feet dry.

"Be it on your own head," Charlie murmured as he passed into the chapel, shaking his head in disbelief. He had already made up his mind how to embarrass everyone and get Father Gregory Scott's attention. Now, inside, he eyed the monks in their long stalls tiered on either side of the chancel. Charlie, and a handful of assorted postulants, sat beneath the tower, in the transept—quite close, close enough to see the snoozing monks, make out their features and identify some of them.

> O Father, that we ask be done
> Through Jesus Christ Thine only Son
> Who with the Holy Ghost and Thee
> Doth live and reign eternally.
> Amen.

The service moved forward; Charlie's eyes roamed around the chapel and he started to think about money. Even in the nineteenth century it would have cost a fortune to build this chapel, let alone the whole monastery. Above the choir was a life-size rood, exquisitely carved and totally realistic. This was not a comfortable re-creation of the crucifixion, but a hard and bloody depiction of a barbarous act, with Jesus' face contorted in agony and his hands and feet hideously mutilated as he dropped in and out of consciousness.

In the half-light of the chapel with its glimmering candlelight, Charlie thought he saw the figures moving around the cross; heard Jesus groan and saw his head lift, then droop to his shoulder. Mentally Charlie shrank back in horror.

In the chancel, behind the altar, great carved and painted panels depicted the birth, death, and resurrection of Christ. Everything here, he thought, was aimed at realism, from the features of the figures to the drops of blood from the crown of thorns. These things were dedicated to hard fact: truth, not fairy stories.

A pretty penny, Charlie reckoned as he peered up at the great vaulted ceiling. Even if the architect and the artists had freely given their time and skills, the overheads had to have been enormous. The quarrying of the stone, the building techniques, the equipment, the builders and skilled craftsmen required, would have been hugely expensive.

He was in awe of the amount of work involved and the beauty of it, the same kind of awe you feel in Westminster Abbey or Notre Dame, in Paris, or the great basilica of St. Peter's, Rome. In the end it all came down to money. This was a big and enduring church, and the monastery would still cost a great deal just to be kept ticking over. Maybe in the nineteenth century things would have been easier, there was money for religion in those days, but now—he asked himself—where does the cash come from? And from where did the other money appear; he thought of the cash Hilary had been depositing at the bank for Gregory Scott. It had to come from somewhere: the smart little oceangoing yacht perhaps? he wondered.

A hundred or so men lived here on this rock: worked, ate, and slept in this place. Even if the monks themselves produced every mouthful of food, the cost of maintenance would be prohibitive. And there would be further costs. Always look at the lifestyle, Charlie had been taught in his other existence. Is there enough money to maintain the lifestyle? If so, for how long?

As the voices swelled around him, he threw back his head and smelled the traces of incense and melted wax and, in the midst of it all, caught sight of Father Benedict's face, flickering ugly in the candle flames, his expression so stern you could use it on a poster to keep law and order.

He had been an unsmiling man back when young Lieutenant Charlie Gauntlet had known him in his earlier incarnation: Corporal Colin Knight of the military police. At that time, he thought, Corporal Knight had all the traits of a stickler for discipline and a firm upholder of military order. Only now could Charlie see how the full man had come to maturity. This lethal, feared military policeman had grown into a fully fledged religious hunter-killer: a rottweiler of heaven. This was not something that Charlie Gauntlet was inclined to dwell on. He had found the military policeman creepy back in the early fifties; the fact of him now, in the present, was horrifying.

The plainchant spiraled down and one of the younger monks began to read the biblical passage chosen for that night:

"And there was war in heaven." He had a flat, somewhat disinterested voice. "And there was war in heaven: Michael and his angels fought against the dragon; and the dragon fought, and his angels, and prevailed not; neither was their place found anymore in heaven. And the great dragon was cast out, that old serpent, called the Devil, and Satan, which deceiveth the whole world: he was cast into the earth, and his angels were cast out with him."

What were people meant to think of that? Charlie wondered. How could they think of it? Even the pope had said we should not picture God as an old man with a long white beard, nor the devil as a scaly creature with horns. Yet how else were ordinary, well-read, educated people to understand? We cannot comprehend endless time and space, so how the divine being, the prime mover of all things, and his adversary, together with their varied armies of angels? Nowadays, people who did not even believe in God seemed to believe in angels: a vast angelic cult was out there in the world, and a large support group willing and able to make hard cash from those believers. No wonder people had relegated God to a character of myth or fairy tale. As these thoughts wandered through Charlie's head, a voice seemed to whisper in his ear, "Man has created God in his own image."

"The blessing of God Almighty, the Father, the Son, and the Holy Spirit, be amongst us and remain with us always." Gregory Scott raised his hand, making the sign of the cross, in time with every other monk in the chapel. Inappropriately, on the movie screen of his mind, Charlie saw Esther Williams and a swash of bathing beauties swimming in unison, to the direction of Busby Berkeley. Now we have the team ritual monks of Ringmarookey, he thought. Heads bent under their cowls—hup-two-three, hup-two-three. The father superior led the monks in procession from the choir stalls toward the nave.

Charlie stepped out directly in front of the father superior, just as he had planned, head tilted, shouting into the monk's face.

"Father Superior, I came here over twenty-four hours ago! I've been kept in a cell with the door locked. I asked to see you as a matter of urgency when I arrived and you haven't responded. I ask you again now, in front of your brethren, and add to this request a note of urgency. Time, Reverend Father, is of the essence." This last was a phrase he had so often used when a legal eagle to that strange world that a once famous spook had called a wilderness of mirrors.

In a collective intake of breath, the younger monks received the shock of this interloper challenging the father superior in their chapel.

Gregory Scott raised his cowled head and looked into Charlie's eyes. When he spoke, it was softly, and so all the more menacing.

"This is God's house, Brother. This is not our way, and time as we know it has little meaning to God. Go and read what has been left in your cell for you." Scott went to move on, but Charlie still blocked his way.

Behind the father superior, Father Benedict made a swift motion with his head and right hand. Two monks stepped from the line, burly bruisers, lifting Charlie into the air, pinning him against a pew.

"Keep quiet and no serious harm'll come to you." The one who spoke had garlic heavy on his breath, while his lips curled in that contemptuous manner beloved of people who physically have an upper hand.

Charlie grunted, tried to heave himself free, and was immersed in agony as the other bouncer got him in a thumb hold.

"Out! Now!" Gregory Scott hissed. "Charles, this is my domain. You do not give me orders. I'll see you when I'm good and ready to see you, and let me add, you are *not* a prisoner. You can leave here whenever you like. The sooner the better."

They dragged Charlie away and he only caught a glimpse of Scott's hard and lined face, dark within the rough material of the cowl, slewed above him at an impossible angle as he was removed from the chapel, dragged along the cloisters, and deposited back in his cell. The pair of monks were efficient and did the job with no further comment, leaving Charlie with the impression that their training had been by someone other than a man under Christian discipline. In the end they dumped him onto the floor of his cell, sprawling him over the stone flags.

The light had been turned on again, and someone else had been in the cell since he'd left for compline. He could scent the man as soon as they left him alone, banging the door closed, leaving a hint of garlic in their wake. In spite of this, Charlie got the scent of another person. Whoever had been there had swapped the red folder of transcriptions for a new smart blue folder. Apart from the exchange there were other tiny indications that a stranger had been present. It was as though the air had been disturbed by the stranger's body, leaving a trace, an invisible molding, and a wake in the cell. Just as the pit viper senses the change in its prey's body temperature, so Charlie's senses tracked an unseen target.

The arrogance of the father superior made him certain that these monks had secrets and strange links with what he could only think of as an illegal part of society. When you boiled it down, it had to be a matter of money. Wasn't that why he'd put a question mark over the presence of the luxury motor yacht? Was the yacht a conduit? Money in by sea and out via a little Cessna piloted by Hilary Cooke with an *e*?

He could still smell the trace of incense in his nostrils, just as he also felt the cold creeping deeply into his bones. He put on the light quilted jacket he had worn since leaving Heathrow, then wrapped the blanket around himself and stretched out on the bed, doubling the pillow against the iron bedhead and opening the new blue folder.

The moment he began reading, Charlie realized that Naomi's narrative had moved to a new, more urgent plane.

Jesus is coming into Jerusalem.

In a few days it will be the feast of the Passover. Romillius, my lord, this is the feast in which my people celebrate their escape from Egypt when the Angel of Death passed over the houses of all Israelites. God punished the Egyptians by causing the death of all firstborn. At that time my people were told to smear blood on their doors so that the Angel of Death would not come near them. Nowadays, families band together and celebrate this by sacrificing a lamb, which they eat, with unleavened bread, wearing the clothes in which they travel. Passover is one of our holiest festivals, very important to us, and for Jesus to show himself is dangerous.

Last night I met the brothers James and John, two of Jesus' followers, and they told me he planned to be in the city. They are both greatly concerned for they fear Jesus' presence is going to put his life in danger. He has already said he will be taken like a common criminal, for he expects to be arrested and killed. He says things must follow their course and the prophecies will be fulfilled.

A strange thing happened before they left me to travel to Bethany where Jesus is staying. "Aren't you the girl who anointed the Master with spikenard?" James asked me. "Yes," I told him. "You saw me. You were there." Then, as they left, he called me Mary. There is some confusion in his mind and I did not dare correct him.

Later, Old Saul, who comes to do heavy work in the house, arrived to see if he could mend the stair to our upper room. He said the whole city is buzzing about the great teacher, Jesus, who is coming soon. "Some were saying that he is the Messiah, the Christ who is come to set us free," he told me.

Charlie turned the page and, unsuspecting, was plunged into a new piece of drama.

Romillius, my lord and master, you have only just left me and I feel dread and fear for I do not understand why you have asked me to repeat everything to Petros: everything you have just told me. The only reason I can think of is that you know, or at least sense, that your life is in danger. When I asked you if this was so, you would not even speak of it. Please, my lord; please understand that I love you with all my heart, so I am greatly afraid for you. But I shall do as you ask, and Petros will write it down.

You came without warning and I had no reason to think you had been anywhere near Jesus. Another centurion had been with me—the tall one with the dark hair and the scar, the one whose mother was born in Britannia, whose parents were of that country. He left only just before and you caught me unaware. You did not want to lie with me. I could see that at once. But I did not expect you to charge me with such a task for the good and safety of Rome. I shall, of course, do what you command, but I plead now that I should be allowed to go to Rome with you, for what I am to do is an honor and also a service to Rome.

I am to leave straight away and go to Bethany where we know the Master, Jesus, is lodged at the house of the widow Martha. Once there, and speaking to him in private, I have to tell him that I am an emissary from the Roman governor Pontius Pilate. Pilate, and the senior officers of the garrison in Jerusalem, are disturbed at the news that Jesus is planning to come into the city for Passover. His Excellency the Governor fears that the religious leaders of the Israelites will attempt to have Jesus arrested to stand trial. Pilate has no wish to harm the Master. He believes the chief priests and the members of the Sanhedrin would be happy to see Jesus executed by the authorities, who would have to take action against him. Pilate has no reason to hurt the Master, so pleads with him now: do not come into Jerusalem at this time. Doing so will only put you in danger.

I leave now, my lord, to carry out this task. May the Lord God watch over us both.

In London, in the Dolphin Square flat, Bex had a second restless night. She could not settle without Charlie, so she made herself a milky drink at bedtime, believing her mother to be right about these things. "A milky drink—Horlicks or Ovaltine—will send you to sleep quicker than any sleeping pill," her mum used to say; just as she also used to say that if you banged your head a set number of times on your pillow you would wake at the same time as the number. It was rubbish, of course, and Bex found that the milky drink was also rubbish—in her case anyway.

As it was, her mum had turned out to be the carrier of erroneous advice in a number of areas. "Nothing good comes of girls who wear black underwear," she had once counseled her daughter, who was willing to prove that excellent and wonderful things did in fact happen to girls who were tarty smart under their frocks.

At two-thirty Bex got up. It had happened in exactly the same way on the previous night. Now it was two-thirty on Sunday morning; she got up, put on her long white robe, the one with the hood that Charlie had so admired. He would quote Christopher Robin at her all the time ("mine has a hood and I lie in bed and pull the hood right over my head"). It was one of Charlie's more endearing traits—quoting from books much loved in childhood. She had bought him a Folio Society copy of *The Wind in the Willows,* for instance, and you'd have thought it was a first edition worth thousands. Then she wondered if she had done the right thing because he quoted from it interminably.

Having got up and swished around the flat in the long robe, she decided to pour herself a stiff, medicinal brandy. She got pissed quickly on brandy, so quite logically she reasoned that it would help her toward temporary oblivion. She looked around for something to occupy her while the alcohol was taking effect, and her eye finally lighted on the stiff envelope full of photographs that Charlie had asked her to send on to him at the monastery. He had even suggested a profligate act—sending them by courier, which would have been hell's expensive. Maybe that should be her line when she greeted him: "You wanted the pictures; well, I've brought them for you." She could do that because nobody there would associate her with the law. Unless, of course, Charlie had been indiscreet, something she thought unlikely.

She slit open the envelope and slid the black-and-white matt prints onto her lap. They were grainy, and not of a high quality, and they were all of similar groups of men draped around each other in various states of what she thought of as camaraderie. A very young Charlie Gauntlet figured in each of them: young, innocent-looking, with a military haircut and in uniform, the single pips of a second lieutenant weighing heavily on his shoulders. In most of the prints he stood next to an older officer, a major, tall, slim, and slightly forbidding: a kind of warning signal in the pix, there for more than a keepsake.

The major was in all the photographs, but most of the other men were different in each picture: picked and mixed, except for a couple of tough guys in uniform, big fellows, tall and muscular: the kind of men who would have drowned cats and pulled the wings off flies. They were policemen: military policemen wearing the white, blancoed gaiters, belts and sidearm holsters with lanyards snaking from pistol butts to necks, their stiff-peaked caps square on the head, braided with crimson bands. Both were corporals and looked right bastards, and in some of the photographs they obviously posed with their charges: threadbare men and women who forced themselves to look happy

263

with unspecified smiles and hard grins. Strangely, it was like looking at contemporary photos of the more dangerous parts of Europe.

She remembered a quotation she had read in one of the Sunday newspaper supplements: "A photograph is a secret about a secret. The more it tells you, the less you know." When she had time on Sundays, Bex would assiduously read the newspapers. She saw it as a means to further education.

In two of the prints the same young woman stood between Charlie and the major: a thin, ferrety woman in an insubstantial gray dress with an old coat thrown around her shoulders. The coat, Bex thought, was there in an attempt to appear racy and sophisticated, but her eyes looked into the camera lens with a terrible used stare, giving a sense of desperate entrapment. "Lord," Bex thought, "Lord, I hope that wasn't on account of Charlie." You could see from the way she held herself, and the blankness of her expression, that this girl's life and experience was channeled into pleasing males. Bex could immediately tell that the thin woman was opening her legs regularly for her guards. "I wonder," she thought. "I wonder if Charlie . . . ?"

Bex looked at the pictures for a long time. This was the Charlie of the early 1950s; Charlie doing his National Service; going through the motions of being a soldier. He had never talked to her about that period of his life, except to say that he had done one year at Cambridge and was then forced to do military service before returning to his beloved law.

Suddenly, Bex realized that she was starting to droop over the prints, that sleep was coming quickly, so she shuffled back to the bedroom, threw off the robe, and climbed between the sheets, dropping sweetly into the healing balm of oblivion.

Only to be shaken roughly awake by the clamor of the telephone. As she reached out dopily for it, she saw the luminous dial of her watch, telling her it was a little after four-thirty in the wee smalls. Who the hell . . . ? she wondered.

It was Patsy Wright, wide-awake and worried. "We're going up to Ringmarookey as soon as they can file a flight plan. Our man on the island has just sent up a distress rocket. I'll be outside in fifteen minutes."

CHAPTER 18

My lord Romillius, I have seen Jesus and bring his reply to you so that you can give it to the governor, Pilate. My news is not good and I fear greatly for Jesus—for his life and the lives of all who follow him. Not only have I carried out your commands, but also I have done them in the manner in which you instructed. I believe you would have been pleased.

Neat little, sharp as a glass shard Charlie Gauntlet read on, experiencing a slight shudder, which he put down to the coldness of the monastic cell. In reality he knew it was about sharing: on the brink of staking claim in some extraordinary plot far outside the biblical framework with which he was familiar.

When I arrived in Bethany, I sought out the house where Jesus is lodging. His needs are being cared for by two sisters, Martha and Mary, who quarrel endlessly. Martha is tall and thin with huge energy and a wart on her chin. She complains that Mary lets her do all the cooking and work in the kitchen. Mary is small and stout, smiles constantly, and lets Martha's complaints slide off her like water from a fish.

When I got to the house, I was told that Jesus was out teaching, leading the people in prayer and healing in an open place a little beyond the town. When I said I carried a special message for the Master, the serving woman, who was called Susanna, asked me to come in and gave me some cold meat, bread, and a cup of wine, for I was tired and hungry after the journey.

Susanna talked most freely of Jesus and his followers, and I—

remembering how you had counseled me—gave nothing away, but rather encouraged her to speak. I fear that when the others are here in the house, which is large, she gets little opportunity to talk—she makes up for it now. She says that Jesus is usually out and about from early in the morning until late in the afternoon, and I can see why, for the town appears to be bursting with people who have followed him here. The streets are crowded, there is no place at the one inn, and people are making money from letting out their rooms to travelers. They do a brisk trade.

I saw many in the streets who were obviously sick, crippled, or maimed, brought here especially to see Jesus. Blind people are led about by friends or relatives, and a great sense of happiness is among the crowds: they are excited and at the same time respectful.

Susanna told me several stories of how Jesus has healed the sick. She has seen it with her own eyes, and I believe her, for she is an ordinary woman who has not the wit to invent some of the stories. She has watched the lame throw away their crutches and walk again; watched Jesus make the blind see, restore hearing to the deaf, and in one case, she has heard a dumb man speak again. As I say, I believe her because I have seen wonders myself, but also there seem to be many others whom he has not healed. She gives details, which she could only know if she was present. For instance, he said to one, "Take up your bed and walk." This man had not walked for several years, yet he did so when Jesus commanded it. Then a man whose sight was returned to him said he could see men like trees walking.

Just outside the house there were thirty or forty people waiting. Some were blind, and four or five were too sick to stand, so their beds were litters on the ground, close to the door. I should report to you that these same people who were outside when I arrived were still there when I left. So, if Jesus is the Messiah, the Christ, God come down to make himself known to us, then he does not heal *all* people. Some are left by the wayside of life, not healed, not brought out of sin and into life eternal. It would seem that the just and the unjust are treated in an indiscriminate fashion, the reason for which is known only to God.

Can one believe this? Charlie wanted to write in the margin. In a universe that produces so many interlocking wonders, can we believe in a God who visits random good and evil on his creations? Can we believe in a God at all? A picture of magnified snowflakes came into his head, then the horror of his mother dying of cancer, diagnosed one September and killing within three months. The long hours of agony, the mind fuddled with drugs. Again in his head he saw film footage of bodies, the western front during World War I; then the Kosovan and Bosnian refugees from the end of the last century; and a voice whispered in his ear, "Free will. That's the reason. God gave man free will and it is man's inhumanity to his own that brings the hell." Charlie knew this was some university argument from his past, and he went back, uneasy, to reading Naomi's narrative, which continued dramatically.

Romillius, the other thing you should know is that Jesus continues to upset many people. In particular he is making enemies among other teachers of our faith: arguing with the priests and holy men, belittling them. He has especially angered the Pharisees, who put a reliance in the Holy Law of our people and preach the strict way of life and obedience, almost to the exclusion of everything else. Also he has many enemies in their rival party, the Sadducees. Wise and learned men from both factions have tried to trick him with ingenious questions, for these men are experts in argument when it comes to the holy books. In particular the Law. Yet Jesus has been able to beat their contentiousness.

Strangely, the Pharisees and the Sadducees are normally at each other's throat in argument, but they seem to be united in their attacks upon Jesus. I know this is all true, about the enemies, because you may remember the odious Thomas who was steward to Caiaphas the High Priest and became one of my clients. Well, that Thomas told me Caiaphas was forever trying to find ways to entrap Jesus, for he, with the other priests and members of the Sanhedrin, believed that Jesus was guilty of blasphemy and also questioned further teachings, causing many arguments and fighting among those at the heart of our religion. So, you must tell Pilate that these men are really dangerous and not to be trusted. They will stop at nothing to have Jesus arrested and punished.

Susanna was telling me more of Jesus' teaching when he returned with three of his closest followers: Simon, Barnabas, and a man I had not seen before called Judas, who comes from a southern village, Kerioth. This last is very pleasant, laughing and joking all the time. Even Jesus laughed heartily at his jokes, then Jesus was called away to talk with Martha, who had also arrived back, in some turmoil, with her sister.

The thing I notice most is the happiness. Everyone near the Master has a smile, and there is laughter everywhere, real laughter from the belly: nobody looks gloomy, sad, or serious, except when they talk of Jesus' future.

Later Judas began to ask me about the Roman garrison, plying me with questions about the way order is kept in Jerusalem, the names of the officers, and the disposition of the nightly watch. At first I did not know how he expected me to be familiar with these matters, but soon it became clear that he knew who I was, how I earned my living, and that my money comes usually from officers of the Roman garrison. Then he began to stand a little too close to me, making remarks that could only have one interpretation, and I became greatly embarrassed by him. He is not the first follower of Jesus who has displayed a little lust, and I don't suppose he will be the last. My kind always sets them off, and I wish I could find some other life. It is humiliating how often they treat me with contempt when others are near, yet when they are alone with me, things change. In this case it is a pity, because Judas seems a nice and good man. In the end I had to ask Simon if I could speak alone with the Master. This was arranged and I was taken to him so that eventually I gave him your message as though it came directly from Pontius Pilate.

At first I thought he was angry with me, but then he smiled

and placed a hand on my shoulder. "Naomi," he said quietly. "Naomi, I have to do my Father's work. You know this. You have heard my teaching. It is necessary for me to go to Jerusalem at this time. Please understand this. I *must* go so that the ancient prophecies can be fulfilled: all this is necessary. At Passover there must be a sacrifice."

I said that everyone was afraid for him. He said he understood and repeated that it was his obligation. "If you believe in me, there is no need to fear for me. I have told you already that to believe in me and follow my way will never be easy. I shall always be with you, though not as you see me now, and I shall give you strength to experience all the bad things that will happen to you because you believe in me. Believing in me, and following the path that I signpost for you, will be the most difficult part of your life."

Then something strange happened. He asked me if I knew of any large room in which he and his closest disciples could hold the Passover meal, which of course also requires some preparation. Without thinking I said they could use the upstairs room in my house, so he asked how he could get in touch with me.

By this time I was embarrassed again. I am overflowing with sin and this is a holy man. To be in his presence is difficult for me; I stand next to him and feel like a diseased woman nudging close to a healthy person. I am afraid that I will pass on my evil, the root of my sins. He cannot hold Passover in my house, Romillius, he cannot. It would not be right and it can only bring shame upon him, but I was too confused and perturbed to say anything. I simply told him about Old Saul, who can always be found near the Damascus Gate early in the morning. "If you give a message to Old Saul, he will bring you to my house, and I shall make all things ready for you," I said.

I must now speak to Old Saul and instruct him to turn away Jesus, or any of his followers. It would be a terrible scandal if he came to my house. If he did, and if it were known, then the disagreements he has with the Pharisees and Sadducees would be multiplied by hundreds.

I became so upset by what he was asking that I began to weep, and he tried to comfort me so that I blurted out what was troubling me. "My whole life is founded upon the sins of the flesh, Master. I would like to follow your way and spend my time according to the Commandments and the Law of God, but if I try to do that, how can I live? It is sin that puts bread in my mouth and clothes on my back."

He told me what he always says. "Go, and try not to commit the same sin again." I repeated what I had already told him. "Lord, I shall have no bread for my mouth and no clothes for my body if I cease to commit these sins."

All he did was repeat what he had already counseled me. "If you trust in God, he will provide for you," he said. Then Martha came bustling into the room and he was dragged away to adjudicate between her and her sister yet again. There was nothing else left for me but to return to Jerusalem.

As I was leaving the house, Simon Peter called me back and asked what I had been saying to the Master. I told him and he shook his head. "We are in turmoil, Naomi. Jesus is convinced that he must be in Jerusalem for Passover, but we think it is most dangerous." He looked at me long and hard. "Yet there is one way in which he could be kept safe."

I wanted him to instruct me in this one way and I said so. Then Simon Peter took me by the arm and drew me outside the house and to the rear, where we sought shade under a tree from the afternoon heat.

"There is a man named Joseph who comes from the city of Arimathea and who, in secret, has been a disciple of Jesus'."

I did not know where Simon was leading me, so I asked what was wanted of this man, Joseph. He told me that Joseph was close to members of a sect of our religion called the Essenes.

Now, these Essenes separate themselves from the world. They live together as groups, and their lives are dedicated to the Law of God, to prayer, and to healing. They are strict with themselves and each other, but they carry with them an abundance of love. These things Simon Peter knew and told me. He says that the

Essenes live and judge each other only on their love one for another. They grow what is needed in the way of food and keep animals for the benefit of the group as a whole. Simon Peter asks that you, Centurion Romillius, go and look for Joseph of Arimathea, and when you have found him, you must ask if he will go to a community of Essenes and plead with them to take and hide Jesus among their people if this is needed.

(So, Charlie thought, Joseph of Arimathea: that sudden, unexpected figure who appears in the Christian Gospels as the man who offers to bury Jesus in a tomb already prepared for himself, is now being linked to the Essenes in some grand plot.

Ideal people, the Essenes, sort of a Jewish monastic order, except the sexes were not segregated. There were several communities around Palestine at the time of Christ, including one near the Dead Sea, close to where the famous Dead Sea scrolls were discovered. Charlie knew this because he had read an article on the Essenes. Very well read, Charlie Gauntlet. He did not know everything about Joseph of Arimathea of course, but who does? Even Christians who have read of him in the Bible sometimes do not know what significance is attached to Joseph's offer to take charge of Jesus' body after the crucifixion. The burial was not an easy business, for it was almost Passover and the Jewish laws concerning dead bodies were explicit; and yet Joseph did what was necessary. More, he had carefully prepared a tomb against his own death, and this he gave freely and used for the body of Christ.

Charlie probably didn't know the rest—didn't know that all four Gospels tell of this secret disciple, and how later writings put him close to the Virgin Mary at the time of the Ascension. They also finger Joseph of Arimathea as the patron of the English holy site of Glastonbury, where Joseph's staff is said to be the root for a sacred thornbush, thrusting this good, righteous, and rich disciple into the heart of the Grail legend.)

Go at once, my lord. Do not delay, for he is coming into the city as soon as the Sabbath is over. I pray you to have this man

Joseph meet Simon Peter as soon as Jesus is within the city walls. Who knows what will happen when he arrives? I hope fervently that one of these groups of Essenes will protect him should it be necessary.

They came for Charlie at around three in the morning, the same couple of bruisers who had brought him back from the chapel. He was dozing uneasily, for the latest developments in Naomi's tale had left him in a dubious, indecisive mood, as though he were on the brink of some world-shattering discovery, which in a way he was.

Fuddled with sleep, and bewildered by the cold, he was totally unprepared for the pair of religious bouncers. They hoisted him up, screwing one arm behind his back, causing a burst of pain that took him back to the viciousness of childhood bullying. This had been a favorite tormentor's trick, hands around the wrist, then the arm pushed behind, high up the back so that you did anything asked of you and went anywhere you were told to go. Later, this would be incorporated with the "Chinese burn," a twisting of the wrist skin in two different directions. "We'll give you a Chinese burn and a penny stamp" were words that had filled the nine-year-old Charlie Gauntlet with dread. The "penny stamp" was a crushing boot to the foot.

As he was frog-marched along the cloisters, Charlie Gauntlet felt faintly ridiculous. You could never call Charles an ostentatious person, yet his height and build made him prone to pomposity, and as they took him wordlessly toward the father superior's study, he forced down half-formed pompous remonstrations until he began to wonder at the idiocy of the situation.

Violence had never been part of Charlie's makeup, for he had never been pushed into using force, nor did his work call for it. Yes, at times during interrogations, a subject had become physically out of control, but at those moments someone else had always been able to assist. The same was true on the rare occasions when he had been forced out of the office and into the field—or into those shrinking parts of the world that were regarded as the field. In his last decade of employment by the Foreign Service, Charlie had made four trips to Belfast, six to Paris, and two each to Hong Kong and KL. The glamorous world of foreign travel had not been loaded in his favor, and he rarely enjoyed those times, for they were always hedged about with sly little routines that kept everyone on their toes. Physical violence had never been his style, but he knew all the details, could have recited every move in his sleep. Some people got a charge from the danger and violence. Not Charlie. If anything, he was built in the opposite mold.

The bellicose monks, still smelling strongly of garlic, finally reached the father superior's study door, and Charlie was aware that they did not even pause to knock. One of them opened up while the other gave him a quick push that took him, on his knees, to the floor directly in front of Father Gregory Scott's desk. He heard the door close firmly behind him as he slowly got to his feet, dusting off his knees as he did so.

"Ah, Charles." The father superior leaned over the desk, spectacles perched on his nose and a wolfish smile almost transforming the thin face. Gauntlet remembered him as he used to be and thought, Where be thy gibes now?

"Charles, I'm sorry. The boys . . ." Scott let his reedy voice trail off, coughed, then recovered. "How shall I put it? Get a little out of hand is a bit of a cliché."

"But that's exactly what they do."

"Yes, get a little out of hand. Muscular Christians taken to extremes. The novice master calls them Friar Bacon and Friar Bungay—from the play, you know. Charles, I'm sorry. You were left in your cell. It was an accident, I've only just been given the facts."

"How very embarrassing for you." Charlie continued to brush dust from his knees. He did not believe Gregory Scott for one moment. "And how damned inelegant of me."

"Charles, what appears to be the real problem?" Father Gregory Scott's eyebrows lifted into a questioning curve. "You were very steamed up in chapel. So, what's wrong? What's important?"

"I don't like being locked up, for a start."

"Family rule, Charles. Family rule got out of hand."

"Only when you choose it, I think."

"Maybe, but I do assure you it's for your own good."

"And then there's the case of your Father Martin."

"An old man."

"Not this one. This Father Martin's a big, bearded bastard with a hooked hooter. Old friend, old colleague of ours, I think. But you must know that he walked into the hospital in Glasgow and threatened your friend Hilary Cooke."

"Ah, no. No, I didn't know that."

"Ah, indeed, Reverend Father. This Father Martin wanted documents he thought you'd entrusted to our female Biggles." Countless generations of English schoolboys have been stirred by the adventures of the intrepid fictional aviator Biggles.

Gregory Scott gave a nervous little laugh. "That's good, female Biggles."

"It's not all *that* good, Gregory. But I do believe I deserve some answers."

"Such as?"

"Nearly fifty years on I find you still flanked by two of the military-police corporals who ran errands for you in Germany when we were sorting out the sheep from the goats. That's too much of a coincidence. And where's Kit Palfrey, by the way?"

"Ah, you've missed him. He's here, Charles. He's fine. Tucked up in his cell with a bottle of single malt."

"I thought the Russians had sorted out his problem with the demon drink."

The smile again, giving a flash of yellowing teeth. "They had. We introduced him to his old friends again."

"Isn't that against the rules?"

"Technically, yes. 'Look not upon the wine when it is red, when it giveth his color in the cup. For at the last it biteth like a serpent, and stingeth like an adder.' Poor Kit, it was certainly stinging him like a dozen adders when I last saw him."

They were both silent for nearly a whole minute, as if they were silently circling each other, waiting for the grappling moment. Finally, Charlie broke the silence, like smashing through a mirror. "Pinball Wizard" flashed through his head.

"Gregory, what happened to Sergeant Hammer? Hammer of the North, what happened?"

"You know what happened. He died. It was a long time ago, Charlie."

"I came in and he was on the floor of your office, Gregory. Sergeant Hammer was on the floor. You were standing over him, and one of your precious corporals was looking on. What happened, Gregory?"

"He had a heart attack. But you knew that at the time. There was an argument and he died suddenly. Unexpected. That's what the doctors said after the autopsy; it's what the inquest—"

"Yes, but was it the truth, Gregory? Is that what really happened? He was messing with the woman Sissel, wasn't he, Color Sergeant Hammer?"

"So?"

"Sissel was yours, Gregory. We all knew that. He poked his nose in—and more than his nose—"

Gregory Scott made a disgusted noise and turned his head away.

"—poked his nose in and got his comeuppance, yes?"

"It's a long time ago, Charlie. Sleeping dogs."

"Yes, it's a long time ago." A pause. "But it's all really about dosh, isn't it, Gregory?"

"Dosh?" Quizzical.

"Dosh, spondulicks, greenbacks: folding or in coin. That's what it's about, isn't it?"

Gregory Scott looked down into Charlie's eyes, locking with him, like enemy radar lighting him up, he thought. Then the old, scholarly monk gave a small nod and puffed his lips, as though playing some imaginary wind instrument. "Isn't everything?" he asked quietly. "Isn't everything about money?"

"Hardly. You've become a man of God, Gregory, so you should be apart from such things."

"What a pity we parted company when you went home for demob, Charles. You could've kept abreast of the times. You have no idea about how I came to this place, what route I took to God and Calvary. Nor, come to that, the path trodden by our old comrades-in-arms, Corporals Knight and Day—sorry, I should say Dayosolavek. You knew that?"

"Of course."

"You knew that remained his real name? Never changed: Beridi Dayosolavek?"

"Really, is that pertinent?"

"Very, Charles. You see—and you'll find this difficult—I have little or no control over Father Beridi Dayosolavek OSJ, and even less over Father Benedict, our novice master, onetime Corporal Knight."

"You expect me . . . ?"

"To believe this? Yes. That way lies your salvation, Charlie Gauntlet. That way and a careful study of Naomi's recorded words. They're relevant, and I need to know what this Father Martin did to Hilary."

"Nothing as yet."

"He asked for . . ."

"The documents she was carrying for you."

The priest nodded. "She give them to him?"

"No, but we took a look at them together."

"I see. Then you know . . ." Scott seemed to change his mind, shook his head as though trying to rid himself of some insect that had entangled itself in his thin hair. "Charles, the man who calls himself Father Benedict is, I suspect, on his way here now. You should know that neither he nor the man who posed as Father Martin in Glasgow have ever been near a seminary, let alone a bishop to ordain them." The old lupine grin, and now Charlie could see it was really a somewhat frightened smile, and the eyes were less hostile; more perturbed. Gregory Scott looked away suddenly, as though he could not meet Charlie's eyes.

"Charles," he said, dropping his voice low, almost a whisper. "Charles, I'm only alive by the grace of our two old comrades. This is a dangerous place for you to be; but as you're here, I really think you should confine yourself to reading the translations made by the good Fathers Hugh and Harry." Scott stopped abruptly as his door slashed open.

"Talking about me behind my back?" The malignant shape of Father Benedict stepped from the darkness outside, the two muscular monks hovering in his wake.

CHAPTER 19

Ronnie Richardson and Tessa Murray traveled from Paris to London by Eurostar under impeccable French passports. They spoke French to each other and appeared to understand only minimal English. Early in their relationship Ronnie had made Tessa learn French by giving her a Linguaphone course. He then brought her to Paris and sat her down for five weeks, surrounded by native Parisians, so that she could learn the accent. Now, years later, people born and bred in the City of Lights would have great difficulty distinguishing Claude and Therese Fernet from the real thing. Alone, they referred to themselves as "the Fernet-Brancas" after the unpalatable French drink alleged to be an infallible hangover cure.

They were skillfully disguised, though not with false beards and hairpieces. Tessa's hair was heavily grayed, pulled back from her face and tied severely in a bun. This device added a good ten years to her age. She wore a ludicrously short leather skirt and impossibly high heels, heavy eye shadow and thick blusher, giving herself an almost bizarre appearance. She was also slightly plump around the midriff—wearing a padded undergarment Ronnie had made for her three years before. The transformation was wonderful. Old friends could walk past her without a sign of recognition. On one occasion, when trying out the disguise in London during the previous year, an acquaintance had recognized her, then, on coming closer, was covered with embarrassment, apologizing and saying that she looked "just like an old school friend, but now I can see you're much older." Then, the woman had realized she had made a dreadful gaffe and went away even more confused.

Ronnie Richardson used a special comb to thin his hair, which he also touched up with gray. He did not wear spectacles, but had inserted colored contact lenses, which made his eyes a startling light gray. Ronnie was a great believer in altering your appearance by drawing attention to a new person. To the change in hair and eye color he added a third feature, becoming a cripple, complete with wheelchair and frayed temper. Years before, he had been confined to a wheelchair for some weeks after breaking both feet—he had fallen from a third-story window and landed square on his heels (did he fall or was he pushed?). Like all men who have been wheelchair-bound, he soon found that unless you assert yourself, you are treated like someone who is mentally handicapped.

So, they changed from being a forty-something couple to a pair set firmly in late middle age, cantankerous and unattractive with few redeeming features. Within an hour of their arrival at Waterloo train station, they were swallowed up, becoming two entirely different people.

They switched cabs three times before dropping off at Ronnie's flat halfway up New Cavendish Street, where they transformed themselves into what Richardson described as a pair of sad old sheep: Martin and Molly Meadows, whom you could hardly detect with a fine pair of binoculars, and certainly not with your eyes. Their documents were American, as were their voices: New York nasal and proud of it. By teatime they had booked into the Ritz, where they became immediately invisible: gray people in forgettable clothes; people who had difficulty in catching a waiter's eye, which is quite a trick at the Ritz, where they provide an ever-ready service.

"Only for a couple of days," Ronnie promised, for to tell the truth Molly Meadows was not Tessa's favorite character. "Get the lie of the land; decide on the plan, then we'll move on." He ordered champagne and smoked salmon from room service. They were both terrible smoked-salmon addicts. "Could live on this," Tessa said with a cat's purring smile, settling in to enjoy the adventure. Odd how she had also started to delight in the planning, the setting up for the killing. There in the Ritz watching Ronnie doing the organization, she was stuck with the enormity of it all. She, Theresa Mary Murray, was as guilty as a murderer because she reveled in the act.

They stayed in their suite while Ronnie worked the phones, calling contacts who knew him as Martin Meadows, international reporter, newspaper and TV station owner. Ronnie Richardson had been meticulous in building up connections in various parts of the media and elsewhere. Under several false names and occupations he had constructed lists of some complexity, for he had separate inventories for each alias in every European capital, plus New York, Miami, Chicago, and L.A.

One of Richardson's obsessions was the constant refurbishment of his many pseudonyms and each of their circles of associates. This was the part he enjoyed most of all: the duplicity, the organization of his hidden lives. His contacts ran from the print media to police, doctors, and professional people of all kinds; even providers of macabre and unique services. He had spent years building this strange and devious network, which was so intricate that he had to keep records of which character was known to which reporter, cop, or fixer in any given city. This data was constantly updated, hedged about with secret passwords and keystrokes on his powerful Macintosh G4 computer.

The last thing he had done as they prepared to leave the Villa Myrte was transfer all this information from his desktop to a Palm III PDA no larger that a packet of cigarettes, after which he erased the Power PC's hard drive and used a program he had written himself to scramble any traces on the drive. Even the most wired computer expert could not resurrect what had once been there as it was constantly being overwritten, again and again, by the Book of Revelation, which filled the drive to overflowing. Within five minutes the ten-gigabyte hard drive had been overwritten seven times.

Now, in the security of their suite at the Ritz, he pulled up on his Palm III the lists connected to Martin Meadows under London and was, seconds later, speaking to the producer of a respected BBC current-affairs program.

"Hi, Barry, Martin Meadows here. I'm in London for a few days. You got a list of the Bortunins' photo ops for this visit next week? I need to be clued in. . . . Yes, I know you can't let it out of your sight, Barry. I'd just like the salient times and places. . . . Well, give them to me now, I have a pen hovering over a notepad as we speak, so be a good fellow.... Yes, okay.... Right." This was strictly against all rules of procedure at the Beeb, and Barry would have been horrified had he known to what use the information was being put. In the space of half an hour Ronnie made three such calls and filched various parts of the schedule for the Russian president's visit to London. Later in the week, when they checked out of the Ritz and moved to a large hotel off Piccadilly Circus, Ronnie carried a complete itinerary for the president's visit. He knew where the presidential group would be, and at what time, for the entire four days due to begin on Monday.

It was now even easier to get lost because the staff at reception here, in the Regent Palace, were constantly changing and nobody took any notice of who came and went in the huge beehive of a place.

By this time, of course, the overstretched Security Service and the Metropolitan police were on the lookout for someone all right, two people, in fact: a man and a woman answering to the descriptions of Ronnie Richardson and Tessa Murray, who by now looked nothing like themselves. They even passed less than four feet from a pair of Security Service watchers who were combing the larger hotels, taking quick shuftis at guest lists in an attempt to spot any possibles. The woman of this pair actually looked up and into Ronnie's eyes, then looked away without a flicker of interest. This was not her fault: she was well trained, but you couldn't expect miracles. The way Ronnie looked to her in that hotel foyer bore little relation to the way he was reported to look in the official description and artist's reconstruction. It is a large place, the Regent Palace, so large that it even has a special chute down which the body of any unfortunate guest who dies in the hotel can be quietly taken away, far from prying eyes.

That evening Ronnie explained to Tessa, in outline, exactly how he intended to take the lives of President and Madame Bortunin. If it was to be done properly, much had to be accomplished before Monday, when the Russian delegation flew in to Heathrow. Talking about the fine details of his plan aroused Ronnie. Tessa had noticed this before and knew what to expect, for he always became sexually stimulated when discussing a meticulously detailed plot. So she took him in her hand, then her mouth, and then into her body, with her clothes draped around the room following Ronnie and Tessa's inventive sexual ritual, which involved the furious ripping off of clothes—in particular the pretty filmy silk underclothes she had worn. Sometimes it seemed that Ronnie and Tessa took more pleasure in the preliminaries and the foreplay than the final plunging and lunging of their bodies.

When they reluctantly broke apart, enraptured by each other, it was like coming up through deep water and breathing hard on reaching the surface, gulping in great lungfuls of sweet air.

"This time next week it'll all be over," he whispered.

"You promise?"

"I promise it'll all be over." Another long drag of air. "I'd better call Dublin."

But when he did, there was no reply. He did not worry about it. Jimmy Maclean was often out of the office on Saturdays, not always, but around one Saturday in four. He would not bother Jimmy at home, he decided, he would get him sometime on Monday.

Alchemist should have been concerned because things were far from well in Dublin.

In the early part of that first decade of the new millennium, people went to elaborate lengths to keep secrets. The secrets themselves were becoming rarer and rarer each year. Anyone with a secret to guard was fearful of being taken by those in opposition. This was true in many walks of life, from politics to crime. Methods of interrogation had become so sophisticated that only those at the heart of the secret-breaking business—in the security and intelligence areas—knew how to separate truth from fiction.

Alchemist had been exceptionally careful in guarding himself with an invisible network of steel. He had remained hidden for a long time. Now, because of the stupid, undisciplined act of a minion, his flank had been exposed. First Tessa had been identified. Then, because of solid groundwork, Jimmy Maclean had been fingered.

True, Bex Olesker had lost Tessa in Dublin, but Bex, in turn, was surrounded by others who, like pilot fish, had swum ahead of and behind her. The result was that before Tessa reached the muddy and battered Rover in St. Stephen's Green, two image-stealers obtained a series of photographs that identified Maclean. Bex and the watchers who moved around her were not intercognizant. They had been so compartmentalized that one would not recognize another.

So, on this Friday afternoon, the tall man with the fine brown frame met in Dublin Castle with a fairly senior officer of the Garda Síochána—the Republic's police force. His voice was cultured, dark and brown, with an accent to die for: cut glass, the finest, with polished vowels and consonants that regularly hit middle C.

"I wanted to make sure," he said to the Garda man who would not look him in the eyes.

The Garda officer muttered, "There'll be all hell to pay if he's not your man."

"Oh, he's our man all right, you can be certain sure of it. We know. Could take him on other charges now, but we'd like to save a possible bloodbath. Nobody'll know. You don't have to do anything. Just keep out of the way. Don't draw attention to him being missing if anyone calls it in. Just stop it dead because he'll be back home before Monday."

The name of the man with the dark brown voice was Rupert Alexander, and he came from a wealthy family that had originated in Senegal. He was the eldest and they sent him to the U.K., packed him off to Eton, then Oxford. There was plenty of money and they said he would never go short, but he lived on the accent and the education. When the money ran out, he still had the education and the presence. He was the jewel in his family's crown, and the beautiful speaking voice was like rich honey studded with rubies. "Once it's been done, the Met'll request him to be held, I should imagine," Rupert Alexander said.

"What do I have to do, then?" the Garda man asked.

"I've told you, Kevin, not a thing." Rupert gave his all-singing, all-dancing, and all-twinkling smile—in glorious Technicolor. "Not a thing. Just stay in your office and respond to nothing: don't answer the phone; don't acknowledge anything. We'll take care of it."

And they did; Rupert and five of the boys spread themselves across two cars. They picked up Jimmy Maclean in the little hallway of his nice suite of offices in Fitzwilliam Square, and they did it so professionally that it was beautiful to behold. Jimmy wasn't at all happy about it, mind. To be honest, he had more than a sneaking suspicion that these people were Brit Security Service having an illegal fling in Dublin, but it all happened quickly, and in truth, it scared the living shit out of him.

"What the hell *is* all this?" he asked nobody in particular and rather loudly. He was angry, but they overpowered him with incredible speed. They knew it had to be fast, because he was a brave little bugger and would not be averse to shouting and hollering in the street, so they got him into the car kicking and shrieking, yet nobody peeped; nobody was alerted.

Mickey Herring drove the first car and he put his foot down, quick and hard, just as Rupert threw the bag over Maclean's head and jabbed the needle into his arm. Little Jimmy Maclean, smart as a whip and cocky as a jockey on a winner, just crumpled up and went to sleep.

"Head over to Dun Laoghaire, yes?" Mickey asked, his voice little more than a whisper. Rupert had given them only a sketchy picture of what was to be done and where they would do it.

"There's a house up in York Road," Rupert told him, softly saying the number. "About halfway up on the left, opposite the Christian Brothers. That should do the trick. You can get right up close to the front door, and we'll help him in. But be quiet about it."

Later Rupert said there would be two nurses waiting. "Two nurses and a nice doctor who's come all the way from Bristol. Lovely woman, does it a treat, this kind of thing. Poor old Jimmy'll never know what's hit him; never remember what's gone on. And we'll have the whole weekend, but it'll be done by tomorrow night."

"Know it all by then, yes?" Mickey asked.

"Everything," Fatty Brimstone cooed.

"Every last detail," Rupert assured them.

The doctor was called Pinhorn. Dr. Emma Pinhorn, and she came from a village just outside Bristol, quite near Cheddar as it happened. Knew her stuff did Emma Pinhorn, had done all the courses and was well up on all the drugs. Knew her Temazepam from her Mogadon and could use chloral hydrate and all the others; knew the dosages and exactly how much would send a person out for how long. She would look at a man or woman and could judge the right amount like an old professional hangman could work out the required length of the drop.

They put Jimmy to bed: strapped him down; put warm hot-water bottles by his feet; soft pillows; every convenience. On the stereo they had Heinichen's Dresden concertos playing softly: oboe, violin, and flute. It was important to play music that was possibly just out of the subject's intellectual range. Julie, the big-boned country girl, made sure he was strapped down and could not move, wouldn't want to anyway; while small, silver-tongued Kate directed her smile at his face, so that would be the first thing he'd see when he woke up.

He just about saw her. Didn't even feel the needle for the second lot; then the third. Came round and went off again, borne along magic floating stairways by loving and invisible hands. When he finally woke, at eight o'clock on the Saturday evening, it was with this same half-peaceful, floating sensation, struggling up into the air thick around him and the angelic face smiling at him.

From behind the face a sweet voice told him, "Jimmy, this is terrible important. Tessa's forgotten the instructions. Who's the target, Jimmy? Who's the bull's-eye?"

Silly girl, he thought. She knew damned well it was the Bortunins: president of the Russian Federation and his wife. Both of them. But he wouldn't tell anyone. Not Jimmy Maclean. Jimmy was silent as the grave. He did not know that he'd spoken the words out loud, slurring them in his deep-drugged half-sleep.

He didn't hear the intake of breath from Rupert Alexander; only the voice, soft and comfortable. "And who's paying?" the silver tongue asked him. "Who's paying for the snuff then?"

Ha, he thought. No way would I mention it to anybody, but this is a dream, isn't it? Sons and Daughters of October. Nasty little monkey called Chermyet, Illych Antonovich Chermyet. Pudgy, sweaty little bastard.

"Go back to sleep, Jimmy darling." Little Kate looked at Rupert and grinned while Emma Pinhorn nodded.

It was so easy when you had the right stuff and the right people.

Within seconds, Rupert was in the next room. He did a little caper and punched air. "Yessss! Yessss!" Then he was on the scrambler to

London. "I wouldn't be surprised if they wanted to call it off," he said before he told them. Then he laid the news on his boss.

"They won't call it off," his boss said. "This is our big chance to catch Alchemist in flagrante. For God's sake put Maclean back exactly as you found him. We don't want him tumbling to it."

"Don't worry. Only the best, and I believe we have some special new wake-up juice. The Yard'll want to request his immediate arrest and presence in the U.K., and I'd rather not prolong it. He'll fight it like buggery. But we don't need him anymore. We've got what we want. Breakthrough time now we know who and who's paying." Rupert broke his golden rule and swore aloud on the phone. He never swore aloud when his boss was on the line, but he did now. "Shit," he said with pleasure. "Bastard obviously thinks it's romantic: lives for cash. It's about as romantic as syphilis, and you can get it a bloody sight cheaper in Chechnya, Kosovo, or Sarajevo. I'd bet this scumbag's making millions."

"Sure," his boss muttered. "Sure you can pick up a killer for a song in Sarajevo or in Chechnya, but not with this style and the Shakespearean quotations."

In London, Rupert's boss put down her telephone.

And in London they fed the name into one of the magic machines: Chermyet, Illych Antonovich. The machine thought about it for a couple of human heartbeats, then spat it all out. Chermyet was known both at Thames House and Vauxhall Bridge Cross. Calls went nipping across the river, and then Chermyet's name was flashed into embassies and legations all over the place. Marked man, Chermyet. Marked with a cross of blood.

Home for Jimmy Maclean was a splendidly appointed bungalow in an enclave surrounded and kept secure by the Garda, who had turned their backs and blindfolded themselves for the time being. Mickey Herring and Fatty Brimstone did the job faultlessly. Rupert briefed them and they even had a peep at some photographs before they went in. A fellow they knew had made certain Jimmy had not planned anything on his own for that weekend. They got him home, stripped him, and popped him between the covers in the early hours of the Sunday morning. You could see Dublin Castle lying below them from the big picture windows in his bedroom. When Jimmy woke up, drunk and slurring, he had a terrible thirst on him and felt heavy-headed, even unwell, late that night. He also had an enormous erection, but he got over it and settled in for a long sleep. Funny, he thought. He did not usually drink to excess. Nor could he remember the details. When he woke again, a worm of concern was nagging away at him.

The Garda arrived around six on the Sunday evening and pulled him out, cautioned him, and carted him off to Dublin Castle; put him in a cell and charged him with conspiracy.

"If the Brits try to get you to London, you'll resist it no doubt, Mr. Maclean?"

"Sure I will." Jimmy gave the officer a wink. "But that's why you've charged me, right? I'll have to face this one before you'll even think of handing me over. What's it all about anyway?"

"If you don't know, we're not telling you, Jimmy, and that's the truth."

Right, Jimmy thought. He wondered what was going on. His memory was dodgy, but he seemed to recall a girl with the face and voice of an angel. It was a couple of days before he really began to worry.

Return to Ringmarookey. It is a little after four o'clock on the Sunday morning. The father superior's door slashed open.

"Talking about me behind my back?" The malignant shape of Father Benedict stepped from the darkness outside, the two muscular monks hovering in his wake.

"We have no reason to talk about you behind your back." Gregory Scott visibly bridled at Benedict.

"Not even to discuss old times around the campfire, Father?" The voice had not changed from that which Charlie remembered from all those years ago: harsh, nasal, astringent. This voice was almost tangible in that you could feel it dragging over you, trying to strip the skin from your face like acid. "So you remember me, Charlie Gauntlet?"

"Remembered you before I saw you. Saw you at that crash site when young Hilary almost got herself written off and said to myself, 'I know that face.' Bingo. It reminded me of the camp. Same smell. Woodsmoke and the leaves gone from the trees." For the first time in ages Charlie thought of his father. His good memories of his father were always of the old man in the garden, digging out trenches for potatoes, or picking the peas, shelling them around the kitchen table with his mother. His dad would get the breath knocked out of him by gardening too hard. He had been gassed in the first war. He'd tell the story of how they got him to the docks on a stretcher and he lay there crying because the boat had gone. "I missed the boat," he used to say. "Do that once and you'll never do it again." In fact a chunk of irony was attached to that experience, for the boat he had missed struck a mine in the Channel and half the wounded on board were drowned.

"You don't change," Charlie told the former military policeman. "You don't change one bit." He could smell the smoke from his father's garden incinerator and the apples laid out in a loft at one and the same time. Memories had their seasons.

"We're old and aged in the wood now." The former Corporal Knight's eyes told their own story. "The one good thing is I don't have to call you 'sir' like I did all those years ago."

"No, but that doesn't alter the natural superiority." Charlie smiled as he said it, trying to make a little barbed joke.

Father Benedict (né Colin Knight) gave him an unpleasant look and turned back to the father superior. "I've just read the latest take from the Naomi diaries." Benedict's smile was wretchedly unpleasant, like an old man's hand lingering where it should not even have strayed. "It's wonderful. We should make a mint with this."

"I didn't know mints were involved." Charlie tried to sound innocent. In his head he saw cases full of cash in a dozen different currencies. He also saw the letters Gregory Scott had written to the bank manager in Melrose: *Dear Arthur, Hope all goes well . . .* Then the other letter . . . *This is the latest take, first draft only.* And so on and so forth, and the name, Beridi, written on an envelope.

"Then you're naive, Charlie. It's keeping company with all these monks that does it," Father Benedict rasped.

"Really." As though Charlie had no interest in it.

"Yes, really, Charlie. There's always money in a good solid monastery, or didn't you know?"

"I think you should get back to your cell. Get some rest, Charlie."

Gregory Scott was speaking as though trying to smooth out something between him and the onetime military police corporal.

"Am I a prisoner?" Somewhere, in the back of his head, Charlie reasoned that there was a distinct possibility that he could already be a dead man. Father Benedict was not a priest but some kind of interloper. And by now Charlie suspected that the monastery of St. Jerome was a giant Laundromat, washing money whiter than the whitewash on the wall. (He heard the words in his head: "Whiter than the water where you washed your dirty daughter, we'll be whiter than the whitewash on the wall." His father had sung it in the bath. Hear him all over the house you could.) If this was the case, they really would not want him outside, in the real world. He accepted that once here he wasn't in the proper world.

"Of course you're not a prisoner, Charlie." Gregory Scott still couldn't look him in the eye.

"You sure?"

"We wouldn't keep you in here against your will."

"No? No, of course you wouldn't." And several images came into his head. A gun being fired close to a prisoner's head; Christ on the cross, the face sagging on the shoulder; and again back to the camp near Frankfurt and Sergeant Hammer stretched out dead on the floor of the CO's office with the big corporal leaning against the wall looking on. "You mean you're going to let me go?"

"Presently," the novice master said unconvincingly. Then he repeated it: "Presently."

By this time the two stocky, muscular monks had moved into the room. "Time you was in bed," one of them said, looking at Charlie with some distaste.

"Yes, time you was all tucked up, Charlie." The other monk, he could see, had what used to be called a cast in his right eye. You didn't see that so much these days. Perhaps they had found some way of treating slight squints; they had found so many cures for what were once quite serious handicaps. Babies born now, early in the millennium, could expect to live around 130 years, so advanced had medical science become.

"Come along, Charlie. You want to go faster so we can all get a rest?" As the monk with the squint spoke, Charlie realized for the first time that they both had accents. The *w* was pronounced *v* and they stressed some vowels unlike a born Brit. He had initially thought this was a regional thing, but on hearing them now he knew that they were Middle European: Czechs or Poles or Albanians or Romanians, something like that.

As they led him away, unprotesting, Charlie glanced back over his shoulder. "Sometime I need to talk to you about Sergeant Hammer," he said, and watched Gregory Scott wince as though he had been slapped in the face. There goes the neighborhood, Charlie thought. There go my chances of promotion; there goes my life possibly. Depends, he thought. Depends on what really happened in that office. Again he saw the large, chubby sergeant dead on the floor. When was that? Fifty-one or '52? Whenever, it was important. Heart attack they said. Even the coroner said so. But, well, he'd been playing around with Sissel, Sergeant Hammer had. And until then Sissel had been Major Scott's private preserve. In a way, Charlie thought, Sissel was like an updated Naomi, lassoed and corralled to do the major's bidding: to slip among the camp's hundred or so inmates and bring back tales to the major's bed. It was difficult now, looking at the old priest, to remember this was once a man consumed with jealousy and lust for a thin, black-haired woman who was trying to buy herself a way back to her hometown with the only currency she had to offer.

When they got to Charlie's cell, the door was open and one of them pushed him in, quite gently, slamming the door behind him. A new, thick folder lay on the bed, so Charlie made himself comfortable and started to read on.

In London the machines had been working overtime. After identifying Chermyet, they set out to put a trace on him. Finally he came back as last identified at a restaurant in Sochi, on the Black Sea, eight days ago. The last resort, some wag had labeled it. All-same Key West, the last resort. Could be anywhere by now. Suddenly Chermyet became the most sought-after man on the planet. He was even given a pseudonym: Checker One.

And the Royal Air Force flew Bex Olesker and Patsy Wright from

Northolt into Glasgow. There, a big Chinook helicopter waited for them, the crew checking things out, busy, swarming around the beast.

"You Wright?" a young pilot officer shouted at Patsy.

"Well, I'm not wrong. Not often anyway."

The message was to tell them not to leave without being briefed by a bristling squadron leader IO who had all the gen. They went into a flurry of buildings and finally huddled round a table in a room where military aircrew were coming and going all the time.

The squadron leader said there were all kinds of problems and that he had been entrusted with passing on a couple of names. "The Oscar One is the Russian Federation president and Madame Bortunin. That make sense?"

"Perfect sense." Patsy's eyes slid across to Bex, who nodded, her face betraying shock as she took it in. "Anything else?"

"Yes. It implicates a known leader of the Sons and Daughters of October. That make sense as well?"

"Yes. There should be a name."

"There is. Chermyet. Illych Antonovich Chermyet. Checker One. After that I was told to fold up my tent and steal away." The squadron leader had a big Battle of Britain mustache with waxed ends. When he smiled, as he did now, the ends seemed to curve upward. "They actually said that I should kill off the brain cells where that information is stored."

"A word to the wise, old boy," said Patsy at his most languorous. "I should take them pretty well literally. Tie a stone round that particular memory and drop it into the deepest ocean, and I do not jest."

The squadron leader could tell that Patsy was not playing around and thought he could just feel the heat from hell brushing his cheek.

At a little after nine on the Sunday morning, the Chinook lifted off and headed west over the sea.

CHAPTER 20

Romillius, my lord. Oh, how wonderfully happy I am. The tribulation we went through over Jesus coming into Jerusalem was like a dark cloud that we regarded with great fear. Now the cloud has lifted. I can hardly believe what happened today: how the people shouted and cheered and welcomed Jesus into their midst. I felt humbled because Jesus sent one of his people, Phillip, with a message telling me to come and be with the two Marys as they came near to the city gates, so I was there when the people crowded out to greet him, and it amazed me. I was much moved because I am nothing but a common harlot and Jesus forgives what I am and welcomes me into his company. Yet I know I cannot be fully saved until I give up the sins of my life and walk in the way Jesus teaches.

As you must know, word spread through the city, saying that Jesus is the Messiah and was about to claim his rightful place among us. It was a moment full of wonder and also a little mystery, for we cannot possibly fully understand what he, Jesus, has brought into the world.

I wish you could have seen what happened: how the people marched in a great throng and stripped leaves from the trees, throwing them down in the dirt and dust in front of the ass that carried the Lord Jesus toward the city.

The people rejoiced and were full of laughter, singing, and dancing as our lord and master Jesus rode toward Jerusalem with the men who watched over him. "Hallelu," they sang. "Hallelu et Adonai." And as they sang, they clapped their hands and made a joyful sound.

Jesus smiled and received the honor of the people as though it was his due—which it is.

He has with him all twelve of the men he calls his messengers. They are the twelve men chosen to go into the world and spread the news that he is come to save us from extinction and lead us into the Promised Land of paradise. His followers are led by the man Simon Peter, whom I spoke with in Bethany, the man I plotted with to be in touch with Joseph from Arimathea.

All was happiness and joy, yet some of the women wept and were full of sorrow, for one woman said to me that, if the holy writings were indeed prophecies, as her husband who was a learned priest had told her, then this Jesus would be betrayed, sentenced, and put to death—dead and buried. I cannot think of that, for today has been the best day of my life ever. Yet tomorrow, my lord Romillius, could be a day without equal, a day of terror, anguish, and pain. A good and holy man, knowledgeable in our Scriptures and the Law, came and sat with a group of us by the roadside. Jesus' mother, Mary, was there with the other Mary, and I will tell you, Centurion Romillius, what this holy man said to us.

He said that today the people have welcomed Jesus into Jerusalem, but before the week is out, they will deny him and give him over to the Romans, who will sentence and execute him. Yet even that is a joyful matter, he said. Truly I cannot understand how this can be, but this man is obviously wise and has a great understanding of the writings and prophecies that he says are the cornerstone of our faith. He then read to us a passage from one of the holy writings, from the prophet Isaiah, which was, as I remember it, like this: "He's despised, rejected, thrown apart from other men. He's a man of sorrows, one who knows grief. Men and women will hide their faces from him, yet he will bear all our grief, carry all our sorrows and all our sins." This, he said, is the man you have seen today: this is Jesus of Nazareth. The Christ. So I now truly believe the man Jesus to be the man of sorrows also.

And Mary, his mother, wept when she heard it and said, "Yes, this is true. I alone know for certain what my son is and from where he came." Romillius, I was and am filled with wonder. For I have seen the coming of the Messiah, for it is Jesus himself.

Yes, I have seen the coming and the love of God. Yet in the middle of all this joy there is uncertainty still. While the many people who came and cheered him along the road from Bethany speak of him in wonder, others would see him destroyed. He knows this and calmly accepts it, and it is in his acceptance that I find myself confused.

Tonight the loathsome Thomas, steward to Caiaphas, has been to me, and I managed to persuade him to have love with Azeb, for I find it difficult to be with him: he is like some slimy, creeping creature. He was boasting, saying that the Sanhedrin had met today at his master's house and Caiaphas had made a long speech saying that if they didn't denounce Jesus to the governor and have him arrested and executed, they were putting the entire house of Israel at risk. "It is better for one man to die so that the Children of Israel shall be saved." According to Thomas, that is what Caiaphas said to the council and they agreed.

The only good thing is that Thomas now prefers Azeb to me. She did not like him and began to be difficult after he left. She said that she would not take him to her bed again and she answered back rudely when I remonstrated with her. I hate doing it, but I beat her soundly, some eight hard strokes with the rod, which she did not like, twisting and trying to free herself from my grasp, but in the end it was done and she wept a great deal. As ever when I beat her, she finally came to my bed and I was glad of it for I am very afraid. I cannot reason why I am so full of anxiety, but I am, and little Azeb held me and made me feel less worried and helped me to sleep. I am sorry for her because I saw in her nakedness the great welts from where I have beaten her, livid scars across her rump. I forgive her. Please do the same, Romillius.

My mind is in disarray. I am so happy with the thoughts of what has happened: when I close my eyes, I see Jesus riding in through the gates with all the people singing and bowing before him, and the dust of the journey falling on the old robe he wears, matting in his hair and beard. Then I hear what this Thomas has said, and what the holy man by the roadside told us about Jesus being the man full of sorrows. My heart will break, my lord, I am sure of it. Have you yet got word from the man Joseph from Arimathea?

Romillius, my beloved. I have tonight received your message about seeing Joseph, and I look forward with joy to being with you. Yet I am full of dread at the last part of your message, for you say that we must have great care and not admit any to this house unless we already know them: that we must turn strangers away and not open the door to men we do not know.

I seem to be living as though in a great storm. One day I am taken up to the top of a high mountain where the winds are calm and the air warm. Next I am suddenly cast down in a dark and gloomy valley where there is no sun and only a wild moaning of wind to accompany me.

Two days ago the Master came into the city and everywhere people praised him and rejoiced. How quickly things can alter. Again it is as though he wishes to die as the prophets have predicted.

Two men came to the house tonight—they come here regularly and are rich merchants—and one told of the last time Jesus was here in Jerusalem at the Feast of Tabernacles. This was some time ago, in Ethanium* after the harvest. At that time, they say, Jesus was unknown to them, yet it was then that he became known and talked of because of his miracles and the good news he brought in his teaching. They were here this time when he came into the city like a king: lord of all who saw him.

Today, though, he has gone out of his way to drive a wedge between himself, the people, and particularly the priests and those who are part of the Sanhedrin, because he has all but defiled the holy Temple. They say he was like an enraged man, incensed, shouting, and frightening all who saw him. Now he is not as before. He is wild-eyed, his robe is dirty, and he needs to wash his clothes and body. He appears to have lost all control and respect for himself.

He lashed out at the men who do business in the Temple, in

*Ethanium—a period of time similar to a month, but a little longer. Ethanium would correspond with our September/October. HJOSJ.

the Court of the Gentiles. Some of the men who are money changers had their tables broken so that money was scattered on the ground. Jesus also struck several of these men, wielding a scourge of cords. These people, and others, those who sell animals near the Temple wall, have now brought a complaint against Jesus, and it is said that the Temple Guards are looking for him, and Azeb has just come to me to say she has heard the Sanhedrin has ordered his arrest.

So it has come, what we dreaded.

Romillius, I am telling Petros what has just happened, for I know that you will be here at any hour now and I am frightened. Two of your men came to us tonight. They were Felix and Aurus, who went with me to Caana when I first saw Jesus. They paid with silver, and when I said to them that I did not think you, my lord, would approve of them coming to our house, they just laughed and said that before long you would not have any supremacy over them. I realized then that they were both a little drunk with wine.

Felix said he would take Azeb to the couch, and Aurus obviously wanted me. He became abusive, so finally I took him to my room. He was not able to do much, for the wine had made him lustful but had taken away his ability to perform. I was tempted to mock him, but he had been so critical of you, my lord, that I dared not in fear that he would become more angry and abusive.

Felix was unpleasant with Azeb and struck her on the cheek because she would not do what he asked, which would have been an unnatural act.

Romillius, we need strong men here to guard us against soldiers like Felix and Aurus. What does their change in demeanor mean? What has happened?

My lord Romillius, you have just left me, but my heart is so full that I think it will burst from my body. You have told me to write everything down, so I shall. Everything. I have long thought that you cared especially for me, my lord. Now you have told me you do and that you will take me with you when you return to Rome. I cannot believe that I am so lucky. Indeed,

I am the happiest among women, for you do me incredible admiration and I am grateful to you for all that you do to keep me safe at this moment.

I was so full of your love and feelings for me. Never has any man held me in such a prime place in his life. You came in, kissed my face and neck, fondled my breasts and then my rump, which you covered with both your hands, one hand to each side, which you stroked and kneaded into fire. You lifted my garment and pulled me onto you as though my body were a natural twin to your own. So I felt your stiffness within me, pumping me so that I seemed to be enlarged by your loving male serpent. I shall not forget, my dearest one, how you took me from the wall, like a feather in your arms, and spread me upon my own bed, and with my garment rent open and my breasts rising toward you, I was taken, it seemed, into a seventh heaven of physical wonder.

You, Romillius, deep within me, is all I can think of, it is so wondrous, and I found it difficult to satisfy you. My legs were open wide to receive you, yet I was forced to open them wider and then wrap my legs around the trunk of your body. So we made the race together, you riding me and I depleting you of your prodigious seed as you bucked and throbbed into me.

Nor will I forget how we lay together, close and loving so that you stroked me in the secret places of my body, kissed me on the mouth, and your tongue became a lithe, live part of you as you thrust it into my mouth just as you propel your sex into me and make me cry out with longing for you. I wish to be able to feel you melt into my body and I into yours. I am raw with your great piercing pleasure, yet I want you to impale me again, and yet again, my sweet beloved.

I can scarce believe that you plan to take me to Rome, but I am also greatly disturbed by what you have told me: that you have been removed from your post, that you are no longer in sole charge of those who seek out the truth from among those who plot against Rome. Your men seem to have turned against you even though you are now answerable only to your old friend Pilate, the governor.

You know that I hung on to you like a child clinging to its mother's breast when you spoke to me of the dangers and the plot against both you and the governor. If I have it right, this conspiracy has been made from the heart of those men who wish ill to the savior Jesus.

In the midst of all these bad tidings there was at least the one piece of good news that the man from Arimathea, Joseph, has pledged his help and assistance if we require Jesus to be spirited away and hidden for a season or two. The tone of everyone has changed now. The clouds gather and there is a smell of danger in the air.

I had forgotten that I was meant to warn Old Saul. My mind is in a great whirl, and in even more confusion for two of Jesus' closest pupils came to Saul this morning, at dawn, and he has brought them back here. In turn they will bring the closest of Jesus' followers to us later today, and Jesus with them. They are to use our upstairs room to take a meal here tomorrow night and, possibly, the Passover meal, on the Sabbath, when we will eat the sacrificed lamb together with unleavened bread. We stand up to eat this, and we wear clothes in which to travel—but I have told you this before.

Romillius, a soldier came to the house tonight and we did not allow him in. He was not known to me and he was not an officer, yet he wore his short sword and walked as though he owned all Jerusalem and parts of every other city in Judea also. What will happen to us? The word is that the Temple Guard are now accompanied by a small detachment of the Roman garrison. I have made a friend of a girl who sells herself from a house near the Tekoa Gate, mainly to soldiers of the garrison. Her name is Ruth and she knows of you. She has told me that your men were loyal, but after a sudden change in orders some of your men asked to go back to ordinary garrison duty like you. Only some of the men have become disaffected and the word is that the terrorists who are called Sicarii—assassins—will soon make an uprising. They say there has already been an attempt to kill Pilate. Is this true?

He is taken, Romillius. Tonight he stayed with us, he and his pupils, the twelve messengers. They ate in our upper room. We served the food—Azeb and I. Petros was not allowed upstairs, and we were told that we should serve the food and then leave, but I hid, just on the stairs, outside the door.

There was much talking, then I crept up to the door and looked through the crack. Jesus was solemn once the meal was over. He looked at each of his twelve in turn, exchanged a long look with each of them, then took the bread and tore it into pieces, made a blessing, and said, "This is my body, which I give for you. Do this in my memory." Each of them took some of the bread and swallowed it and murmured a blessing on themselves. Then Jesus poured a cup of wine, made a blessing, and said, "This is my blood, which will be spilled for you. Do this in my memory." And they passed the cup around one to another, each taking a drink of wine and making a blessing prayer for themselves. It was a great and sacred moment: a few seconds that seemed to gather in an entire lifetime.

I stood there as though stricken with illness, and one of them then came running for the stairs and I hid in the shadows and saw him go out. It was the one called Judas who comes from Kerioth. His face was like a mask, or a clever, frightening carving.

Then they all went out, and later we heard that he was taken in the garden—in Gethsemane. The Temple Guards together with the soldiers from the garrison came—a whole crowd of them—with brands and torches that made the light flash and the shadows dance against the walls. Judas showed them the way, and what part of the garden they were in, and he kissed Jesus and they say that was a sign. What will happen to us now? I send this with Azeb. Come to me if you can.

Charlie put down the transcript. He sighed, deeply moved by this simple account, though he was, yet again, somewhat shocked by the descriptions of sex between the girl and the centurion. But, he reasoned, this was the only way in which the girl Naomi could explain the depth of her feelings for Romillius. She was a relatively simple person, and to her mind love would be measured by the passion and intensity of the sexual act.

He closed his eyes and there were vivid pictures in his head: the fire from the torches, the words of Jesus—"Do this in my memory." He could see the twelve at the table, unlike any grouping he had seen before; then Christ with his followers in the garden and the Temple police coming, with the Romans, torches held aloft. The smell from the burning torches and the way the shadows leaped in their fire. Then he could also smell the fear on Naomi.

Far away, he thought he could hear the sound of a helicopter descending somewhere near the monastery.

Nobody came, so he turned back to what had to be the last entries in Naomi's spoken diary: to the death of Christ and the aftermath.

In Glasgow, two plainclothes protection officers, alerted by their colleagues in the Anti-Terrorist Branch, were now on duty, in shifts, at Ward C7 in the Glasgow Royal Infirmary. There was only one way into the room housing their principal, Hilary Cooke, and on their first visit the pair of them went to see her.

To begin with, Hilary could not work out why they were there. She thought perhaps it was to ask her questions about the accident, so when she started to talk about it, DC Pete Brookes told her calmly that they were there to protect her.

"Oh, to protect me from the mad bloody monk?" she asked. "That must be Charlie Gauntlet's doing. What a sweet man he is."

"We're not given all the facts, Ms. Cooke," Brian Appleby, the other PO, said with a smile. "Though they have told us the threat's high and it comes from one of the Ringmarookey monks. Or at least a male in the dress of a Ringmarookey monk."

"You familiar with the monks of Ringmarookey?"

"I wouldn't say familiar actually, miss, but I think we can be trusted to identify one on a clear day," said Pete Brookes.

"With a following wind," Brian Appleby added.

Hilary nodded energetically. "Well, you can't miss this one, he's a big bugger."

"Don't worry, miss, I'm sure we can take care of a monk no matter what his size."

"Oh, please call me Hilary."

"Best to stick with *miss,* if you don't mind, miss." Protection officers are discouraged from getting too emotionally close to their principal. This was a cornerstone of the rules that had evolved over the years. Familiarity may not breed contempt, but it could cloud judgment in moments of crisis.

Hilary gave a little shrug that said, please yourself. "Where'll you be? I mean, you won't be in here round the clock will you? Or will you?" Battered though she was, Hilary was starting to face the threat with some humor.

"Somewhere outside," Brian said. "Not quite lying across your door, but certainly within sight of it. We'll go and take a look round, then we'll let you know."

They explored the corridor and finally decided that, for the time being, they would use an office that was only occupied on Tuesday and Thursday afternoons. A couple of big-wheel consultants held their clinics on C7 then. But neither of the great men otherwise used the little office.

After a telephone call a techie turned up in a plain van and installed a silent alarm on Hilary's door, and a look-see mirror that allowed the POs to sit in comfort within the office and still keep an eye on the private ward next door. Among the many advantages of this low-tech kit was its cheapness when compared to CCTV.

"Round the clock," Pete told her. "We'll be there round the clock."

"Should I get lonely in the night, will you come in and chat me up?"

"Well," he began, looking dubious. He had reason to take care, for he was married—and not happily. He suspected his wife would be delighted to catch him out in some adulterous crime or misdemeanor of the heart so she could sue him for divorce and custody of the three-piece suite and the kitchen utensils. Pete loved his wife, who was young and wore tight dresses. He loved her more than she loved him: hence the unhappy marriage. If you weighed them in the balance, she would be found wanting. Very careful with other women, Pete Brookes.

Hilary stepped in quickly. "Don't look so worried." She laughed. "Can't really see myself chasing you round the bed, trying to get a bit of nooky." She grinned and waved a hand toward her raised, tractioned leg. She felt much better now that a couple of big, hairy policemen were there to look after her. "You got a gun?" she asked, then remembered the old joke and giggled. "Or are you just pleased to see me?" More giggles, but not from the police.

"Yes, we're armed, miss." Appleby nodded.

"Show it to me." She gave him her pale and interesting grin. "And the gun."

Pete Brookes gave a little chuckle. "Incorrigible, miss." He lifted the corner of his jacket to reveal the Glock nine-millimeter in a waist holster on his hip. These days Glocks are the weapon of choice for many law enforcement officers and their opposite numbers in the criminal and terrorist worlds.

"My, you have got a big one, Officer." Hilary was nothing if not obvious.

They told her there was absolutely nothing to worry about; that they would be around all the time; that they were well trained; that the threat, if it came at all, would most likely come either late at night or at dawn. "The rest of the time we just remain alert," Appleby said.

Hilary thought they were very comforting, even though they were careful to tell her they would only be in her life for a short spell. "We're not going on your Christmas card list for the rest of our days, miss," Appleby said, grinning.

The threat did not come late at night, or at dawn. It came shortly after nine o'clock on the Sunday morning.

Father Martin, OSJ, aka Beridi Dayosolavek, aka Corporal Bertie Day, aka Father John, OSJ, aka Father Sebastian, OSJ, was a nutcase. In fact, he was the worst kind of nutcase; he was a psychopath of the mad and bad persuasion. He was dangerous in that he was convinced deep down within him that Hilary Cooke had those letters and parcels of cash on her: with her, there in the hospital. He was determined to lay his hands on those letters, particularly the fat ones stuffed with cash. Nobody could stop him because he was well over six foot three inches tall, built like a standing stone, with hands like hams, and he was perfectly prepared to perform actions of great violence on Hilary Cooke, or anyone who got in his way.

He came rolling along, looking as though he were doing God's work on a Sunday morning, heading straight for C7. His reasoning was that nine o'clock was a time when everyone would be busy on the ward; that also it was a Sunday, which meant a new shift would have started a month on days and so would be getting acclimatized. He would undoubtedly be above suspicion, because he was dressed in the habit worn by the Order of St. Jerome—a tailored cassock with a tippet and a broad belt from which hung the crucifix. On a cold morning like this, he also wore his cloak with its lion's head clasp. The cloak billowed out around him, making him look like a huge top as he marched with purpose toward the ward.

Pete Brookes had taken over from Brian Appleby at a little after seven-thirty. He sat back in his chair, drinking a cup of black coffee and taking an occasional squint at the mirror and the alarm. He was relaxed and did not think any threat was imminent. He was wrong, and the alarm went off at precisely 9:12:32. We know that because one of the features of that particular alarm is that it prints out a small slip showing the time and date whenever the alarm is activated.

The light began to blink rapidly, and Pete Brookes's eyes flicked up to the mirror. He saw the long skirt of a cassock twitching and disappearing through the door of Hilary's room. Pete drew the Glock and was out of the chair, through the door, and at Hilary Cooke's door before you could recite the first two lines of the nursery rhyme "Jack and Jill," or some such nonsense.

Like many of the protection officers in the United Kingdom, Pete had never drawn his weapon at a threat, but he had done all the drills and had no problem with drawing it now. He stepped into the little room and saw this huge figure dressed as a monk leaning over Hilary Cooke with one hand bunched, rock hard, above her face. Pete also took into account Hilary's face, which was contorted with fear.

"Armed police officer!" he shouted. "Stand away from the bed and place your hands on your head! Down on the floor!"

The monk glanced up, did not like what he saw, growled like a trapped animal, and wrapped his hand around a chair, which he lifted above his head and hurled in the direction of Pete Brookes, who stepped out of the way. "Down on the ground now!" Brookes yelled. "Hands on your head! Lie down now!"

The monk growled again and pushed a hand inside his cassock, at which point Pete Brookes without hesitation shot him twice in the head—the double tap, just as he had been taught. This was the right thing to do to protect his principal, and he knew it when a little gun-metal blue revolver skittered from the dead monk's hand.

The monk's head exploded, in a mash of blood, mucus, bone, and matter. A cloud of fine blood hung in the air for a second as the now useless body dropped to the floor with a bone-crack crunch and the stench of an abattoir filled the air.

Hilary Cooke began to scream.

It was to be a lead news story for the next three days.

On that same Sunday morning Ronnie Richardson and Tessa Murray took a cab out to Heathrow Airport. They carried briefcases and Tessa wore a smart backpack done in Gucci leather matching her briefcase. They also carried raincoats and wandered from terminal to terminal, taking a cup of coffee here and a snack there. They covered a lot of ground and finally hired a silver Vauxhall Tigra from Hertz, which they took back to Piccadilly.

They checked out of the Regent Palace and drove up past the Albert Hall and into the forecourt of The Royal Garden Hotel, which looks out on Kensington Gardens. They checked into the Royal Garden and were shown to a stylish and splendidly appointed suite.

"This is the life." Tessa enjoyed staying in luxury hotels.

"When I've done the *presidentsky* and his lady, we can live in hotels for the rest of our lives, if that's really what you want." Ronnie reached over and kissed her, long and lingering, the way they both liked it: but in the back of his head death lurked, a dreadful shadow.

While they were doing all this in London, Charlie Gauntlet, on the Scottish island, was reading what appeared to be the final pages of Naomi's diary.

303

CHAPTER 21

Romillius, I pray for you and for our lord Jesus. I hold you both in my heart and trust that your plan will succeed. Nobody must ever know, so I am unhappy at telling Petros, but you have commanded it and I must obey.

From what you have told me, I understand that should Pontius Pilate be forced against his will to sentence Jesus to death, you will be in charge of the execution detail. If this happens, you will see to the crucifixion of our lord and master, but you will do your utmost to have the body taken down before he is dead. To do this you will use Passover as an excuse. You might even be forced to give the master a slight wound, but you will *not* carry out the final breaking of legs, as is the custom. The thought of what could occur fills me with horror. Even speaking of it to Petros makes me tremble.

If this has to happen, when you take Jesus down from the cross, you will hand his body to the man from Arimathea, Joseph, who, together with Mary, Jesus' mother, and one of his messengers called John, will take him away for burial in Joseph's own tomb, which is prepared.

Later, you will return to the burial place under cover of darkness, with two of Joseph's most trusted men, who will be needed to roll away the stone that seals the tomb. Jesus will then be taken secretly to the Essenes, who live together as a family by the Dead Sea. These good people will nurse Jesus back to health and keep him close to them for as long as is necessary.

Jesus has not been told of this plan, nor will he be told of it.

Charlie Gauntlet gave a long sigh. If this document was real, and if it was a mirror reflection of the events in Palestine two thousand years ago, then a huge cornerstone of the Christian faith could be hauled into a new doubt. If these words were true; if they were dictated by this woman living in Jerusalem at the time of the crucifixion; if the centurion Romillius was the officer in charge of the barbaric execution; and if he had brought Jesus down from the cross before he was dead; then the mystery of the resurrection was suspect. Many in the twentieth century had found the resurrection difficult enough to swallow. Now, with the coming of Naomi's diary, the atheists would have a field day.

A lot of ifs, he thought, remembering a passage from one of the Gospels: the bit about a soldier piercing Jesus' side with a spear. He clearly recalled the words "and forthwith came there out blood and water." Back when he thought about these things, Charlie had felt this was one of the small details adding a patina of truth to the story of the crucifixion and resurrection. Now, if the reason for it was to demonstrate, falsely, that Jesus was dead, it altered a massive thrust of history. If Naomi's spoken diary was proved to be dependable, then people had no need to make a leap of faith to find God. The whole idea of the resurrection was blown away.

These thoughts disturbed Charlie, who could not help thinking that, if it were so, then the monastic order of St. Jerome, indeed no Christian community or congregation, would be happy about this document going into the public domain. Their assignment would rather be to prove that the document was suspect, even fraudulent.

He paced the cell—turning every four strides—his brow wrinkling; feeling the first twitch of a headache, far away but coming closer just between the eyes. He pushed roughly at the door, and to his surprise it swung open so that he could walk into the cloister and head toward Father Gregory Scott's study.

It was cold, damp, and blustery, and as he rounded the corner, Charlie saw Bex and could hardly believe it was her. At first he did not recognize her because he had never conceived of her in this setting: it was a total surprise. His brain said, "It can't be her," while his instincts told him it was. And it was true, there was Bex half running, loping toward him, head back and a raincoat wrapped around her, insubstantial in the chill of the morning. He thought it was a dream or a hallucination. "I'm imagining it," he said to himself. "This can't be real."

Then they ran toward each other, like Hollywood lovers meeting in a great reunion scene at the end of a film: embracing and hugging close, Charlie lifting her from the ground for a second, smelling the scent of her and the sweetness of her hair, feeling the familiar flesh under the raincoat. Then he kissed her, an imitation of penetration. He tasted the salt of her tears and the clean, minty toothpaste, then he pulled away.

"How in heaven's name . . . ?"

"You'd better come." She brimmed full of happiness, her eyes damp. "You'd better come and listen. Patsy's doing the honors."

"Patsy? Patsy Wright? Patsy's here?"

"We came to collect you. Joe Bain was alarmed and not a happy man. We've been running an op here." Grabbing at his arm a little like a child, hanging on, almost swinging. "Patsy saved my bacon in Switchbackland. But I think he's got a hidden agenda."

"Usually has." A long intake of breath, a gulp of air. "Crikey, I've missed you, Bex."

She told him that she loved him and clung even harder. She's worried, he thought to himself; come to that, I'm worried. These monks are bloody weird.

Patsy Wright was leaning over Father Gregory's right shoulder, looking at something as they entered the study. Patsy glanced up, a little guiltily, Charlie thought, until he saw the others ranged around the room: Fathers Harry and Hugh, with Kit Palfrey sitting on a carved, high-backed chair in the corner. The chair could have been made for Richard III, Charlie thought; the head of a wild boar was carved in the center of the tall back. Words sidled through his head: "The cat, the rat, and Lovell our dog, rule all England under a hog." Richard III's emblem was a wild boar. My mind is stuffed with trivia, Charlie thought, and recalled a schoolmaster's report that said, "This boy has a ragbag mind."

"Charlie?" Patsy framed it as a question. "Charlie, you okay?"

Charlie shrugged. "Cold but mild mannered as ever. What's going on, Patsy?" Charlie saw that Patsy had one hand resting on Gregory Scott's shoulder in a kind of proprietary way. Still the same old Patsy: the toughened steel hand in the serviceable white cotton gloves.

"You shouldn't be here, Charlie." Patsy squinted upward, head still turned toward the pages on the desk. "How the hell did you . . . ?"

"I persuaded him," Kit Palfrey spoke softly from his corner, as though he had a lot more to say. "Persuaded him against his will really. Used him. There were reasons."

"You should've known better, Kit. This is a bloody minefield—sorry, padre. Padres," Patsy corrected himself, his deceptively gentle face smiling at the two studious monks, Harry and Hugh.

They beamed back as though pleased to be included. Neither spoke, but that was their way, and for a second Charlie wondered at the buzz these two men of God got from delving into the past, reading old manuscripts, translating not just words but tenets of faith.

Gregory Scott smiled a distant smile, but did not even turn his head.

"Why's it a minefield, Patsy?" Charlie asked. In his experience with Patsy Wright, a conversation like this was really to inform those who listened rather than to exchange knowledge.

This time Patsy Wright raised his head and looked directly at Charlie. "Did you ever know anything infested by the likes of Kit Palfrey that wasn't a minefield, Charles? You know everything he's touched in the past three decades has turned to dross."

"That's not fair, Patsy." Palfrey spoke out of the corner of his mouth, like an old lag in a prison yard, or a bad ventriloquist. He appeared to be genuinely hurt by what Patsy had said.

"What's not fair, Kit?" Patsy's tone changed to gruff and stormy. "What's not fair, bringing Charlie here to vouch for something he knows damn all about? Letting him wear government colors when he's no right?"

"Worn them before," Palfrey began.

"But not anymore, you slimy little man. You had no right. It's like dragging a blind man into the middle of Regent Street in rush hour. Charlie's not briefed, has no idea what we're up against . . ." Patsy stopped as though lost for words, one hand raised, the fist clenched, balled. He turned back to Gauntlet. "You know what's going on, Charlie?"

"Not the foggiest, Patsy, but—"

"There, you see." Swiveling at the hips, turning to face Bex in the corner. The priests' heads turned as if they were watching a game of tennis.

"But I can hazard a guess," Charlie said.

"Well, guess away, old love, because I reckon this is the original tangled web we weaved and deceived with."

For a second, Charlie felt like an escapee trapped in the cone of a searchlight: in a minefield. "Okay." He looked around the room. "Okay, I'll have a stab at unraveling it. First off, I think the good father superior has been in bed with the wrong people."

Gregory Scott began to splutter.

"Oh, Gregory, I didn't mean literally in bed. Well, possibly some fifty years ago . . ." Charlie let the idea hang in the air like smoke. Father Gregory simply looked away and shook his head.

"You want to tell us about it? After all, you started to tell me, I think, when you revealed that our former comrades Bertie Day and Colin Knight didn't have the benefit of a bishop when it came to their holy orders. Your actual words were 'Neither has ever been near a seminary, let alone a bishop to ordain them.' You want to go on, Father?"

Out of the corner of his eye Charlie caught sight of Father Harry's face, stricken, shocked.

Then, quietly, almost as though he had some terrible ailment, Gregory Scott began. "You'll think me so foolish . . . so very foolish, but I was afraid of public scandal, and they knew. The buggers knew . . . I'm sorry. My parents were like that and I swore I was never going to find myself in the same trap, but I did. You know, Charlie, how they can lean on people."

Charlie stepped into the space in which Father Gregory paused. Now the old Gauntlet courtroom skills returned. For a moment it was as though he stood, bewigged and gowned, in front of a jury once more. His talent had always been for interrogation, out there in a court of law, or more often in the quiet of one of those places where paralegals worked for the government. "I should really explain. I have an unfair advantage. You see, years ago I served under the father superior. A long time ago, when the world was young, Major Gregory Scott was my CO, so I'm what you might call privileged." Now Charlie faced the old monk. "Shall I continue, Gregory?"

A nod, the slight, almost dismissive movement of a hand.

"This is only what I suspect." Breath. Pace. Turn. "When I was a young officer, I was posted to a holding camp for displaced persons, not far from Frankfurt. We had an assorted lot there: men and women, no children, thank God, and very few Christians. I don't believe you were a Christian yourself, were you, Gregory?"

A shake of the head. Still no eye contact. "I didn't find God until the early sixties, when I also found my true academic vocation."

Off pat, thought Charlie, as if Gregory had learned it by heart, conned it by rote, or was filling in one of those interminable government forms that had created a whole new breed of professionals: men and women who helped you fill in the forms they had invented in the first place.

"So, Major Scott was our CO and I'd hardly given him a thought for around fifty years: didn't really even recognize his name or face when I first arrived on Ringmarookey." Pause. Count of three. "Now here's the interesting part. I was reunited with the father superior—courtesy of Kit Palfrey—and strange to tell, there were two other old comrades within striking distance.

"We had a small military police presence at that holding camp years ago, in the shape of two somewhat sinister corporals: Corporal Day and Corporal Knight. Yes, Colin Knight and Bertie Day with all the attendant jokes."

Turn again toward the father superior. "You didn't tell me of their existence here, did you, Gregory? I got the feeling that you didn't want to let on about our two corporals. I had to make the running. After I spotted our gallant Corporal Knight disguised as the novice master, I had to give you a bit of a push, right?"

"Absolutely." The voice a shade stronger, as if Scott was coming to terms with whatever was gnawing at his conscience.

"And those two didn't really trust you either, did they?"

Back a snake. Back to the shaking of the head.

"They trusted neither you nor your winged messenger, Hilary Cooke. One of them even tried to sabotage our Hilary's aircraft?"

This time the father superior looked up into Charlie's eyes. "Possibly. We have no real proof, and there are a couple of other monastic toughs as well. Brothers Vitus and Lapsi."

So the novice master's thugs had names.

"We do have proof, I think, that the former Corporal Day tried to put the arm on Hilary in the Glasgow Royal Infirmary."

Patsy Wright coughed, then spoke. "He's tried it once too often if he's a seriously tall, formidable toughie."

"Oh?"

"You arranged protection for the girl, I think?"

"I spun the Anti-Terrorist Branch a yarn, yes."

Patsy raised his eyebrows. "I had a call on my mobile. A protection officer shot him dead as he was threatening Ms. Cooke, just after nine this morning. He'll get in all the papers, and lead writers of the world will unite against the brutal methods our wonderful policemen have to adopt when faced by an armed killer."

"One down. One to go. And a couple of . . ." No trace of regret in Charlie's voice. "Father Gregory, what did they have on you, the two ungallant corporals?"

No response. It was as though Gregory Scott was pondering an answer of Byzantine proportions.

"Was it concerned with Sergeant Hammer? Perhaps you'd speak more freely if we were left alone. Yes?"

The father superior shook his head, looked up at Charlie, then down again, not breaking eye contact. Quietly he said, "No. I'd find it difficult whatever the audience. Some of it'll find itself into the confessional anyway. I'm in need of absolution. In desperate need."

"Sergeant Hammer?" Charlie prompted, catching Bex's eye as he spoke.

She had never seen Charlie in action before, so now she thought how good he was, then wondered why she was surprised. He's like a boxer pounding away at his opponent's weakest part, she considered. It was a Charlie she had never known.

"Sergeant Hammer?" Charlie repeated.

Gregory Scott made a small waving motion with his right hand, as though trying to rid himself of a troublesome insect. "Partly," he said, stronger now. "To my shame. . . . Partly . . . and there was no need. . . . My real problem was greed."

Only then did he settle into telling his story: first haltingly, almost crippled for words. Then as the need to unburden himself grew, the old priest became more fluent in the tale of his lust and greed.

"I was caught almost unaware," he began. "I'd gone up to Oxford as what today they'd call a very mature student. I'd always been pretty dotty about Egyptology, and I wanted to specialize. First I was grasped by papyrology, then on to detailed work on the fringes of Egyptology and the ancient biblical texts. You will recall that the Dead Sea scrolls were discovered in the late 1940s and early '50s, so it was an interesting time for those of us just starting to plumb the depths of papyrology.*

"Incidentally, it was during this time that I met Kit Palfrey's brother, Cawdor, who later introduced me to Kit. You ever met Cawdor, Charlie?"

"Keep to the main highway, Gregory." Charlie tapped him forward, nodded, the image of Cawdor Palfrey filling his mind: a big, clumsy, ham-fisted man, the absolute opposite to Kit.

In her head Bex saw Charlie goading a camel, the Sphinx behind him. Charlie, she thought, is a bit of a travelogue himself.

"Around that time I went through a kind of Damascene conversion to Christianity. Later I knew my true vocation so I trained and completed the ordination examinations at St. Stephen's House and continued to live and work in Oxford, until I came here, to join the Order of St. Jerome."

---

*The first of the Dead Sea scrolls was uncovered at the ruins of a settlement at Khirbat Qumran in 1947, and later others were found in sites farther south, in Murabba'ât, Seelim, and Masada. Among these scrolls are biblical texts of immense interest to scholars.

"Where, eventually, you once more met Corporals Knight and Day?" Charlie prodded.

"Indeed." Scott closed his eyes for a few moments as if his brain were stewed in pain. "Two and a half years ago I was in Glasgow. It was shortly after I'd been elected father superior, and I'd just flown back from the General Synod in London. As the father superior I hold—like a Benedictine abbot—the ecclesiastical rank of bishop, so there's some real muck to rake if someone turns over the stones in my past life. Anyway, I was in Glasgow. Waiting for an hour at the airport. Waiting for young Hilary Cooke to fly me back here. I'd never have recognized Colin Knight, particularly in his disguise as a priest, but it soon became clear that this was no accidental meeting."

"Engineered . . . ?" Tentative.

"More masterminded. He and Day had clearly thought the whole thing through. Day, as Charlie knows, was originally born a Chechen and remained the brawn of the pair. Colin Knight was the brains plus a certain amount of somewhat perverted and sadistic muscle. The thing that mattered was that they had access to huge amounts of cash, emanating from inside Russia and from Bosnia, Chechnya, and Croatia—this was soon after the supposed cease-fires, and large sums of money were coming to Knight from Zagreb, Sarajevo, and places like Grozny and Tiflis. You didn't have to be Einstein to figure out that the cash was ill-gotten. It was all in hard currency and negotiable traveler's checks, and I don't mean piffling little amounts. I'm talking serious cash—fifteen, twenty thousand a day in some cases. Yes, of course it was basically Russian Mafia money, and the amounts had to be illegal because they were, in the main, larger by the day than some of those countries spend on policing in a month."

"So they made you an offer you couldn't refuse?" Charlie Gauntlet did not have a breath of a smile in either voice or lips.

The father superior went back to the nodding. Then, slowly: "Yes! Yes! Yes, Charlie. They made me an undeniable submission, but not until they'd had a little dabble around blackmail."

"Sergeant Hammer's death?"

"As you've already suggested, Charlie, Sergeant Hammer's death. You were there, after all . . . weren't you?"

"Not quite there, Gregory. I came in just after it happened, but Colin Knight *was* there. And a lot of people pointed the finger at you, didn't they, Reverend Father?"

"Even though it was death by natural causes."

"People thought you had the fix in somehow." Pause as Charlie's mind soared upward. "Gregory, shall I fill in the blanks for the others?"

An angry flurry crossed the priest's face. "I think I can deal with matters, Charles."

"Keep your hair on, Gregory."

"It was natural causes. He had a serious heart attack in my office. Died on the floor near my desk."

"But . . . ?"

Once more, the thin, old monk pointed at the facts, facts that were demonstrably true. "But only Knight and I saw him die."

"So your new novice master knew something that we didn't. He also had a master plan. For megabucks, as they say."

This time the father superior gave a wry little smile. "Yes, indeed, Charles. Yes, he did."

"Tell us how that came about."

"Well, first I pleaded that it couldn't be done. How, I asked them, could I run several thousand pounds and dollars a day through my books? They told me that all I had to do was run it through a bank, dollars and pounds wash whitest. I still disagreed and they pointed out what a lovely story Sergeant Hammer's death would make."

"And would it?"

"Make a good story? Of course it would, my dear Charles. 'Elderly Monk Tells of Murder and Love Nest.' What d'you think? They wouldn't worry too much about the facts."

"But *we* would, Gregory."

"Yes, all right. All right. There was a row. A fight?"

"A row. Okay, so what was this row about?" Charlie clearly saw the death scene: Hammer spread on the floor and Gregory standing over him with shocked eyes.

"What are all domestic rows about? Money or women."

"Which particular one in this case?"

"Come on, Charlie, you know. Women. No. It was about *a* woman."

"Sissel?"

"Of course, Sissel. What d'you think, Charlie? Of course, Sissel."
All this in his reed-blown, old-man's cracked voice.

Charlie's turn to nod: to Bex, then to the two silent priests, and last
to the apostate Kit Palfrey. "You see, there was this girl called Sissel."
Settling into the story, comfortably.

Bex, by the door, immediately knew what she had looked like, this
Sissel. Thin, sharp features, narrow shoulders; jet hair; burning eyes
and her worn coat thrown across her shoulders in a kind of cavalier
fashion statement. Bex reached into her brown leather shoulder bag
and pulled out the packet of photographs, handing them to Charlie,
who quickly riffled through them, peeling one off and handing it to
Father Gregory.

"Recognize her?" Then, turning back to the others: "The father
superior was tupping a thin, young girl called Sissel. That's the top
and bottom of it. Sissel. I believe that's a Norwegian name, or some
such, but she was the one in the barrel that week, and Major Scott—
as in Gregory Scott—Major Scott was giving young Sissel the benefit
of his charms, if you follow."

"There was also a noncommissioned officer with a lecherous bent,"
muttered the father superior.

"Sergeant Hammer. Hammer of the North, as the galloping major
called him. Taking liberties with Sissel, wasn't he? Smooth Sergeant
Hammer with his pencil-thin 'tash and his floppy little kiss-curl, eh?
Sergeant Hammer was giving Sissel a right good seeing to, wasn't he?"

"To put it mildly, yes. And to my shame I called him to account.
Struck him: hard in the face, on the shoulder, and just above the heart.
A flurry of fists. Very hard. Killed him. Heart attack. Great bruise
on his ribs. Triggered the heart attack. They quizzed me about that.
Didn't come out, but I was suspect. . . . And what was important, I
knew."

"And Colin Knight knew? Knows?"

The nod. "Yes, Colin Knight knows. The folly of an old man's pride.
What a fool I was for Jesus' sake." Head lifted, thrown back with a
thin laugh. "How stupid," Scott piped. "As if any of it mattered. I
thought I was saving the Order of St. Jerome from scandal, but I was

really only saving myself from the Sunday papers: the scandal sheets."

"The blackmail won then?"

"Mostly, and wrongly. *Deluded,* that's the word. I deluded myself for cash. They made a very good case for the cash. Ten percent they said we could have—the Order of St. Jerome could have. Lot of bread. Loot." Scott laughed again. "Spondulicks."

"So your monastery became a giant Laundromat?"

"Turned swag into clean money, yes."

"The devil's money, Father Gregory?"

"Totally. The end product of sin, yes. Odd how money obtained through criminal acts suddenly becomes Snow White."

"And you knew exactly where the money came from?"

"Pretty well, yes." Scott almost chanted a litany of criminal cash. When the killing, the militant clash, the unhealthy tally that followed ethnic cleansing and political and religious unrest was done, the sharks slid in to make the big-time bucks. They provided drugs, flesh, booze, money, meeting places called clubs, and the necessary protection for those clubs. After the dust cart comes the Lord Mayor's Show.

"No wonder the Muslim world holds Christians in derision." Gregory Scott looked drunk with anxiety. "We of the West allow everything that they abhor to dance in front of our eyes. Islam holds us in contempt because we argue about our religion but don't seem to practice it."

"Talking of practicing a religion, what about old Kit Palfrey here?"

Patsy Wright took a step forward, laid a hand on Charlie's sleeve, and shook his head. "Kit's okay," he said in almost a whisper.

"Really? All Sir Garnet?"

Patsy nodded. "For years he was our man in the Kremlin, Charlie. Out-of-date now, but in those bad, bold days he was quite a treasure. Jockstrap medals galore."

"Our little hero."

"The glory that was Rome."

"Moscow."

"Whatever."

Charlie grinned. They had played this double act many times. Now

315

he turned back to the father superior. "Old Kit looks okay to me, Gregory. I thought you'd plied him with the demon drink again."

From across the room Kit chuckled, "They're wild men these monks. Leave a bottle of gin in your cell as easily as look at you."

"Just testing, Kit." There was humor in Father Gregory's voice: the genuine article, no Giacondas here.

"Didn't touch a drop." Kit lifted his right hand, circling his head with his forefinger to denote a halo.

"This mean the diary's genuine, Kit?"

"How should I know? I picked it up just as I told you, Charlie. Found it down in the cellars of the Lubyanka. Told you the whole truth about that. But I'm no expert on things biblical. That's why I brought the proofs here, where they know about these things."

Slowly Charlie turned back to Gregory Scott. "Your credentials, Father, are they for real?"

"You think I'd tell you if they weren't? Of course they're for real, Charlie, as are Father Harry's and Father Hugh's. They're biblical scholars, known throughout the world. Noted for their teaching and writings. Why, Father Harry's published a seminal work on the Jewish historian Josephus—*Josephus: War and the Maccabees.*"

Father Harry made self-deprecating movements.

"What more can I say?" The father superior closed his mouth as if he were never going to speak again.

Charlie remembered what he had read—about the plot to save Jesus from death, and the pact made with Joseph of Arimathea to take the still-living body from the tomb to be looked after by the sect living by the Dead Sea.

Charlie looked at the two monks, Harry and Hugh, and they both made tiny movements, as if acknowledging his presence. He did not want to get bogged down in dense theological arguments, so he went back to the question of money flowing like a river through the island of Ringmarookey.

"How did it work, Gregory? Explain the technical side of things. Money in, cleaned up, and then money out." Back to the monastic Laundromat.

"For a while I held them at a distance, Day and Knight, because I

316

couldn't see how it could be done. Even though I certainly wanted it. We were getting deeper in debt every year."

"How *did* you make ends meet?"

"With great difficulty. The Church had rich patrons when Father McConochie first formed the order. Nowadays it doesn't seem to figure highly in Cool Britannia. We tick over with a few grants and the advances and royalties from our books, which seem to get less and less each year. Young Brother Simon says we ought to settle down and write blockbusters. He maintains that we've much more talent in here than Jackie Collins and Danielle Steel combined, with Lord Archer thrown in." Scott shook his tonsured head. "That lad'll carry many terrible sins to the grave, I fear. Simon, I mean."

"You were telling us how it worked, the dry-cleaning business." Patsy now applying a little pressure.

"I held out. I said it couldn't be done; that it would be too complex. But they provided the other players. A tame bank manager who got a cut—"

Arthur, Charlie thought. Good old Arthur. *Dear Arthur.*

"—and Colin doing the books here, disguised as a new novice master. Passing off the cash as income from the hardly existent royalties of fictitious scholarly works, or the take from our many fabricated business activities. Eventually it was candy from a baby, easy. There's no end to human creativity where hard cash is concerned. Like being sentenced to death, it is a great motivator. Concentrates the mind wonderfully."

"How did you get the other monks to buy a new novice master when he hadn't served time with the order?"

"Simple. I introduced Benedict as a former Dominican monk. They bought that, even when they were told what we were doing."

"Told what you were doing?" Charlie's voice soared in disbelief. "You mean all your monks and brothers know about the money going through the books?"

"Of course. We're bound one to another. We're a family. We're also a kind of democracy. It wouldn't have been right to do it off my own bat."

Of course not. There would be a huge difficulty about charging

150-odd monks if the law became involved. Somewhere in the back of his head Charlie smiled: wry and sardonic, a smile for all seasons. Clever Father Gregory, he thought. Father Benedict was the one who really worked the scam. Colin doing the books, as Scott had put it. Yes. Aloud, Charlie asked about the actual physical movement of money.

Real money every time, he was told. Real cash and traveler's checks. "The couriers came in all shapes and sizes, and they used every form of transport. Flew into Glasgow from Heathrow mainly, then dropped stuff off with Hilary, though she had no idea of why or how. Some came in with her, stayed a few days; others came in and collected envelopes from a bank."

Charlie thought of all the odd envelopes addressed to people with names like Alex, Petor, Igor, Kenni, Rudolph, Anton, Valery. Aloud he said, "And some came by sea, Gregory, right?"

"Most-favored method. We even had a couple of submarines last year."

"And an oceangoing yacht."

"Ah, yes, the *Golden Cockatrice.* Fanciful names they have, especially for a Russian."

"A Russian?"

"Yes. Well, a Chechen really. Not registered in Russia of course, nor Chechnya come to that." Pause. Laugh. "But it's all over the place. Monte Carlo mostly if its owner is anything to go by."

"Who is?"

"The owner? A fellow by the name of Chermyet. Illych Antonovich Chermyet."

Charlie caught the significant look passing between Bex and Patsy Wright: it sizzled like a static charge. "He comes here regularly?"

"Once every three months. He's the one who takes most of the money back, so I presume he also generates it. He says he moves it physically. Switzerland and other places. *Golden Cockatrice* comes in, Father Benedict goes into hiding."

"Why would he do that?"

"Oh, the man Chermyet is looking for him. Doesn't know he's here as a monk, Colin Knight. Chermyet claims that Colin has double-crossed him, ripped him off he says in his rather quaint English. The last time I spoke to him he said he would rip Colin's eyeballs out of their sockets and cut his ba— Well, charming, eh?"

"Now you're spilling it all to us, I presume you have your Father Benedict under lock and key?"

Gregory Scott gave them a wide smile, full of guile. "Spilling it? I haven't said a word. I'd deny it all, and I'm afraid we seem to have lost Father Benedict this time. Could be that he's gone off with Chermyet: God have mercy on his soul." Scott crossed himself. Inappropriately Charlie thought, ace, king, queen, jack.

"The *Golden* whatever it is?"

"*Cockatrice* . . . ?"

As they speak, Charlie wonders where the yacht is. He also wonders where Colin Knight has gone. Most of all he wonders why his wife and his old buddy Patsy Wright are in cahoots, and what they are in cahoots about. The look passing between them had the shocking feel of a dangerously shared secret.

"Tricky things, cockatrices," Charlie mutters. "Mythical, half-serpent and half-cock." Colin Knight would go off at half cock if Charlie got his hands on him.

"I wonder if Chermyet's really caught up with Colin Knight," Gregory Scott wonders aloud.

"And what about old Kit Palfrey?" Charlie asks.

"What about him?" The father superior feels lucky: after all, he's negotiated most of the shallows on this rocky run.

"You said you did a favor for Kit Palfrey one time. Wondered what it was." Charlie leaned in toward the old monk, eyes glistening with a springlike expectancy.

Yes, Father Gregory said, looking across at Kit Palfrey, who nodded. It seemed that he had contacts everywhere, Father Gregory, even in the sixties. He told them, "It was soon after I joined the order. Arrived here, on Ringmarookey, in '62 or '63. Made a lot of contacts in that camp we ran together, Charles." Scott's look was distant, as if he were on some mental time machine. "I maintained the contacts. Did favors and sometimes called them in. On this occasion I kind of chartered a ship for Kit. He came here on a fishing boat. I saw to it that another kind of boat took him off. Sort of chartered it." No trace now, and he would not speak of it again. "I knew it wasn't treasonable."

"Really?" Unconvinced, Charlie was listening to the music of what the old monk was saying. The word *boat* stood out and he recognized it for what it was. A *boat,* not a *ship,* which in military terms meant a submarine. Submarines are boats, not ships. So a younger Gregory Scott was able to whip up a submarine to lift Kit Palfrey off the island.

"Ceased to be real, has it, Gregory? About as insubstantial as a bit of nooky in a monk's salad days." Charlie did not smile as he spoke.

"Quite like old times, this," said Patsy. "Pity you've left us, Charlie. Pity you're not official anymore."

After that they sidetracked a little, talked round the question of Hilary's airplane, asking did she fall or was she pushed.

"He had a good knowledge of engines," the father superior told them. "Right from when I first knew him in Germany, he was always tinkering around with cars and motorcycles. Sabotage was quite within his capabilities."

And Charlie also recalled Bertie Day with greasy hands fiddling with engines.

"Leave it to the experts," Patsy told them. "I'd put money on it, though: ruptured fuel line or a little booby-trap device."

"They ran practically everything," Gregory Scott said. "And they wanted more. Hated the fact that, after they'd set it up, I had control over the bank accounts. I never thought they'd be quite that ruthless, though."

They were evil, he told them. Evil and like a couple of machines. "They're comparatively old men now." His eyebrows lifting and falling. "Senior citizens, yet they'd kill like swatting flies. No consciences either of them. They've looped me around their little fingers for too long."

Charlie thought he saw tears glistening in the elderly monk's eyes, though it could have been a trick of the light.

CHAPTER 22

—————

N o reason why you shouldn't know," Patsy said as they walked, chummy, in the cloisters, sheltering from the cold, thin, soaking drizzle that had blown in from the sea. "Your new wife'll probably have nightmares, so you'd better be aware of what's afoot—as they used to say in the comics—because it's more than a game."

He went on to tell Charlie how Alchemist had cornered Bex on Lake Maggiore, and how they now knew of Chermyet's contract to assassinate President and Mrs. Bortunin. Patsy explained everything except his own part in rescuing Bex Olesker. He rarely spoke of his own involvement in adventures. His personal file said that he had an unassuming and capable manner.

"They've even identified the bugger, Alchemist." Patsy took long, somewhat halting steps, and Charlie found it difficult to keep up with him. "He was a professional soldier for years—boy entrant, Green Howards, then SAS until there was an unfortunate incident with an NCO and an accidental shooting. He left the Regiment but remustered in the Royal Marines. Wizard soldier apparently. Walks on water, goes invisible, turns himself inside out like a reversible coat. Amazing bastard, name of Richardson. We've got pictures now, but they're old. Back at the office they've got the magic machines to show how he probably looks these days. Bex is the only person to have seen him head-on recently."

Charlie, who knew a great deal about the attributes of Alchemist, was aware of the legendary necromantic powers of the killer. He also knew that one day the man who was Alchemist would make a mistake, or those who sought him would get incredibly lucky. This apolitical murderer would finally make his violent quietus. Charles was 110 percent certain of it.

"This can't be a coincidence," Patsy rambled on. "It's got to be the same man, Chermyet. We've got an alert out for the yacht. All we can do at the moment, though if he's got Alchemist working for him, he'll know damn all. From what we understand the guy gets his orders, takes the finances—his starter for a million or whatever it is—and disappears to do the job."

Charlie thought, Lord help us. Alchemist on the loose, and this Russian hood Chermyet tied in to the fortune being laundered by the monks of Ringmarookey. Words came into his head, adapted from the great barbarous Anglo-Saxon epic poem:

> Now from the marshes under the misty mountains
> Comes Alchemist prowling; branded by God.
> This murdering monster was minded to trap
> Some hapless human in the high hall.

"You warned the Russian?" Charlie asked Patsy.

"The prez's been warned, but nothing doing. They're still coming."

"So it's all hands to the pumps."

"Something like that. Saturation. We're going to be drenched with SAS, Airborne, and Royal Marines. They'll be everywhere, on rooftops, behind windows, up each other's bums with their hunting rifles, scopes, and exploding bullets. They're going to ferry Bortunin and his missus everywhere by chopper with several decoys. Cars only when there is no alternative. That's why I've got to get back to London with Bex." Patsy looked pointedly at his watch, and Charlie could feel the energy building like an electric charge. Patsy was always one for perpetual motion. "This business with Chermyet was unexpected," Wright said, "but they'll track the bugger down. Can't lose an ocean-going yacht for long. Specially with such a fanciful name."

"And this man Chermyet heads up some organized crime family in Georgia, right?"

"Very big wheel. Capo di tutti bloody capo I shouldn't wonder."

"But he's Chechen?"

"By birth, yes. But these guys nip across the new frontiers like we'd cross the road. They pick and choose; duck, dive, weave around. They're part of the warp and weft of life out there. Corrupt as a hatful of arseholes as well."

"Why would they want to take out the president of the Russian Federation?"

"Hard to say. Probably worried because the man's very popular: going to get the country back on its feet. That's the last thing they'd want. Mind you, Charlie, they're crazy people, so it could be that they're dyed-in-the-wool, born-again Communists."

"Or want people to think they are."

"Sure."

"And you'd already got an operation going on here, on Ringmarookey, among the monks?"

"Jacks-of-all-trades these days, old love. We'd been on the track of loot for quite a while, chasing up money. Known for some time that the monks were doing some creative financial haute cuisine. Unfortunately for them the cash was so big that it might as well have had neon signs pointing to it."

"So Kit Palfrey was your inside man."

"Sort of outside bet more than inside man. Kit really brought those scrolls back from Moscow, you know." Patsy shot Charlie a sideways look, trying to gauge if he was believed or not. "The Old Man took a look at them, out of interest you know. Suggested Kit use them to get in here, what with old Gregory Scott being an expert and all. Kit'd already had dealings with these Holy Joes of course, but you know that." Grin. Tap his coat pockets. Turn. Walk the other way.

Charlie still trotted along beside him.

"Overstepped the mark, though, had no right to deal you in, old boy. Don't really know why he did, but my guess is that he spotted you and decided he wanted company. Saw you'd clocked him as well. Thought it was best to have you on his side." Another pause and turn. "Could be he wanted some legal backup. Didn't quite trust head office, eh? Maybe. Sorry you've been troubled really. It's all a bit hairy and I don't think Bex'll be the same again. It'll hit her when she lets up for a while. When she stops. You're going to have to keep an eye on her, look after her, Charlie."

Charlie thought it sounded dodgy indeed and didn't care for it at all. For the first time since he had met her, he wished that Bex would give up the Job.

When the taciturn Fathers Harry and Hugh had been sent away to catch up on their sleep, Charlie asked if he could have the rest of the transcript to read.

"You realize you've only been given edited highlights?" In spite of his age, Gregory Scott appeared to thrive on lack of sleep. As from Patsy, you got a charge of nervous energy from him. In a cold, dry climate he would be a dangerous man to shake hands with: a walking electric shock.

"Yes, I know. You've been giving me gems from Naomi's diary."

"Something like that. But I'll see you get the main pages. It's very interesting, the idea that Joseph of Arimathea was involved in a plot to take Jesus' living body to the Essenes. He was probably an Essene himself for some time."

"Who? Joseph?"

"Yes. People who know about these things are pretty certain of it. They also think he was a disciple of Jesus'. He was certainly a council member—the Sanhedrin, that is—and he seems to have been well-off. Interesting, how he suddenly pops up, just when he's needed. 'Rich disciple; good and righteous.' That's what the Gospels say. What's going to happen, Charlie?" The question ran on quickly, without a pause, his voice dropping slightly. Patsy and Kit had gone outside and Charlie would join Patsy in the cloisters later.

"What's going to happen about what?"

"Am I going into the pokey, Charles? What d'you think I meant, what's on the menu?"

Charlie thought for a moment. "I'm not really privy anymore, but my instincts tell me they won't want to make too much of a fuss—unless they pick up Chermyet on some very serious charges and get a lot of cash back. What about you, Gregory? Will the Order of St. Jerome survive?"

"Course it'll survive. Passing fancy. Not a fad. We're not God's punk rockers. Roll on today, roll off tomorrow. We don't get so many novices these days, but they do still keep coming, which is surprising really when you consider the way in which so many Anglican priests and prelates are trying to gainsay the faith. We've even got an archbishop who prophesies the death of the C of E in one generation. He's no cause to talk like that. Defeatist and sinful really. Yet I suppose it's all part of the idiot, muddled thinking. I heard priests being referred to as worship leaders the other day. People aren't taught facts anymore."

"I *had* noticed. Is there an answer?"

"Will the Church survive, you mean?"

"Something like that."

"Yes, eventually it'll get back to full strength. These things run in cycles. At the moment we seem to be in the dog days of belief. People have to be galvanized into action by events: pushed along. Already there are straws in the wind of change: demonstrations of people's need for a spiritual life. Haven't you noticed how many folk're getting married when the accent is on just having a partner, not a husband or wife?"

"Buzzword, *partner*."

"Yes, and the real buzzword should be *mystery*. That's what the Church has lost. They've done away with tradition, not set standards, told people that God is all-loving and that he'll forgive anything— even lies, murder, rape, and torture. They say very little about the requirements for God's absolution." Scott gave a little snort.

"So many of our priests want to talk of themselves as ministers first and priests last, when it should be the other way around. They're falling over themselves trying to prod people into pews, and they've lost sight of what really matters—teaching the good news of God, keeping an eye on the rules, and setting beautiful standards of worship: worship sanctified by custom not by clapping along, cheers, and pop songs. Where's the dignity in that? It's like a Christmas game. Your man in the street isn't lured into faith by accessibility, though the happy clappers have convinced themselves. They call people like me 'traditionalists' as if we're something set apart. We've lost the language of the Church, we've lost its wonder and mystery by pretending it isn't

325

there, we've lost the bloody plot, and we're in danger of reducing Christianity to a kind of comfortable old jumper that you can put on or take off as the mood suits you. A miraculous piece of clothing that'll absolve you from all wrongdoing and lead you to some package trip for eternity. Oh, what the hell, Charlie, I don't need to preach to you."

"You probably do, Gregory, but we haven't the time now. Maybe I'll come back with Bex and have our marriage blessed."

"It'd be a pleasure."

Charlie looked up, sensing movement. The lanky Brother Simon stood in the doorway.

"Well?" Gregory sounded stern, unforgiving.

"Three seem to be absent, Father Superior."

"Simon's been doing a head count for me," Gregory Scott explained to Charlie. "Who's missing then?"

"Father Benedict, Brothers Vitus and Lapsi. Just like you suspected, Father."

The father superior crossed himself.

When Bex and Patsy Wright had flown into Ringmarookey on board the Chinook, they had peered toward the oceangoing yacht as it sliced through the breakers about a mile east of the small harbor, picking up speed and seemingly heading toward the Western Isles.

What few people knew was that the Russian toughs Vitus and Lapsi had long been in the pay of Illych Antonovich Chermyet. Their job had been to watch Colin Knight, the self-styled Father Benedict. Chermyet had suspected Knight for a long while and always knew where he could pick him up.

In the early hours, Chermyet decided that the false Father Benedict would have to pay for lining his pockets—for Colin Knight had not been too scrupulous in the handling of Chermyet's funds.

Vitus and Lapsi had laid hold of the novice master and taken him by force down to the yacht, where Chermyet waited silently, ready to inflict punishment and seek retribution.

By shortly after eleven-thirty on the same morning, *Golden Cockatrice* had spotted the freighter off Rathlin Island just as she ducked into the North Channel, running between the coasts of Scotland and

Ireland. For vital minutes they sheltered on her port side, shielding themselves from the shoreline, from radar and any prying eyes. Nobody saw the inflatable leave the yacht and streak toward the freighter. One man was in the stern and a monk lay in what on a larger vessel would be called the fo'c'sle, two deckhands hanging on to the chains they had put around the captive's hands and ankles.

The inflatable swept in toward the freighter, which now rode at half-speed ahead with nets and a kind of boatswain's chair on ropes and pulleys over the side to haul the monk on board. For three days Chermyet had been in constant radio contact with the freighter, which was registered in Odessa and inappropriately named *Tsar Ivan IV*. Had any former tsar seen this salt-caked rust bucket, the result would have been truly terrible.

Now, as the inflatable reached the side of the freighter, *Golden Cockatrice* turned away and headed north at full speed.

In the inflatable, the man in the monk's habit was retching, throwing up over the side, his face green and drawn, eyes ringed red, and snot running from his nose. His illness had little to do with the sea, for Colin Knight had always been a good sailor. He was ill now because of the beating Chermyet and the two Russians had given him in the forward lounge of *Golden Cockatrice*, during which he had admitted embezzling large sums of money. He had even given Chermyet the numbers of secret bank accounts, in Luxembourg and on the Cayman Islands, and the code words that would unlock them. Now, every movement caused the man pain, and Chermyet threatened much worse once they got him on board.

The freighter was bound for Felixstowe, where she would pick up half a dozen containers full of secondhand cars, mostly Ladas, Mercs, and BMWs that had been stolen in the U.K. and would be carried to the Federation of Russian States and sold for king's ransom prices.

This was a regular trip for *Tsar Ivan IV*, though on this occasion she had been delayed three days with engine trouble off the northern coast of Ireland. Nor was this her usual or direct route; rather it was a scenic route that added many nautical miles to the journey. Both the navigation and the "engine trouble" had been on the orders of I. A. Chermyet, the chairperson of the consortium that owned *Tsar Ivan IV*.

This was Chermyet's ride into the U.K.

The man in monk's robes was swung inboard and dropped onto the freighter's deck so that he sobbed with pain. One of the deckhands even felt a twinge of sorrow for the man, for he knew what awaited him below in the empty hold. He had helped build the instrument of death. Now he helped lift him and carry him down into the depths of the ship as Chermyet climbed aboard, swarming up the net that had been dropped for him. Below him the two other men now secured the inflatable, then followed their leader while the small craft was lifted on board. Later that evening she would be needed again, so they disguised her by covering her with a tarp, leaving her near to where she could be swung out again. Chermyet clambered straight up to the bridge to shake his captain's hand.

"Everything arranged?" Chermyet asked in Russian.

"Ten-thirty tonight," the captain said, nodding.

Chermyet gave him a grim smile. "Good. You'll make yourself available to come with me. Now I shall see to our passenger. Posing as one of Christ's brothers brings Christ's reward."

Vitus waited at the companionway. He carried a clutch of thick, sharp wooden stakes, shaped like huge nails, and a sturdy mallet. "Ladislav's gone down with the rope," he told Chermyet, who simply nodded and led the way down, his body turned sideways to more easily negotiate the companionways.

In the aft hold the engine noise was louder, reverberating throughout the ship's hull, a deep, booming thrum that had just increased as the captain had ordered full ahead all from the bridge. The ship rocked slightly and trembled as she picked up the revolutions.

In the hold the elderly man who was Colin Knight lay trembling on the metal deck, his eyes wide and incredulous as he tried to make sense of the great wooden cross that lay nearby. The cross had been fashioned from two thick planks of wood, jointed and nailed together. His mind would not accept that these people could be inhuman enough to use such a thing.

In London, Ronnie Richardson left Tessa Murray in the Royal Garden Hotel while he took a cab to Piccadilly Circus, then walked through

Soho until he found an ironmonger's shop in one of the narrow back streets. The sign above the window said that the owner was a J. Grant and that he was an Ironmonger and Metal Engraver.

The shop was closed, but a fat man with a bulbous nose opened up when Ronnie pressed the bell three times.

"Josh in?" Ronnie asked, keeping his hands away from his body and showing them to be empty.

"Who wants him?" The fat man stared at Ronnie as though he had asked an obscure question.

"Tell him it's Walter from Germany."

The fat man nodded, said nothing, and lumbered away, disappearing through a door at the rear of the shop. Richardson took a step inside the door and sniffed at the metallic smell and traces of leather. He remembered as a child he had great pleasure in shops that displayed and sold leather. He would breathe in the scent of the leather, then chew at the corners of his tongue. This gave him a frisson of almost sexual excitement.

A couple of minutes later the fat man returned, breathing heavily, not happy about exerting himself. "You got a number, Walter?"

"Yes. One forty-one."

"You're to go up, then."

Over the years, Ronnie must have visited this shop some twenty times, yet the routine never varied. Same fat man, same dialogue, absolutely no familiarity.

Through the door a steep, wooden, uncarpeted staircase led up to a long room cluttered with the gray boxes of computers and their peripherals. In one corner stood a small dormouse of a man sliding a tray of glossy paper into a large, sophisticated color laser printer.

The dormouse grinned at Ronnie. "Hallo, Walt. Long time no see. How you keeping?" He had a high-pitched voice, almost unnatural. Having fed the printer like a domestic pet, he walked to his big desk in the center of the room; his movements were exaggerated and almost grotesquely precise, as though he had to conform to a set routine. If he did not, then ill luck would be upon him.

"Hello, Josh." Ronnie waited for the man to settle himself behind the desk. "Got a favor to ask you."

"Favors can cost, Walt."

"Have I ever let you down?"

"You're a pleasure to do business with, Walt."

Driving back from Heathrow, Ronnie and Tessa had gone out of their way to stop at the nearest motorway service station. There they had used a passport photograph booth to have pictures taken. Ronnie now handed the prints to Josh and told him what he wanted, spreading out a couple of sheets of plain paper covered with his neat handwriting. "I want these back when it's done, mind."

The grin did a fast fade from the dormouse's face. "Don't want much, do you? It'll cost."

"How much?"

"Four grand. Used notes, same as ever."

"Five if I can have it by seven tonight."

"Done. Half now."

"You've got it."

After a short exchange of questions and answers concerning the work, Richardson left, hailing a cab in Piccadilly Circus and traveling through the bottleneck of Kensington Gore, back to the Royal Garden.

That evening, he returned to the ironmonger's to collect a small package, which he showed to Tessa after they had dined well in the Garden Room, the penthouse restaurant at the hotel.

Over coffee in their suite, Ronnie explained exactly how he intended to kill President and Madame Bortunin. When he finished the explanation, he went through it again, emphasizing the part Tessa was to play in the plan; he then went through it a third time, after which he asked questions. Things fell into place for Tessa. Over the past two days she had, on Ronnie's instructions, bought certain items and played certain roles. Now she knew why.

After Tessa had asked a couple of questions, Ronnie unlocked his briefcase and handed her a Browning nine-millimeter automatic. Years ago he had taught her to shoot and was confident that she could use the weapon if it became necessary. "You're in up to your armpits now, Tess," he told her. "Let's do it properly. And if anything goes wrong, then don't get taken alive." Somehow it did not sound melodramatic the way he said it.

Finally, he went through the plan one more time for luck, though he had left little to luck.

The man known as Josh was the world champion of forged documents: a grand master in the production of fake letters, IDs, and the like. In a profession now badly damaged by cheap and cheerful computer work, Josh performed what he thought of as a quality service for the high end of the trade.

Over the past days in London, Ronnie had made innumerable telephone calls fitting himself out with everything else he required to do a professional job. Now he was armed with facts, names, places, times, and passwords. He knew, for instance, exactly where the car that would take President and Madame Bortunin from Heathrow safely into central London was garaged; he knew the name of the driver and what his movements would be and with whom he would be in contact. More particularly, Ronnie knew exactly when the driver would pick up the car and who else should be at the pickup point in West London. Knowing all this, Ronnie planned to be by the sleek, armored official Rover long before anyone else.

Kit Palfrey traveled back to Glasgow with Bex, Charlie, and Patsy in the big Chinook, carrying on a shouted conversation with Charlie. Flying in a Chinook is not the same as whizzing from Heathrow to Kennedy in a 747.

"I always say you've never flown till you've bucked around in a military chopper," Kit said loudly into Charlie's ear. Around them the noise seemed almost tangible.

"What're you going to do now then, Kit?" Charlie was interested. He wondered if the government would ever admit to Kit's double life during the Cold War.

"Live quietly in Portugal."

"Singing fados to the moon?" It was a half-remembered line from some unmemorable poem. Charlie recalled spending a couple of weeks in Lisbon, eating cake and drinking too much wine while he ran an intelligence informer through a gymkhana of simple questions, none of which had much of an answer. In the evenings he used to go down to a café in sight of the sea and listen to melancholy fados being sung to the accompaniment of a competent guitarist. The singer was a young girl from a village near Vigo. She singled out Charlie, and when she found that he was English, she became his lover to improve her language skills. He smiled at the thought of how she would breathlessly gasp, "Yes, Charlie, yes, I'm came." She was wonderfully young, with all the sexual inventiveness of an original, and Charlie thought back with fondness to a time when his life seemed endlessly uncomplicated. He could see her clearly, the mole on her left breast and the dark golden areolae round her nipples; he heard her laugh, saw her smile, and vividly felt her sexual tightness on the business side of her trimmed, cropped bush. But for the life of him, he could not remember her name.

He was ashamed of himself.

When they got to Glasgow, Kit disappeared. There one minute, then, with a grin and a wave, he walked off and vanished. Charlie never saw him again.

They had a two-hour wait for a flight to Heathrow so Charlie wanted to drag Bex off to the Glasgow Royal Infirmary to see Hilary. But Patsy was not having any of it.

"Joe Bain'll have my guts for the proverbial if I don't actually bring her right back to his door." Patsy took it all very seriously. So, in the end, Charlie went off by himself.

To his surprise Hilary was sitting up chatting away to the PO who had saved her life. Charlie joined in, but felt left out completely.

When Pete Brookes went off in search of a bathroom, Hilary, bubbling with excitement, told Charlie that he was leaving his wife. "She's run him ragged, Charlie. Isn't it amazing? If someone hadn't tried to kill me, I might never have met him."

Her excitement was infectious and Charlie went back to the airport awash with good humor.

"Hey, Bex," he whispered as they flew to London at twenty-five thousand feet. "I've got a nice surprise for you tonight."

"Animal, vegetable, or mineral?"

"All animal."

"You dirty beast, Charlie." She giggled.

*   *   *

In the hold of *Tsar Ivan IV* the man was screaming. He tried to thrash around, kicking and struggling, shouting in terror. "Please," he shrieked. "Please, for God's sake. I've told you . . . I've accounted for every penny. . . . What good will this . . . ? I'm sorry, I've given you everything."

"Is not yours to give, Colin. You ask *me* what good will it do?" Chermyet spoke far more English than he had owned to in the whore's flat off Praed Street with Jimmy Maclean. "What good'll this do, Father fucking Benedict? I'll tell you exactly what good it'll do. It'll be an object lesson: a discipline. It'll be a visual aid. You British use a French expression, *pour encourager les autres*—to encourage the others. That's what it'll do. It'll encourage the others never to steal money, goods, people, or things that belong to me and my family. It will tell people not to screw around with my family."

Vitus and Lapsi held Knight's left arm against the crossbar while Chermyet raised the mallet and brought its heavy, flat end down on Colin Knight's hand, smashing at bone and tissue. He screamed again, then again, as this time, Chermyet held the sharp-pointed wooden stake and drove it right through Knight's crushed left palm. The stake crushed through flesh and bones, causing unbelievable pain. It was like white-hot lances being held to the flesh, and the pain jumped and stitched itself up his arm. His brain became totally inarticulate when the second stake went in and the ropes were bound around his out-stretched arms.

He could not believe how his body altered at the horror that engulfed him. They broke his feet, then drove stakes through them, smashing bone once more so that a great humming wall of agony engulfed him from his demolished extremities.

They tied him to the cross, then lifted and hauled it up, lodging it against the metal side of the hold, steadying it with guy ropes threaded through metal eyes let into the deck. Knight had no idea how they managed to keep the cross upright, for he did not think he could imagine further pain—until he was hanging from the cross, pinioned to it, outstretched, with his muscles and sinews joining in the clamor that was a river of flaming agony.

He wanted to die.

He screamed until his voice box dried up and he could scream no more.

Chermyet shouted up at the racked body, "Steal from me and die like Christ." He then muttered to his two henchmen, "Throw the whole thing over the side. When you're in the Channel—the English Channel—throw it all into the sea so that the British will know what we do with those who betray us." The men, Vitus and Lapsi, were the kind of people who reacted well to melodrama. Chermyet knew this, as indeed he knew a lot of things.

Colin Knight took hours to die, and every moment of his dying was anguish. And before he died, his sphincter muscles loosened and his bowels gave way and the human waste flooded down the wood mixing with the blood. It is what happens when you crucify someone. That's how it is.

At ten-thirty that evening, as they passed close to the Welsh coast, between Swansea and Porthcawl, the inflatable was run out again and Chermyet climbed down the net. This time the freighter's captain accompanied him. Chermyet was not going to have any mistakes. He knew little about the sea and questioned almost everything people told him. The captain had said he would be able to pinpoint a small stretch of beach and land his leader on it. The beach had been chosen before *Tsar Ivan IV* had left her port in Russia. Nothing to it, the captain had told Chermyet. If there was nothing to it, Chermyet said, then the captain should also put his freedom at risk.

The little inflatable was low in the water, and the small stretch of coast did not come within the range of any shore-based radar. It took an hour to bring the craft close in to the shore. When they were almost on the beach, the captain aimed a flashlight toward the beach and winked a series of long and short flashes.

They waited, the engine cut to idle, until flashes answered from shore. The captain whispered good luck to Chermyet. Seconds later the stocky little figure was gone, swallowed up by the night. In a few hours he would be in London. Certainly in time for the arrival of the president of the Russian Federation.

CHAPTER 23

DS Dennis Tyler was a driver for the Special Escort Group, the police service that provides protection officers for politicians, royalty, VIPs, and visiting firemen. He was trained in observation, physical combat, shooting with handguns and automatic weapons. He could identify practically every make of vehicle, and every weapon he was ever likely to see, knew a great deal about body language and the techniques of protecting individuals in both friendly and hostile environments.

His girlfriend, Anthea Austin, was also a PO, but they never got a chance to work together. In their wisdom, the powers-that-be hold that police officers who are in a relationship off duty should not be on duty at the same time or work in close proximity to one another. Like most police officers, Dennis and Anthea agreed that this was a sensible state of affairs because, no matter how good you are, serving close to your partner can lead to inappropriate actions in an emergency.

Today was a memorable day for Dennis. He had driven important people before—including royalty—but this was really different. He was to drive President and Madame Bortunin from the Royal Suite at Heathrow to the embassy building where the president would be staying during the talks in London.

A woman protection officer, Miranda Evans, had been assigned to his car, and at half past seven on this Monday morning Dennis pulled up in front of the semi in Hammersmith where Miranda lived, only a stone's throw from the house Dennis shared with his seventy-three-year-old mum, who looked after him, cooked his meals, and generally waited on him hand and foot.

Ostensibly Miranda lived alone, but in reality she had a series of friends who helped out with the rent, and provided other interesting experiences. Miranda Evans was very much a girl of the second millennium's first decade.

Dennis tapped the horn as he'd promised, having already saved her a good ten minutes by signing in at the nick for both of them, a job he had done fifteen minutes earlier.

As protection officers they were both permanently armed: he with a Glock nine-milllimeter; she with an H&K semiautomatic pistol. Dennis wore the Glock now, in a cross-draw holster on the left side of his belt so that the pistol was snug against his hip. Shifting in his seat, he reached over to touch the butt, making sure it was settled in a comfortable position.

Tyler wore a dark gray, conservatively styled suit with a white shirt and burgundy tie decorated with gold fleurs-de-lis that—he had checked—was considered appropriate for the occasion. The last time he had driven a member of the royal family, Dennis had had a sizable strip torn off him for wearing a tie embroidered with small pink elephants. Today he was immaculate.

Miranda Evans came swinging down the small path to her front door, neat and slim in a dark suit and a crisp white blouse. Her skirt hem ended a modest one inch below the knee, which was unusual for Miranda, but it was not considered acceptable to wear skirts up to your navel when on duty with either royalty or a head of state. No matter that today they knew Madame Bortunin would sashay down the aircraft steps in a skirt that would probably not even cover her bottom, they were still duty-bound to maintain modesty.

"Hi ya." She slid into the seat beside him, buckling her seat belt, then doing a kind of shimmy to make herself comfortable. If he had not known she was a police officer, Dennis thought he would treat her with caution. He might even give her a wide berth, for Miranda had the outward appearance of being one of the girls—the female equivalent of laddism: an outwardly brash noisiness with a svelte figure and loud assertiveness. Dennis was basically a quiet, no-nonsense young man, and at times, in the canteen for instance, girls like Miranda and her mates would embarrass him and make him feel decidedly uncomfortable.

Later, his girlfriend, Anthea, would ask him about his day, but not about the Bortunins. Anthea would quiz him about Miranda Evans and her disregard for modesty whenever she was on the cars. Anthea was a suspicious girl because her mum had caught her dad in a blatant infidelity in the stockroom of the International Stores where they had both worked. What was galling to Anthea's mum was that this had happened some twenty-four years ago, two days after they had returned from their honeymoon and one week before Anthea's dad left her mum forever. She never tired of telling her daughter of this terrible fate and warning her of a similar destiny.

Dennis had long realized that Anthea was not necessarily the only girl in the world for him. Sometimes he felt trapped, as though Anthea had somehow snared him as a trophy, and it occasionally worried him slightly that, quite against his natural instincts, he often found Miranda and her friends more attractive than Anthea. For instance, he found her very attractive this morning.

"You're looking dead cool today, if you don't mind me saying so," Dennis told her, raising his eyebrows and doing a finger-and-thumb movement to straighten his tie. There was none of this feminist business about not liking compliments where Miranda was concerned. Long ago she had let it be known that the more compliments she got the more thigh she was prepared to flash and the more bubbly she would become. She had even suggested greater compliance, but, in Dennis's case, the possibilities had been left unplumbed. He had no desire to be rebuffed, and his lengthy association with Anthea had taught him that even a long and loving relationship did not automatically give one access to the pleasure gardens of love. The feminist sisterhood remained in despair over Miranda Evans, but the male officers with whom she worked never complained.

"Every little bit helps, and flattery'll get you everywhere." She batted her eyelids. Miranda was an accomplished flirt, but she was also a very professional police officer. Later, when they picked up the bullet-proofed Rover and their principals, they would only speak to one another if it was absolutely necessary. Now, on their way to get the car, Dennis and Miranda were relaxed; not what you would call nervous, but just that tic over normal, slightly apprehensive. Bound to be. Wouldn't be natural if they weren't a shade anxious.

As Dennis drove to the secure garage where the Rover had been kept overnight, they talked about the latest bits of gossip in the canteen, what they had seen on television, and the state of the world in general. After all, they were both young, fit, and ready for anything. If either of them had been your boyfriend or girlfriend, you would have had the right to be uneasy.

"Your Anthea going to give you a hard time 'cos we're driving together, then?" Miranda asked.

"Why should she do that? No." But he was too casual, a shade too laid-back, so she laughed, a great, almost dirty guffaw.

"What?" Dennis feigned bewilderment, and Miranda spent the rest of the drive to the secure lockup needling away at him.

When they pulled into the garage, a second man and woman waited by the Rover, which was polished and shining, obviously juiced up and ready to go.

"DS Tyler?" the man asked.

"Who wants to know?" Tyler slipped the button on his jacket.

"DI Hunter. You *are* Tyler, aren't you?" Hunter flipped a warrant card in a leather wallet at him.

"Yes, guv."

"Sorry about this, Tyler, but there's been a change of plan. We're to drop you off at the nick."

"What d'ya mean? I'm driving the Russkie president . . ."

"I'm sorry, as I said, there's been a change of plan."

Dennis Tyler's mouth fell open. "Oh, shit!" he said loudly just as the uniformed sergeant in charge of the secure garaging came out from behind the gleaming Rover.

"Absolutely right, Dennis. They rung me twenty minutes ago. Sergeant Vosper rang the nick. DI Hunter and WDS Collins have to drop you back there to get new orders. They've got all the paperwork and everything. Signed, sealed, and delivered."

"Where you from then, guv?" Dennis tried to hide his disappointment. He felt that this was some senior officer's vote against him.

"Special Branch, but I live only five minutes away. Mind if we just drop round there for a second? I might've left a pan on the hob."

"Always doing tricks like that. Forget your ears if they were loose," said the sergeant, Collins, pulling a face at Miranda Evans. Miranda muttered something about being pissed off. "I'd been looking forward to getting a photo with that president's wife. She's dead tarty, en't she?"

"I'll see what I can do. They're here for a whole week and we're going to be with them all the way," the DI told Miranda.

Miranda thought that the DI was so relaxed he would fall apart at the joints if he wasn't careful. He also obviously liked the smooth power of the car, the way he drove. The Russian president would get tossed around in the back if the DI handled the motor like this, she thought. She had done the heads-of-state driving course, where you were told to always imagine you had a full glass of champagne sitting above the dashboard. The object was to never spill the champagne. "Whoops, there goes another glass," the instructors would constantly shout as you manhandled the vehicle into a tight turn or hit the brakes too sharply.

Less than three minutes and they were pulling up at a neat little detached house with trees giving it a rare bit of privacy. "Twenty Gunnerbury Road," Miranda read. "Looks nice, guv."

"It'll do. I'll only be a second. Make sure nobody pinches the motor," and then the DI was out and running toward the side of the house. He disappeared inside and they waited gloomily.

Miranda Evans started to whistle tunelessly, one of her more irritating habits, one she indulged in when nervous. Somehow things did not seem quite right. She felt little alarms probing, and Dennis Tyler did not seem able to sit still.

Then, the DI was suddenly out of the house yelling at them from his back door. "Get in here! Quick! Help me!" He ducked back into the house.

Dennis Tyler was the first in. He ran down the short passage, through the kitchen, and into a long front room. As he got into the room, he thought, Funny, he's had all his furniture nicked. Dennis got the impression of a sharp pain in his right shoulder, had a sense that someone was bearing down on him, then lost the entire plot for the remains of the day.

Something similar happened to Miranda Evans just inside the back door, but she got quite a vivid picture of what was going on. She knew that WDS Collins had grabbed her wrist, and she actually saw the throwaway hypo being jabbed into her upper arm, right through her jacket and blouse. Collins took on the form of a vampire and Miranda tried to shrink away.

I've got to remember this, she thought as the darkness came over her and she slid into a peaceful sleep. I must remember . . .

"Upstairs," said Ronnie. "I'll get her upstairs and shackled to the radiator. With any luck they'll both be out for five or six hours."

He lugged the young policewoman up the stairs while Tessa went back to the car. When he had safely stowed the girl away in the front bedroom, cuffed to the radiator, he went down and dragged Dennis Tyler up to the second bedroom. He pulled the policeman's jacket down behind his back, removed the pistol from his belt, and cuffed his hands.

When they had first come to the house, with the real estate agent, on the previous Saturday, they had pleaded to be allowed to keep the keys. "We'd like to come in over the weekend, and on Monday morning," Ronnie had said.

"I really need to do some serious measuring." Tessa had been very Irish, very touchy-feely with the agent, who had picked them up by car at the Regent Palace. Reception had rung them in their room. They would be ideal buyers, the agent thought. People with money: they talked about having room for the two ponies and two cars.

"Our drawing-room furniture and the corner cupboard will be lovely in this room," Tess had purred. "And we could have the Turner over the mantelpiece; over the Adam fireplace. It would look lovely."

The agent got hopeful. He particularly liked people who talked about drawing rooms.

"You ought to get an Academy Award," Ronnie told her later. "Bloody Academy Award you should have. Effing marvelous."

On the Sunday, on the way back from Heathrow, they had stopped off and hidden the handcuffs and chains in the two bedrooms—in the cupboards—so that they would be ready on the Monday.

Now Ronnie ran a piece of metal chain up through the cuffs and used a third set of handcuffs to secure Tyler to the hanging fixture in the built-in wardrobe. Back in the master bedroom he picked up the Heckler & Koch that he had removed from the anesthetized WDC, slipped it in his waistband, went downstairs, let himself out, and locked the door behind him.

So far, he thought, it's worked like a charm. Richardson believed that you could get away with anything if you exuded confidence and carried the right kind of paper. Josh, the forger, had done a fine job with the warrant cards and the letter of authorization. Knockout jobs both of them, and Richardson was proud of his own contribution on the telephone. Ronnie had telephoned the nick and told them there had to be some changes made and who the hell did they think they were? "Because I'm Sergeant bloody Vosper," he yelled down the phone. "And you'd better look smart about it." DI Hunter and WDS Collins were bringing Tyler and Evans back to the nick, he told them. They were to ring Sergeant Randolph at the Thames Valley HQ at Kiddlington. See how many men they'd contributed to the Heathrow operation, then get back to him.

"They believed," Ronnie said with glee. "They really believed me. All that gobbledygook, and they believed it."

He had the Rover cruising down the M4 now, heading out to Heathrow, and nobody could stop them. If the Russian aircraft was on time, nobody would question anything. Ronnie knew exactly what he was doing. Tess would sit back, and he had warned her about the moment of death, that second when the light goes out. The target is there, then gone. In a moment. In a twinkling of an eye.

He quite forgot that she had seen it all in the Villa Myrte the night he had blown poor old Lenny Saxby away.

Ronnie Richardson was getting the buzz. It always happened when he was close to a kill, the buzz, almost like the high you got waking up from being anesthetized, a bit surreal, a shade drunk.

It was the sense of power.

It was the feeling of being Almighty God. And he hoped God would grant the Russian absolution for all his sins. This is the day of absolution, he thought, the day of forgiveness.

They came off at the Heathrow exit, then headed off on the slip road toward Terminal Four. The Royal Suite is a little past Terminal Four, a long, low building with a hard standing for the aircraft just off the taxiway.

Ronnie had spent hours wrestling with the problem of how he could dispatch the Bortunins with some privacy. He needed to get them alone, and within sight of an escape for himself and Tess. Needed that situation for a shade less than two minutes.

He thought the Bortunins would be locked up tight all week, so he had to get them now, at the beginning. Or leave it to the end. There would be no other chances.

When he was a little boy, his mummy had said to him, "Ron, in this world you have to make your own luck. Nobody else'll do it for you. You have to do it for yourself."

Ron was doing it for himself now. Hold back, get them in the car, keep pace with everyone until the motorway, then put your foot down and go. The escort would never know what he was doing. The radio would be off, the road already cleared. He knew which way to take them; had the other car waiting. It was all so close that he could never lose. They wouldn't even get a chopper up in time. In his pocket, Ronnie had the card with the Shakespearean quotation written on it:

> This will last out a night in Russia,
> When nights are longest there.
> —*Measure for Measure*

Ronnie had been right: a minimum disguise, he thought. Late last night he got Tessa to cut his hair and shave it right down just in case the chauffeur's cap got knocked or blown off. He wore wraparound sunglasses, but nothing else by way of pretense.

Tessa was a slightly different case. He had chosen the wig himself. Thick, short, but very blond. She looked almost Nordic. The wig did the job, changed her entirely. No problem there.

CHAPTER 24

Charlie was thrilled to bits. They were home, and safe, only Bex had to be on duty again first thing. "Get this damned visit over, Charlie," she said in a sort of flat monotone. "Get it over, then Joe Bain says I can take some proper leave." This wasn't the old Bex he knew and loved. This Bex was much more serious, preoccupied.

"Sure, Bex, where'd you like to go? Anywhere special? Just tell me, old love, and we'll do it. Slow boat to China? Road to Mandalay? Up the lazy river? Camelot? Anywhere you want. Say the word and we'll do it."

But Bex wasn't really thinking. She was far away. She hadn't really come back yet. Give her time, Charlie. He remembered Patsy's warning.

"Where do they want you? In the morning, I mean."

"Heathrow. They want me there when they arrive—when Oleg Bortunin arrives. Want me in close looking at faces. That's what Commander Bain said. 'Let DCI Olesker watch the faces.' He reckons that it doesn't matter what disguise he's taken on, I'll be the most likely person to recognize him."

"You want company? Want me to come along for the ride?"

She looked puzzled, as though she couldn't understand why on earth Charlie would want to schlepp all the way out to Heathrow with her. "If you like," she said in a tone that translated into "No way, Charlie."

So he drove her out, noticing that she wore a shoulder-holster rig under her suit jacket; noticing that the holstered big Glock was set hard against her ribs on the left side, directly below her armpit; noticing that she seemed more quiet than usual; noticing the wariness that came into her eyes; noticing how she seemed to shrink the nearer they came to Terminal Four.

Armed Royal Marines were on the gates that led down onto the low building and the apron in front of it. As they got nearer, there were signs of other uniforms: men in camouflage jackets on the roof; weapons all over the place; men with clear, watchful eyes.

A sergeant guided them into the parking area: precise, making sure they went exactly where he pointed and nowhere else. A tall man, back like a ramrod, shoulders like a bullock. Face carved from gray stone.

"Better hang on a second." She had cocked the Glock. Charlie saw her put the safety on and slide it back into the holster. Button it down.

She got out and walked to where her commander, Joe Bain, stood talking to another uniformed cop, Patsy Wright, a man Charlie recognized but couldn't put a name to, and a colonel with the Royal Marines' commando flash on his shoulder and the green beret on his head. The colonel looked as if he could kill for England: sunburned face, lived-in, held himself with pride, hand occasionally straying to touch the holster low on his webbing.

Charlie saw them glance over in his direction, almost heard Joe Bain say something, then watched as Patsy walked over with Bex.

"Commander Bain says you're family, Charlie. Says you can come on over before he does the O group."

Charlie was just out of the car when a whistle blasted and a handful of men seemed to materialize from the buildings, the roof, and from a helicopter that stood about half a kilometer to one side. Half a dozen men were standing around the chopper, wearing jeans and ski masks and carrying assorted weaponry. Charlie knew who they were before he saw one of them doubling toward the O group. SAS, the elite. He saw the colonel of marines turn away with a smile. The colonel was thinking that he did not have to wear a ski mask in public.

A pair of young commando subalterns trotted toward the colonel, stopping and saluting, heels together, shoulders so square that you could have used them for a geometry lesson. How wonderful to be young, well-trained, and fit again, Charlie thought. Then he saw Bex smile and changed his mind.

"Move in and relax. My name is Joe Bain and I'm the assistant commissioner in charge of the Anti-Terrorist Branch. This morning I was summoned to a meeting of COBRA, which, as you know, is the acronym for Cabinet Office Briefing Room. The Briefing Room Committee was called into session in the early hours of this morning when it became clear that neither President nor Madame Bortunin was going to take steps against a very serious threat to their safety while they're here in the U.K.

"We informed the president of the situation, and he apparently spoke with his security people, who told him that we have probably the best security forces in the Western world, so he says that he feels quite safe about coming, even though the threat is extreme.

"This being the case, I have to inform you that we have ordered the Russian presidential aircraft not to land here, at Heathrow. In the interests of the president's safety, the aircraft is being diverted to Northolt. Only a very few people are being advised of this action, which is with effect from"—Bain paused, looking at his watch— "with effect from . . . now.

"I have a trained police presence at Northolt, including officers from the Special Escort Group, and two police helicopters. You are instructed to remain here until I have clearance to stand you down. I must also tell you that the press are *not* being informed of this change of plan, so I would ask you to remain alert. It is possible that the sharp end of the threat is actually here, in this vicinity, at this moment. It could well be a mortar attack or an RPG-7 or something similar. I have four patrols moving along perimeter roads. Anyway, I suggest you do not—I repeat *not*—inform the men under your command, as I am anxious to be sure we remain watchful and vigilant. Thank you."

As the various officers made their way back to speak to their men, the black, official Rover came quietly through the gates to the side of the building. It paused, then moved forward, parking just short of the building.

"Hallo." Bain kept his voice down. "Either someone hasn't received my instructions, or we have an unauthorized visitor." He scowled and muttered into his mobile.

Charlie saw the marine colonel's head come up, felt the static, glanced at Bex, who was just turning, her eyes registering surprise, then the frown forming.

Bex was thinking, I recognize that girl in the Rover's passenger seat. In retrospect, Bex thought it all took an age, her thoughts moving slowly down the wrong end of a telescope. Is she one of ours? Not her features or her hair, but I know her by the way she's sitting: right shoulder slightly forward, weight on the left buttock; back straight but her chin tilted arrogantly to a certain angle. Where? Seen her. Seen her recently.

Bex froze again, uncertain, mind humming down the pathways of memory. Then: Jesus, she suddenly knew—"It's them," she said quietly. "It's the woman, Tess Murray, and Alchemist. It's them."

The marine colonel heard, and his pistol was out almost before she finished speaking. As the pistol came up, both hands steadying the butt, legs apart, the man at the wheel of the Rover reacted, slammed the car into reverse, and gunned the engine.

The car screeched backward, burning rubber, and the marine colonel did not hesitate. He fired twice, straight into the driver's face. The windshield frosted over, then was drenched in blood, while the rear of the car thumped hard into the closing gates.

"Stop!" shouted the colonel. "Stop! Get out with your hands up! Leave the car now!" He had switched targets, starting to squeeze the trigger, just holding back, hesitating.

Other weapons had materialized; troops and police, plainclothes officers, men and women, were forming a crescent in front of the car.

In the passenger seat, Tessa Murray sat rigid, her body taut, trembling. Some of Ronnie's blood had jetted from his head to her face. Jesus God, she thought. Ronnie's head had exploded just like that watermelon in that *Day of the Jackal* film. She was conscious of her pronunciation. In her head she said "filum." Anything but the real matter in hand.

Logic tripped through her mind. Ronnie was dead, she knew that and accepted it. They had failed, but at least the death was quick. Her left hand touched the door catch and her right slid under her jacket. She unbuttoned the strap over the butt of the Browning, drew it out, and flicked off the safety.

She had really had enough: didn't want to go on without Ronnie. Until the very last moment she was scared, keeping the truth hidden at the back of her mind. She pushed the door open and turned her body. Feet onto the ground. Now, she thought, push up and away, then start shooting. Take some of the buggers with you.

Tessa was on her feet. She turned. The pistol came up in the double-handed grip and she was squeezing the trigger, both eyes open, looking over the sights toward the first target. Turn from the waist. Don't move your feet, Tessa. Now, just in case, on the off chance, an act of contrition. "Dear Lord Jesus, save me. For all my sins I am truly sorry."

And in that fraction of a second she saw him with his pistol held at arm's length. She even saw it buck and move as he fired twice. Even though some fifteen years or so had passed, she saw him plainly and recognized him before the blinding light struck her brain and she was swept away.

Joe Bain, Bex Olesker, and Patsy Wright held weapons. Charlie was touched that Bex had elbowed him out of the way, standing with both feet firmly apart, shielding his body with her own.

"Thank you, Colonel Docking," Joe Bain called out, and Ralph Docking flipped on the safety and turned away as uniformed police officers ringed him, safe from the cameras. Colonel Docking looked around, clearing his head. He had seen the girl. Oh, Sandymount, he thought. Rory Deacon, all those years ago. "Oh, God," he whispered. That was it, a Sunday morning walking along the strand at Sandymount. How young we were then, a few years ago.

There was nothing in brooding; nothing gained by wondering what might or what might not have been. He walked away, his back straight and the side arm holstered and safe.

In his head he played the loop of memory. The Canaletto print, the tall ceiling with the crack in it. Then the spray of the sea, and the smell of the sea, the great barber's-pole chimneys out at Poolbeg, and the sound of a horse being ridden up the strand, half in the water as it went past the two young people with their hands clasped tight as though they would never let go of one another.

CHAPTER 25

The *Evening Standard* had it on the front page, with a huge headline that screamed, "Marine Colonel Shoots Terrorist Pair, Saves Russian President." Joe Bain told Bex she could take two weeks' leave effective now, and Charlie drove her back to Dolphin Square, sat her down, poured her a large brandy, and again thanked her for taking such trouble.

"Only doing my job, Charlie."

"Not every girl would stand herself in front of her husband in case the shooting started."

"Ah, well, I'm not *every* girl, am I?"

She was immensely cuddly and he told her that as well.

"Perhaps we could do something about that a bit later on," she said, cocking an eyebrow and giving him her overbite smile, licking her lips.

In fact much later—after she had made them poached eggs on toast and new potatoes—they had quite a roughhouse in the warm and loving bed she had left on the night of her wedding. In the end she did not get up again until almost noon the following day.

Next day in the post, Charlie found a flat package addressed to him. Surprise, he thought, wondering how Father Gregory had managed to get it to him this quickly. Then he looked at the postmark and saw that it was from Melrose on the border. Was the canny old monk getting money moved around and giving Arthur, the bank manager, the tip-off?

The package contained a few pages of translated manuscript and an envelope addressed to Charles Gauntlet, Esq. *Covering Letter*, it said.

* * *

Naomi had dictated all those hundreds of years ago:

I saw you, my dear Romillius, with your men and with Jesus, and I wept like a child for him. Azeb had been out to buy food, and she returned with the news that Pilate had sentenced the Master to death: to be crucified with two common robbers. We were told that Pilate had sent Jesus to King Herod, hoping that he would reprieve him, but the priests, together with the Sanhedrin, led by Caiaphas the Chief Priest, demanded that he be put to death.

We were also told that Pontius Pilate washed his hands in front of the crowd to indicate that he was against what was being done. So, in the end, he would take no responsibility for the action.

It is brutal and shameful what is being done; made worse by the dreadful mockery your friend Pilate has visited on Jesus. I saw that he wore a purple robe and that horrible crown of thorns. I also saw the notice that Pilate had written. All the time we hear about the Roman way, but this is barbarous. I came near to the Place of a Skull and once there could hardly believe how terrible it was. All three condemned men cried out as the nails pierced their flesh and bones, and it was especially bad for Jesus, you could tell.

I stood quite near to him briefly as he was being taken up to the place of execution. I wept, for he looked so dreadfully ill and his back was lacerated in great bleeding strips where the soldiers had flogged him.

Our good Lord seemed not to be there, bewildered, unable to look people in the eye, and without dignity. It is strange how quickly people have turned against him.

He staggered under the weight of the cross they made him carry, and I heard him cry out again in agony as they were putting the terrible instrument in place.

Like me, Romillius, you will have become disturbed as the weather has suddenly changed. This afternoon it was unusually hot, sultry, with clouds coming in over the mountains. Both Azeb and I were exhausted and our heads hurt, deep within, just before that terrible storm broke with its thunder and lightning. The lightning seemed to tear at the clouds and the rain sounded like an army of horsemen galloping across the city. I thought we were all going to be swept away, it was so violent.

Azeb tells me one huge bolt of lightning landed upon the Temple itself. People have been frightened, and there is talk that putting the Lord Jesus to death has been an awful and greatly wrong thing to do. So bad that Jehovah is visiting his wrath on us.

Your messenger has just left me and I am speaking to Petros. Romillius, I am heartbroken that you could not save Jesus' life. I know you tried, but the poor man had been so worn down, I suppose in the end he simply wanted to give up.

The man you sent said that at the end Jesus shouted out, "It is finished." Is that true? I questioned the soldier, but he tells me that he was not there when this happened.

He also said that the man from Arimathea, Joseph, was allowed to take the Lord Jesus' body away and that his mother went with them.

They have, your soldier says, washed the body, put it in a clean cloth, and laid it in the tomb that Joseph had made for himself.

How terrible it all is. My eyes are sore with weeping. What a kind, good man Jesus was. He would hurt no person. There are moments when I cannot believe he is gone, for his presence seems strong and close to me. What shall we do? I have moaned and wept with grief and Azeb has also shed bitter tears.

Your second messenger has left and I do not understand. Are we in danger just because we allowed Jesus to eat here with his followers? What can all this mean? Yes, I will come to you now because you say we must leave for Rome.

Father Gregory wrote:

My dear Charles,
This is all we end up with. Nothing complete or clear except

for Romillius's letter, which is with the diary. You will recall that
he said Azeb and Petros had been murdered, and that the story
was about that Jesus had risen from the dead. We hear nothing
of this from Naomi. Indeed, we do not even hear of Naomi arriving to meet Romillius, so it is a total mystery, which is truly as it
should be, for God works through mysteries and is difficult to
understand.

Jesus told us that it would be hard to believe in him. It is, and
that is all we can say. I am in no doubt that Naomi's MS is old,
ancient in fact. My concerns do not lie there. My doubts and
anxieties are wallowing in the girl's theology, which is more
nineteenth century than first century. It is very strange.

For those of us who labor in God's vineyard, it is enough. All
that has gone on, my dear Charles, is for the power and for the
glory. Soon I shall be leaving all pain and mystery behind for I
am tamed unwilling by time. What do I mean? You will discover.
God bless you. Pray for the absolution of my sins.

Remember that those of us who are swamped in our faith
really do not need any extra proofs, for the proofs are all around us.

In a luxury suite high in the Carlton Tower Hotel, Illych Antonovich
Chermyet sat facing a group of powerful men.

"You see," Chermyet said in his accented Russian. "You see, I was
right. It has all come about as I suggested to you. The outrageous man
whom they called Alchemist is dead. This was quite predictable. He
could not have lasted forever, and it has happened. The British have
scaled back their security. The Bortunins even did this idiotic business
of what they call a walkabout this afternoon outside the Parliament
building.

"Now, I presume we are all still of the same mind, so my people will
deal appropriately with President and Madame Bortunin while they
are still here in London. We can go on from there as planned, gentlemen. Might I suggest it should happen outside the Mansion House,
just before one o'clock on Thursday? That will give you all plenty of
time to be back in Russia. Good? Yes?"

ABOUT THE AUTHOR

Before becoming an author of fiction in the early 1960s, John Gardner was variously a stage magician, a Royal Marine officer, a journalist, and for a short time, a priest in the Church of England. "Probably the biggest mistake I ever made," he says. "I confused the desire to please my father with a vocation which I soon found I did not have."

Educated in Berkshire and at St. John's College, Cambridge, he became a theatrical journalist in the late 1950s chronicling the years when Sir Peter Hall was reorganizing the Royal Shakespeare Company in Stratford-upon-Avon, giving it a London base at the Aldwych, and forming the semipermanent ensemble. Gardner also lectured in Shakespearean production in Canada and the United States.

In the early sixties he wrote a series of highly acclaimed comic novels featuring a cowardly secret agent called Boysie Oakes, then moved on to more serious books. In the early eighties, however, he was invited by Ian Fleming's literary copyright holders to write a series of continuation James Bond novels, which proved to be so successful, worldwide, that instead of the contracted three books, he went on to publish some fourteen titles.

In all, Gardner has forty-two novels to his credit—many of them best-sellers (his *Maestro* was a *New York Times* Book of the Year). *Day of Absolution* is his first book in three years, following a serious battle with cancer. Work in progress includes a dark and disturbing novel (*Bottled Spider*) set in the 1940s.

John Gardner has variously made his home in the Republic of Ireland and spent ten years living in the United States. Following the death of his wife in 1997, he has moved back to the United Kingdom. He now lives in Hampshire. He has two daughters and a son.